# Disappearance

by

Jeanne Selander Miller

# BY

# JEANNE SELANDER MILLER

For Sylvie—

May you come to know your
inherent worth

and

spend your days in golden light

# Chapter 1
## Amy

"I guess I'd been thinking about it for a while, just not in any serious way."

"No wait, start at the beginning."

"The beginning of, what, my entire life?"

"No, but we may get back to that. How about just that day?"

"Oh, *that* day … well, let me think. It's been a while now and you know how memory is."

"No, not really."

"It can play tricks on you, memory plays fast and loose with the facts, leaves things out that may or may not be significant. Memory is overcome by emotion and always favors the storyteller. Just as long as we're clear about that."

"You're stalling, is there something you don't want to tell me?"

"Of course."

"Perhaps it would be best if you just begin."

"Okay. It was the middle of July, and it was already hot and it was only nine AM. I was standing at the sink washing up the breakfast dishes. Judy Collins was playing over the speakers and I was singing along softly, lost in daydreams of my own.

"*... my father always promised me that we would live in France, we'd go boating on the Seine and I would learn to dance...*"

"Alexa, turn this shit off. Alexa, play Waylon Jennings." The music changes and some old country song about good ole boys breaking the law fills the quiet and disturbs my peace. My husband, Nash, walks into the kitchen and any feelings of peace or serenity I might have had, have just blown right out the window.

I look over at the kitchen table that I've just cleared and washed. Now it's piled high with Nash's baseball mitt, a faded pair of swim trunks, and a ratty old pair of gym shoes. God only knows where those have been. I don't know how many times I had to correct the kids when they were growing up about not putting their shoes on the table. Good lord, that's where we eat. I bite my tongue as I move his stuff onto the floor.

"When are we getting that money from your old man's estate?" He asks as he pulls a two-liter bottle of Coke from the fridge and drinks straight from the bottle. He burps loudly and returns the half empty bottle back to the fridge.

"I don't know. I'm sure my brother will let me know once the estate is finally settled."

"What in God's name is taking so long? Add it up and divide by two. This should be settled by now, it's not like it was a surprise that he finally kicked," Nash says as he scrounges through the pantry for something else to eat even though we've only just finished breakfast. "I put a call into Hank, his brother is a realtor down in South Carolina, you know I'd just love to have a place in Myrtle Beach."

The silence grows between us. I don't trust myself to speak, but the only way this man is getting his hands on my daddy's money will be over my dead body. Dad had been onto Nash. Dad had his number long before we ever talked about it. All the money Dad left me has been designated to go directly into a trust where I am the sole beneficiary. Dad and I talked about this years ago, but I have yet to tell my husband. He thinks *we* are going to be rich.

"My father hasn't even been dead for two weeks and you're already spending *my* inheritance."

Nash gives me a look and I know he'd like to slap me right into next week. If it wasn't for my father's generosity he'd be all over me like the wrath of God. For the first time since we've been married I have something he can't force me to give him. It infuriates him.

I turn my back to him and put the dishes back in the cupboard.

He clears his throat loudly to get my attention over the latest country song about some guy and his truck which plays loudly and fills the kitchen. "Hey, I just got off the phone with Casey and Will, and we've decided to head up to the river for the weekend. It's supposed to be another hot one, the women and kids are coming, too. So get a move on, they're meeting us here in an hour and we're gonna caravan to the campground."

"They're coming here?" I ask for this the first I'm hearing of it.

"Pack the cooler. We're gonna barbecue," Nash barks at me without a please or thank-you. "I'm heading down to the Grog Shop to pick up the essentials."

Oh great, another drunken brouhaha with my in-laws and *his* friends. I reach for the dish towel and dry my hands. The day is already hot and muggy and we don't have air conditioning or I'd never have agreed to go. It crosses my mind to feign a headache or something but the thought of another day trapped here at home is almost more than I can bear.

Once again Nash had already made the arrangements without consulting me. I shouldn't be surprised. Why in the world should I think today would be any different? I've been the go-along, get-along girl ever since we met. And that has been decades ago now. He's already invited his pals and his siblings, their spouses, and their broods of undesirables.

"It's my day off and I'm not sitting around here all day just watchin' the grass grow," he grumbles as he heads out. "I'm taking your car," he calls back to me. The door to the garage slams.

He's irritated that I'm less than thrilled about *his* plan for *our* retirement. He talks incessantly about moving to the shore so he can attend football games and relive his glory days at our alma mater every fall weekend from now until we draw our last breaths. I hate football. I've seen enough of it to last me a lifetime. The very thought of it makes me nearly suicidal. Maybe I should have said so long before now.

Still, I have to agree with him, the pervasive boredom of this suburban living can be deadly, particularly now that the kids have grown up and left me alone with their father. He's always complaining about how we never do anything anymore as if that's somehow my fault. He seems to believe it is my responsibility to keep *his* family together. But whenever I suggest visiting my brother in California, or our daughter in Colorado, it's always too far, too expensive, and too much trouble to be bothered.

But if not this, then what?

Lost in my daydreams of lost opportunities and a different life, I pull together some of the things I'd planned to cook for dinner—chicken, I guess we could barbecue it, some potato salad, and pickled green beans from the garden, and put it all in the cooler and packed the ice in around it. Next, I pack the camping gear in the back of the truck.

The whole notion of camping with Nash's friends and family leaves me tired. Really? Let's just pack everything up and schlep it down to the river and cook outside and then schlep all the rubbish and dirty dishes home so I can wash it all up and put it away. The whole idea of going camping with *his* family and his pals is overrated and that's just about the kindest thing I can say about it. It's never a day out or a day off for me, this whole picnic and camping thing does nothing but create more work for me and to say nothing of the joy of spending time with people who have always made me feel like an unwelcome outsider even after nearly forty years of marriage.

Nash returns with three cases of Rolling Rock and a couple of fifths of Jack Daniels. "Put the beer on ice, then let's get out of here," Nash says as he heads back out to hitch up the trailer. I hear the trucks, trailers, and horns honking. My in-laws have arrived and are ready to go. I fill a second cooler with beer and cover it with ice. Standing there with the bottles of Tennessee whiskey, one in each hand, I pause before putting them in the cooler.

Nash Cooper can be a vile and nasty drunk. He has trouble holding his tongue when he is sober, let alone after he's been drinking. Is it any wonder the kids have moved away?

I turn and put the liquor under the sink behind the paper towels and the bottle of dishwashing soap.

~ ~ ~

"Once we arrive at the river, Nash pulls into the campsite. All the menfolk head down to the river to swim and cool off leaving the women to set up camp. The old pop-up trailer still smells faintly of mildew. It must have been raining the last time Nash used it. It smells musty but it's clean. I know because I scrubbed the old girl down after Nash brought it home from his last fishing trip. At least that's where he said he was. I don't know what he was fishing for but I found a pair of women's panties in the bottom of his sleeping bag when I went to air it out before packing it all away again. That old redneck must have developed a hankerin' for big bottom girls given the size of those panties. He can have all the big bottomed girls he wants as far as I'm concerned as long as he keeps his hands and *little mister* away from me."

"Little mister? You're kidding, right?"

"What is it with men, naming their genitalia? Nash acts like his penis has a mind of his own and is beyond his control. I was sick of his juvenile behavior."

"Certainly not all men."

"I couldn't say. I've been married well over half my life, so my experience is limited and my sample size is small."

"Anyway, go on…"

"The men went swimming and then off to drink some beer and play a little softball while the women set up camp, cracking open a few beers of their own, and getting the grills going.

"Betsy was going on about her 40th anniversary and how Billy was taking her on a cruise. They hadn't decided where just yet, but she had her heart set on a ten day cruise of the Mediterranean. After all, they'd never been out of the country and they were not getting any younger. Billy wanted to go to Alaska, but it would be too cold in December. So she might just get her way.

"Then we went over to see Candy and Tim's new camper. While everyone was oohing and aahing, I slipped

away unnoticed to change into my bathing suit, then
headed down to the river to cool off.

I wade out into the middle of the river.

The river is swollen after all the rain.

The cool clean water brings a welcome relief.

I feel my temperature dropping.

Soon I will be numb.

I long to float there indefinitely

in the cool moving water,

buoyant,

feeling nothing at all.

It's better now,

just better.

The arguments and the litany of disappointments

Nag at me for attention

Not today

Not now

I'd already given enough of myself

to the misery of others' creation.

I let the water take me

Downstream

Away from the cloying reality of my life

The current is swift

It isn't long before those who'd brought me here

have disappeared from my sight

I won't be missed

At least not right away

I left without a plan

There will be time for that later.

As I float further and further from the picnic

grounds

And I know—today is the day

I feel a sense of freedom

Quite unlike anything I've felt before

I can almost visualize the chaos I've created

Quite unintentionally

Yet I am responsible just the same

The cool water rushes over me

And the shame or guilt I should feel

are washed away.

Shame and guilt,

For what?

Taking control of my own life

For just once I am doing as I please


Can I deal with the consequences?

The harsh and angry words,

the accusations

that are sure to follow

Perhaps I am already too far

down the river

to even think of going back


It's not that I *don't* love them—

My family

But perhaps it's too simplistic

To think of it as love

I was suffocating

In the judgment and expectations

Spoken and implied

I didn't *not* love them

I just wanted a different life

A life they are quite incapable of providing

So, if I want it

Now is my chance


Wet and chilled

I emerge from the cool rushing water

Resting a moment on the soft sand

Pushed up on the shoreline by the eddy

The sun has warmed the sand

The warmth of the late afternoon sun

envelops me like a blanket

I drift off towards sleep.

And wake to the sounds of dogs barking.

# Chapter 2
## Nash

"Shit man, what were you doing, playing with yourself. My golden would have caught that ball."

"Shut up," I say as I give Ted a shove in the shoulder before I throw my glove under the bench and take a seat to wait for my turn at bat. It's 3 to 2 them. I take a deep breath.

"You're just lucky we're only playin' for beer. If I had anything more ridin' on this game we'd be sendin' you back to help the women," Marshall says with a good natured laugh.

I try to think of something clever to say. "Damn sure your wife is back there just waitin' for me." I can dish it out with the best of them. We've been trash talkin' since junior high. Still I beat myself up for my screw-ups. I'm pissed. "Shelby wouldn't turn me away," I say with a laugh.

"You touch my wife, you sonofabitch, and she'll clean your clock," Marshall says and all the guys laugh.

Goddamnit." I grounded out at first, then fumbled that goddamn fly ball. I heard those mofos laughin' at me.

These assholes have been playin' ball every summer since Little League. I coulda kicked their ass back in the day.

"You better get a hit this time, Slugger," Wayne says as I go to put on the batting helmet. "Put some of that weight behind it and knock it out there."

I was quick and strong, back when I was playin' football and training in the weight room, but that was a long time ago. Lugging around this extra 100 pounds sure doesn't help. I tap my belly and it jiggles, "What can I say, my goddamn wife knows how to feed her man. I swear she's trying to kill me, always bakin' bread and cakes and all."

"Nothin' to do with all that beer," Ted laughs as he takes both hands and shakes his own beer belly.

I've heard enough of their bullshit, so I walk away and pick up a couple of heavy wooden bats and start swinging them hoping to loosen up my shoulders before I'm up.

I know I'm out of shape. It was Amy who wanted three kids.. Then there was all the time I spent goin' with the boys to their practices and games. I should have been taking care of myself and goin' to the gym. Maybe I would have if Amy wasn't always nagging at me to fix something around the house, her and that goddamn honey-do list of hers.

This little internal rant is cut short when out of the corner of my eye I see Betsy and Maggie running this way, followed by all the other gals. They're all waving their arms and carryin' on like a bunch of ninnies. "What the hell do they want?" I say to no one in particular. The last thing we need is this squad of aging cheerleaders out here. Maybe they're just here to watch, Maggie's always had a thing for me.

Wayne is tagged out at second and I'm just gettin' to the batter's box when the game comes to a halt as the women take the field, they're all crying and carrying on.

"What's going on?" I ask as Billy tries to comfort his hysterical wife. I can't understand a word she is saying. She is sobbing and out of breath from running out here.

Then I hear her say my wife's name, "Amy, Amy…"

"What did you say?" I shout at her. "What's happened to Amy?"

Now Betsy is hyperventilating and appears to be heading into a full blown panic attack.

"Back off Nash. What's your problem? Just calm the fuck down," Billy barks at me as he tries to settle his wife's hysteria. By now the other women have caught up and they begin to relay the story.

"We can't find Amy?" Shelby says as she begins to cry. All the men in the outfield have come in and gather around home plate as the story unfolds.

"Don't worry about Amy," I say. "Trust me she's fine. She probably went for a walk. She got one of those Fitbits and is always talking about how many steps she does and how many more she still needs to do. Don't worry she'll turn up…"

Lacey cuts me off. "No Nash. She's not fine. She went down to the river to swim and that was over an hour ago. The river is high and the water is fast. Her flip flops and towel are still on the shore with that book she was reading. We've looked everywhere for her. She's not in camp."

"We need to find her …" Polly stops mid-sentence before putting any more words to her fears.

"Shit." I was up to bat and hoping to redeem myself. I take the batting helmet off before going back to the bench to retrieve my glove. Leave it to Amy to screw this up, too. "I'm sure she's just gone for a walk," I mutter under my breath but the others are not having it.

Marshall pulls out his cell phone. "I'm calling 911. Everyone spread out and start looking for Amy." Marshall is taking charge and issuing directions, then he steps away

15

from the crowd so he can talk to the dispatch and explain what's going on.

"Do you really think this is necessary?" I ask. "Shouldn't we just wait before calling the police?"

"What the fuck are you talking about. She could be injured and the sun will be down in less than an hour. We need to find her before dark," Zeke snarls at me and I can see the hatred flash in his eyes. Lacey is Zeke's wife and Amy and Lacey are friends. What has that bitch been saying about me? I'm gonna need to play this another way. I turn on a dime.

"Right, what was I thinking? Oh God, poor Amy. Let's head down to the river," I say playing the role of the worried husband as best I can.

The shore of Sacandaga River, where Amy was last seen, is a good ten minute walk from the ballfield and another ten minute walk to the campground and our RVs. Some of the others have run on ahead. I try to keep up, but I'm quickly out of breath. I make another promise to myself to lose some weight and get back in shape.

Standing with the others on the shoreline. I see my wife's things. "Amy's a good swimmer," I say, trying to reassure those who are already here. I watch the river for a minute as I try to come to terms with what is happening. The river *is* moving fast and there is a rocky outcropping

16

not far downstream. "I suppose she could have hit her head." Shadows from the tree-lined shore have cast the river in the darkness. Fallen branches and logs are caught up along the river bank threatening to give way at any moment in a rush of rapidly moving water. Watching the power of the river, the reality hits me, "Amy could be hurt or worse."

The others fall silent.

I want to feel worried, fearful, and sad. I know I should. Amy really could be hurt, but all I feel is numb. What if...? I can't allow myself to even begin to think these horrible things, nor can I stop my mind from going there. What if she's dead? What will become of her old man's money?

Standing there looking into the dark deep water, we hear the sirens. "Thank God, help is on the way," one of the women says and begins to cry as the other women reach out to hold and comfort her and each other. The police are the first to arrive, followed close behind by a fire truck and a team of paramedics.

One of the younger cops asks, "Mr. Cooper, can you give me a description of your wife?"

This cop is still a kid, no older than my sons. "She's my age, 67."

"Height and weight?"

"She's about five foot eight, and skinny."

"Hair color?"

"She has blonde hair. She dyes it."

"Do you have a picture of your wife?" The young cop asks.

I show him a photo of the whole family that I have on my phone. "This is Amy." I point out my wife. "This was when our son Sammy got married. She doesn't really look like this."

The cop takes my cell phone from me and looks at the photograph. "I know Sam. We have some mutual friends. You said that she doesn't look like this, what do you mean?"

"She was all dolled up for the wedding in this photo. You know, she's had her hair done, she's wearing makeup, and that fancy dress. Besides, she's older now."

"When was this taken?"

"I don't know, nine or ten years ago."

"Don't you have anything more recent?" he asks me and I can hear and feel his judgment.

"Why would I carry a photo of her, I see her every day," I say.

"I have a photo," one of the women says. "This was taken last week."

Then he asks a bunch of other stupid questions that I can't answer.

"How am I supposed to know what color her swimsuit is? Look if you find an old gal floating in the river, it's probably her." I say a little too rudely. The cop glares at me and I see a look cross the faces of the others, they're appalled.

"What?" I say in a tone that invites no comments. I need to cool it.

"Okay Mr. Cooper, we've called in our K-9 team to help us locate your wife. Could you find us a piece of her clothing, something she's worn recently so our dogs can identify Mrs. Cooper's scent. What was she wearing before she went swimming?"

"I don't know."

"She had on a pale pink cotton t-shirt and a pair of shorts," Candy says. "Want me to see if I can find them in your camper, Nash?" she offers sweetly.

I nod. Now here is a helpful woman.

"We're going to need to mobilize forces and look for your wife before it gets dark. Why don't you folks head back to the campground? Change your shoes and put on some bug spray. We need to get this search and rescue organized. Good thing there are so many of you, we'll be able to cover more ground if everybody helps. Head on

19

back and ask to see Officer O'Leary, he'll let you know what he needs you to do."

The sun is already starting to set and the sky is red and gold. I walk back to the campground with this cop. What did he say his name was? I can't remember. He isn't any older than my kids. He speaks kindly to me but I sense he doesn't really like me. I hear the others whispering, they're just a few steps behind me and their voices are low and muffled. They are supposed to be my friends, but I can't help but feel that they don't like me very much either. I really need to play this differently. I need to be the grieving husband if these people are going to help me out. Maybe I can use this situation to my advantage.

Good God, Amy, where the fuck are you?

# Chapter 3
## Amy

I open my eyes, squinting into the blinding glare of the late

afternoon sun as a small white terrier stands his ground and barks at me as if he has just located an unwelcome intruder. I struggle to sit up hoping this little beast's bite isn't nearly as bad as his bark when the shadow of his master emerges from the tree-lined shore and completely obscures the sun. A chill comes over me as I try to determine where I am. I have the distinct impression that I am trespassing.

I am not a large woman, and as I lay there reclining on the beach in a still damp swimsuit I begin to feel rather vulnerable.

I pull my feet beneath me and stand up as this man, or maybe she's a woman as she bends over and clips a leash to the yapping little dog.

"That's quite enough Skye," she says to the dog.

I get to my feet and take a step away from the barking dog as I wrap my arms across my chest in an attempt to cover myself or at least my over-exposed cleavage.

The androgynous person smiles. "Welcome to Covewood. I'm Ellery McMasters. You must be the person they're searching for."

I'm pretty certain this person is a woman, at least I think she is. Her hair is gray and short. She wears no jewelry or makeup, only loose fitting jeans, an old blue flannel shirt, and running shoes. Are those breasts appear hidden by the folds of her shirt? If so, they are the only visible manifestation of her gender.

I struggle for something to say to explain who I am and why I'm here as I try to come to terms with the fact that there are people looking for me. "Shit," is all I can come up with.

She laughs as her face breaks into a wide welcoming smile. "I take it you'd rather not be found."

I close my eyes and nod my head. Without saying any more this person seems to understand.

"Come now. Let me find you a blanket. You must be getting chilled."

Without waiting for a reply she turns and her little dog leads us away from the river and back into the woods where a small cabin sits amongst a stand of hardwoods.

I'm still uncertain if I am with a man or a woman. I decide it doesn't matter. I struggle with the need to classify and use the correct pronoun.

I follow a few steps behind gingerly attempting to avoid the small sharp twigs that poke the tender soles of my feet.

There is a small fire still smoldering in the firepit outside the cabin door and an old coffee pot sits over the fire on an iron grate. "Sit," Ellery says and gestures towards a large stump outside the fire circle.

I do as I am told. I start to shiver in the shade of the trees as Ellery heads into the cabin. I watch Ellery walk away. There is a softness about her. I decide she is a woman, albeit a reluctant one. She returns momentarily with the blanket she has promised me. She hands it to me, still keeping me at arms-length. Only then does it dawn on me that perhaps she has as much reason to fear me as I do to fear her. I wrap myself in the well-worn patchwork cotton quilt covering my near-nakedness and wallowing in the warmth the blanket provides.

"Would you like some coffee?" she asks.

"Please," I respond.

"Hope you can drink it black. I haven't any milk or sugar."

"Black is fine, thank-you." I always take my coffee with cream and sugar. Right now I'm feeling anxious and apprehensive. I have an overwhelming sense of urgency to figure this all out, before I'm found and found out. Coffee may be a bad idea, particularly this late in the day. Still, I need to stay alert and vigilant. The coffee will help.

Ellery adds another log to the fire and stirs the ashes. I watch her as the flames spring to life and we wait for the coffee to be reheated. Her age is equally difficult to determine. Her face is lined and crows' feet appear around her eyes when she smiles. She appears to have completely abandoned any need for social convention. She moves with purpose, her voice is gentle and her words are spare and well chosen.

Still, I know she is waiting for me to offer some kind of explanation about why I'm here.

Once convinced the coffee is hot, she pours two cups, then hands me mine before taking a seat on the stump beside me.

The fire crackles and pops as we drink our coffees. The coffee is strong and bitter, left too long over the fire, heated and reheated. I drink it anyway as I attempt to face up to this new reality. The questions begin to take shape in my head— What have I done? Now what?

No words are spoken when the silence is broken by the whirring of a helicopter flying low, just above the canopy of the trees. The search lights glow as the chopper travels slowly hovering above the river's bank as it heads upstream towards the campgrounds.

"They're looking for you," Ellery says as a matter-of-fact.

I know this, but say nothing. She looks me in the eye and I hold her gaze.

"Do you want to send word to anyone that you're okay?"

I shake my head and a tear slips from my eye.

Ellery nods her head slowly, "If you don't want to be found, then I think we should go inside." Without waiting for a reply she stands and walks towards the cabin. I hesitate as I watch her walk away, I am completely out of options.

I follow.

# Chapter 4
## Amy

Night has fallen and Ellery lights a couple of lamps which fill the cabin with a golden glow. Again, I hear the sound of dogs barking. This time the sound is distant, coming from upriver, perhaps near the campground. Police dogs, no doubt, out on search and rescue. Sure didn't take Nash very long to throw his prodigious weight around. He probably called in a favor from some of the cops in his bowling league.

I wonder how far away they are.

How far down the river did I travel?

How soon before they find me?

Ellery's little dog, Skye, peers out the front window. She is on full alert.

"Is she a Westie?" I ask.

"Sort of. She is of questionable parentage. Her mama was a West Highland terrier and a bit of a run around." Again Ellery laughs in a lighthearted way. "I supposed we have that in common. I don't know who her father is any more than I know mine. We're a couple of misfits, she and I. She's good company all the same." She stops a moment and ruffles the fur on the dog's head. The little dog looks up at Ellery and a look of mutual affection passes between the two. I can't help but feel a twinge of envy. It has been so long since anyone has looked at me with anything that resembles either love or affection.

Ellery heads into the bedroom and comes out with a flannel shirt and a pair of sweatpants. "Better too big, than too small," she says as she sets them on the footstool. "You can change in the bathroom if you like." She points to the closed door off of the kitchen.

Once I've changed, I return to the sitting room.

"Perhaps we should start with your name, I need to call you something," she says.

Again I hesitate.

I hesitate before answering, as if this is a difficult question. I sit there a moment longer trying to decide just how much I want to tell this woman. I take a deep breath to steady myself before I begin. "I'm leaving my old life behind. I guess that means I can choose a new name, a new name for a new life. You can call me Kaye."

"Why Kaye?"

"I went to Cahill School when I was nine years old. I guess that was when the indoctrination began. That was when and where I first got lost, where I lost my freedom,

27

and eventually lost my way. Maybe if I go back to Kaye Hill I will find what it is I've lost, and needs to be recovered."

Ellery nods as if this seems reasonable.

"I've been on the A track all of my life. I've always been the good girl, you know the type, I always followed the rules and played nice, until today. It's time for a change and a new plan."

Ellery looks me in the eye and holds me in the silence that grows between us. Eventually a slow smile passes her lips and she says, "That's the thing about life, as long as we're still here we can do so. We can start over and recreate a life of our own choosing."

She speaks with an air of confidence that leads me to believe she knows what she's talking about. I can't help but wonder if she speaks from experience. I look around this small, simple cabin with furnishings that might once have been gathered from someone else's attic, and at this woman who hides her gender beneath a masculine façade. If we indeed choose our own path, and create our own lives, why in the world would anyone choose to live as Ellery does? Before I can even begin to come up with an answer, she says, "You must be brave, you know, leaving one's life behind takes courage, particularly to leave with as little as you have."

This time it is my turn to laugh. "I've fantasized about leaving for years, decades really. I'd formulated one plan after another, but the timing just never seemed quite right. Today the opportunity presented itself and I realized as I floated further and further down the river if I didn't go now, I would talk myself out of it again and I might never take the chance."

Again the sound of the barking dogs can be heard in the distance. This time the sound is louder and I know they are getting closer.

"I went as far as getting a passport, although I've never used it, and I have some money. I guess that has always been a bit of a stumbling block, at least until now."

A quizzical look passes over Ellery's face, but she keeps any questions she may have to herself. I didn't know that today would be the day, you know, the day that I would leave."

"Where is home?" Ellery asks.

"Home? I haven't felt safe or at home since I was a child. But I've been living with my husband over in Beaver Ridge for the last 40 years."

"Beaver Ridge?"

"It's the name of our subdivision. It's in Clifton Park, outside of Schenectady. It's not on a ridge and there hasn't been a beaver living anywhere near there since they plowed it all down and built 97 homes, each one just like the next."

"Ah, I see," she nods her head as she visualizes, "life in the suburbs."

Again we hear the barking dogs.

"The river has probably thrown them off your scent, at least temporarily. But, you know they'll come looking for you. It'll be best if you're not here when they do, if you're serious about disappearing and starting anew. You're welcome to come back 'til you figure out what's next, but you'd better get going. You can use my truck."

"What will you tell them if they come here?"

"Leave that to me. I've been living a lie most of my life, I've gotten pretty good at it by now. I don't suppose one more little lie will keep me from the pearly gates." Ellery laughs as she reaches into her pants pocket and hands me the keys. "Maybe you should go get a few things, being as how you haven't packed as much as a toothbrush. I'm bettin' your house is empty now, now that everyone is out searchin' for you."

I stand and hike up the extra-large sweat pants that are puddling down around my bare feet.

"I'll turn on the porch light when it's safe for you to return. If the light is off, just wait. Take the back roads, the truck has GPS. You'll be okay."

"Thank you, Ellery," I say as I head towards the door. I want to give her a hug for all of her unmerited kindness. But I decide against it. She doesn't even know me, or I her.

"See you soon, Kaye." Skye follows me to the door, her little tail a waggin'.

Again we hear the dogs. They are hot on my trail and getting closer.

The door closes behind me and I hear Ellery turn the bolt and lock the door. Before I'm even to the truck, the porch light goes out.

# Chapter 5
## Kaye

I walk slowly up the gravel driveway towards the parked

vehicle allowing my eyes to adjust to the light. The night

sky is as dark as I have ever seen it and I'm afraid I might

stumble over something in my bare feet. I turn my face

toward the sky and a million stars begin to appear almost

out of nowhere. Out here in the wilderness, away from the

lights of the city and the suburbs, I am awestruck by the

majesty of the night. There are times when my problems

seem so overwhelming, yet standing here with the Milky

Way so visible overhead, I realize how small and

insignificant my concerns really are.

I remind myself to try and keep this in perspective.

I climb into Ellery's truck and adjust the seat so I

can reach the pedals. Ellery's GPS is similar to one I'm

already familiar with. I type in my address and a map

appears on the screen, it's only then that I see that I'd

floated further than I'd realized. I start the truck and head

for home. This GPS attempts to send me towards the

highway, but then it indicates there is some kind of a slowdown up ahead and advises an alternate route.

I turn on the radio and the local station is broadcasting about the missing woman. I cringe as they butcher my name. Maybe I should be glad the public is out looking for a sixty-eight year old woman named Amelia Hooper, rather than Amy Cooper. Nash couldn't even get my age right. I won't be sixty-five until the first of next month. He's the one who is sixty-seven, not me.

"She was last seen in the picnic area at the Sacandaga Campgrounds about four o'clock this afternoon. The police believe she may have drowned in the Sacandaga River or may possibly have met with foul play." Then the broadcaster encourages the listening public to contact the sheriff's department if anyone knows of my whereabouts.

I guess Nash is getting pretty nervous thinking about cooking his own dinner and trying to figure out how to use the washing machine.

I follow the directions as indicated  on the GPS until I see a cluster of police cars with their lights on up at the break of the hill. I take the next side street and decide to stick to the back roads. There's another bridge about twenty-five miles upstream from here. They'll probably be looking for me or my body downstream. I turn and head north. This route takes me miles out of my way, still it seems a little safer. I have not come this far only to be found now.

The GPS reroutes me. Lost in my own thoughts I follow the directions towards home as I mentally run through the list of what I need to take with me: Passport, cash, my new credit card that I've yet to activate, and some clothes.

I left my purse and my wallet in the camper, there's no way I can retrieve them now. I guess my passport can serve as identification.

I have a pretty substantial pile of cash that I've been saving, as I have always hoped that the day would come when I would finally get the courage to leave. It should last me a little while, as long as I'm careful. Besides, my brother, Douglas, said our inheritance from Dad should be available any day now, if it's not already.

I'd be happy if they just assume that I'm dead, maybe then they'll stop looking for me. That will never happen if someone notices that all my things are missing. But Nash will have no idea if any of my clothes are missing, it's been decades since he's noticed what I was wearing. I decide to take a change of clothes. I don't want to look conspicuous, like I do right now in this oversized sweat suit. I will buy what I need once I decide where I'm going.

I think about driving into the subdivision, but decide against it. It's not that I really know my neighbors, or they know me. However, I do know this, they have an overwhelming tendency to stick their noses into other people's business. No doubt they are having a field day with this.

I pull into the parking lot for the elementary school behind our house. The school is closed for the summer holiday and won't be re-opening for another couple of weeks. I go and hide on the top of the plastic slide on the playground. No one can see me as I am encircled in the yellow plastic designed to keep little children from falling from the top. From here I can see into my neighbors' houses. I wait and watch as one by one their lights go out and I assume my neighbors are heading off to bed.

I know this schoolyard as I walk in this neighborhood and around the perimeter almost every day. I've been going to yoga here at the school three nights a week for almost ten years now. Tonight, I stick to the shadows cast by the trees. There was a time when the kids were little that Nash had built a ladder over the chain link fence so the kids could just climb the fence to get to school. I smile at the memory, that seems like another lifetime ago.

I may be turning 65 in a few short weeks, but I don't feel old. Still I'm glad the fence is only about five feet high. I climb the chain link fence that separates our backyard from the schoolyard. My toes are killing me as I poke my bare feet in the holes created by the interlinking steel mesh, then I hoist myself up and over the top. I land in a heap in the grass. I get to my feet, noticing that I've scraped my leg coming over the top but no real damage done.

Under the cover of darkness, I make my way to our back deck. The hide-a-key is just where I left it, under the terracotta pot of red geraniums. The key is for the door to the garage and the door inside the garage is never locked. We always use our garage door openers to get inside. Feeling like a prowler, I put the key into the door lock, and turn the latch then let myself into my own home.

I don't turn on any lights. I don't want to alert anyone that I am here. My heart is racing as I slink around in the dark. It doesn't take me long to find what little I need. A change of clothes, undergarments, a nightgown, some basic toiletries, and a bottle of Shalimar. I have worn this fragrance for as long as I can remember. My father first bought it for me when I went to study in France. The memory brings on another round of tears. I wipe them away with the sleeve of Ellery's oversized sweatshirt and

36

put the perfume in an old canvas shopping bag along with everything else. Kneeling on my side of the bed, I reach my hand between the mattress and the box spring and find what I am looking for— my mad money. I knew the day would come when I would finally have had enough and would find the courage to leave. I just didn't know it would be today. I've been preparing for this day all of my adult life. I put the envelope of cash into the shopping bag.

I sit for a moment on the edge of the bed and there is a framed photo of my children, back when they were little and I believed that everything was possible and something good awaited us. A tear runs down my face as I hold the photo close to my chest before putting it into the bag with everything else. How can I leave my children behind? Struggling with the magnitude of leaving and leaving without a word, I put my bruised and bleeding feet into an old pair of running shoes.

The irony isn't lost on me.

I'm running away from home and I'm running for my life.

# Chapter 6
## Kaye

Lost in my own thoughts, I slowly make my way back to Ellery's cabin. There is a part of me that knows this is a bad idea. People are looking for me, however, I still have her truck. She trusted me with it, at the very least I owe it to her to return it.

Sticking to the two-lane back roads, I slowly make my way. It is so dark out here on these narrow mountain passes. I drive slowly around the curves in the low light. The last thing I need is to get a speeding ticket or hit a deer and bring some police officer to the scene of an accident.

It is already after midnight when I drive past Ellery's driveway and stop for a moment. Still on the road, I can see her porch light is on. At least I think it is, am I at the right house? I back up, then pull down the driveway. This is it. I turn the truck off and sit quietly in the dark before I gather up the canvas bag holding all of my worldly possessions and make my way down the driveway towards the house. The house is dark. Has Ellery gone off to bed? I take another couple of steps when the spot lights go on. I freeze. She has them on a motion detector. Skye starts to bark and announces my arrival and Ellery steps out onto the porch.

"Quick, get in here," she commands and I do as I am told.

She turns out the porch light and closes the door behind us. "Thank you," I say as I hand her the keys to the truck.

"I was startin' to wonder whether you were comin' back," she says with a smile.

The little cabin is dark, except for the fire in the fireplace. Ellery gestures towards the chair nearest the hearth and I take it. She settles herself on the sofa and Skye jumps up and snuggles into the wide soft folds of her lap.

"I'm sorry," I say. "I hope you weren't worried. I had to take a detour as the police had set up a road block by the exit to the highway. They were stopping cars and searching them with a flashlight. I took the back roads and headed north to the Algonquin Lake bridge." Ellery just nods her head.

"Did you get what you need?" she asks.

"I think so," I respond.

She gets up and walks towards the kitchen and returns with a folded dish towel. "Looks like you cut your leg."

39

I look down at my legs. The blood has soaked through the sweat pants Ellery loaned me and has dripped down onto my foot and running shoes.

"Sorry about your sweatpants." She shrugs letting me know this is no big deal. "It looks worse than it is. I had to climb a chain link fence. I caught my leg as I went over. I guess I'm not as agile as I once was."

Ellery laughs. "Who is? Can I get you something to eat? You must be starving. Or would you rather get yourself cleaned up first?"

"All of the above," I say.

Again she laughs. "Why don't you go get in the shower and I'll warm up some soup. There are towels and soap in the bathroom. Use whatever you like."

I nod as she walks back into the kitchen. I grab my bag and head for the bathroom. The warmth of the shower feels so good as my core temperature slowly begins to rise. There is shampoo in the shower and I wash my hair. She uses some inexpensive drugstore brand. It is harsh and unscented, no doubt my hair will frizz and look like straw. But at least now I am warm and clean.

I let the water wash over me another moment as my mind wanders. I am not accustomed to great luxury anymore. The life that I've been living bears no resemblance to the way I was raised. But I have always pampered myself with gentle, fragrant hair and body washes. Ellery does not. It is the one area of my life where I indulge in a little bit of self-love. I have allowed myself to become invisible, unseen, and my needs and desires have not been considered. I know this is not all my husband's fault, for I have allowed it.

No more.

I turn the shower off and notice that the scab that had begun to form on my leg has loosened in the warm running water and my leg is bleeding again. I use the dish towel Ellery gave to me to stop the bleeding before drying myself off. I wrap my hair in a towel and put on my nightgown.

When I return to the living room, I see that Ellery has set the table in the corner near the kitchen with a plate of biscuits, a butter dish, and a jar of raspberry jam. There is one tablespoon and a homespun napkin long since past its prime. She carries a ceramic soup bowl with both hands being careful not to spill. "You're in luck. I went to the farmer's market yesterday and made myself a pot of vegetable soup and a batch of biscuits this afternoon. The raspberries grow wild here in the woods. I just need to get to them before the bears do." She gives me a generous and welcoming smile as I take my seat at the scrubbed pine table that has been waxed to enhance its antique patina.

"Eat," she says and so I begin.

The soup is delicious. I hadn't realized how hungry I was. I hadn't eaten since breakfast. I guess stress is an appetite killer. At least it is for me. I break open the biscuit. She has warmed them in the oven. I spread the butter and jam. The butter melts and drips down my fingers. I wipe them on the napkin and dig in.

Ellery sits in silence while I eat and sips a mug of tea. "Would you like a cup?" she asks. All I have is Lipton."

"No thanks. I'm still pretty wired from the coffee. Any more caffeine and I'll never sleep."

She nods and the silence grows between us. "They were here about an hour after you left. I guess the dogs picked up your scent from either the shoreline or from around the fire pit."

"The police? What did you tell them?" My anxiety is rising. I push the empty soup bowl towards the center of the table.

"The canine unit. They asked me a few questions like: Have you seen this woman? And then they showed me a photograph of you. I simply told them no, that Skye and I had been inside since the mosquitos descended upon us. This seemed to satisfy them and they continued on their way."

"Thank you. I'm sorry to have dragged you into this."

She shrugs as if it is no big deal. "My life is pretty quiet out here. I don't get much company and I like you." She pauses. "I'd like to help you. There were people who helped me and now I believe it's payback time."

She smiles as I take this all in. I really don't know what to say. I'd like to ask who helped her and what she needed help with. Before I can formulate my questions, she asks me, "Do you have a plan?"

All I can do is shake my head no. Tears threaten to escape my eyes and I dry them with my napkin.

"I think *we* should make one. But you look exhausted. Let's put this off until tomorrow morning, but not any later. I fear the police may be back if they can find no other trace of you. Now off to bed, get some sleep. I'll clean up and see you in the morning." She points to a door off the kitchen.

"Thank you for your generosity and kindness," I say, holding her gaze for a moment. I stand and move towards the door she indicates. "Good night Ellery."

"Good night Kaye."

This name change is going to take some getting used to.

The room is small with a single bed and a well-worn patchwork quilt. I pull the blankets back and turn off the light on the bedside table before I crawl into the soft flannel sheets. I think I am asleep before my head hits the feather pillow.

# Chapter 7
## Kaye

I wake in the night with a fright. My heart is pounding out of my chest. Nash is looking at me and he is raging mad. Convinced it was just a bad dream, I sit up in bed only to realize I am not in my bed, in my room, or even in my own house. As the dream starts to fade and slip from my consciousness, slowly an awareness of everything that happened yesterday and last night begins to fill in the empty spaces in my memory.

I am in Ellery's cabin in the woods, in her guest room, in this cozy bed and Nash has no idea where I am.

I pull back the muslin curtain and look out the window. The full moon peeks out from behind the trees all bedecked in their summer loveliness and I breathe in the peace and quiet of this place. The air blowing through the open window is cool and fresh. My heart rate has slowed and fear dissipates. I remember how Ellery has offered to help me with a plan. We will do that in the morning. Convinced of my safety, I snuggle back down beneath the flannel sheets and fall back asleep.

The sun is not yet up when the smell of coffee calls to me. I lay there for a moment as I hear Ellery puttering about in the kitchen. This bed is so cozy, I'd love to sleep the day away. But all things considered, this is not an option.

I dress quickly in a pair of worn jeans and a sweatshirt. This will be too warm later in the day, but it feels good now as the air is brisk this morning. Before I pull on a pair of white footies, I reexamine the cuts on my toes. I really did a number on them climbing that fence in bare feet. Then I put on my old, now blood-stained running shoes. Aside from the bloody shoes, I look positively inconspicuous for I am dressed in the uniform of every other Adirondack tourist, I might even pass as a local.

Entering the kitchen, I see that Ellery is sitting at the table with her morning coffee. She, too, wears a sweatshirt and faded jeans. The first signs of daylight can be seen to the east as the sky is red and just beginning to lighten. It's 5:30.

"Good morning, Kaye," she says to me and I return the greeting. "Red sky at night ..." she begins the old adage and I complete it ...

"Sailors' delight, red sky at morning, sailors take warning." And with the mention of her name Ellery's little white dog scampers into the kitchen. I bend down to pet her. "Did you think we were calling you, Skye?" The little pup wags her tail. "Good thing I'm not sailing anywhere today," I say and give Ellery a smile.

She smiles and gives a nearly imperceptible shake of her head. She is thinking something although I'm not sure what that might be.

"Did you hear the rain last night?" Ellery asks.

"No. I woke up only once. The sky was clear then. I fell back to sleep and slept soundly."

"Rained pretty steadily for a couple of hours. I got up to close the windows, and you were sound asleep. Since I was awake, I listened to the police scanner for an hour, or so. They called off the search for you about 2:45. Too dark and too much rain."

I'm glad to hear that. Still, it makes me feel disposable. I keep these thoughts to myself.

"Help yourself to the coffee," Ellery says. "And have a seat, Kaye. I've just re-warmed these biscuits from yesterday."

I pour a small cup, as black coffee is not my favorite. I slather the biscuit with butter and honey and it is almost as good as the ones were last night.

"We need to get on with that plan," Ellery says. "As much as I welcome your company, you need to get out of here."

47

I nod in agreement. "I had a terrifying dream that Nash was after me."

"I assume you have your reasons."

"We've been married for forty years. We met when we were in college." I hesitate and ask, "Do you really want to hear this?"

"Go on," she prods.

And so I do. "We did all the collegiate stuff. Nash was considered quite a catch back then. He was the quarterback on the football team with dreams of playing pro-ball. I know it sounds rather cliché. But I was attracted to his confidence. He was so different from anybody else I'd ever known. I guess I didn't understand just how different he was and how different we were from one another.

"He was funny and we did fun things, at least initially. Like so many other couples we were friends with in college, everyone was planning their futures, either separately or together. And as expected, we got engaged over the Christmas holidays of our senior year. I already had reservations about marrying him, but I consented and we planned for a long engagement. I thought I'd have time to figure it out. I was graduating in the spring, but Nash had been red-shirted as a freshman. He had another season of football ahead of him and a few more classes to finish up. I don't know what I was thinking, I should have known. All the signs were there."

Ellery sits quietly sipping her coffee. She waits a moment for me to continue, but I fear I've already said enough.

She asks, "Did he hit you?"

"Not at first. But he would get jealous if I spent too much time talking to another guy and he was a mean drunk. And he drinks a lot."

Ellery nods her head, "Give me an example." Encouraging me to continue with this old saga.

"Initially, he was just mean. He called me names that hurt my feelings and made horrible accusations that were unfounded." Ellery looks perplexed. "You know… he accused me of sleeping with his friends and stuff like that and it just wasn't true. Once he sobered up, he would apologize and be overly affectionate. Once we were engaged, he refused to wear a condom, claiming it *ruined* everything for him but that wasn't it. If I became pregnant, then I wouldn't stray or leave him. He was controlling and he wanted control of me."

"Did he actually say this?"

"Not to me, but my sister-in-law told me. Apparently, Nash was shooting off his mouth when he was drunk about keeping *his woman* barefoot and pregnant."

Ellery shakes her head and I feel embarrassed for being such an idiot.

"What can I say, I was young and naïve and he was my first real boyfriend. I ended up getting pregnant the month before graduation and we were married in the summer before he went off to the training camp in August.

"Nash was injured in the first game of the season and never played again. He never even finished the last few classes he needed to graduate. I now know he was grieving the loss of his future and his identity as a football star.

"I was about five months pregnant; we'd been married less than three months and Nash was drinking. That was the first time he ever laid a hand on me. He came home drunk and accused me of messing around with his brother. He roughed me up, you know..."

"No, tell me."

"He just pushed me around until I lost my balance and fell and hit my face on a door knob. He later apologized, and blamed it on his drinking. He promised never to do anything like that again. He said he would never have done such a thing if he wasn't drinking. I wanted to believe him. But things escalated since that first time and have gone from bad to worse. We moved back to his hometown where he took a job in his father's auto supply store until his father passed away. That was about 25 years ago and he left Nash the business."

"I'm sorry Kaye. It's hard to imagine staying in a situation like this for forty years."

"We had kids and I couldn't risk leaving him. I didn't have any real money of my own when the kids were little and he always threatened that if I ever left him that I'd never see my kids again. Even if he didn't kidnap them and take them away from me, he is a powerful man with friends in high places. In the best case scenario, we might have had shared custody and I couldn't even imagine leaving my children alone with their father, particularly, my daughter. Nash could say terrible things to her. I stayed to protect her from him. He was unpredictable and still is. He has unmitigated anger and access to weapons. I was and still am more than a little bit afraid of him."

"So, I guess going home is out of the question," Ellery says with a sardonic smile.

"You might say that," I return her smile. "Sorry for going on and on about my own personal nightmare. I've been holding my cards pretty close to my chest for decades, I guess I just needed to talk about it."

"No problem. Since we're using the card game metaphor, I think you need to put all your cards on the table so *we* can come up with a plan to keep you safe. Can I tell you something?" Ellery asks.

"What?" I respond.

"I really admire your courage."

"Thank you," I say. "I've always thought of myself as a coward for not standing up to Nash. I don't think anyone has ever thought I'm the least bit courageous."

"Easy for others to pass judgment on things they know nothing about. It's far more difficult when you are being bullied and beaten and fear for the safety of your children. You need to disregard the opinions of others, for truly, it's none of their business. The gossip and judgments of others says far more about them, than they do about you."

I smile and nod my head. I can only imagine the judgments and gossip Ellery has had to endure.

"But as I said before, you are not safe here. Where do you want to go? And do you have any money?" Ellery asks.

She is pragmatic and gets right down to the problem at hand. There is wisdom in this, for it is not only a problem for me, but even my being here also creates a problem for her. She has lied to the police to protect me and God only knows what kind of upheaval that might create in the life of this generous and kind woman.

"My father passed away a few weeks ago, my mother has been gone for over ten years. My brother is the executor of my parents' estate. He and I are the only named beneficiaries. We will inherit what remains in the estate, and I believe it's substantial although I don't know exactly how much. I won't have to worry about money. My father couldn't stand Nash. A few weeks before his death he sat me down and told me that my inheritance was going to be directed into a Swiss bank account. It was set up for me years ago and the money should be transferred there any day now. So, I guess I'm going to Switzerland. In the interim, I have enough cash to last me for a while and a new credit card that I've opened using my daughter's address in Denver. I haven't activated the card. I will only use it in an emergency, it feels risky. I really just want to slip away without a trace."

"Sounds like you have this pretty well thought out, but you'll need identification in your new name, Kaye Hill. If you use your passport or that credit card under your old name, they will find you. Everything is connected via the internet; privacy is an antiquated concept."

"How do you know so much about this?" I ask as Ellery is already two or three steps ahead of me.

"Do you think my mother named me Ellery?" she asks.

I shrug. "I've never known anyone named Ellery before."

"My given name was Cassandra Marie. Can you imagine me with such a feminine name? She couldn't have come up with a less suitable name if that had been her intention. She might as well have named me *Tinkerbell*." She laughs and I smile. "I changed my name and my identity years ago when I moved out here to the north woods. I was sick and tired of being bullied and subjected to the judgment of others who did not know me and certainly did not love me. You and I are not that different in some regards. Get your bag, we need to leave. Now."

"Where are we going?" I ask.

"You're going to Montreal. I have some friends up there. You're going to need some travel documents."

She's right of course. I head for the bedroom and get the old canvas bag with all my worldly positions before stopping in the bathroom. I catch a glimpse of myself in the mirror and decide to braid my hair in one long golden plait down my back. I never wear my hair like this, just changing things up.

When I leave the bathroom Ellery is standing by the door ready to go. She hands me a pair of dark Ray Bans and navy-blue baseball cap that says Mirror Lake Lodge in white lettering. "Ever been there?" she asks.

"Never heard of it."

"It's in Lake Placid. A little too rich for my blood these days, but once upon a time I was a frequent visitor."

I want to ask her a million questions but …

She must sense my hesitancy as she grabs her keys and heads towards the door. "Now is not the time. We'll have time to talk once we're on our way."

# Chapter 8
## Nash

The storm clouds seem to come in out of nowhere up in the Adirondacks. They come fast and furiously and there is always a risk of flooding. There was another downpour about three this morning adding even more water to the rushing river. The riverbanks are slippery and muddy and Officer O'Leary was concerned about losing another person to the river. Besides, you couldn't see a damn thing, so they decided to call off the search until the weather cleared. It is supposed to be nice in the morning.

I was soaked to the skin and exhausted. By the time the search was called off, everybody in our party was packed up and ready to go home. They'd eased their consciences and fulfilled whatever obligation they might feel they owed Amy. I'm sure I'll not be let off the hook so easily.

I change into some dry clothes before I begin the drive home. Thankfully one of the women packed up all our camping shit while I was out with the troopers searching for Amy. Some of the other women cooked dinner, kept the campfires burning and waited, while hoping and praying my wife might walk out of the woods. The next teary-eyed woman who tells me not to give up hope is going to get herself somethin' to cry about.

I pull onto the expressway with the pop-up in tow. Maybe when some of her old man's inheritance comes through I'll get myself one of those souped-up RVs like Candy and Tim just got. Not for the first time, I wonder if the fact that Amy's gone missing will impact when we, or I, will get the money from her father's estate. Lost in my thoughts, I'm brought back to reality when I see a police car at the exit with its lights on. There is a barricade across the road and a cop is stopping everyone.

I roll the window down. I haven't seen this guy before. He shines his bright flashlight in my eyes.

"License please," is all he says.

I reach for my wallet in my back pocket and hand it to him.

"Nash Cooper?" He says as he turns the flashlight from my license to my face.

"Yes sir. I'm the dead woman's husband."

He scrunches up his face and decades' worth of frown lines appear across his forehead. "Dead? Do you know something that we don't know, something that would confirm your wife's demise?" This sounds like an accusation. This guy is all business. He stares me down, unsmiling.

Oh God, the last thing I need is to be considered a suspect in Amy's disappearance. "No Officer. I do not. I just left the campground. I was part of the search party and we were unable to find any trace of Amy. I guess, I just fear the worst, that's all."

"That's all?" he says and curls his lip and sneers at me. He hands me back my license and lets me go.

I can't help but wonder what he knows…about me. As I head for home, there are police cars stopping drivers at all the exits near the campground. They are concerned Amy may have met with foul play. I've seen enough cop shows to know it's always about sex or money. It's hard for me to imagine, who would have any interest in my wife in either regard. God only knows I'm not interested and I'm her husband. And she doesn't have any money, at least not yet.

I wonder if anyone's checked the hospitals? I suppose that's standard operating procedure in a case like this.

What am I gonna tell the boys? I guess I'm gonna *have to* call Andrea, too. It's still the middle of the night in Denver. She will probably fall apart. She was always way closer with her mother than she ever was with me. One of the boys can call her. I have enough to deal with right now.

It's about sixty-five miles home. It will take me every bit of 90 minutes to get home given there are police cars everywhere. I watch my speed and my mind wanders. If she's really gone, I'm already certain I'll never remarry. But how long should I wait before I can start dating again? I start thinking about the women I'd like to sleep with.

Lost in my own thoughts I make my way towards home.

I pull the old camper into the driveway in the early morning hours, sometime just before dawn.

Where the hell has Amy gone? I thought for sure we would have located her body by now. Maybe she'll be found this morning.

I'm not even out of my truck when I see headlights in my rear-view mirror.

Whoever it is has followed me into my driveway.

It's a cop.

Can't a guy get a moment's peace? Officer O'Leary, that pompous prick, said someone would be by in the morning, I didn't think they meant five AM for god's sake. I step out of my truck as the cop approaches.

"Nash Cooper?"

"Yes Officer." Who the hell was he expecting?

We shake hands as we size each other up in the bright headlights shining from the cop car. He's about half my age and half my size, wearing the gray uniform, purple tie, and a stupid hat that looks like he should have arrived on horseback. He's a trooper.

He flashes his badge. "I'm Detective Roy Randall, from the New York State Missing Persons Unit. Can we speak inside?"

I nod. Like I have a choice. "Let me open the garage door," I say as I open the driver's door of my truck and click the remote on the visor. The door opens and the garage lights go on.

He follows me in through the garage. I hit the button and close the garage door behind us.

The door is unlocked, as always. We make our way down the hallway, past the laundry room and a half bath. I turn on the hall light, then the one in the kitchen. "Have a seat," I point towards the kitchen table. "I need to take a leak." He does as requested and I head for the bathroom.

What the fuck does this guy want? Amy is missing and she sure as hell isn't here. I catch a glimpse of myself in the bathroom mirror. Who is that old guy? Being out all night combing the banks of the river for my wife has taken its toll on me. I splash some water on my face and dry it with a hand towel.

When I return to the kitchen the officer is perusing the kitchen like he's at an open house and thinking about making an offer. What the hell is he doing poking around in my house? Again, I point to the chair I left him in when I went to use the john. I take the seat across the table from him. "What did you say your name was?"

"Roy Randall, Missing Persons Unit."

"Any chance we can do this later? I've been up all night and I'm exhausted. I really need to sleep."

"I'm afraid not Mr. Cooper. I have some questions I need to ask about your wife and a team from our forensic lab should be out here in about an hour.

"Forensic lab is that like CSI or something?"

"Yes, the same. Your home is not considered a crime scene, at this time, but we will need to search your home to be able to rule out any foul play."

"You are wasting your time and mine. You should be dragging the Hudson River for her body, not snooping through her underwear drawer." The officer rolls his eyes and gives his head a nearly imperceptible shake. "Alright, already let's get on with this so I can go to bed. It's been a long day."

"I imagine it has Mr. Cooper." He pulls out a notebook and a pen. "Your wife's first and last name…"

61

"Good God, are you people incompetent or just idiots? How many times am I going to be asked the same questions?"

"I realize this may seem redundant but you were working with the local Northville police department up where your wife went missing. Given that your wife went missing over twelve hours ago and has not been located up in the north woods, the Missing Persons Unit has been brought in to help with the investigation. Time is of the essence and we need to get this information out for wider distribution. Things that may appear to be inconsequential to you may be significant, our forensic team often finds things the rest of us have overlooked."

I want to tell this guy to shut the fuck up and get the hell out of my house, but my better judgment prevails. "Her name is Amy Cooper. Amy Elizabeth Cooper."

"Age?"

"67, no wait she's a couple years younger than me. We were in the same class at UNC, but she skipped a grade and started early. I think she'll be 65 next month." Then he proceeded to ask all the same questions I was asked last night.

"Full description of your wife…"

"Any distinguishing marks, scars or tattoos?"

I pause momentarily and decide not to mention that she broke her forearm a year ago and had to have surgery with pins and a plate. She has a long red scar where they operated on her arm. She thought it was my fault, but it never would have happened if she wasn't so mouthy. Going off like she did, I had to hit her. No red-blooded American man would let his wife talk to him the way she was talking to me. She knew how to piss me off. She'd done it before. She deserved it.

"Mr. Cooper?..." The officer speaks my name to draw me back into this conversation. "Did your wife have any distinguishing marks, scars or tattoos?"

"No, no she didn't."

And then the questions start to get a little more difficult...

"Tell me about your marriage..."

"Was your wife faithful to you?"

# Chapter 9
## Ellery

We head out to the truck. It must be about 6:00 AM as the sun has already risen and can be seen across the lake but it's still pretty low on the horizon. Things have cooled off since the storm passed through and it looks like it is going to be a beautiful day. Kaye carries nothing but that ragged canvas satchel she arrived with last night. Things must be pretty bad at home for her to be running away, changing her name, and leaving behind everything and everybody she has ever known.

I told Kaye that I admire her courage, and I do. It took every ounce of courage I could muster to leave my mother and my family. It seems like another lifetime ago, and in so many ways it probably was. I understand more about her situation than she probably realizes. There were differences, to be sure, but there are similarities, too. I ran away from a life that did not suit me, in truth, it probably would have killed me. I did it and Kaye can, too.

Kaye climbs in the front seat and pulls the door closed behind her. She latches her seat belt and then begins to rustle through her bag and pulls out a fifty dollar bill and thrusts it towards me. "We're almost out of gas," she says. "Sorry, but I was too afraid to stop and fill it last night for fear that someone might recognize me."

I must have looked perplexed as Kaye continues, "It's not like I know anyone around here, but they kept repeating that radio broadcast about the woman who went missing from the Sacandaga Campgrounds and how anyone who knows anything should contact the sheriff's department." Again, she holds the fifty out for me to take.

"Keep your money, you're gonna need it," I say. Reluctantly, Kaye puts her money back in her bag and we drive on in silence towards the town of Speculator. This woman is pretty trusting to allow a complete stranger to assist her in her escape, for all she knows I could be driving her straight to the sheriff's department. Her willingness to do so speaks of the desperation she must feel.

I'd like to ask her more. I have so many questions.

But for now I want her to feel safe.

So, I keep my questions to myself.


It isn't long before we're at the gas station. I slow down to peruse the situation before I pull in. It's quiet and it's all *pay at the pump*. There isn't another soul around this early in the morning. Even the Mountain Market hasn't opened yet. No doubt they have closed circuit cameras to keep people from driving off without paying.

"Stay in the truck and pull that ball cap down. No sense getting spotted now," I say as I pop out of the truck to gas up. It takes a while to fill the twenty-one gallon tank. I'm feeling a little apprehensive standing here, all the while trying to convince myself that I'm doing nothing wrong. She hasn't committed any crime and neither have I.

At least not yet.

Once we are back on the road, I turn onto State Route 8. "Where are we going?" Kaye finally asks.

"We're going to see some friends of mine. You'll need to trust me," I say and I think about how long it has been since *I* have trusted anyone. Kaye just turns her head away from me and keeps her eyes on the road. Her eyes give nothing away. She is well-practiced at keeping her thoughts and feelings concealed. Still, I don't think my request to *trust me* is sitting very well with her.

The narrow mountain road is in desperate need of repair like so many are around here, as it twists and turns around the mountains, rivers and lakes. First we head south, then the road turns and we head northeast before taking a short stint on the Northway and then onto State Route 74 and towards Bridgeview Harbor on the western shore of Lake Champlain. We should be there in a little under two hours. I spoke with Henri last night, and he will meet us there.

"This morning when you came into the kitchen, you said something about red skies at morning and sailors take warning…"

"Yes," is all Kaye says. She waits for me to continue.

"We can't just drive into Canada, I'm certain the border patrol has been notified to be on the lookout for you. As soon as they scan your passport, you'll be on your way home to dear old Nash, that heavy-handed man you're still married to."

Kaye blanches at the very thought of it. "I guess, I haven't thought this through very well."

"That's okay, you've had enough on your mind just masterminding your escape and ending up on the river bank of an elderly, benevolent, non-binary person's meager estate."

Now Kaye and I are both laughing.

"Yes, that was indeed my well-executed plan. I only have one problem with your description of it all."

"Do you? And what might that be?" I ask.

"You referred to yourself as elderly. Just how old are you?" Kaye asks.

67

Again, I laugh as I say, "That is your question? Most people are far more curious about my gender, sexual preferences, my lifestyle, and the list goes on from there. But you want to know how old I am... okay, we can start there. I'm 68."

"I understand a little about ..."

"Non-binary?" I say. Clearly, Kaye is struggling not to offend.

"Yes. You see I have a daughter, Andy or Andrea. So I understand a little about what you call *non-binary*. Nash doesn't know or at least he pretends not to know. His words can be hurtful, cruel really."

Kaye doesn't offer anymore and I decide not to pry or be intrusive. I know how this goes, she'll tell me more if she wants to or needs to. The pause in conversation lengthens as silence fills the space between us.

Then a look of relief passes over Kaye's face before she changes the subject back to something safer. She continues, "You are only a couple of years older than I am, and I certainly don't consider myself elderly."

"Age is really just a number. The truth is I'm an old soul living in a 68 year old body. Is that better?" I say trying to soften the label suggesting that neither of us is elderly.

"Much. I'll be 65 in a few weeks and I refuse to think of myself as elderly. I have squandered so much time living in fear and regret. My time is right now, and I have plans for this next chapter of my life," Kaye says a with heavy dose of gumption and pluck.

"I see. Good for you. Let's get you across the border so we can get you some identification and you can begin this new life. The life of Kaye Hill."

"Yeah, well I guess, I didn't think this part out very well either." Kaye shakes her head and mutters something about her own stupidity.

"None of that, we haven't time for it. Besides, I have a plan. My friend, Henri, will meet us at the Bridge Marina on the western shore of Lake Champlain. He's a charter fisherman and he owes me a favor. You will board his fishing boat and sail right into Canada, hopefully avoiding the border patrol."

"Will we be safe? What if we get caught? Isn't this illegal?" Kaye asks and I can hear the quiver in her voice as she begins to fear the consequences of what I am proposing.

"Playing by the rules these last forty some years hasn't proven to be very safe for you either," I state as we cross the state line into Vermont. The morning sun is brilliant in the eastern sky as I lower the visor on my truck and tug on the brim of my old ball cap.

Kaye looks over at me. "This feels a little like Thelma and Louise," she says.

I laugh. "Or Thelma and Lou."

She laughs, too.

"I have another friend who will meet you on the Canadian side and take you into Montreal. It's all been arranged. Let's just hope the *Coasties* are busy doing something stateside this morning."

"Coasties?" she says, clearly she is unfamiliar with the jargon.

"You know, the Coast Guard."

"I thought the Coast Guard was stationed on the oceans."

"They patrol the Great Lakes and Lake Champlain, too."

"Red sky at morning, sailors take warning," Kaye mutters just loud enough for me to hear. "I hope that isn't some kind of an omen." She pulls the ball cap down over her eyes and pushes the old Ray Bans up her nose as she turns and looks into the bright morning sun.

# Chapter 10
## Nash

The questions continue and my aggravation is increasing as the officer asks the same questions over and over again in slightly different ways. He's trying to confuse me and get me to admit to something, anything. But I haven't done anything to confess to, maybe I wasn't the best husband, but her disappearance didn't have anything to do with me.

It couldn't possibly, could it?

We've been married for over 40 years, if she was going to leave me, she would have done so long ago and she sure as hell wouldn't have done it like this.

Would she?

There's something about the way this cop asks the questions that makes me feel guilty of something. I fear he might go on like this forever until I confess to something just to shut him up and make him go away. Instead, I put my head down on the kitchen table and ask, "Do I need a lawyer?"

"I suppose that's up to you Mr. Cooper."

I don't know any lawyers, we don't run in the same circles. But, I know a few folks who've had run-ins with the law. Maybe Terry or Stan know someone. I look at my phone, it's not even eight o'clock. Still a little too early to call.

My phone has been on silent since the officer stopped me in the driveway. There is a long list of missed calls, including many from Joey.

"Shit. I didn't want him to hear about this, not from someone else," I mutter to myself. "Look officer…"

"Detective," he corrects me.

Self-righteous little prig. "Detective," I say with a sneer I can't control. "I need to call my kids and let them know what's going on. My phone is blowing up with missed calls. Calling a lawyer will have to wait."

The detective nods his approval. "Okay, Mr. Cooper. I'll wait outside and give you a little privacy. Besides, the forensic team should be here anytime."

I walk into *our* bedroom and sit on the edge of the bed. This room smells like Amy, a little like flowers, a little like spice. The scent still lingers and I almost expect her to walk in from the bathroom. It's hard to believe she was here yesterday and now, just like that she's gone. In this moment I fear I may break down and cry. How will I tell the kids that their mother is gone? The reality hits me hard.

I wasn't good to her, I haven't been, not for a long time. She didn't deserve to go, not like this. It was all supposed to have been different. I don't think I can tell Joey— not yet. I'm not ready.

I take a moment to scroll through my voicemail. The last message came in over an hour ago. My mailbox is full.

While listening to my voicemail, another call from Joey comes in. Oh God, I don't want to do this. I answer anyway. "Joey," I say and my voice cracks.

"What the fuck, Dad. What happened to Mom?"

Before I can respond. He continues, "The police showed up here a couple of hours ago. We'd all gone to bed and they were banging on the door and shining spotlights in Kyle and Kirk's room, shouting 'Open up it's the Sheriff.' It was terrifying and the kids were crying as these two armed cops in Kevlar vests pushed their way into our home looking for Mom. For the love of God, why didn't you call me? They were grilling me with questions about you and Mom. They wanted to know whether she was hiding out here because of you. Now, I'm getting all these calls from reporters about how Mom floated down the river and they think she drowned. The police just came back about an hour ago checking to see if she had shown up or if I'd heard from her."

"What do you mean? They thought your mother was hiding from me? Where did they get that idea? I'm confused, who's been talking shit about me to the police?"

"How do I know, Dad? Where is Mom? What happened?" Joey can hardly get the words out, he is so upset.

I've got a girl who acts like a guy and now my son is crying like a little girl. Amy and all her gender neutral bullshit. God help me, I can't deal with any of this right now.

"You know as much as I do. We'd gone up to Sacandaga camping. The guys were playing ball and your mom went down to the river for a swim. That was the last time anyone saw her."

By now my son is sobbing and I am fighting hard to choke back my own tears. "But Dad, it doesn't make sense. Mom's a good swimmer."

"I know Joey, but there's been so much rain lately and the river was high and faster than I've ever seen it. Maybe she hit her head or something."

"Wouldn't they have found her body?" He's crying so hard he can't even speak.

"It was raining so hard last night. It was hard to see anything. I've only been home for about an hour. I was out all night helping with the search."

"Maybe she's injured, I'm going up there. Maybe I can help with the search."

I know my kid. He's hard-headed, but soft-hearted. Losing his mother like this is more than he can bear. There's nothing I can say to stop him.

"Have you talked to your brother?" I ask Joey.

"No, what would I tell him? I think *you* should call him and Andy, too. You are their father." I can hear the anger starting to seep through his tears. What the fuck did I ever do to him? To any of them? "I suppose ..." Joey continues, but his words trail off behind the tears.

"You suppose what?" What a little prick, I suppose he is going to try and blame this on me and try to make me feel guilty. For what? Being a bad husband. This has nothing to do with that. I'm not having it.

"Never mind, just call Sam and Andy."

"I'll call Sam, but do you think you could call Andrea?"

"Do you mean Andy?" Joey snarls.

"Of course, I mean Andy."

"Never mind, I'll call them both." Joey says in disgust.

"Thanks Joey."

"Jesus Dad, they're your children. Just because we're all adults doesn't let you off the hook. You're still their father and Mom is missing. Forget it. Just forget it. I'll call them on my way up to the Adirondacks. Let me know if you hear anything, anything at all." And with that the line goes dead.

What a jerk. He didn't even say good-bye.

Sitting on the edge of the bed, I think about calling him back. I lay down to rest my eyes. I'm so tired. It stings a little that he hung up without saying good-bye. Joey was always lookin' to hang out with me when he was a kid. It was always "Dad this" and "Dad that." He always wanted to play catch. He was the only one who ever wanted to spend any time with me.

Now that Joey has a family of his own, I can see he's a much better father than I ever was and a much better husband, too. Maybe he just tolerated me, the other two just didn't hide their feelings as well.

Just as I begin to drop off to sleep, I hear the doorbell. Shit it must be the forensic team. What do they think they're going to find here? It takes all the strength I can muster to get up and out of bed. Before I can even cross the room and open the bedroom door I can hear the cops in my living room.

"Sorry about this Mr. Cooper," says the detective from the Missing Person's Unit that I spoke with earlier. What was his name? I can't ask again. "They're going to need access to your bedroom and bathroom." The crime scene investigators are lined up in two rows of two behind the detective just waiting for me to step aside.

"Can I take a shower and change my clothes first?" I ask.

"No sir, and we're going to need the clothes you're wearing and a DNA sample to rule you out as a suspect."

"A suspect?" I am incredulous. I can be a shit, I know this. "I didn't do anything. My wife is floating somewhere in the Sacandaga River. It's an accident. No crime has been committed. Don't you people believe in accidents anymore?"

"Please step aside Mr. Cooper. We will bring you a robe or a pair of sweatpants to put on. We need to get on with this."

One of the investigators hands me a plastic bag marked evidence. "Take off all your clothes and put them in the bag," he commands.

"Everything?" I ask. He can't mean everything.

"Everything," he says, leaving no doubt that he wants me to strip down to nothing. Before I head off to the hall bath to change, another woman pushes past me and enters my bedroom, then quickly emerges with my old plaid robe that always hangs behind the bathroom door.

She hands it to me. "Put this on and wait with Detective Randall in the kitchen. This won't take too long."

I sit there at the kitchen table feeling ridiculous and emasculated, sitting naked beneath my old ratty bathrobe, amongst all these officious uniformed officers. I wonder if they do this on purpose, to make you feel vulnerable and powerless. For god's sake I don't even have any pants on.

"Where's your wife's toothbrush?" the same woman asks, emerging from our bedroom.

"How should I know?" Hers is the pink one, isn't it there?"

"No."

"She must have taken it with her to the campground," I say. This seems like a reasonable explanation to me.

"How about a hairbrush?"

"If it's not there, she must have packed it to go camping." Still this seems a little odd to me as I know she has a second makeup bag with all her stuff that she leaves in the camper. I remember that girl, I think her name was Cheryl, was using Amy's stuff that weekend we went to the Moose River.

"That's okay we found some hair in the shower that looks too long to be yours. We can get a DNA sample from it."

She turns and addresses the detective. "We also found a bloody footprint, just a partial print really, on the bedroom carpet. Not much. We're sending it to the lab, we'll compare it to the DNA in the hair and try to determine how long it's been there."

"Did your wife injure herself recently?"

"Not unless you consider getting knocked out and drowning in a rushing river a recent injury." As soon as the words are out of my mouth I regret it.

All the officers turn and look at me.

If looks could kill.

They don't see a grieving husband, they think I'm a real asshole.

# Chapter 11
## Kaye

There are so many things I want to ask Ellery, but I'm not really certain how to begin. I'm afraid if I don't ask now that I'll run out of time. So at the risk of being rude I just begin…

"You said this man, Henri, owes you a favor. It must be a pretty big favor, if he's willing to help me cross into Canada." I decide against stating the obvious as we both know what we are attempting to do is illegal.

"Hmm," Ellery responds as she turns and looks at me. "I'm not sure how much to tell you, you might be better off not knowing some of this." She pauses and I'm not certain if she will continue, but then she does albeit reluctantly. "I've known Henri most of my life. You see, Henri and I grew up together in a little village on the shores of the Richelieu, in

St. Paul de l'Île -aux -Noix. Lake Champlain flows into the Richelieu River in Quebec where the waters join the St. Lawrence Seaway before making its way into the Atlantic Ocean. Henri was destined to be a boat captain, just like his father, and I worked at the marina in my youth before leaving home.

"Many years ago, Henri got involved running drugs between the states and Canada and got himself into a world of trouble, as many young people do. He stayed with me for a while in my cabin until his father could come and get us. He changed his name, and he needed papers. Once back in Canada we contacted friends in Montreal who helped us. I helped him and in return he has helped me.

"His father sent him out to St. Andrews-on-the-Sea in New Brunswick where he joined the merchant marines. He was at sea for over a decade. When he came back his father had passed on and Henri was using a different name. He was completely unrecognizable, even in our small provincial community of St Paul's. He left as a young man and while away the years and the seas had aged him. He keeps his own counsel and minds his own business. He's a mountain of a man. Nobody messes with Henri.

"He's a good man, just one who made a mistake. He learned from his and has great compassion for people in need of it. I spoke with him last night. He'll meet us at the Bridge Marina on Lake Champlain and take you to the marina at St. Paul de l'Île-aux- Noix where you will rendezvous with Claudette. She will take you into Montreal to get your papers."

"You're not coming?"

"No, I'm already under suspicion since the K-9 unit picked up your scent at the cabin. I think I'd better head back."

"Okay," I say feeling disappointed. I really like Ellery. She's kind and good-hearted. "I don't know what I would've done without your assistance."

"I know, sometimes we just need a friend, someone to go out on a limb and help."

I sense there is something more Ellery wishes to tell me. The silence grows between us until she continues…

"Henri did that for me. The summer I was working at the marina, I was just seventeen. There were two men, boys really, who bullied me. At first it was just juvenile banter, you can imagine the kind of things macho teenage boys might say to someone like me. I wasn't exactly their idea of what a young lady should be. It was the seventies and I was a bit of an anomaly in this provincial town. But that kind of thing takes its toll on you. Don't let anyone tell you differently. One night as I was leaving the marina they jumped me. They intended to rape me, apparently they thought if I knew what I was missing, they could fuck me and change me, into what? A proper girl?"

"Oh God, I'm sorry," I say as images of someone trying to hurt Andy, like that, flood in.

"Henri came to my defense and beat the shit out of both of them with an oar off one of the dinghies. I remained undefiled," she laughs. "It was a long time ago, but I have not forgotten. Fearing their retribution, I knew it was time for me to leave. You see, over the years I have learned that real friendship is reciprocal, sometimes you are the giver and sometimes the beneficiary. When Henri calls, I answer and he does the same for me."

I nod as I am not sure what to even say.

"I told you this may be more than you wanted to know," Ellery says as we make our way through the little town of Crowne Point and I begin to see signs for the Champlain Bridge. "We should be there in five minutes, give or take. Do you speak French?" she asks changing the subject.

"I do," I tell her. "I studied French when I was in college, but I'm sure I am more than a little rusty as there hasn't been much opportunity to use it in the suburbs of Albany. Still it has always been my dream to live in France."

"Maybe now you'll get a chance."

"I really can't begin to thank you. I'd like to keep in touch, if that's okay with you."

"Once you get a new phone, download *Signal*. It is the safest option we currently have. Only use your new first name and never mention anything that might indicate who you are and how we became acquainted, for both of our protection. Henri, Claudette, and I will deny any knowledge of you and likewise you will deny any knowledge of us. That is how this whole thing works, mutual protection."

"*Je comprends*," I answer. "Might as well get some practice in while I can.

Ellery smiles. "How's your memory?" she asks.

"Still pretty good," I say with an air of pride. "I've lost many things but my memory is still intact. Why?"

"You'll need to memorize my phone number so you can find me on *Signal*. I find a mnemonic works best. The first letter of each word corresponds to a number. For example Apple corresponds with the number 1, and Ball corresponds with the number 2, and so on."

"You've really thought this through," I say feeling like I've just stepped into a spy novel.

"It's been necessary as the stakes are high."

"My phone number is—324-324-2232 or Edith always has enough cash, how bad can Edith be."

I repeat the words slowly, committing them to memory. "Edith always has enough cash, how bad can Edith be."

"It's a little awkward, but I had to come up with it while you were sleeping. Once you get into Canada, Claudette will help you get a burner phone."

"What's a burner phone?"

"A disposable one, a temporary one until you land somewhere and are safe and able to begin your new life. But keep in contact with me, I want to know you are safe, in case I need to get in touch with you or if you need something."

We pull into the parking lot of the marina and Ellery parks the truck beside an old boat trailer that looks like it has been abandoned. "This is where we say good-bye. Henri will meet you on the dock."

"How will I know him?" I ask. My anxiety is mounting as my heart begins to race as I think about what I'm about to do.

"He'll know you. You are expected."

My eyes fill with tears. "I truly don't know how I will ever thank you, Ellery."

She opens her arms to hug me and then she releases me after only a brief embrace.

"Remember what I said about friendship being a reciprocal relationship? There may come a time when one of us needs something from you."

I nod and feel as if I have just entered into a sacred oath.

"Now go Kaye Hill and live that life you've only dreamed of."

I step out into the morning sun carrying only my old canvas satchel. Before I even begin to make my way to the boat dock, Ellery puts her truck in reverse and then pulls out onto the dusty, gravel road and is gone.

# Chapter 12
## Kaye

I watch as Ellery's truck disappears into the dust she leaves behind. In spite of all of our promises, I can't help wondering if I will ever see this kind stranger again.

I take a moment to look around the parking lot, to my great relief there are no police cars here. Ellery is gone. I guess I'm really going to do this.

Heading towards the docks, I think about my children and how I am walking away from them, too. But just for the time being, just until I am settled and safe. A lone tear slips down my cheek as I open my old canvas shopping bag, the framed photograph of my children is still there. My fingertips caress the frame. I utter a small prayer of gratitude. Perhaps this will be my talisman, my touch stone, connecting me with those I love.

Maybe I am a crazy woman, impulsive and irrational. How many times did Nash hurl those nasty accusations at me making me doubt my own perceptions, my own sanity? What are they calling that now? Gaslighting, I think. Still, I fear if I don't act on this opportunity, I may talk myself out of it, again. Just as I have so many times before.

Images of my children fill my head, followed in close succession by the sound of Nash's voice criticizing them and enumerating a litany of all the ways *they* have disappointed *him*. Andy, Sam, and Joey are no longer children. They are grown and have all moved away. Andy to Denver, Sam to outside of Philadelphia, and although Joey isn't far away like the others, I rarely see him. The boys are busy with their own families now. I tell myself they left to avoid their father. Still I'm certain they hold resentments towards me, too. Justifiable. I have long been a broken shell of a woman no one in their right mind would want to emulate. The rejection still hurts and I miss them. Each of them has flourished in their own way outside of the darkness of the home they were raised in. I know they won't be coming back. There is no reason for me to stay. I never see them anymore. I know that nothing will change as long as their father is in the picture. Unfortunately, he is not going anywhere, so I must.

I hope my children will forgive me.

Walking across the parking lot, I see long abandoned trailers and a multitude of boats up on blocks or hoists of some kind. All are awaiting repair before they wither away and are used for scrap. A sense of sadness threatens to overwhelm me. If I don't do this now, I'll end up rotting away just like these once cherished vessels. I, too, am in need of repair, extensive repair. If I don't see to it, no one will.

The morning sun glistens across the crystalline waters of Lake Champlain. The water sparkles. Someone is pulling out of the marina in a large wooden sailboat leaving a small wake behind. The waves splash rhythmically against the dock and the boats sway gently on the incoming waves. I hear a motor sputter as the man raises the mainsail and it flaps in the offshore breeze. It's a beautiful day for a sail.

I walk on towards the docks where beautiful boats of every variety fill the slips and there are people lovingly tending to them, washing down the decks, and polishing up everything in need of a shine. None of this is lost on me.

Where is this man I'm supposed to meet? I walk slowly down the pier looking at all of these beautiful boats each flying their various burgees, the triangular pendants from their yacht clubs. Dad used to have one from Seawanhaka on his Catalina when he sailed out from Center Island into Oyster Bay. The memory of Dad brings a smile to my face. He had wanted me to leave Nash since he first laid eyes on the guy. I can't help but feel that wherever he is, that he's happy I've finally found the courage to go.

No one here on this dock is paying me any mind. I turn and walk back towards the shoreline when something draws my eye from these grand pleasure crafts to the working boats over on the next pier. There the fishing boats, a couple of ferries, and a big green barge loaded with lumber. All are tied up to the pier. It is then that it dawns on me that I may have assumed too much. I walk over to take a look, but for what? Or for whom?

From the shadows in the cabin of a large fishing boat emerges a big man. He moves slowly up onto the deck of his boat. He must be at least six foot five. He raises his right arm to wave at me. Even from here I can see the strength he possesses.

No doubt this is Henri. I am expected.

I swallow hard. I'm really going to do this? Then I raise my arm and wave back.

Once he has made contact, Henri retreats into the cabin and waits as I make my way to his boat. The boat is tied to the dock with the bow pointed out into the lake. Henri is prepared to go. Across the stern, I read the name— *Été Lune* and beneath the name, *Saint-Laurent de l'Île-d'Orléans*, the home port for this vessel. I quickly translate, "Summer Moon". I like it. Other boats have rods propped up along their decks, all prepped for a day of fishing, but not the Summer Moon. This clearly is a fishing boat, but we won't be fishing today.

As I approach I hear Henri call out from within the cabin. "Key Ill?"

At first I am confused until it dawns on me that he is saying my name, Kaye Hill, albeit with the accent of the *Quebecois*. Had I thought any of this through I might have chosen a different name, one that translates into something more pleasing to the ear, say Madeline.

"Oui," I respond standing on the dock peering into the darkness of the boat's cabin.

He switches to English. "Welcome, please watch your step." His voice is soft and gentle with the sing-song intonation of his native tongue. He steps from the darkness and takes me by the arm assisting me onboard.

Ellery was right, he is a mountain of a man. His clothes are clean but well-worn and roughly patched. He looks older than I expected. His face is tanned, both weathered and lined. He has a full beard and thick white hair. He exudes an air of chivalry about him that I am unaccustomed to.

"Please, come in." He holds the door to the cabin and ushers me inside before closing the door behind us.

It takes my eyes a moment to adjust to the dim light. The space is small with both of us inside. In the darkness, I stumble backwards as I back into a narrow bench that runs the length of the cabin.

"Please sit down," he says and I do as I am told. "I've gathered a few provisions. There are sandwiches in the basket on the table and a thermos of coffee. Please help yourself. The head is through the door." He gestures to the only door in the cabin and I nod. "I think we should be on our way. We'll have time to get acquainted once we're out in open water. Right now I think it is best if you stay in here. It's safer, for both of us." Again, I nod indicating my consent and understanding.

"I don't know how to thank-you," I say quite uncertain what else I can say to express my gratitude.

He smiles at me and his pale blue eyes exude a level of kindness and concern, and I feel safe for the first time in a very long time. "Any friend of Ellery's is a friend of mine. This is what friends do for one another. We'll talk later," Henri says as he backs out the cabin door, then he stops to add a few more instructions. "I will announce myself before entering the cabin, so you will know it's me. If you hear any conversation at all, go directly into the head, lock the door, and don't say a word. Just wait."

I must look confused as he adds, "That is what we call *les toilettes sur un bateau*, the head."

I smile. *"Oui."* But this I already understood. This is not the source of my confusion or concern. There are no answers or guarantees. We are embarking on something illegal and therefore dangerous. I know, there may be unforeseen consequences. Still, I keep my concerns to myself.

Henri leaves me in the dark cabin. I hear the click of the door being locked from the outside. The only light is a yellow glow from a small lantern that hangs on a hook above a drop leaf table. The cabin is cast in shadows that play with my imagination. I close my eyes and say a prayer for safe passage and deliverance to my new life, whatever that might look like.

# Chapter 13
## Joey

I hang up on my father. I can almost hear my mother's voice from somewhere deep within my memory. *You know that will only make him angry. You know what he's like when he loses his temper.* I've spent my whole life tiptoeing around Dad, trying not to set him off. God help me if I end up being like *him*. I take a deep breath and try to ground myself and let this anger go. Still, my heart is racing and my blood boils. What has become of my mother? An image of her lying injured on the bank of the river fills my consciousness and I wonder if this is some kind of a premonition or if she is trying to send me a message.

I head into our bedroom where Natalie is lying in bed propped up on a pillow nursing our baby girl, Laurel. "I have to go," I tell her. She holds my gaze but says nothing. "I have a bad feeling about this." She nods giving me her consent to do whatever I deem necessary. Natalie and I have been married for six years, but together for over ten. After ten years and three kids, you learn to read another person. Sometimes nothing needs to be said: some things are just understood and words only get in the way.

I change into a pair of cargo shorts, pull on a tee shirt, and lace up my old running shoes before heading over to the bed to kiss my beautiful wife good-bye. I can't imagine how I would feel if something like this happened to her, and she was missing. I'm starting to get choked up again and turn away before she sees my tears.

"Where are the boys?" she asks.

"Watching cartoons."

"Tell them I'll be out to get them some breakfast once Leah is finished with hers," and then she adds, "Call me, Joey. Let me know if you hear anything. Anything at all."

I nod and leave the bedroom. The boys barely look up from the television when I tell them, "This is your last show. I want you to play outside today. Mommy will be out to get your breakfast in a few minutes."

Neither of the boys say good-bye. I pray they will not grow up and feel about me like I feel about my father. The very thought of it threatens to bring on another round of tears. I can't think about that now.

I jump in the car and program the GPS. Before I know it, I'm on I-90 headed toward the Sacandaga River. Lost in grief and guilt, I plead for some kind of divine intervention as I promise to be a better son if only... if only Mom can be okay.

Dad is so difficult. He can be so self-centered. Although it's been years since he's laid a hand on me, he wields his tongue like a saber, striking down anyone and everyone who dares to disagree with him on anything. I can't stand him, and I know Andy and Sam feel the same. Still, we have left Mom to fend for herself. I can't believe I may never see her again. The tears come fast and free now that I no longer have to keep that stiff upper lip. Fuck that.

Once I feel I have cried out all my tears, I decide it is time to call Sam and Andy. I check the clock on my dashboard. It's nearly eight o'clock here, which means it's only six in Denver. That's pretty early for a Saturday. I call Sam first. I let the phone ring and ring but he doesn't pick-up until the call shifts over to voicemail. I decided not to leave a message. He'll see that I called when he gets up. This isn't the kind of message I want to leave on my brother's voicemail.

Heading toward the toll booth it dawns on me that I don't have any cash. Shit. I certainly hadn't planned on this when I paid the babysitter last night. Can this day get any worse? No sooner does the question form in my head that I want to issue a retraction as I know it could get a helluva lot worse, and I don't want to think about how this day might unfold. Instead, I head through without cash or an EZ Pass. God only knows what the penalty for this will be, probably at least a hundred dollars per toll. I haven't time or any inclination to stop. Just fuck it, I have more important things to do right now.

I take a deep breath and call Andy. She picks up on the first ring.

"Hello?" A groggy voice answers. Clearly, I woke her.

"Andy, it's Joey. Sorry to be calling so early."

"Joey, is everything okay?" Andy is practically shouting at me. I can hear the panic in her voice.

"No, Andy. No," before I can even get the story out I start crying again.

Now Andy is comforting me and she still doesn't have any idea why I'm calling. Slowly, between my heart wrenching sobs, the story of Mom's disappearance comes out.

"Oh God, no…" Andy is crying too. "Where's Dad?"

"He's at home, dealing with the police. The forensic team had just shown up at the house."

"What? Do they think Dad had something to do with Mom's disappearance?"

97

"I don't know Andy. I think they're just ruling him out as a suspect."

"A suspect? Do they think there was foul play?"

"I don't know Andy. All I know is that Mom is missing and she may be hurt or worse."

"If he had something to do with this, he'll need more than a lawyer. I swear to God if he hurt Mom, I'll kill him."

"You'll have to get in line behind me, and probably Sammy, too."

"Call Dad back and tell him to get a lawyer. Does he know enough to keep his big trap shut, for once?"

"Well, God knows it would be the first time."

As I expected, Andy informs me that she'll be on the next flight into Albany.

"Can I pick you up?" I ask.

"No, just get up there and see if you can help find Mom. I'll rent a car. Keep your phone on and I'll text you my flight info and you can let me know where to find you. I have to go. I need to book a flight. I'll call you when I'm headed to the airport. Call Sammy. Oh God, Joey, please find Mom and let her be okay. I love you and I'll see you soon."

And with that the line goes dead.

# Chapter 14
## Andy

The vision of my mother's pale body thrown up on the rocky shoreline of the raging Sacandaga River takes shape in my head. I shake my head to dispel the image. Oh God, please let them find her. Please let her be okay.

Tears fill my eyes as I walk back into the bedroom and see Michelle laying there with her long dark hair cascading across my pillow, sleeping peacefully in my bed. She has no idea that my world has just blown apart, and I don't think I want to tell her. This thing between us is so new, and I don't know her well enough. It's too soon to bare my soul and introduce her to my dysfunctional family, particularly my father. I'm not sure if I even want *this* to work … whatever *this* is. But if I introduce her to the inner workings of the Cooper family, I know *it* doesn't stand a chance. She'll be gone before I even have a chance to miss her.

I pull on my jeans and grab a tee shirt. Looking in the bathroom mirror, I run some water through my short hair. My face is still a little soft, but I have a bit of that five o'clock shadow. I decide not to shave. I kind of like it. The scars on my chest are still tender and red, but they are healing and eventually will fade. At least this is what Dr. P says and he should know. I pull on my tee shirt and turn out the bathroom light.

I wonder what my family will say. I haven't seen them in almost two years and I haven't told them any of this, not even Mom. Now that I've had top surgery, I'm looking rather manly. I swallow hard thinking of Dad, there is no way he will ever accept me now. He's never accepted me, so why should I expect him to change?

Still I wanted to be through the transition before I saw Mom. She loves unconditionally, she always has. She might not understand, but she will still love me. This I know for certain. Then reality crashes through this conversation I am having in my head, none of this matters now because Mom is missing and might be hurt or worse. God, I wish I had told her. Why in the world did I keep this from her? Why? I was planning to invite her out here after I'd been on hormone therapy for another six months. I wanted to tell her in my own way and on my own turf. I wanted her to see that I'm a grown up and how this is the right decision *for me*. I didn't want her to have to lie to Dad, even if it was a lie of omission.

I push the regrets away, this will have to wait. This is not the time, I need to get going.

My gym bag still sits, unpacked, in the corner of the bedroom. An extra set of clothes, some toiletries, and my wallet, with my credit card and ID, are inside. I grab the bag and my car keys. I'll call Michelle from the airport.

The traffic is light this morning. I open up the APP for CheapOair and book my flight to Albany while waiting for the traffic light to change. I always use CheapOair, so they already have all my relevant information and autofill takes care of the rest. The first flight out is on Free Bird Air. I hate flying Free Bird, they charge extra for everything including a seat. Do they really think the FAA would allow a passenger to board and stand in the aisle? It looks like a good deal when you look at the advertised price. Woo hoo! It's only $175 for a one-way nonstop ticket from Denver to Albany. But by the time I pay for my seat and my carry-on bag the additional cost adds another hundred dollars. I'm aggravated by the idiocy and the money grab of the airlines, but I have bigger fish to fry this morning.

My flight leaves in ninety minutes. I park my car and take the shuttle to the terminal. I have my e-ticket on my phone and only my gym bag as a carry on, so I head through security. There are two guys standing in the line behind me, they whisper behind their hands.

Do they think I cannot hear what they are saying, or do they just not care?

"Is that a man or a woman?" one guy says to the other.

"I think it's a hybrid, you know something not found in nature. Not man or woman, simply an *it*." They both laugh and others in the line turn to look at me.

I've heard this kind of thing all my life. They question my gender and their words hurt. I straighten my shoulders, but don't turn around. There are two of them and just one of me. I don't like the odds and I'm not looking for a fight. Not while going through security and under the scrutiny of the TSA, no I don't need a fight today and not ever. Right now, I just want to be left alone.

By the time I get to the gate, they have already begun to board the plane. I have no time to use the restroom, grab something to eat or drink or to even text Michelle. Damn, by now she should be up and she's probably wondering where the hell I am. I've left in the middle of the night before, just not from my own home. Another nail in the coffin of another relationship that just didn't work out. I'll text her when I get to Albany, maybe she'll be understanding or at least forgiving.

# Chapter 15
## Kaye

It doesn't take Henri long to get underway. The motor sputters a moment before engaging and then I feel the gentle swaying of the boat as we pull out of the marina and head out to open water. The cabin is dark and dank. I'm chilled to the bone and look for something to wrap up in. There is a fleece blanket folded neatly on the end of the bench. I'm guessing this bench also doubles as a berth when Henri is out on the water overnight. I wrap myself tightly in the blanket waiting for the shivering to stop. Usually just touching this kind of fabric, made of petroleum-based polyester fibers, makes my skin crawl and gives me the creeps. But today, I am grateful for it. The blanket smells freshly laundered. I breathe in the faint fragrance of lavender soap. I don't know what I was expecting, but not this.

I lay down on the berth and wait for Henri to call for me. Lying there it dawns on me that I may be down here for a while. Still, I wish I'd had the presence of mind to ask him how long he expects it to be before we are in

Canada, but I did not. Given that we are at the southern end of Lake Champlain it could be at least three hours, unless we run into some type of delay, like bad weather, mechanical issues, the Coast Guard, or some immigration official. I try to push these thoughts out of my head. I'll probably be down here until we cross the international boundary and are safe on the other side.

Safe. The word takes up space in my head as I wonder what it even means. When was the last time I felt even remotely safe?

Henri seems like a solid, solitary man. Images of him standing at the helm with his hands on the wheel navigating this boat north on into Canada begins to take shape in my mind. Although, I've only just met him, he seems to be a man used to spending his days alone out on the water. I'm sure he likes the quiet and has no need of a woman, like me, chatting on and on about the situation she is running from or running to. How many times did my father tell me that information should be shared on a need to know basis, and Henri has no need to know how I've made a mess of my life or what I intend to do about it.

I think about starting over and re-creating a life of my own choosing. I've dreamt of this for decades, and my future is now. I have been unspeakably lonely in my marriage, unknown and unseen and rarely given a second thought or consideration. I'd better learn to be content living on my own and in my own company, at least for a while. I can't afford to make another big mistake. I am no longer a young woman, my time and my life are precious. Being alone is not the same as loneliness, I need to embrace the solitude.

But there are still some fairly major obstacles to overcome and I need to keep my head and be smart. As they say, I'm not out of the woods yet.

The hum of the motor drowns out the voices on the radio that I'd heard earlier. Gradually the chill begins to leave my body. In the darkness of the cabin, I begin to drift off towards sleep.

# Chapter 16
## Ellery

It takes me just under two hours before I am pulling into my driveway. There are two police cars already there and a van with a K-9 unit logo on the backdoor. For a moment, I think about putting my truck in reverse and getting out of here. It is then that I see one of the officers holding Skye, and the poor dear is trembling. I grab my binoculars from the console between the seats and put the cord around my neck. Then put the truck in park and make my way down the walkway towards the cabin where the officers are waiting.

"Good Morning," I say to the guy holding my dog, with all the reserve I can muster. "May I have my dog, Officer?" Skye nearly jumps into my arms as I reach for her. I bring my face close to the top of her head reassuring my pup as she quakes in my arms. "She's a rescue and doesn't like men. No doubt, she was abused before she came to live with me." I say as I hold her close to my body and pet her gently.

The officer sniggers when I make the comment about men, but he decides to let it go without comment. "Are you Ellery McMasters?"

"Yes. What can I do for you?" I ask. Although, I'm pretty certain I know why they are here.

"I'm Officer Malone and this is Officer Griffin." The first man extends his hand but quickly withdraws it when he realizes I have no intention of shaking his hand as I'm still trying to settle my dog. "We're investigating the disappearance of Amy Cooper, a sixty-four year old woman who was last seen yesterday in the Sacandaga River Campgrounds a few miles upriver."

"Some officers came by my camp last night." I think about saying something about the search and rescue dogs and that I haven't seen anyone named *Amy Cooper* but decide against offering any additional information as these are different cops then the ones I spoke with yesterday.

"The canines picked up her scent at your fire circle and again in your driveway."

"Yes, the officers who were here last night told me that. I did have a fire last night, but turned in early as I do most nights."

"May we come in?" the second officer asks.

"Why?"

"We have a few more questions…"

107

"I'll be happy to answer any questions you have . . . right here."

The first officer looks over at his partner before he continues. "Where were you last night?"

"I told you, I was inside my house. I had dinner and went to bed early. I didn't see or hear anything." The space between us grows in the silence as I wait for their response. When it is clear that they are waiting for me to continue I add, "Now is there anything else you'd like to know?"

Let's just get this whole charade over with. They pretend to be kind and concerned and only here to help and I plead ignorance. I have no intention of saying anything to incriminate myself or tell them where Kaye is.

"Where were you this morning?"

"I was birding up on Pillsbury Mountain." I lift the binoculars off my chest to corroborate my story. "I went up to the summit looking for the nesting grounds of the Bicknell's thrush." They have no idea what I'm talking about and I decide to leave it at that.

"Did you see the bird you were looking for?" the shorter one asks.

"No, they are rare and pretty elusive. Even from an old birder like me. Besides, it was too foggy." Maybe it had been a premonition, or maybe I'm just used to trying to stay one step ahead but I'm awfully glad I had thought about having an alibi while I was driving back home this morning. Still it surprises me how easily the lie slips off my tongue, even I might believe it if I didn't know any better.

"Still we'd like to come in Ms. McMasters, it is Ms. isn't it?"

"What is it that you gentlemen hope to find?" I ask and my voice is a bit more clipped than I intend. Skye senses my agitation and begins to growl.

"Can't say for sure at this time, but a woman is missing and she was here…" He lets the implication hang there.

"Then you'd better get a warrant," I say as I turn and walk back towards the house.

When I am nearly out of earshot I hear the short one call after me, "Do you like women, Ms. McMasters?"

I keep walking as I carry Skye, unlock the door and go inside letting the screen door slam behind me.

# Chapter 17
## Nash

"We're finished in here, at least for now," the tall guy in the paper coveralls says to the detective in charge as he leaves my bedroom with a plastic bag full of miscellaneous stuff.

"Now can I have a shower?" I ask.

He nods in my direction. His eyes give away little, but I sense he doesn't like me very much. What the hell, I didn't do anything. My wife is missing and you'd think this asshole would cut me a little slack. I leave the forensic team crawling around the rest of the house and head back into my bedroom. I free myself from my old robe. Standing there in nothing but my boxers, I look out the window. The sunlight is pouring in and the room is already heating up. It's gonna be another scorcher and it's not even ten o'clock. Another of those CSI guys is creeping around my backyard. I close the blinds. I'm sure he doesn't want to see me standing here in my underwear any more than I want to see him poking around my house and talking to the neighbors. What is he bothering them for?

I lie back on the bed. It still smells of Amy's perfume, that French kind she always wears. What's it called? I can't remember the name. Her old man always bought it for her for Christmas. The kids sent her another bottle when he died last month. I look over at her dresser, but the crystal bottle is gone. Did she take it camping? Maybe. How would I know? I inhale again. This room still smells like her. I close my eyes, just for a moment…

"Nash. Nash Cooper."

I awake in a panic to the sound of impatient pounding on my bedroom door and someone calling my name. It takes me a moment to surface from the depth of my dreamless sleep and try to put the pieces together as to why I'm in bed in the middle of the day and who's pounding on my bedroom door. Slowly the day's events take shape in my consciousness. I don't know how long I was asleep or what has transpired in my absence.

I glance at the clock before opening the door. It's three o'clock and Detective Randall is standing there. "What?" I say, sounding as incoherent as I am.

"Get dressed Mr. Cooper, we need to ask you some questions down at the station."

"Did you find Amy?" I ask as I reach for the robe that lays over the end of the bed. The detective looks all neat and trim, his clothes are still all crisp and pressed even in this humidity and I couldn't appear more slovenly if I tried. I had intended to shower and shave, but I fell asleep instead.

"No sir, I'm sorry we have not."

I nod indicating my understanding. "Can I shower and drive myself down once I've had a chance to clean up?"

He just looks at me as if deciding what to do. "I'm afraid not. You need to come with us. Now"

"Am I under arrest or something?"

"Not at this time, but we have a few more questions we'd like to ask you. We've talked with a couple of your neighbors…" The pause lengthens as I wait for him to elaborate on what those busy bodies have been saying about me, until it becomes obvious he has no intention of doing so.

"Jesus Christ, do you really think I had something to do with this?"

He doesn't respond. But he looks at me, full of disdain and contempt, good God this guy thinks I've offed my wife.

Anger erupts from somewhere deep within and before I know what I'm doing I'm shouting at him. "I was playing baseball when *she* disappeared in the river for God's

112

sake. There were no less than twenty people who saw me there. While you're down here screwing around with me, Amy's probably lying on the banks of that bloody river up in the Adirondacks or maybe by now her body has been eaten by a bear." The detective grimaces at the visual I've just planted in his head. "I'm not going anywhere with you or saying anything else without talking to a lawyer." I clench my fists, my face flushes hot, and my heart pounds.

The detective moves his right hand towards the revolver holstered at his waist, just in case. He looks me square in the face, never letting his eyes leave mine. He speaks slowly and methodically, careful not to inflame me any further. "Suit yourself Mr. Cooper. You can either put on a pair of pants and come with us willingly or we can take you out of here in handcuffs and your underwear. The choice is yours."

The younger cop reaches his left hand behind his back and pulls out a set of handcuffs.

"I want a lawyer," I say louder than I intended to.

"You can call someone from the station. Now would you like to put on some pants or do you intend to go in your underwear?" He sneers at me as he waits for me to respond. I reach for a pair of shorts that lie rumpled on the floor next to the bed. They are the same dirty pair I was wearing yesterday when this whole fiasco began. I can smell the stench of my own body odor. I want to gag. Fear threatens to overwhelm me and I want to run. Any pride I once had is gone.

The detective turns slowly to leave the bedroom with his hand still on his weapon and says, "Don't let him out of your sight," to the officer standing just outside my bedroom door.

I catch a look at myself in the mirror over the dresser. My hair has turned a nondescript shade of gray. It's thinning and greasy. The lank strands clump together as I attempt to comb it over with my fingers to cover my ever receding hairline. I desperately need a shave. My scruffy beard has gone nearly white making me look old. Just old. Even the hair on my chest has turned from dark to gray. When did all of this happen? I pull on my shorts and open the dresser drawer and find a stack of neatly folded t-shirts. Amy's handiwork. I pull on a faded navy t-shirt with a Buffalo Bills logo. At least, now, my protruding belly is covered.

I think about changing my dirty shorts for a clean pair when the young cop says, "It's time to go, Mr. Cooper."

"Can I change my shorts?" I ask.

"No." Is all he says, leaving no space for any discussion.

The junior officer is no older than my youngest son. He walks behind me with the force of something pressing on my low back, pushing me forward and out of the bedroom and out of the house. I don't know if it is his hand or his gun, but I do not ask. I just walk forward.

The neighbors have gathered in their own driveways, whispering to one another and bearing witness to my humiliation. Another officer is standing outside the patrol car talking loudly on his radio. But all I hear is the sound of my own heart pounding wildly in my chest. I can't bear the shame. I want to beat the crap out of this kid and that pompous detective, too.

"It sounds like you and your wife have had a rather tumultuous relationship over the years."

# Chapter 18
## Kaye

I don't know how long I've been asleep when I wake to the long slow deep bellow of what I can only presume is some kind of a fog horn or an approaching vessel. Coming up on my knees on the bench where only moments before I had been sleeping, I peer out the window of the lower deck. My line of sight is just above the now gray water. The day has turned cloudy and I can't see much except the eastern shoreline as one beautiful vacation home after another quickly disappears from my view. Just ahead one of these lakefront estates flies the maple leaf on the red and white Canadian flag. Are we nearing the border? I take a deep breath to ease the panic that is threatening to overwhelm me. I need to think, just think.

I lay back down on the bench and pull the blanket up and around my shoulders.

The only sound I hear is the gentle hum of the motor and the splashing of the water as it laps against the hull of the boat. The boat keeps moving forward— full steam ahead. I hear nothing from Henri— not a word.

Should I assume everything is okay? Surely if we were approached by the Coast Guard or Immigration the boat would have stopped.

I close my eyes trying to settle myself and before long the movement of the boat across the water gently rocks me back towards sleep as a sense of peace enfolds me.

When I wake again, Henri has come down to the lower chamber and he is gently touching my shoulder and whispering the Francophile version of my name, *"Key, Key."* It is only then that I realize that the boat has stopped. "We are here, at the marina in *St. Paul de I'Île-aux-Noix."*

"Did we cross customs?" I ask.

"Yes, did you hear the horn on the barge about an hour ago?'

I nod.

"There is a floating custom's station, that blue and orange barge at the crossing into Canada. Did you see it?"

I shake my head no. "But I did hear the horn."

"I'm sure you did. That horn could raise the dead. I secure a summer permit every year so I can boat on either side of the international line. Very rarely do they board the boat, but it has happened. Sometimes the DEQ is there checking for fishing licenses and the like."

"DEQ?"

"It stands for the Department of Environmental Quality, in Canada the equivalent is the Ministry of Fisheries and Oceans. They checked my licenses a few weeks back, so I must already be in their database under the column marked *law abiding citizens*."

We both smile.

"Today they just blew their horn and waved me on through. Still I think it would be wise if you stay below and out of sight for a little while longer. I received a text from Claudette and I'll need to take your picture for your new documents."

"Okay." I reach into my canvas bag holding what remains of my earthly belongings to find my hairbrush. "Mind if I tidy up a little before you take my picture?" I ask as I begin to loosen the elastic that holds my now messy braid.

"No problem," Henri says as he uses thumb tacks to cover the porthole with a white sheet. "We need a backdrop."

I brush my hair out and drape it over my shoulders. I wish for a clean blouse to put on, instead of this old sweatshirt, but alas all I have are the clothes on my back.

"I think the braid," Henri says as he eyes me up and down. "We need you to embrace a new look, as you are leaving your old life behind.

I nod and begin to re-plait my long blonde hair. "I haven't worn my hair like this since I was in college."

"Perhaps you should, it suits you—both young and fresh."

I give a little embarrassed laugh as it has been so long since I have felt either of those things.

Henri opens the cabin door to let in a bit more natural light and takes three or four pictures with his cell phone camera. Then together we select the one we both agree on. He edits the image so it is in black and white. "*Tu es belle.* You are so photogenic," he states as if this is beyond dispute.

I think he said I was beautiful and I cannot help but smile. It has been so long since anyone has even noticed me, let alone offered me a compliment.

"I must go and find Claudette, but first I must have your passport."

A sense of foreboding runs through me, but passes quickly. Henri and Ellery have gone so far out of their way to help me. The time for caution has long since passed, I need to trust him. I reach into my bag and hand my US passport over to Henri.

"Do not worry, dear one, you will have it back *tout de suite*, along with a new *Canadien* one in your chosen name. I promise you." Henri holds my hand and gives it a squeeze

119

offering me a little reassurance. "Claudette should be nearby. I won't be long."

# Chapter 19
## Ellery

I slam the door behind me. I have bigger issues right now than a couple old boys who can't believe that every woman on the planet is interested in what little they have between their legs. Fuckers. I'm sick and tired of it. I haven't got time for it. Not any of it, not right now, and not ever.

Those good old boys will be back here with a warrant and their dogs and God knows what else. I need to think. What did Kaye touch when she was here? I start with the bedroom. I strip the bed. The sheets smell of perfume. It must have come from Kaye. I put the cotton quilt, the sheets and pillowcase into the washing machine, then go into the bathroom and grab all the towels and put those into the washer, too. I add the unscented laundry soap, it's all I have. I wonder if it will be enough to get rid of Kaye's scent.

Opening the medicine cabinet, I find some eucalyptus oil that I bought last winter when I had a head cold. Henri swears by essential oils. I don't think I ever even opened it. I add twenty or so drops into the washing machine. The smell is clean and pungent. This certainly would clear anyone's nasal passages.

Next I move into the kitchen and double wash all the dishes before putting them back in the upper cabinets, way beyond the nose of any nosey canine.

At the last minute I decide to cook some smoked venison sausage with garlic, onions and every variety of dried spice I can find. Maybe it'll confuse any of the hounds that the cops might bring along. It isn't long before the aroma fills my little cabin. Skye sits attentively at my feet while I cook. She smacks her chops and drools a bit, hoping I'll give her a taste.

Just as I finish hanging the clean bedding out on the line, in roar two police cars with lights a flashing and an SUV with the words *K-9 Unit* emblazoned on the side panel of the truck. I finish hanging the last of the wash before I make my way over to see what they want. I stuff my hands in the front pockets of my pants to keep them from shaking. I know why they're here. I do my best to appear surprised and confused, but I don't think I'm terribly convincing.

The guy, who made the rude comment earlier about whether I liked women, approaches me while his partner does his best to keep his German Shepherd away from me and Skye. I picked up my little dog. She trembles in my arms for the second time today.

"What can I do for you, gentlemen?" I find it difficult to keep the contempt out of my voice. One of the cops smirks as he hands me the warrant. I pull my reading glasses from the front of my t-shirt so I can read the small print. This document gives them permission to search my home, my property, and my car.

Oh shit. I'd forgotten about the car.

My heart races and I feel a trickle of sweat run down my back. I take a deep breath in an attempt to calm myself. Trying my best to appear annoyed rather than afraid, I think I might be able to pull this off. I'm a pretty good actor and still my gut wrenches in fear as it belies the image I desperately attempt to project.

Given that I have no recourse, I step to one side and a forensic team enters through the front door in search of something, anything that might indicate that Kaye was here. I wait with Skye by the fire circle.

Meanwhile, the officer and the dog search the grounds. He leads the dog over to the clothesline but the formidable beast does not react.

I sit on the stump beside the fire circle stirring the ashes tossing in dried pine needles from the forest floor hoping they will ignite. Perhaps the smell and smoke of burning balsam will obscure any scent of Kaye that still lingers. Officer Malone approaches, and Skye begins to growl and acts like she wants to take his leg off.

"Does she bite?"

"She's been known to," I say as she bares her teeth at him.

He steps back. "How come you're washing the sheets today?" he asks.

"Because they were dirty."

"You always do your washing on a Saturday?"

"I do my wash when I have the time and when it needs to be done. When do you do your wash?" I can't keep the contempt from spilling forth. "This is a fascinating conversation, Officer, but surely you must have something better to do? Can we just get this over with so I can have my supper?"

He grumbles something about me being a bitch and walks away.

The dog is on a long leash and is sniffing around the perimeter of the house.

The dog begins to bark as they approach my front door and the two men exchange a knowing glance before the dog handler opens the door and brings the dog into my house.

It seems like an eternity before the cop with the dog comes back outside. He makes eye contact with his partner who has given up chatting with me and is now leaning up against the patrol car. The canine cop shakes his head. "The whole house smells like a Texas barbeque joint. Admiral's more interested in what she's cookin' for dinner then findin' that missing lady," he calls out.

The two members of the forensic team leave the house with a couple of sealed plastic bags.

"Hey, what are they taking?" I shout as they walk over and confer with the guy in charge who is hovering near the patrol car.

He turns and glares at me before sending one of his lackeys over with a handwritten ledger of what is in the bag on a piece of pink NCR paper. I pull my readers from the top of my head to read: a pair of white sweat pants, a dish towel, and some used Kleenex from the bathroom waste basket.

I take a deep breath and try to think. What in the world do they want those for?

Shit.

I gave Kaye a dish towel when her leg and foot were bleeding.

She borrowed those old sweat pants when she got out of the river.

Damn.

I ease myself back down on the stump. Turning my gaze to the fire circle, I begin to stir the smoldering ashes with a dead branch from a maple tree as the remnants of last night's fire re-ignites.

What the hell have I gotten myself, and the others, into this time?

Lost in my own dilemma I hear Rin-Tin-Tin begin to bark like he's just captured some escaping criminal. The cops race up the hill one right after the other leaving the cop dressed in his suit, tie, and dress shoes scrambling up the gravel drive in their dust.

From the fire circle I can see that all the car doors are open. I'm sure the keys are still in the ignition, just like they always are. The tail lights flash as someone steps on the brake pedal and starts the car.

Before I can walk up the hill to see what the commotion is all about, the officer in charge is walking back down the hill to meet me.

"Ellery McMasters, we'd like to bring you into the station. We need to ask you a few questions about the disappearance of Mrs. Amy Cooper."

"Am I under arrest?" I take a deep breath and run my hand through my short white hair as I try to think.

"Not yet."

"Let me get my dog her dinner and a sweater."

He nods. Like a shadow, he wordlessly follows me back into my house.

# Chapter 20
## Kaye

I wait for Henri below deck as I listen to the voices of other boaters returning from a day on the water. There is a mixture of French and English. The voices are distorted by all the other sounds of the marina: the water lulling against the hulls, the cries of gulls, exuberant children, and those who are tired, hungry, and just plain ornery. To my great relief there is no official present calling out smugglers, illegal immigrants or other law breakers like myself. I settle in, realizing I may be here for a while. I wish I'd had the forethought to bring a book and my reading glasses. This is such a ridiculous notion, I nearly laugh out loud at my need for my creature comforts. I escaped bringing nothing with me except last year's worn bathing suit that I was wearing. I paw through my old canvas bag perusing the things I did decide to bring in my hasty departure from the house. I take out the crystal perfume bottle of Shalimar from the bottom of the bag and mist some behind my ears and inhale. I love the scent, I always have. If Ellery hadn't loaned me her truck I wouldn't have any of this. A sense of gratitude threatens to bring me to tears. I'm lucky to have the few things I do.

There in the bag is the photo of the kids. It was taken years ago. They look so happy all filled with the innocence of youth. All three of them are dressed in their softball uniforms. I hold the framed photo close to my heart. I miss them already.

They must be worried about me. I never meant to…

I never meant to what? I never meant to hurt them or anyone else.

I just needed to be free of my life with Nash. He roughed me up; more than once. If he even thought I'd dare file for divorce and take my inheritance with me, God only knows what he'd do. I don't even want to think about it. Still the verbal barrage of threats he made over the forty years of our marriage plays on and on in my head, like a tape stuck in an unending loop.

I shake the thought from my head as I look out the portal over the water. It looks to be late afternoon as the sun has turned the water a golden color as it slips its way westerly across the sky.

I will contact Andy when I'm safe. She can let the boys know where I am once I get where I'm going. There are still so many obstacles that need to be overcome before

I can say for certain where that will be. As much as I want to tell them not to worry and to relieve whatever anguish they may be feeling, I can't risk it. Not yet. I can only pray that they will understand and find it in their hearts to forgive me.

Before I can put my photo back in my canvas bag, I hear Henri on the dock. He is chatting amiably with another man in French. I had hoped maybe he was arriving with Claudette. The boat shifts towards the dock as Henri boards and a moment later he is knocking softly on the door of the cabin below the deck.

"Henri?" I ask, just to be sure.

"*Key, c'est moi. Ouvre la porte,*" he laughs softly then reverts to English. "It's me. Open the door, my dear one."

I open the cabin door as the late afternoon sun fills the lower level with warmth and golden light. Henri steps inside but leaves the door open. "I think we need to get a bit of fresh air in here. It feels a little like a cave or a cellar. You must be chilled, no?"

"Really, I'm fine, Henri. No need for concern."

"Very well, I have brought you a light supper as well as some news," he says as he raises a canvas shopping bag in my direction. "I think it is best if we stay below deck until dark. We have come this far, no sense drawing attention to you now."

He states this as a matter-of-fact, yet his face seeks my approval. I lower my eyes and nod. He is the captain of this ship and my very presence is not only a problem for me, but for him, too.

He raises the drop leaf table and lays the canvas bag upon it. Then with the flourish of a most gracious host, he lays the table with a clean linen tablecloth and linen napkins, wine glasses, china plates and flatware from a wicker basket beneath the table. Only a moment later he is pulling a bottle of wine, a baguette, a variety of cheeses, and a salad from the canvas bag.

"Really Henri, you shouldn't have gone to all this trouble," I say as I slowly fold my arms across my chest. A flicker of anxiety threatens to ignite as I wonder what his expectations might be. Perhaps, I have been too naïve, too trusting.

"Please sit. You must be hungry. You need to eat. You will have a long night ahead of you."

His words play on in my head, '*a long night ahead.*' Does he expect to be compensated for his kindness and my deliverance? A shudder of dread runs through me.

Still, I do as requested.

"Are you chilled?" Henri asks as he closes the cabin door and the darkness closes in. Then he opens the two portholes to bring in the soft breeze of early evening, before he lights the two lanterns that hang on either side of the boat's interior. He looks again in my direction and smiles, then he opens the wine and pours each of us a glass. I think about the wisdom of refusing but before I can say anything . Henri says, "A little wine with dinner, most civilized. You may need it for courage and strength. It will not hurt…"

I nod and lift the glass. Henri lifts his, too. "*Santé.*" We clink glasses as he drinks to my health.

"Let's eat first and enjoy our repast. I can fill you in on my meeting with Claudette once we have finished. Relax and enjoy, everything is going according to plan."

What plan? Whose plan? I take another swallow of the wine and a piece of bread and cheese. "Delicious, thank you," I say to my host and again he smiles at me.

"I have given Claudette your passport and the photo we took earlier. She will be back for you later this evening, once the sun has set."

I take another sip and offer a silent prayer of thanks. So far… so good.

# Chapter 21
## Nash

"You're gonna wish you'd let me shower," I say to the snooty young cops in the front of the patrol car.

"I see what you mean," the driver calls back over his shoulder, not taking his eyes off the road.

The other cop opens the window *and* turns up the air conditioning. I guess they can smell my stink, too. Whatever.

The driver programs something into the GPS, but given the protective shield between the front and back seats, I can't read it. Besides, I forgot my reading glasses. The driver pulls on to I-87 North which seems a bit odd given the police station is on Maxwell Drive just off of Clifton Park Boulevard.

"Hey, where are you taking me? You said we were going to the station?"

"We are but not the Clifton Park station. The State Police are handling the investigation. We're headed up to Mayfield near the Sacandaga campgrounds. That's where your wife went missing, so this case is in their jurisdiction."

The other cop chimes in, "We're with the New York State Missing Persons Unit—just consulting really. Just lending a hand." Both of the cops start to laugh as if this is some kind of an inside joke. I don't laugh because I don't get it.

"Mayfield, what the ... I haven't been to sleep yet."

"Suck it up, you had a nap. You were snoring loud enough to wake the dead," the driver says with a sneer.

"We should be there in about an hour. Why don't you close your eyes and try to get some sleep now," the other cop says.

"And your effing mouth, too," the driver says under his breath.

I want to deck that smart ass.

"Give it a rest," the ride-along rookie chides his partner.

By the time we get to the State Troopers headquarters in Mayfield it is nearly dark. It's been a very long couple of days. I'm dirty, exhausted, and starving.

"I said I want a lawyer," I say as one of the cops unlocks the back door to let me out.

"We heard ya. You'll get your phone call," he says as he escorts me down the hallway.

134

"And how about a sandwich and a Coke? I'm starving."

"I'll see what I can do," he says. We pass an old woman in the hall. Her hair is shorter than mine and she dresses like a guy. She's being escorted by another cop. She looks as pissed off as I feel.

"What'd that old dyke do?"

"Shut up, Cooper," the younger cop says as he gives me a firm shove in the back. The woman turns her head and stares at me as if she has just crossed paths with the devil. I turn away. Man, if looks could kill.

"What?" I snarl, not expecting any response.

No one says a word until the ride-along cop unlocks the door into some kind of interrogation room. It's just like those rooms you see on all the cop shows on TV.

"Take a seat, someone will be with you shortly."

The room is sparse with only a government issue table and three plastic chairs. There is nothing on the wall but a one way mirror. I wave and sneer at whoever might be on the other side. I give them a good five minutes before I start demanding my rights. "I want a lawyer," I shout kinda loud. When no one comes, I increase the volume until I'm shouting the same thing over and over again. I decide to pound on the door to let these punks know I mean business.

"I'm not a criminal. I'm the grieving husband for God's sake!" I scream through the locked metal door still pounding on the door with alternating fists until my knuckles are bloody.

# Chapter 22
## Andy

By the time my flight arrives in Albany it's already after six

Eastern Standard Time. At least there will be a couple more

hours of daylight. I know I should be grateful for a direct

flight and getting across the country as quickly as I have,

but I find no place for gratitude in my heart. The flight was

rough as we passed through one thunderstorm after

another. They must have been the remnants of the storms

that ravaged the East last night.

Where the hell is Mom?

I hope Joey has some news for me.

In my heart, I plead for her safety.

Please let Mom be found.

Let her be safe and well.

I'll call Joey as soon as I get in my rental car. I can't

call him now. I know I'll need some privacy in case … in

case he has bad news. Tears begin to fill my eyes with the

very thought of bad news.

Still, I power up my phone as I walk through the

terminal. Nothing. No service—and this is the airport

serving the capital city in the great state of New York? Good Lord, welcome to the technological revolution.

I didn't have time to get anything to eat before boarding and the economy airlines didn't have enough of their *snack-packs* left for the cheap seats back near the toilets. As I exit the main terminal, the only carry-out restaurant that is open is a *Chick-fil-a*.

No. Just no. I won't give those ignorant homophobes one thin dime. I'd rather starve.

Instead, I go to a vending machine in baggage claim and grab a bottle of water and a *Twix* bar. I wait for my bag as an older couple lean in toward one another and snicker behind one hand as they speculate loudly about my gender and laugh at their own little joke about my being *be-twix and between*.

Just because they're deaf and can't hear one another doesn't mean I can't hear them. If they only knew how rude and hurtful their little joke is they'd be going straight to the confessional begging for forgiveness. I turn and walk away as soon as my bag arrives. Is this the equivalent of turning the other cheek? How many times am I supposed to do it? Seventy times seven if my memory serves me. God knows I must be getting close.

Once I reach my quota will it be okay if I tell these hypocrites exactly what I think?

I step out of the terminal and head for the parking garage to pick up my rental car at the Budget desk. I finish the remains of my candy bar. My phone buzzes in the pocket of my jeans, as calls and text messages that were made while my phone was in airplane mode begin to ambush me.

Both my hands are full, and I'm already sweating as I carry my suitcase and my laptop into the parking deck. I will turn up the air conditioning and get my phone out once I get inside the rental car. Thankfully there is no one in line ahead of me.

I pull out my phone and see my messages have not loaded completely. I growl in frustration, if ever there was a time that I needed to be in touch it would be now. Must be the interference of all the concrete in this parking structure. I pull out of the garage and into the cell phone lot. It's probably faster to just call my brother rather than slog through the myriad of waiting messages.

He picks up on the first ring. "Andy, where are you?"

"I just got in."

"Andy?"

"Yeah, it's me."

"Your voice sounds different, are you okay?"

"More or less. Anyway, I'm in the rental car. Where are you?"

"Didn't you get my messages? I've been trying to get in touch with you for hours."

"No, Joey. Like I said, I just got in. Just tell me what's going on."

"They've taken Dad up to the State Troopers' in Mayfield."

"Hold on. You need to bring me up to speed. First things first—have they found Mom?"

"No." I can hear his voice crack, and, I know, he is about to lose it.

"Are they still looking for her?" I ask as I start to cry.

"Nothing organized. They've posted notifications with her description and a photo, and there are intermittent bulletins on the local TV and radio stations asking anyone who may have seen her to notify the State Police." I can hear the desperation in his voice as I'm sure he can hear it in mine. I take a deep breath and try to get myself under control. There will be time to grieve later, but not now. We still don't know *anything*, I remind myself. Now is not the time to give into fear.

"Did you get a hold of Sam?"

"No, I forgot he took Ellie and the kids up to Nova Scotia to go fishing. They're not due back until next weekend. I left him a voice message to call me. I told him that it was important. God only knows if he even has service up there."

Joey seems to have gotten himself under control, at least for the time being. Better to stick with the concrete things we know for certain and focus on what we can actually do rather than allow ourselves to travel into the unknown which is filled with fearful speculation.

"Okay, where are you?"

"I'm at the State Troopers' Headquarters in Mayfield. They brought Dad in for questioning a little over an hour ago."

"Do they think he had something to do with Mom's disappearance?" I ask as my despair gives way to anger. "If he hurt Mom, I swear I'll kill him."

"I don't know, Andy?"

"Does he have a lawyer?"

"I don't know. I don't know *anything*. I've been sitting in this godforsaken waiting room drinking bitter, cold coffee and thumbing through *Sports Afield*."

"What? What's *Sports Afield*?"

"A hunting and fishing magazine that's at least three years old."

"Oh, spare me," I mumble with a heavy dose of sympathy. This might appeal to our brother Sam, but Joey and I couldn't feign the least bit of interest on a good day, and today is not a good day. "Let me program my GPS so I have some idea where I'm going." Opening *MapQuest*, the town of Mayfield, New York appears on my phone. I hit the button for directions from my current location. "There it is. I'm about an hour away."

"I should get off the phone. I need to save my battery in case…"

"In case what?"

"I don't know. Someone has learned something about Mom…"

"Okay, I'll be there soon." I hang up head west onto I-90. Ugh, I-90 is a toll road. I reach into my back pocket for my wallet to see if I have any cash.

Some things were easier when I was a woman and could carry all my important stuff in my purse. Slowly the realization threatens to overwhelm me. This day is going to get even more difficult as I haven't seen my brother or my father in the last two years or told anyone in my family about my transition. Joey will be cool. He and Mom have always loved me, and I know they always will, no matter what.

Dad and Sammy will be a different story.

Once I've passed the toll booth and am on I-90, I listen to my voicemail. Most of the calls are from Joey. I delete them as he and I have already discussed everything of importance. Then there is a call from Michelle. I take a deep breath. Heaven only knows what she might be thinking as I abandoned her sleeping in my bed without a word and now the entire day has passed without a call or any explanation. God, she must hate me. I play the message, but she doesn't say a word and after a long moment or two she just clicks off.

I hit reply as I try to think how much I want to tell her. She doesn't pick up. My call goes directly to her voicemail.

I hadn't realized until this very moment how much I wanted to confide in her and let her in on what has happened and how afraid I am that something terrible may have happened to my beloved mother. But all I am capable of saying is, "Michelle, something has happened, and I had to leave. I'm sorry. It was… is… a family emergency. Please call me. I'm in New York. Please call me." I break down and an audible sob emerges from the depth of my soul just before I am able to hang up the call.

I run my fingers through my short hair, then caress my chin feeling the stubble as the tears come freely down my face. Oh Mom, where are you? Please God, let her be alright. Her life has been so difficult, it can't end like this. It just can't.

# Chapter 23
## Kaye

I drain the last of my wine and Henri lifts the bottle and looks me in the eye.

"Should we finish this?" he asks.

I smile and shake my head. "No thank you, I've had plenty."

Henri gives me a nod and recorks the bottle. "Then I think I should clean up, and you should get ready to go. Claudette should be here shortly and a new adventure awaits you, *mon amie.*"

Henri begins to clear the table and puts the remainder of the food away in the canvas shopping bag. I excuse myself, gather up the bag with my limited belongings, and head for the washroom.

I close the door behind me. There is barely enough room to turn around, still there is a small, gilt-framed mirror hanging above the sink. I unbraid my hair and begin to brush it out.

I can be such a paranoid idiot. I guess it comes from living all those years with Nash, where nothing was ever freely given out of the goodness of his heart. All that talk about the reciprocal nature of friendship from Ellery and then Henri, and then the tablecloth and napkins and wine with dinner. It all felt a bit too… what? Intimate? I was afraid I was going to be asked to pay up for all the risks taken and kindnesses received. How? With my sixty-four year old body? I can't imagine how that could be adequate recompense for all their benevolence. Still I was concerned, intrigued—but wary and reluctant. Is it possible to be so conflicted? It doesn't matter now, for that is not the case. Henri isn't interested in me, at least not like that, not in any sexual way. He seems to expect nothing of me. I should be relieved, still it has been so long since any man has even noticed me, really seen me—until tonight. It was kind of nice. I glance back in the mirror to re-braid my hair, my own smiling reflection looks back at me.

As I start to brush my teeth, I hear a knock on the cabin door and the low whispers of a woman's voice. A rush of adrenaline causes me to panic. Is it the authorities? Or Claudette? I turn off the water in the sink. Standing in this cramped space trying not to move or make a sound, I swallow the toothpaste. I wait in silence.

"Key, it's okay. *C'est* Claudette. Come out and say *allo*," Henri says as he taps gently on the bathroom door.

"I'll be right out." I turn the water back on and use my hands to take a drink and rinse my mouth.

I open the door. Henri stands there in the hull, the evening light coming through the portholes has grown dim. A small woman with long dark hair sits in the shadows.

"*Bonjour,*" I say, stepping towards her.

"*Key…*" Henri addresses me as the woman stands and pushes past him and extends her hand.

"*Je suis* Claudette," she says as she shakes my hand.

Her grip is firm but her hand is soft and her nails manicured and finished with a burgundy polish. She is at least twenty years younger than I. She's petite, small-boned, and very slender—almost waif-like. She's dressed in a dark mini skirt and fitted black tank top and sandals. Her toenails are polished in the same color as her fingernails. The contrast between us makes me want to slink back into the bathroom. I feel like a cross between a Viking warrior and a street fighter as I tower above her and I become acutely aware of my old stained sweatshirt, short and ragged fingernails, and my old, now bloody, running shoes.

She looks me up and down. "*Tsk tsk.*"

Clearly, I don't meet with her approval and I feel ashamed. She turns to Henri and speaks rapidly in French. I miss most of it, but I get the gist of it.

She can't take me out looking like this.

She turns to the bench behind her and retrieves a shopping bag.

Henri raises his shoulders and shrugs. Then he hands me the bag, "Claudette has brought you some new clothes to wear. Think of it as your disguise." He gives me a smile, sort of. One that says, I'm sorry. It's clear he feels embarrassed for his role in my humiliation, but clearly still feels the wisdom in altering my appearance.

I look in the bag. There is a navy dress with silver buttons and a belt, a brightly colored silk scarf and a pair of navy wedge espadrilles. The dress is knit and a medium. It should fit. I check the size of the shoes. They are an eight and half, close enough.

"*Changes-toi rapidement,*" Claudette says as she turns her palms up in frustration. There is no need to translate. I take the bag and head back into the bathroom. It doesn't take me long to change into the clothes I have been given. The dress falls just below my knees. I fold my old clothes and put them back in my canvas bag and head back into the main cabin.

"*C'est mieux.*" Claudette approves as she smiles at me for the first time. Her teeth are as perfect as the rest of her.

Henri smiles, too.

Claudette approaches me and re-ties the scarf, tossing one end of it over my left shoulder. Then she crouches down and unbuttons the lower four buttons on the dress so it opens above my knees. She takes off her own earrings, large silver hoops and hands them to me.

My ears were pierced long ago. I still wear earrings, although not all that often. I gently lace the hoops through the lobes of my ears, grateful the holes are still open.

"*Assieds-toi.*" She gestures to the bench. I take a seat as directed. Claudette pulls out an oversized cosmetic bag and begins to do my makeup with both speed and precision. Once she has cleansed my face with some kind of a pre-moistened towelette, she plucks my eyebrows, applies face cream and then foundation with one of those makeup brushes that I've never used and only seen in magazines. Then she starts in on my eyes using shadow, eyeliner, and mascara. She hands me a hand mirror and a lipstick in a dusky rose. "Put it on," she commands in heavily accented English.

I use the mirror to apply the lipstick. I look transformed.

She picks up my braid and again gives me a *tsk tsk* in disapproval. "What can be done?" she says to no one in particular. Again she says something to Henri in French

149

that I can't quite catch, something about not being a miracle worker.

Henri steps over to me and extends his hand for me to stand. He embraces me with tenderness and gently kisses the top of my head while whispering so only I can hear, "You are lovely. Do not let anyone allow you to feel differently. Now go with God and enjoy your life."

Claudette grabs my canvas bag and puts it, along with all of its contents into a chic navy leather satchel then thrusts it in my direction.

"Everything you will need is in the bag: your papers, passport, airline ticket, a bit of money—euros, and cell phone. Your flight leaves in a little more than four hours. Montreal to Paris. Once you get to Paris…" Henri does not say anything more, but I know.

Once I get to Paris, I am on my own. I nod to assure Henri that I understand.

Then he continues, "We are about an hour from the airport. You'll need to leave now, if you are going to make your flight."

"You're not coming?" I ask, feeling apprehensive about traveling with this powerhouse of a woman. She is gruff, small, but mighty. I don't like her, and I'm pretty certain that she doesn't like me either.

"No, my dear, I am not. Do not be afraid. Claudette will get you where you need to be. You can trust her." Henri reaches for my hand and gives it a squeeze.

"Okay," I say as much to reassure Henri as reassure myself.

I feel like a child. Both naïve and incredibly vulnerable. Still, the enormity of what I am undertaking threatens to derail my confidence and unravel all of these carefully executed plans.

"Do not use the phone until you get off the plane. Then, you'll need to call Ellery. She will be waiting to hear from you. Do you remember her instructions?" Henri asks.

I nod. "Edith always has enough cash, how bad can Edith be?" I say reciting the mnemonic Ellery had me commit to memory so I will remember her phone number. I give Henri one last smile.

"You've got it, *mon amie*." He smiles again and gives me a wink.

"*Vite. Vite. Allons-y*. Let's go," Claudette says impatiently with one hand already on the handle of the cabin door.

"Good-bye Henri. Thank you for everything," I say as tears threaten to spill forth from my eyes.

"Don't. Your makeup!" Claudette snarls as she hands me a tissue to dab my eyes

151

Again Henri smiles at me, "Until next time."

Stepping off the boat, I follow Claudette out onto the dock. I can barely keep up with her as I attempt to walk in these three-inch wedges. I'm close to five eleven in these shoes. I feel like a giant next to this woman. The dock is gently swaying beneath my feet. It's been a long time since I've worn heels.

Claudette is three or four feet in front of me when she steps off the dock and onto the cement walkway of the marina. She turns and looks over her shoulder at me. Once I am next to her on solid ground she growls at me, "Keep up." Then she thrusts an emery board into my hand and says, "And do something about your nails."

# Chapter 24
## Kaye

Like most French Canadians, Claudette is conversant in English. Her English is better than my French. I haven't used my French since college and that's been decades ago. Still, I understand more than she thinks I do. She chooses to speak French with Henri as a way to exclude me from the conversation and make me feel inadequate.

I hang my head feeling embarrassed and a little ashamed. For what exactly? I acknowledge that my appearance was a bit unkempt, clearly not up to Claudette's standards. And for that matter, it was not up to mine either.

But I have just done the bravest thing of my entire life and I will not let this arrogant little woman diminish that or me. I straighten myself up and pull my shoulders back as I walk with all the grace and finesse that I can muster in these ridiculous three-inch platform shoes.

As we approach her car, a late model black Peugeot, she clicks the remote and I hear the door unlock as the interior lights go on. "Get in," Claudette says as she walks to the driver's side of the car and puts her bag into the back seat before getting in to drive. It only takes a moment for us to be buckled up and heading out of the marina towards Montreal.

It becomes clear that she has nothing else to say to me. Taking the emery board she'd thrust upon me, I turn my face towards my lap and begin to file my nails. My mind turns to other matters as I vigorously rub the emery board back and forth across my broken thumbnail. We still have about an hour's drive to the Pierre Trudeau International Airport and I have a few questions whether she wants to talk to me or not.

Once my nails have been shaped and look presentable, I put the emery board back into a pocket in the new leather bag then continue to rifle through the bag to find my passport.

"This bag is lovely," I say, hoping to express my gratitude and break the uneasy silence.

"'Tis nothing. Only a faux *Atelier Auguste*. But it's passable."

I look at the metal insignia—*Sévigné*.

"You'll never pass for a Parisian." She turns her head away from the country road and takes a moment to look me up and down. Her lower lip turns down and I know, in her eyes, I just don't quite measure up. "But you might pass for a tourist, provincial perhaps. If you take a little effort with your appearance, we can only hope you'll look a little less… like an American."

I let the obvious insult go and say nothing, at least for the moment. The truth I must acknowledge is, whether I like it or not, this woman is doing me a huge favor.

Then again, maybe the favor is not for me, as this woman owes me nothing.

Today is the first time she has ever laid eyes on me. She is repaying a debt owed to someone else, Henri or Ellery perhaps. She isn't happy about it, but she does it just the same. Both Henri and Ellery had said something about the reciprocal nature of friendship. I let this thought linger.

I pull my passport from the beautiful satchel Claudette *gifted* to me. My new passport is encased in a navy leather cover that matches the satchel. Claudette has a point, my old canvas shopping bag and bloody running shoes truly did lack that *je ne sais quoi*.

I look at the new passport. It's Canadian and has been issued in my new name—Kaye Hill. The birthplace is listed as Trois-Rivières, Quebec. Somehow I've been made five years younger—just approaching my sixtieth birthday. This pleases me and a slow smile forms on my lips. In the photo I'm wearing the old sweatshirt, but fortunately the stain has been cropped out. I look like the old me rather than this new improved version of my former self. Oh well.

155

"How did you get me this passport?" I ask.

"Information will be shared on a need to know basis, and *madame*, you do not need to know." She snarls and keeps her eyes on the road as she accelerates. "We are all safer if you are kept in the dark on this. *Mes amis,* let's just say he owes me a favor. *Compris?*"

"Okay," I mutter under my breath as I'm not certain I want to be *friends* with any of these people. What will be asked of me? I fear it may be a little too late to worry about that. What is the old saying? In for a dime in for a dollar…either way at this point, I'm all in.

We leave the old country roads, turning onto an expressway we head in towards the city. I look through the bag expecting to find a cell phone but do not. I think about my promise to Ellery. I said I would call her.

Feeling confused and presumptuous I shift uncomfortably in my seat before daring to ask, "I thought there would be a cell phone, I promised Ellery that I would call once I got to Paris."

"You must buy a phone and an international calling card. Look for the kiosk at the train station. In your wallet there are two visa gift cards. They are untraceable and will cover the cost of the phone. Once you get yourself established you can use the same phone and set up a more permanent account. There is also a bit of cash, euros, for traveling expenses," she says in a dismissive tone.

I repeat the mnemonic once in my head, then again out loud as I commit it to memory, "*Edith always has enough cash, how bad can Edith be?*"

There are others I will need to call, but not now. I will call my children once I am in Paris, once I am safe.

By now someone has notified my kids that I am missing.

What have I done?

My stomach cramps as I think about how worried they must be… but are they? I haven't really seen any of them in so long. If they were really worried about me would they have stayed away? I know they love me, but things were never easy for them, any of them, but growing up in our home was particularly difficult for Andy.

She's never had it easy. She resembles her father, both big and strong. Never feminine enough to be granted her father's approval. He subjected her to unspeakable cruelty and perpetual criticism as he mocked and taunted her. Is it any wonder she's moved away and I haven't seen her in almost two years?

Both Joey and Sam take after my side of the family, especially Joey. He's tall like Nash, but fair and fine boned. He, too, bore the brunt of his father's ridicule as he teased

157

him relentlessly about being overly emotional and acting like *a little girl* as if this was the worst insult he could come up with. While Nash was actively picking on Andy and Joey, Sam slipped silently beneath his father's radar doing his best to go unnoticed.

Clearly, no one will nominate me for the *Mother of the Year*. How could I have let this go on? I should have left years ago but I was afraid. I'm nothing but a coward. I guess I've always felt the children would be safer if I was in the picture. I didn't want our children to spend time alone with their father—God only knows what he might have said or done if I wasn't there to run interference or buffer the blows.

I guess we all are destined to live by the choices we make.

I rarely see the boys or my grandkids. How can I blame them? Both of my daughters-in-law, Natalie and Ellie, have carefully orchestrated their families' lives to keep their little ones out of harm's way, or beyond the reach of Nash.

I can't help but wonder how you can miss someone you hardly ever see. Still, I know, I will miss them. I will miss them in ways I can't even begin to imagine. But they are all launched, I've done my job.

Maybe, just maybe, they all will come and visit me once I am settled. Hope and dreams are mine, and I refuse to abandon either. My future must be better than the past. I couldn't stay, I just couldn't.

I reach in my bag for a tissue to wipe my eyes then take out the plane ticket.

I'm taking an overnight flight that arrives in Paris at 11:45 tomorrow morning. The plane leaves in three hours. I turn my thoughts to the ordeal associated with getting on an international flight and the fact that I am traveling with a fraudulent passport and have no luggage. Will I be conspicuous? Will this draw questions and undue attention? Will I need a story about where I am going and how long I will be staying and why I only have booked a one-way ticket? It has been so long since I have traveled to Europe, not since I was a young woman, not since I married Nash.

"Do you think I'll need a story for the immigration agents when I arrive in Paris?" I ask, hoping Claudette will help me out.

Instead, she snarls at me, "That, *madame*, is up to you to figure out. I have provided you with a Canadian passport in your chosen name and a long term visa which will allow you to travel in any of the Schengen countries for one year. After that you are on your own."

I turn my head away from Claudette and towards the side window. I assume since she has booked my flight into Paris, that France is one of the Schengen countries. I will need to find out more about this. She treats me like an idiot and maybe she is right to. I have entered into this without having thought it through.

I read the signs on the highway, the advertising this and that, and try to remember my high school French. Claudette drives quickly, changing lanes, and passing the slower moving cars without a moment's hesitation. She appears oblivious to the stress her driving causes me, or perhaps she just doesn't care. The light posts appear rhythmically, one after another after another in rapid succession, against the night sky until the sign for the *aéroport* appears.

Claudette puts on her turn signal to exit the expressway. Still silent, she navigates her way towards the place labeled *departures* in the international terminal. She pulls up to the curb and stops the car underneath the sign marked—*Air France.*

"*Bonne chance, mon amie.*"

"*Merci* Claudette…" Again tears fill my eyes as I try to think about what else I want to say.

"*Oui, oui,*" she says impatiently. She has no interest in my gratitude or a long good-bye.

160

It is time for me to go. Just go.

I open the car door and step out onto the curb dressed in clothing selected by someone else, in shoes I can barely walk in, and carrying nothing but the navy leather satchel. I close the car door and step up onto the sidewalk. I raise my hand to wave good-bye. I stand on the sidewalk and watch as Claudette pulls the shiny black Peugeot away from the curb and merges into the onslaught of airport traffic.

She does not look back.

Her task is complete and I am on my own.

# Chapter 25
## Andy

I texted Joey on my way to the police station. He's

supposed to meet me there. I check the GPS, Alexa or her

Google counterpart who informs me that I have arrived at

the State Police Headquarters in Mayfield.

At first I think this can't possibly be right, on one

side of the street is a building with rotting plywood

covering the windows. Across the street is a brick building

with columns that are too small for the portico, making the

whole thing look out of proportion. The lettering on the

portico indicates I have indeed reached my destination—

State Police. However, the letters p and o in police are

missing leaving the sign to read *State lice*. This hardly instills

any confidence in me.  The place is small and looks like it

might once have been a restaurant that went out of

business or maybe an abandoned funeral home. Perhaps

this is law enforcement's equivalent of a one room

schoolhouse. Welcome to the Adirondacks.

I pull off the two lane road and into the parking lot.

Behind a rusty blue dumpster I see where four police cars,

each from a different jurisdiction, have been parked. Joey's blue Volkswagen Jetta is there, too.

I lock the car and take a deep breath. Today will be one of those days that will live on in family lore—the day their daughter and their sister came back home to New York as a man.

I take a deep breath. I only wish this was the biggest issue facing us today.

Walking up the sidewalk and even before I'm in the building, I hear my father bellowing from somewhere inside.

"I'm not a criminal. I'm the grieving husband for god's sake."

I'd know this angry voice anywhere as it still permeates so many memories of my childhood. Good Lord, I'm nearly forty years old and haven't lived in my parent's home since I left for college. Hearing him raging, even when it is not at me, causes my heart to race and the keys to the rental car jingle as my hand begins to tremble.

What does my therapist call this? I'm triggered.

I take a long slow deep breath, straighten up, and shove my shaking hands along with the keys into my pocket. For God's sake I'm a fully functioning adult, I will not be intimidated any longer by this man who fathered me, yet has never had any idea what it means to love and nurture anyone.

Just inside the door a receptionist sits behind an elevated desk. She does not wear a uniform, instead a simple green dress, civilian attire. From her elevated perch, she looks down at me trying to figure out who I am and why I am here. I approach the desk.

"May I help you?"

Not quite sure how to begin I stumble over my words as my story spills out. "I'm Andy Cooper and that man yelling is my father. My mother is … missing." In spite of my best efforts tears fill my eyes. I wipe them away with the back of my hand while this woman waits for me to continue. "I just flew in from Denver and I'm here to help." A look of confusion crosses her face. "Not help *him*, I'm here to help find my mother."

"I'm certain Detective Randall will want to have a word with you. I'll need to see your driver's license and you'll need to sign in," she says as she pushes a clipboard with an attached pen beneath the plexiglass barrier that protects her from John Q. Public and the *likes of me*. I fill out the form answering the required questions: name, address, phone number, email address, nature of my business, then push the clipboard back beneath the barrier. I reach into my back pocket to retrieve my wallet and my driver's license. This is the third time today I have been asked to use it as identification. First to board the plane, then to rent the car, and now to gain admission into the police waiting room. I take a deep breath and sigh as I hand it to the receptionist.

I wait while she scrutinizes everything as my father continues to holler in the background.

Trying to find the silver lining in the midst of this dark cloud that envelops me, I'm relieved that this whole fiasco didn't take place six months ago when I was in the process of getting my name and gender changed legally. My name has been changed from Andrea to Andy and my designated gender is now listed as X on my driver's license.

The receptionist disappears behind a closed door with my license and the clipboard.

In New York, my gender would simply be listed as male. That would certainly make things easier for me. Still, I'm glad I don't live in Florida, as I understand there are a myriad of hoops they make people jump through in order to get new documents in that state, including a note from a physician.

I'm filled with angst and conflicting emotion. I'm embarrassed to acknowledge that the out of control screaming idiot is a member of my family. I'm overwhelmed with dread that something awful has

165

happened to my mother. And lastly what will my family think of the fact that I have transitioned and couldn't trust any of them enough to tell them until I was already well on the other side of this lengthy and difficult process?

The woman in the green dress stands and comes out from behind the closed door and around the desk. She hands me back my driver's license and says, "I'm Evelyn Harris. Why don't you come with me, Andy, and I'll show you where your brother is waiting."

I follow her down the corridor as her low-heeled black pumps click rhythmically on the linoleum floor. She indicates a door on the left before departing. "I'll let Detective Randall know you are here."

Looking through the window in the door I see Joey with his elbows on his knees looking down at the floor in a windowless waiting room. He sits on an old government issue vinyl chair holding a paper cup filled with vending machine coffee.

Could this whole scenario get any more depressing?

I quickly shake the question away because the answer is—of course it can.

# Chapter 26
## Nash

The door to this interrogation room opens as I holler and

rap on it. A young cop practically knocks me over as he

pushes his way into the room. I stumble backwards. This

kid is a beast. He looks like a bouncer from the Lionheart

Brewery or some other steroid-laden gym rat.

"Hey, watch it, buddy!" I say as I attempt to regain

my footing. Who does this kid think he is? "What took you

so long? And where's my goddamn lawyer?"

"Sit down and shut your mouth or I'll handcuff you

to that chair," the cop barks.

"Are you planning to gag me, too, Mr. Tough

Stuff?"

"Don't push your luck. Your lawyer has been called

but he can't be here until tomorrow morning. So you can

either talk to us or sit tight and shut your freakin' mouth."

Now I'm pissed. "If you think I'm going to just sit

here all night waitin' till my lawyer decides to show up, well

you have another think comin'."

He stands in the doorway with his hands on his hips and a shit eatin' grin on his face. "You should know, Mr. Cooper, that we can hold you for up to 96 hours before charging you. Your wife is missing, she could have met with foul play or may even be dead and you, sir, are a prime suspect. So you might as well get comfortable, 'cause you're not goin' anywhere."

I pull out the metal folding chair and lower myself down with an audible thump.

Shit. Just shit.

This bozo just stands there guarding the door. He looks like he'd like nothing better than to punch my lights out. I clench my fists and release them a couple of times. The last thing I want to do is give him a reason to strike me. I need to think …

The silence between us lengthens and in spite of the flicker and buzz from the fluorescent lights, the space between us fills with a palpable gloom and a sense of desperation threatens to overwhelm me.

"Okay, then get me one of those public defenders. I know my rights!"

"Look Einstein, you can only get assigned a public defender if, or should I say when, you are charged and bound over to stand trial. Get it?"

I nod my head, I get it. "Is my son here?" I ask quietly.

"Yes, both of them are in the waiting room."

"Sam *and* Joey?" I ask.

"I didn't get their names."

"Can I see them?"

"Sorry, not until your interview has been completed or you've been released. Besides, they have both already agreed to talk with Detective Randall from *Missing Persons* about your wife's disappearance. He should be with them shortly."

I drop my face into my hands, God only knows what those two will say about the state of our marriage.

"I didn't hurt Amy, honest I didn't."

The cop gives me a look that says, *I've heard this all before.*

He doesn't believe me.

He turns his back on me and walks out of the room.

I hear the jingling of his keys as he locks me in.

# Chapter 27
## Ellery

Sitting and waiting, it's been at least twenty minutes since they locked me up in this stuffy, windowless room with the cinderblock walls painted a color that must be called *institutional beige*. You'd think with all the taxes paid to the State of New York they could do something about the ventilation, at the very least provide a fan. I'm starting to sweat. I mop my brow with the hem of my tee shirt.

I check my phone. There is no service or internet.

I haven't been charged with anything and I have no intention of talking to anyone about anything. I've watched enough cop shows to know that they have a way of twisting your words and getting you to confess to things you know nothing about and certainly haven't done. I just need to stall and wait this out until I hear from Kaye.

Again, I check the time on my phone. Only a minute has passed since I last checked. Kaye should be in Canada by now and probably on her way to the airport. God willing … if everything has gone according to plan.

Sitting there my mind wanders and I think about that unkempt white dude who sized me up when we passed in the hallway. Who the hell is he to look down his nose at me? I nearly gagged as he walked passed. At least I had the common decency to take a shower, that guy smelled like last week's rubbish left too long in the bin. The cop escorting that lowlife looked like he'd already put up with enough of his nonsense. I saw how the cop gave him a shove when the dude looked me up and down and asked, 'What did that old dyke do?'

Still, I can't help but wonder what that guy is doing here in this Podunk police station.

And then it dawns on me, just like solving a crossword puzzle where one piece of information gives way to the next. The answer is obvious. How could I have missed it. And still it is unbelievable—that stinky old dude is the infamous Nash, Kaye's notorious husband.

I close my eyes and attempt to send her my heartfelt message: *Get going, girl. Don't look back. You deserve so much better than the likes of him. Just go!*

Nope, these good old boys won't be getting anything out of me.

With that I hear the lock turn and two uniformed officers enter the room.

I feel like I'm on a movie set. Each of us ready to play our assigned role and these boys must have been sent over from central casting. They look like they've been cut from the same cloth, except one is short and the other tall. Their uniforms are pressed and those shit-kickin' boots all spit-polished and buffed to a shine. They're all set and ready to catch themselves some criminals.

"Ellery McMasters?" Shorty asks, as if now my identity is somehow in question.

"Yes," I answer, offering nothing further.

"What can you tell us about Amy Cooper?" Tallboy asks.

These yahoos still have not given me the courtesy of introducing themselves.

"Nothing. I don't know anyone named Amy Cooper," I respond. That is sort of true, as Kaye is no longer using that name. Is there such a thing as *sort of true*? "Who is Amy Cooper, anyway?" They're fishing and I need to know just what they know.

"We'll be asking the questions, *Mizz Mc Masters*," Shorty quips, elongating the z with unmitigated disdain as if to refer to me as Ms. is an affront to all womankind.

I nod and hold his eye until he turns his gaze away.

"Mrs. Cooper is a sixty-four year old woman who has disappeared. She was last seen yesterday in the

172

Sacandaga Campgrounds. She was heading down for a swim in the Sacandaga River and has disappeared," Tallboy explains.

"The river has been very high and fast since that rainstorm last week," I offer as I try to appear cooperative.

"We searched the river all last night and haven't recovered a body," Shorty says.

"That doesn't mean she isn't out there…" I suggest.

"True. But people don't just disappear…" Shorty says, as if I need him to draw me a picture. I know full well what he is implying.

"Of course they do, people disappear every day. Often of their own free will. This woman is an adult, 64 years old, right? Maybe she just disappeared and has no desire to be found. As far as I know, it's not against the law." I offer a possible explanation.

"What do you know about the law, Mizz McMasters? Are you a lawyer?" Tallboy asks.

I purse my lips to keep myself from telling off this asshole. Instead I say, "No sir."

"Do you know Nash Cooper?" The first cop takes his turn in this round robin of interrogation.

"Nash who?" Maybe this youngster isn't as green as I thought. If he has already met the infamous Nash,

173

perhaps he can understand why Kaye split and doesn't want to be found.

"Nash Cooper, the victim's husband," he responds and holds my gaze just in case my face might give something away.

"Wait a minute, a moment ago she was a missing person and now she's a victim, how did that happen?" I'm being snarky again. I need to stop it or this will not play well for me. These two irritate the hell out of me and I can't seem to help myself.

Shorty ignores my question and instead asks one of his own.

"Our canine unit picked up her scent outside of your house. How do you explain that?" Tallboy asks.

I see how this is going to go with the two of these bully boys alternating questions.

"How should I know? I expect your dogs picked up the scent of deer and squirrels, too. Am I supposed to explain to you what they were doing crossing my land as well?"

The cops turn and look at one another and then back to me. I need to watch my tone. How many times have I been cautioned to do just that? I take a deep breath and wait. All the while reminding myself to keep it short and sweet.

We sit in silence. I have nothing more to say as the silence between us draws out— becoming more and more uncomfortable.

Shorty nods to Tallboy. "Have you ever been to 3742 Beaver Ridge?"

"What? Beaver what? I don't know what you're talking about. Is that an address or something?"

"3742 Beaver Ridge. It's in Clifton Park." Shorty elaborates.

"Do I look like a rich suburbanite, a soccer mom perhaps?"

They both look me up and down as if trying to decide whether my question is worthy of a reply.

"3742 Beaver Ridge is Amy Cooper's address. Can you tell us why it was programmed into the GPS in your car?" Tallboy asks.

I swallow hard. Oh shit. Before I can even begin to come up with any kind of an answer Shorty is badgering me further.

"It is very interesting that you don't know Amy Cooper as our forensic team found blood on a towel in your bathroom and on the floor mat in your car."

"So…"

"It's Amy Cooper's."

"I have nothing else to say. I want a lawyer."

175

# Chapter 28
## Joey

I don't know how long I've been in the waiting room when at last the door opens. I don't know what I was expecting, but it certainly wasn't this. It's been over two years since I last saw my sister. I guess I just wasn't prepared. I could kick myself for my own ignorance. Let's just say I didn't handle it well.

"Andy…" I gasp as I try to come to terms with what she has done. I can't help but stare at her. She has a five o'clock shadow and her breasts are gone.

"Hey Joey. It's been a while… too long really," she stumbles around trying to find something to say that might ease the mounting tension between us.

"Good God, what have you done?" In spite of my best efforts, tears fill my eyes and I am nearly shouting at her, him, whatever.

"I'm sure it must be obvious. I know we haven't seen one another lately, but this can't come as a complete surprise. You haven't been living under a rock. I'm trans,

Joey. I've been in transition for the last two years. Why do you think I haven't been home?"

Now Andy is crying, too.

"Oh God, what have you done?" The look on Andy's face makes me recoil. God I wish I could take my words back and try again. I have hurt her deeply. "I didn't mean it like that. I love you. I always will. This changes nothing…"

"It's changed everything for me. For the first time in a very long time, I feel like me. I feel authentic, no longer a poser, trying to be someone I would never truly be. Please be happy for me, Joey."

I stand there looking at my sister as I try to wrap my head around what she has just told me and come to terms with what she means by *trans*. She's always been a big girl taking after Dad, but now she looks… what… strong, I guess? Buff really, she looks more like a guy than I do with my progressively softening Dad-bod.

She opens her arms to hold me and comfort me, just like she did when I was little and Dad was drunk and yelling at one of us.

"This is hard, Andy. I don't understand why. Why would you feel the need to do something like this…something so drastic?"

Somehow we move as one sitting back down on the old vinyl couch as she pulls me close and whispers in my ear. "Joey, it's like wearing a shoe that doesn't fit. Everything about it just rubs you the wrong way. It will never be comfortable, and you know it; you just know it. Once you realize what the issue is and that *it's* solvable, you take that shoe off. Then you know you can never put it back on. It feels so good to be free of it. It was just too painful."

She sounds so practiced. She has probably used this analogy before, perhaps a hundred times with others burdened by the same questions that haunt me.

We sit there in silence as I try to figure out what to say without making this whole situation any worse. I guess I've always known. It's just that we never talked about sex, sexuality, gender and a myriad of other things. When we were growing up these things were never discussed in our home. I'm nearly ten years younger than Andy and she left for college when I was still a kid.

"Still, you could have let us know. It couldn't have been easy... to go through... *this*...all alone."

"Oh Joey, I wasn't alone. I have friends. Friends who helped me. In a city the size of Denver, gender dysphoria and trans folks are a lot more common than here in the suburbs of New York."

"Do Mom and Dad know? What about Sam?" I cringe when I think about how my brother and my father might react. They're not exactly open-minded, never have been and I don't see that changing in this lifetime.

"No, I haven't told any of them." Now it's Andy's turn to cry. "I wanted to tell Mom. I know she will love me, no matter what. But I wanted her to see that I was okay, better than okay. I'm happy now. Mom would want that for me. I didn't want her to worry. Now, I'm afraid I'll never see her again."

Andy and I cling to one another. "I love you, Andy. I just want you to be happy. Hey, what am I supposed to call you now?"

"Andy, just Andy. I changed it. I'm no longer Andrea on any of my legal documents. Just Andy Cooper."

"What about Dad?"

"He has bigger issues to deal with right now than the fact that his only daughter is now his eldest son."

We laugh in spite of everything. "Isn't that the truth."

I reach for Andy's hand and hold it between both of mine for a moment before I gently release it as some of the ramifications of this new reality begins to dawn on me. "Oh God, I guess there is a whole new set of parameters dictating how we should interact. I can't go grabbing your

179

hand and hugging you like I did when you were my sister. Can I?"

"Of course you can. Are you concerned someone might think you're gay if they see us holding hands?"

"I'm not that insecure…at least I don't think I am. I do love you, *brother.*" I laugh and so does Andy. "Just trying it on for size. I want to see if I can really get used to calling you that."

Andy laughs. "Be patient with yourself. I'm still getting used to all the changes accompanying my new identity, too. You'll be happy to know my preferred pronouns are *he* and *him.*"

"I'm still getting used to referring to you as my *brother,* I don't know how I would do if you were using *they* and *them.*"

"Let's leave that discussion for another day," Andy says.

I reach for his hand to hold it for a moment.

"When am I going to see your new baby? Leah, right? She must be about six months old by now."

"Later today I suppose. You'll stay with us, right? It may be a while before we get this fiasco sorted out."

"Thanks, that'll be great."

"Natalie and the kids will be so happy to see their *Uncle* Andy."

"I wish I could say the same about our dear old dad."

"Yeah, that's gonna be a tough one."

Andy drops his head then takes his hand to his mouth as if he is trying to keep himself from speaking his mind. "He's never approved of me. I've long since given up on trying to meet his expectations. What's that old quote? *'What other people think of me is really none of my business.'*"

"Well, for what it's worth, I think you're pretty great, always have and always will."

"Thanks, Joey."

I reach over and squeeze Andy's hand as the door to the waiting room opens and a uniformed cop shuffles in and gives us both a look like he is disgusted to find us holding hands.

"We have some questions we'd like to ask you two. So, which one of you *fellas* wants to go first?"

I drop Andy's hand as my brother stands and follows the cop out of the waiting room.

# Chapter 29
## Kaye

After all my fretting, anxiety and worry, I board the plane to Paris without incident or delay. It is only once I'm in my seat with my seatbelt fastened that I'm able to relax, at least for the time being. I'm greatly relieved to have a window seat, as I turn my face away from the flight attendants and my fellow travelers. In less than 6 hours we should arrive in Paris, it will be morning by then and I will need to be on my toes at least until I pass through immigration and can lose myself in the energy and vibrancy of the city. I haven't been to Paris or anywhere in France since I was a girl, a young woman really. I have to laugh, there was a time in my young life when I would have chastised someone for calling me a girl. Now if anyone called me a girl or the French equivalent, a *jeune fille,* I probably would kiss them in sheer gratitude. Back when I was a young woman, I had such grand expectations for my life. But they dissipated like the morning mist on a hot summer's day, along with all my feminist ideals. When I became pregnant and decided to keep my child and marry her father, my life and any agency

I might have had over my own destiny were gone. It might have been different had I married someone else or if I had been someone else. I can't put all of this on Nash. There were reasons why I acquiesced to his will. Still, I just never realized it would take me forty years to get back to my original plan for my life, get back to feeling like I had some control in my own life, and get back to just being me.

Let the adventure begin.

The plane rolls down the runway and in a moment we are in the air leaving Montreal and on our way. I close my eyes and begin to hum that old song by Judy Collins again. How many times have I sung this song as I wallowed in the throes of suburban domesticity. Nash never noticed or never cared to even ask why. Why this song, again and again? The words play on in my head and a smile comes to my lips as I look out into the darkness of this summer night.

*My father always promised me that we would live in France, we'd go boating on the Seine and I would learn to dance...*

I'm on my way Daddy.

Thanks to you and your benevolence.

Promises made and promises kept.

I, too, have made promises that I am bound by. Tomorrow, once I am through immigration, I will call Ellery and then she will call my children to let them know

183

that I am safe. Just like we planned. Everything is going according to plan.

# Chapter 30
## Andy

I follow the cop down the hall.

He's a small man, mid-thirties give or take, but he exudes that arrogance and authority that have given cops a bad name. Maybe it's part of the *small man syndrome,* I think it comes from always needing to prove oneself *man enough.* Man enough for what I'm not sure, maybe man enough for the job, maybe it's simpler than that, maybe just man enough.

I get that. I'm over six feet tall, strong and lean at 180. Still, I know people look at me and wonder if I'm trans or worse they know and they judge me for my choices. I'm not a small man but I get this guy. I also find myself needing to be man enough, whatever that means.

We enter a room with a couple of disheveled desks. The waste baskets are overflowing with the bags from yesterday's fast food and discarded Styrofoam coffee cups. The room smells, some sort of rank combination of stale recycled air, decaying food, and body odor. I may have inherited my father's height and bone structure but I also inherited my mother's sense of smell.

What did Sam used to say? Mom could smell a fart behind a barn door. I chuckle at the memory, God knows she could never have tolerated this mess and foul odor. She'd have set this place to rights in no time and given these cops a good talkin' to about the virtues of being neat and clean. Poor mom had so little control in her own life. She took great pride in controlling what she could, like her home and her children. It's funny now that she's gone that I can see the world through her eyes. I vow to try and make her proud of me, I owe her that much.

The cop gestures to the chair by his desk.

"Have a seat," he says as picks up a dirty napkin and wipes a coffee spill off the corner of his desk before he pushes the napkin into an old paper coffee cup and throws it in the trash. It falls out of the overflowing can and lands on the floor.

I bend over to pick it up and put it back in the trash can.

"Just leave it. The cleaning lady will be in tonight."

I cringe at the disrespect he exudes for the woman who cleans the office and the work she does. I know this disregard for women and the work they do, I've experienced it most of my life. Really, why would I ever want to be a man?

"Sorry, we have to meet in here. All of the interrogation rooms are occupied." He shuffles through the papers on his desk and then looks for something to write with.

I'm surprised, given the size of the police station out here in the middle of nowhere, that they would have more than one interrogation room. I let that go. The real question is— other than my father, who else is being interrogated?

"I'd like to ask you a few questions."

I nod.

"Your name?"

"Andy Cooper."

He looks down at his notes. "Andrea Cooper?"

"My legal name is now Andy."

He looks at me and nods as if it is just dawning on him as to who I was and who I am now.

"I'm a trans man. Amy Cooper, the missing woman, is my mother and Nash Cooper is my father."

"No one told me ..." he stumbles over what to say next.

"No one in my family knew about my transition, I haven't been home for a while. Now what is it that you would like to ask me?"

Then this young cop from rural America launches into a litany of disjointed questions. It's obvious to me that he's in over his head. He probably has never conducted a missing persons investigation, certainly not a murder investigation where there is no body, let alone dealt with the likes of me. If he wasn't so arrogant I might have a little sympathy for him as he is clearly out of his depth.

As he fires his questions at me I try to answer succinctly and get to the heart of the relevant information. I attempt to steer this interview where it needs to go so everyone can get back out there and try to find my mother.

"I live and work in Denver," I offer hoping to get this thing rolling. "I'm an attorney and for the last five years I've worked at the Law Offices of Prescott, Evelyn and Conrad."

"Well la-di-da, I suppose that keeps you pretty busy. Too busy to get back here and see your family?" he smirks.

He thinks he knows me, in truth he knows nothing about me, my life, or my family.

"It's been over two years since I have been back in New York to see my family. But, I talk with my mother every Sunday, well most Sundays."

"Do you think your mother drowned? We've had a lot of rain and the Sacandaga is running pretty fast."

Wow, this guy is incredibly insensitive. I swallow hard before I answer to keep from choking up. "My mother is a good swimmer. She's fit. She swims all summer at the public pool in Ballston Spa, walks and counts her steps, and practices yoga. I didn't see the river and how fast it was moving, but my mother is strong and healthy."

"Did she ever talk about ending it all, you know—killing herself, or anything?" he adds a note on the legal pad as if this is just another routine question.

"Suicide? Not a chance." I answer quickly. Initially, I'm pissed. This junior cop is not getting off with an easy answer. I glare at him for even suggesting such a thing. Still I have to admit, if only to myself that I hadn't considered this even a possibility. I was so depressed in middle school. I was mocked and bullied every day. Mom and I made a promise to each other that we would *never* hurt ourselves.

He drops his gaze to avoid the fire in my eyes. Searching his notepad for the next prescriptive question, he asks, "How would you describe your parents' marriage?"

"My parents' marriage? What can I say, you've met my father. How she deals with him is beyond me. But they've been married for almost forty years, if she was going to leave him don't you think she would have done so long before now?"

"Is he abusive?"

"He roughed her up a few times when we were kids. I think it's mostly verbal. But, I really don't know. Mom never complains to me and I don't live there. What can I say, he's a mean SOB."

"Could he have..." he stumbles over his words ... "done away with her?"

"Do I think he *killed* her? Is that what you're asking me?"

The cop nods and looks me in the eye.

Again I swallow hard and tears fill my eyes and threaten to fall. "I don't think he has it in him. He's a bully. All about exerting his will and control, you know the type. Do I think he is capable of killing her? I don't think so, but what do I know?"

"Come on buddy, man up," he says fearing I may break down. "I understand your mother's father recently passed away and she's going to inherit from his estate. People *do things* when there's money involved. This could answer the question of motive."

"I don't think my grandfather's will has even been read. At least I don't know if it has. Grandpop has only been gone a few weeks and there hasn't even been a memorial service yet."

My dad is such a greedy bastard, would he really... I can't imagine. Still, it begs the question.

I add, "I assume my mother and my Uncle Douglas will inherit equal shares of my grandfather's estate. I don't know how much he was worth, probably a sizable amount. Still, I'm sure my dear old dad can give you an exact accounting."

"Do you think your mother may have found someone else, you know, a love interest?" he asks with a smirk.

I want to wipe that shit eating grin off his face. This is my mother he's talking about. But then I think about it a little more and the very notion makes me smile—a kind and gentle lover for my mother.

"Someone else? Well, that certainly would be the best case scenario. She finally meets someone, her equal, who sweeps her off her feet, and she runs away with him and they live happily ever after." I smile, but then sadly shake my head. "Sounds a bit like a fairy tale, and I think we're both a little too old for fairy tales, don't you?"

"Has she taken up with other men? Or women?"

I can't imagine my mother with a woman. Is he just being provocative? More likely he's just an ass. "As far as I know she's never had an affair, but who could blame her if she did?"

"Where do you think she is?"

"I have no idea. She's a beautiful woman, inside and out. Someone may have hurt her, she may have been abducted, or maybe she is still out there, injured and just waiting to be found."

Most of his questions are sort of expected, until he asks, "Do you know Ellery McMasters?"

"Who?"

"Ellery McMasters. She's an old woman who lives up on the banks of the Sacandaga River."

"Never heard of her. Is she involved?"

"I'll ask the questions, Mr. Cooper." The cop scribbles furiously on the yellow legal pad. "Where will you be staying while you're here?"

"At my brother Joey's. Do you need the address?"

"No. We have it. Don't leave town. We may need to talk with you again."

I do my best to keep the contempt I feel for this man off of my face. This asshole sounds like a character actor from every B-rated cop show I've ever seen.

"What?" he says. Is there something else you want to say?" he snarls in my direction.

I just look at him and I know he is reacting to my *resting bitch face*. I've been called out on this since I was in middle school. I can almost hear my father say, 'wipe that look off your face.' Hey, I thought I was being helpful and cooperative, but I've never been a very good actor. This guy has just burned my last good nerve. He is wasting precious time dilly-dicking around while my mother has yet to be found.

The cop stands indicating this interview is over.

"Can I see my father now?" I ask. I'm not really certain I want to do this, but it seems like the appropriate thing to do.

"No. We've had to postpone the interrogation until his lawyer gets here, and it sounds like that may be a while."

"Has he been charged with *something*?" I ask, not quite certain what that *something* might be.

"At this time we are treating your mother as a missing person. We have not concluded that a crime has been committed. However, your father is refusing to answer any questions without a lawyer and we won't be releasing him until we have some answers. We can hold him for up to seventy-two hours without charging him, not including weekends and holidays."

"I see," I say. I mentally calculate just how much longer he might be here. "It's Saturday night so the clock won't start running until Monday morning, theoretically he could be here until Thursday morning without any charges being filed. Is that right."

"You're smarter than you look, big guy."

193

I bite my tongue to keep from telling this punk how I feel.

"Why don't you and your brother go home? We'll call you if we have anything to report."

I check the time on my watch, it's getting late. No doubt the sun's been down for over an hour. "Have the rangers called off the search and rescue for today?" I ask pretty certain I know the answer.

"Yes. I spoke with the ranger an hour ago. They plan to start again in the morning, if the weather holds. They are calling for another thunderstorm and heavy rain around midnight. You should prepare yourself... if they haven't found her in the first 24 hours, it's highly unlikely that they will, at least not alive."

# Chapter 31
## Kaye

I wake as they turn up the lights in the cabin and see that

the flight attendants are coming down the aisle serving coffee and croissants. It must be morning. I raise the shade that covers the window and I'm surprised to see the sun is up. I didn't think I would sleep, but I guess I did. The coffee is marginal but the croissant is delicious. I haven't had anything to eat since last night when Henri and I had dinner on his boat. The sweet memory of Henri lingers and brings a smile to my face. What a kind and gentle man.

Time passes as we approach our destination and the other passengers wake and whisper softly to one another.

In another 40 minutes the pilot's voice is coming through the public address system and asking the passengers to refrain from using the restrooms, stow their personal belongings, raise the tray tables, and fasten their seatbelts as the flight attendants prepare the cabin for landing. I'm surprised how much French I still understand. Even when I don't know every word, the remainder becomes clear due to the context.

After we disembark we are ushered straight to immigration. The lines are long and as I wait my anxiety builds in anticipation of some sort of issue regarding my identity. The possibilities run through my overactive imagination: Maybe the facial recognition software used for entry into the country will alert the authorities, or my fraudulent passport will be flagged by the border patrol agent, and I'll end up detained in some French penitentiary. My anxiety mounts with each step I take closer and closer to the immigration control officers.

I silently rehearse the details of the story I intend to tell if I am asked why I am here, where I am staying, and for how long.

I hand the female officer my Canadian passport and my long-stay visa which Claudette has secured for me. The woman looks me in the eye and begins to question me in French. "Où êtes-vous un citoyen?"

"Canada," I respond with my best French accent. She isn't buying it. I only have to answer her first question before she switches to English. I guess my accent gives me away as an Anglophile.

She proceeds with a litany of questions and I begin to perspire. I keep my answers short with no embellishment giving this immigration officer only as much information as she has asked me for.

"Why have you come to Paris?" she asks as she holds my gaze to see if I am telling her the truth.

"I'm just passing through on my way to Nice to visit friends."

"How long will you be in France?"

"I plan to be here for about a year."

"Where will you be staying?"

"I will stay with friends while I secure an apartment in Provence."

"What do you intend to do during this year abroad?"

"I have just retired and I plan to enroll in a French language immersion program and learn to paint."

She scrutinizes my paperwork and concludes that I am not a threat to national security and stamps my passport.

"This will allow you to stay for one year, after that you must reapply at the Canadian consulate. She returns my visa and my passport and dismisses me with a "*bonne journée.*"

All of this fear proves to have been for naught as I slip through immigration without incident. I offer up a prayer of gratitude for Claudette. I really didn't like her very much, she was haughty and arrogant and still she has thought of everything. I remind myself not to be too quick to judge.

I breathe a sigh of relief as I head for baggage claim and the exit marked customs with only my navy leather satchel. I hand the declaration form that I filled out on the plane to the customs agent. He doesn't even look at it and I exit the building with the throngs of other travelers with some place to go.

Now what?

It's only eleven o'clock and too early to get a hotel room. I'd like nothing better than to have a hot bath and a nap, but that will have to wait. I pull the wallet from my matching carry-on bag. Claudette has thought of everything. Inside the wallet are two fifty euro notes. Enough to get me a cab to the Louvre and a real cappuccino.

I wait in the line for a cab outside the airport, still convinced that someone will apprehend me and force me to go back to my life with Nash. I try to breathe through this, telling myself that I only need to get in the next cab and away from the airport, then I will be safe.

Then I will be safe...

I repeat the words over and over in my head like a mantra.

I climb in the back of the cab as the driver flips on the meter. *"Musée du Louvre,"* I hear myself say. He programs the destination into his GPS and we are off. To my great relief he makes no attempt at conversation. I turn and look out the window. I want to be that invisible woman, absolutely forgettable. Just another tourist he picked up at the airport and took to the *Louvre*.

The drive takes us almost an hour so I have plenty of time to see the city as well as observe the silent driver as he wends his way through the streets of Paris. It is a beautiful summer's day. The cabbie's license is displayed in a yellowing plastic envelope. His name is Malik. He appears to be in his mid-forties. His dark hair is thinning, but he is very handsome. He appears to be of middle eastern descent, perhaps French is not his first language either.

I am starting to get nervous as the ride from the airport is further than I thought and more expensive. I'll hardly be just another inconspicuous tourist if I can't pay the fare. The meter in the taxi already reads 58 Euros and that does not include a tip.

We pass *Le Jardin des Tuileries* when I spot a Travelex money exchange and ask the driver to stop. I'll exchange some of the cash I've been saving. God knows I'm going to need some of it if I am to travel into Switzerland and claim my inheritance.

The cabbie pulls over to the curb.

First things first, I give the driver 100 euros. *"Donnez-moi vingt euros et gardez le reste. Merci."* I ask for twenty back and tell him to keep the rest.

At first he looks confused. It must be that my American accent makes my broken French incomprehensible. He hands me a twenty euro note through the plexiglass divider and smiles. *"Merci, bonne journée madame."*

I exit the cab with all my worldly possessions in this navy blue satchel. Walking across the street I begin to think of all I need to accomplish today. One of the first things I'll need to do is get a new pair of comfortable shoes that I can actually walk in.

I think about calling Ellery as I promised. It's nearly half past noon here, but only six-thirty in the morning in New York. Still a little too early to call her.

Besides, I can't be wandering around Paris with only twenty euros to my name. I can't even buy my own lunch for that. So, I head into the local branch of Travelex. I have no idea what the exchange rate even is. It doesn't matter right now. I need cash, euros specifically.

I start to make a mental list of what I need to do today: secure a hotel room, buy a couple of changes of clothes, and some toiletries.

I'll need to locate the train station and buy a train ticket to Geneva, then locate the United Bank of Switzerland or UBS branch there. My father set up a Swiss Bank account at UBS years ago.

*Just in case ...* he used to say. *Just in case.*

He never liked Nash. Can't say I blame him. I have no idea how much money is even in the account.

*Don't worry. There will be enough. You can start over, anytime you are ready. Anytime ...* I can almost hear his hushed voice as he whispered the words in my ear the last time I saw him. My eyes fill with tears as I wipe them away with the back of my hand.

My US passport, in my old name, resides securely within the center pocket of my handbag. I'll need it to access the account.

I push the memory of my father from my thoughts. I need to keep my head about me as this whole thing is getting more and more complicated.

I continue running the list of all I have to do before I can get on my way. I'll need to get a cell phone. I want to get a smartphone. At the very least, I'll need GPS so I don't get lost. I'll need access to the internet...

Then it dawns on me— at the very least, I'll need a credit card in order to get a smartphone.

That may have to wait until I get to Switzerland.

201

I remove an unmarked envelope containing a stack of one hundred dollar bills from the inner pocket of my bag. I brought it with me when I snuck back in the house for my passport and some clean clothes. I once thought of this as my *mad money*. Every time Nash did something unkind or disrespectful I would stash a bit more of my grocery money away for a rainy day. This has been going on throughout my entire marriage and clearly it was a frequent occurrence given the amount of cash I've collected.

A smile crosses my face as the morning sun gleams through the window. Who knew it would be a sunny day when I would at last dip into my savings and begin again.

At last it is my turn at the teller's window. I exchange three thousand U.S. dollars into euros using my fraudulent passport issued in my new name. I sign *Kaye Hill* on the receipt.

Before yesterday, the only crimes I had ever committed include one speeding ticket and a few parking violations.

Who knew disappearing would be this easy?

I take a deep breath as the teller returns my passport before pushing a large stack of 50 euro notes beneath the glass partition that separates us. I tuck them into another fabric pocket within my bag and close the zipper.

With my bag tucked tightly beneath my arm I walk to the sidewalk café within the *Tuileries Garden* for a real cappuccino and a light lunch.

Ah, it feels so good to sit down.

I slip off these ridiculous heels.

# Chapter 32
## Ellery

I wake up still dressed in the clothes I wore yesterday. I take a moment to pull together the pieces of my life and figure out how I have come to be lying here on this nasty stained mattress. This old woolen blanket is enhanced with the stench of someone else's body odor and moth holes. I toss it onto the floor. The events of the last couple days come back to me like a computer download.

I'm here in this cinderblock holding cell, and, God forbid, I may be for another couple of days unless I'm charged with some kind of a crime in Kaye's disappearance. Oh God, I don't want to think about that....

I look at the clock hanging on the wall, it's quarter to seven. This old clock looks like one that once hung on the walls in the classrooms at St. Mary's, my childhood grammar school. I watch as the red second hand makes its way around the clock face. I used to wait and watch the seconds tick by just waiting for the bell to ring so the teacher would release us. This waiting feels much the same as it did when I was a child; the seconds hang there moment by moment as my life passes by and my freedom is restricted. I've never felt particularly claustrophobic, but I sure feel it now.

I sit up. The very thought of resting my face on this dirty old mattress makes my skin crawl as I think of all the others who might have slept here before me. I sit up and press my back up against the cinderblock wall and wait.

But what exactly am I waiting for?

Surely they won't charge me with Kaye's murder. They don't have a body. People have a right to change their lives and walk away from a life that is no longer working for them. It's not illegal. It's certainly not a crime. I walked away from mine, changed my name, and up until yesterday, I lived a life of my own choosing. Kaye has the God-given right to do the same with her life.

At least I think she does.

I hear some church bells begin to ring. Sunday morning, and bells are calling all the devout churchgoers to Mass. I count as the bells toll. I look at the clock again. It's eight o'clock and I wonder when Kaye will call. She should be in Paris by now.

My cell phone was confiscated by the police before they put me in this holding cell. I was told it would be returned *if and when* I was released.

This little snafu wasn't something I had planned for. I guess she'll just have to leave a message on my voicemail.

The carillon of bells plays softly in the background. It's an old hymn I'm familiar with and then, before I even realize I am doing it, I'm singing along,

"Be not afraid. I go before you always.

Come follow me, and I will give you rest.

If you pass through raging waters in the sea

you shall not drown,

if you walk amid the burning flames

you shall not be harmed..."

and then the words fail me and I hum along until I remember...

"Know that I am with you through it all.

Be not afraid."

The carillon plays on and tears fill my eyes and threaten to fall.

Is this a message for me?

Have I just had a divine encounter with The Almighty?

It sure seems like it.

I wipe the tears away and, somehow, I feel more at peace with whatever may come my way and strengthened in my resolve.

I can deal with this.

Although I haven't prayed in a long, long time. It's been years really. It's been so long ago now that I may have forgotten how. Still, in light of what I've just experienced, I offer up a prayer to whoever might be listening,

"Please protect my friend, Kaye, on her journey to a new life. Keep her safe. Amen."

I don't know why I feel so committed to her and her survival, but I do.

The water was rushing by carrying all sorts of detritus pulled forth from the river bed when I first saw her. There she was, washed up on the banks of the Sacandaga. She was so vulnerable. And I knew, I just knew ... I was supposed to help her.

God bless Henri. How many times have we done this? Must be seven or eight now. He never questions me or turns me down. He doesn't ask many questions about who they are or why they are running or why they need our help. He only asks where he should meet us and when. Even Claudette, with her fancy new life, remembers that she was once a victim of human trafficking and desperately needed help to leave that pimp who'd beat her senseless. So, as much as she would like to forget her past and be free of her responsibilities and obligations, she never turns us down. She's generous and helps when she can.

207

Henri says this is our ministry.

I don't know.

To call this a *ministry* sounds too sanctimonious to me. Henri helped me when I needed help and in return I once helped him. It's as simple as that. There are times when people find themselves in some pretty horrific predicaments, so when we're needed, we do what we can to help. That's all.

It's as simple as that.

# Chapter 33
## Nash

I wake to the metallic sound of a key turning in a lock. It takes a minute for me to remember where I am. Good God, if being locked up in this hell hole, for a crime I didn't commit and know nothing about, isn't bad enough now these assholes won't even let me sleep. I turn over to face the door as the bed springs creak beneath the weight of my body.

"Ohh," I groan aloud as my back aches and threatens to seize up from sleeping on this three inch pad masquerading as a mattress.

"Rise and shine Sleeping Beauty," the first guy says with a laugh and the fluorescent light from the hallway beams into my dark cell nearly blinding me.

"What do you want now?" I shout at the jailer. "First you keep me up all night with your inane questions and now you wake me before dawn."

"Sorry to interrupt your beauty sleep Princess, God knows you need it. But here at the Mayfield Hilton we have an early check out, and, sir, your time is up."

209

"What the hell are you going on about?" I rub my eyes as they slowly adjust to the light. The big burly guy's body fills the doorway and I know he isn't anyone I want to mess with. He's obviously a gym rat with muscles on muscles and a good thirty years younger than I am. But he's smiling a big shit eatin' grin.

"You're being released. You get to leave, you know, you can go home."

"What?"

"Which part of *'you can go'* do you not understand?"

"I just thought...oh never mind." I slowly push myself up to a sitting position. My back is killing me.

"Officer Brownell needs to see you in the interrogation room."

"Did they find my wife?"

"You can ask him."

I follow the jailer down the hall to the same room I was held in late last night.

I take *my seat* at the table. I've come to think of this as *my seat* as I occupied it for hours and hours last night before they decided to keep me.

The jailer steps out and locks me in.

So much for being able to leave and go home.

What's happened? Last I heard I wasn't goin'
anywhere, at least through the weekend. What about all that
talk about charging me Amy's murder?

It isn't long before the lead cop arrives. He unlocks
the door and sits down. This is the same asshole that grilled
me last night. He looks like I feel. His once pressed shirt is
now rumpled and there is a coffee stain over his protruding
belly, not that I'm one to talk. He looks like he could use a
shower and a good night's sleep.

He pulls at his crotch and adjusts himself beneath
the table. He doesn't look any happier with me than he was
last night. He glowers at me and I get the distinct
impression that releasing me is not his idea.

I'm tired of waiting. He's the one who called for
me, not the other way around, but he just sits there, not
speaking. So, unable to wait a moment more, I begin with
my questions.

"Did you find my wife?"

"We did not."

"So, the jailer said I was free to go...," I say as I
hope he will get with the program and tell me what I need
to know so I can get the hell out of here.

"Look here Mis-ter Cooper," he draws out the
Mister as if it pains him to offer me this little bit of respect.
"I don't like you. Personally, I think you're a cheating

scumbag who beats on his wife. I think you offed your wife. She was set to inherit a substantial sum of money from her father's estate, and greedy people have been known to kill for much less. So we have motive but we don't have enough evidence to hold you, at least not at the moment. I don't believe for one moment that you're not involved, in some way, in your wife's disappearance. I just need more time to figure it out, and trust me, I will. So don't go anywhere, Nash."

"I didn't kill my wife."

"In the meantime,  we're still holding Mizz Ellery McMasters."

"Who is Ellery McMasters?"

"Don't play dumb with me, Nash."

He says my name like he has just tasted something foul. "I have no idea who you are talking about."

"The old dyke? Your accomplice? Ring any bells?" He snarls at me and holds my gaze. "Look, your wife's DNA is all over her riverside cabin on the Sacandaga and your home address was programmed into the GPS in her truck."

"I said, I don't know the woman, or whatever you want to call her."

"Amy's blood was found in your house."

"Look, she lives there! Maybe she cut herself in the kitchen," I offer as a possible explanation.

"Like I said, Nash, you are free to go. Just don't leave the area."

# Chapter 34
## Nash

The detective pushes himself away from the table. If he wasn't such an asshole, I might feel sorry for the guy. He looks beat. He passes the jailer in the doorway.

"Get him out of here."

The jailer holds a clear plastic bag which contains the stuff I brought in with me, and that isn't much as I'm still wearing yesterday's clothes. I grab my phone and put it in the front pocket of my shorts, then check my wallet to make sure no one took anything. I count my cash, seven dollars. It's all here. I shove my wallet and my car keys into the other pocket, then hang my reading glasses on the front of my dirty tee shirt.

"How am I supposed to get home?" I ask the jailer. "You guys brought me here in a cop car, against my will I might add."

"What do I look like, your mother? You're a grown man, figure it out," he says and walks away.

"Great." I walk out to the reception area and I pull my phone from my pocket to see who I can call to pick me up. "Damn. My phone is dead."

The receptionist says, "You can make your call from my phone."

Finally, someone is being nice to me. I smile at her. "Thank you ma'am, but I don't know anyone's number anymore. My numbers are all stored in my phone these days."

"Your sons were here last night. Let me see..." she pulls out a clipboard and runs her manicured index finger with that sexy red polish down the log-in sheet.

I take another look at her and mentally undress her. Maybe beneath that frumpy green dress ...

She catches me lookin' at her and gives me that look. I've seen it countless times before. Then I know, she's just another cold bitch. She probably hasn't been laid in a month of Sundays.

I pull myself back to the situation at hand. "I thought my son, Sam, was away fishing with his family."

"No, not Sam, but Andy and Joe. Let's see, I have phone numbers for both of your boys."

"Andy, what is she doing back here?"

"She?"

"Never mind." She must have arrived lookin' like some kind of a lumberjack. I can only imagine her showing up here in a flannel shirt, baggy jeans and some old shit kickers for boots. "Were they together?" I ask the receptionist as I weigh my options.

"Yes, sir. At least they left together. They left a phone number in case we have any news about their mother, your wife. Would you like that number?"

Good God, I don't want to talk to Andrea. At least not yet. She'll probably blame me for her mother's disappearance, too.

"No." I decide to call the store. I look at the clock on the wall. It's five after eight. *Tony the Toad* should be there opening up. Brad can manage alone for a couple of hours. Sunday mornings can get pretty busy with all those DYIers and weekend mechanics tryin' to save a buck and workin' on their cars.

I gesture for the phone and the receptionist pushes it around the plexiglass. I decide to call Tony anyway. It's not like I have other options. I punch in the number and wait. Besides if he breathes a word of this to anyone I'll fire his ass.

The phone rings three times before someone picks up, "Cooper's Auto Supply. This is Tony. May I help you?"

"Listen Toad, it's Nash. I need you to pick me up."

"Hi Nash."

"I'm at the police station up in Mayfield."

"What?"

"I'll explain later. Have Brad hold down the fort until we get back. Take the delivery truck and get your ass up here."

"We've just opened and we're pretty busy..."

"Now."

"Yes sir. I'm on my way.

I take a seat in the waiting room. This is not something I'm particularly good at—waiting. I decide to try my luck with the receptionist again. There on the window is her name plate.

"Evelyn," I say her name softly and seductively. Over the years, I've found that women like it when you speak to them like that, particularly when you want something from them.

She looks up from her laptop. "Yes," she answers. She's all business. This time she is looking me up and down from behind the safety of the plexiglass shield. She looks disgusted with me.

Stuck up bitch, she thinks she's better than me. Maybe it's my dirty clothes. Maybe it's because I need a shower. Maybe it's because of all the weight I've gained.

Another day maybe she'd go for me, I still clean up pretty good.

Then as if she can read my mind, she says, "Is there something you need Mr. Cooper? I know you've been released but that doesn't mean that any of us think you are innocent. So don't even try to cozy up to me. You don't stand a snowballs' chance in hell. Do I make myself clear?"

"Yes, ma'am."

"Now is there something that you need or can I get back to my work?"

I was right about her. She's a cold bitch. "Can I borrow a phone charger? I have an iPhone."

She reaches inside her desk, then pushes a USB cord and plug under the glass.

I return to my seat and wait for my phone to charge.

I wonder how that detective knew about Amy's inheritance. Who'd he talk to? And what about all that shit about me beating my wife? I may have pushed her around a little when she got sassy with me. She may have gotten a little bruised up, 'cuz she's a frail little thing. Who'd she tell? She musta told someone. How else did these cops find out? I can feel my blood pressure rising, like it does when I get angry. I look down at my clenched fists. I feel like smashing something. If I ever *really* beat Amy, trust me, she wouldn't be around to talk about it.

Then my own thoughts come crashing down all around me, for that's exactly what they think happened.

My phone boots up and I enter my password. I wonder how many other people use their birthdates? I have dozens of text messages and phone calls. I scroll through the messages, mostly people offering condolences and offers to help. All I have to do is ask. I chuckle, like I'd need their help and it would be a cold day in hell before I'd ever ask.

A text from Andy, asking me to call her.

A text from Joey and another from Sam.

I take it that all the kids are in the loop. I'll call them when I get home.

And then there is a message from Amy's brother Douglas. It came in early this morning at about three AM. I'm sure by now that pompous prig knows that Amy is missing. Why else would he be calling at that hour? Somehow I doubt that he is calling to offer me his condolences. As much as I would like to just delete the message, instead I click on it and listen.

"Nash, it's Douglas. I've just spoken with Detective Randall from the Missing Persons Unit. I understand you are being released in the morning, but the detectives think you killed Amy for her inheritance. You're not only a vile miscreant but you're also an imbecile if you think you'll ever see any of my father's money. He was onto you and so am I. The State of New York may not have the death penalty but if you've hurt or killed my sister, rest assured there will be hell to pay. So, you'd better watch your back because I know people who know people."

And just like that the message is over. Did he just threaten me? I go to replay the message again and it has disappeared.

I should have known the Little Prince of Silicon Valley would know better than to leave a threatening message on my phone. Pansy ass.

I've known guys like Dougie Watson all my life. He's just another geek and a nervous Nellie who'd piss his pants if I ever came after him. I laugh out loud as the vision of him fills my head —standin' there in a puddle of his own piss, wearing wet pants, and begging me not to hurt him. Maybe that's what I ought to do if he tries playing hardball with me.

I'm not afraid of him, he's the one who should be afraid of me. God knows Amy was.

Still, I wonder what will happen to all that money if Amy is dead. Wouldn't it go to her next of kin? Clearly, that should be me, after all we've been married almost forty years.

Maybe I should get a lawyer to look after my own interests.

I'm old enough to retire, close enough anyway. Those big chain suppliers are killing us, maybe I should just sell the store. I won't get much for it now. Not since NAPA and AutoZone opened up on either side of town. Should have sold it ten years ago, back when it was worth something. Now I owe almost as much on it as it's worth.

I could do it, if I can get my hands on some of that money. Maybe I should buy a house on the beach somewhere in Florida or maybe the Carolinas. Then I could still get those season tickets to watch *my* Tar Heels play some football. The very notion of starting over brings a smile to my face. That woman sitting there behind the plexiglass is gonna wish she'd hooked up with me when she had the chance.

I'm scrolling through the property listings for a beachfront home when *Tony the Toad* walks into the station. He's here to take me home.

# Chapter 35
## Ellery

It wasn't difficult to overhear Kaye's husband, Nash,

carrying on in the corridor this morning. His voice is loud enough to wake the dead. They're letting him go, not enough evidence to hold him. I guess that's good, takes me out of the position of havin' to tell them what I know. After all, other than being a monstrous human being, he didn't have anything to do with Kaye's disappearance. He may have killed that poor girl's spirit, but he didn't murder her. In good conscience, I couldn't just sit here and allow him to be arrested for something he didn't do. Now, I guess I won't have to worry about that.

I hope they'll be comin' to let me out of here next. I could use a strong cup of coffee and a hot shower. I stand and bend over to stretch my back before I go to take a look out of the plexiglass window in the door.

As I'm peering out the slit in the door and into the corridor one of the jailers opens the door and practically launches me to the other side of my cell.

"Hey, take it easy," I say as I rub my forehead where the door struck it.

"You'd better toughen up, given where you're headed," he says without apology.

"What?" I'm confused.

"You didn't really think you were gonna get away with it, did you? Come on, Detective Randall wants to see you in the interrogation room." He steps behind me and gives me a shove, just enough to set me a bit off balance.

I want to tell this guy to keep his grimy paws off of me, but think better of it. Instead, I straighten up and emit a low growl as I glare at him. He's not the least bit intimidated by me. He holds all the power, and he knows it.

The detective, who interviewed me before I requested a lawyer, stands as we enter the interrogation room.

"Ellery McMasters, you are being arrested for the murder of Amy Cooper."

"What? Murder? You've got to be kidding me. I didn't kill anyone. How can you arrest me for murder if you don't have a body?"

He pauses a moment and holds my gaze.

Does he think I'm going to tell him where her body is? "Have you found her body?" I ask.

"Not yet," he admits, "but we will." Then he continues, "You have the right to remain silent. Anything you say can and will be used against you in a court of law. You have the right to an attorney. If you cannot afford an attorney, one will be appointed to you."

In spite of my best efforts to control my emotions, tears begin to flow down my face as the young jailer walks behind me and pulls my hands behind my back, with more force than is necessary, before securing them with his handcuffs. Even restrained, my arms continue to shake. I don't know if it's fear or rage that causes me to tremble, probably both.

"What about my dog? Who will take care of Skye?" I ask through my tears.

"Listen lady, once we get you transferred to the Fulton County Jail and they get you processed through central booking, you'll be able to make a couple of phone calls, then you can check on your dog."

"Hang on," the detective says to the hard-ass jailer. "She's already been here overnight. No sense making the little pooch suffer. You got a neighbor or someone who'll look after him?"

"I do, Pat Duffy. He works up at the Mountain Market in Speculator."

"I'll have Evelyn look up the number and give him a call."

"Oh, thank you," I gush, overcome with emotion. "I've watched his dog a few times when he was out of town visiting his grandchildren. He'll take care of Skye until I get back."

The jailer smirks and shakes his head. I know he's thinking that I won't be coming back. With that, a woman in a green dress appears in the doorway and gives a nod to the detective, I assume she's indicating she's on it.

"Oh, Skye," I call to my pup in anguish as my heart is breaking, "I'm so sorry."

"Now let's get you up to *county*. You'll be goin' before the judge tomorrow morning."

I drop my head feeling both shame and humiliation as the jailer leads me down the hallway and then outside towards a waiting patrol car.

The day is bright and sunny. It's gonna be another hot one. I squint as the light hurts my eyes after being held so long inside the windowless police station. I turn my face as someone in a car parked on my right lowers his window and shouts in my direction, "Is that the lesbo who killed my wife?"

I cringe at the accusation. It is all I can do to keep my mouth shut. I want to defend myself so badly. How

225

could he, of all people, accuse me of such a horrific thing? He's the one who drove poor Kaye to flee from her own home. He is despicable and should be the one who is handcuffed and marched off to the county jail, not me.

The officer opens the car door then places one hand on the crown of my head so I don't knock myself out as I struggle to climb into the back seat of the patrol car without the use of my arms. I thank him for his consideration and he gives me a bewildered look as he gently closes the door and I hear the click of the automatic door lock.

By now Nash is out of his car. He stands there red in the face and sweating like a pig while screaming at me over and over again, "That lesbo killed my wife!" He shakes his fist as the police car, with me in it, pulls out of the parking lot.

The last thing I hear as we pull onto the gravel road is this misogynistic creep yelling, "Lock her up! Lock her up!"

"Clever, wherever did he come up with that?"

The two cops in the front seat start to laugh. There is a thick plastic shield separating the front and back seat that protects the officers from the likes of me. Neither of them address me as they drive through town towards the county jail and the courthouse. I close my eyes and take a

226

moment to think. I have to keep my head about me. I didn't hurt anyone. How can I make them believe me and still protect Kaye, at least until I know she is safe? I wonder if she's called me like we planned.

I'm just about to ask if one of them has my cell phone when they begin to speak softly to one another. They are whispering and must be saying something they don't want me to hear. I keep quiet and feign sleep.

"I still like the husband for this. He's obviously a hot head and an asshole."

"Obviously, but we gotta follow the evidence."

"My gut tells me we're wrong, this woman ... no connection with the victim, kind, courteous, loves her dog... I don't think she has it in her."

"Prime motives for murder, you know, are money and sex. Maybe she was into the vic'..."

"Maybe. But I'd still put my money on the husband. He's got anger issues and he could've killed her for the money. According to the victim's brother, their old man just died and left Mrs. Amy Cooper a pretty penny."

Resting my head on the back of the seat, still keeping my eyes closed, I decide I'll ask about my phone later, once this all gets straightened out.

## Chapter 36
## Andy

I wake in the morning to find a long email from my

girlfriend, Michelle. I guess I had begun to think of her as

my girlfriend as we have been seeing each other for a few

months now and intimate for a number of weeks. I thought

things were going pretty well, but given this email, I guess

she feels differently. Michelle wrote that she's a lesbian, as

if I didn't know this. She said she wants to love me, but

she's confused.

You'd think it would be easier for a trans person

with a lesbian partner, but there's a great deal of prejudice

against trans people in both the lesbian and gay

communities. Makes me wonder if I'll ever find a loving

partner. There is a part of me that would like to stay in bed

and pull the covers up over my head and have a good cry,

but today that is not an option.

I hear Joey's boys in the kitchen. The aroma of

coffee and bacon frying wafts down to the guest room. I'll

just have to deal with the emotional fallout of getting

dumped at a later time. My mother is missing and my dad is

in jail as the cops think he is somehow involved in her disappearance. As they say, I have a few other things on my plate today.

Joey's wife is wonderful. She was accepting and loving as if it was truly no big deal that her sister-in-law is now her brother-in-law and Kyle and Kirk followed her lead. God bless 'em all. It won't go so well with Dad or Sammy and his family, this I know for certain. I wish I didn't care so much, but the truth is, I do.

I pull on a tee shirt and a pair of basketball shorts over my boxers and head to the bathroom to shave, take my meds, and get cleaned up for the day.

By the time I reach the kitchen the boys have already finished their breakfast and Natalie is seated at the table nursing little Laurel. Joey jumps to his feet. "Can I get you some breakfast? A cup of coffee?"

"That would be great," I answer and take a seat at the table where Natalie has already set a place for me. I'm happy to see that Joey doesn't assume all the chores associated with domesticity belong to his wife.

He brings me a cup of coffee and asks, "Omelet? We have tomatoes and fresh basil from the garden. Maybe with some cheddar?"

"Sounds great."

I turn my face towards my brother as Natalie shifts the baby to her other breast and takes a sip of her coffee before she speaks, "We heard from your father this morning."

I turn and look back in her direction, "You did?"

"Yes, he called when you were in the shower. They've released him."

"Okay...," I wait as I am sure there is more to this story.

Joey refills my coffee as he waits for the omelet to cook through. "He said, they didn't have enough evidence to hold him but they warned him that he shouldn't go anywhere."

"They must think he had something to do with Mom's disappearance or I don't think they would've told him that. Do you think he's involved?" I ask out loud, not certain whether I think he's capable of it or not. "He's always been a son of a bitch, maybe not to you and Sammy but he sure was to Mom and me."

Joey turns back to the stove to plate my breakfast and turns off the gas burner. "There's more," he says as he puts the plate with the omelet and a couple of strips of bacon down in front of me.

"What?" I'm not sure I want to hear this.

"According to Dad, they've arrested a woman for Mom's murder."

"They think Mom is dead?" The tears begin to pour down my face as I wipe them away frantically with my paper napkin. "Did they find her body?" I'm losing it. I push the plate with this beautiful breakfast my brother has just prepared for me into the center of the table. I can't begin to even think about eating.

"No. They don't have a body," Natalie whispers as their beautiful little daughter sleeps in her arms.

"Then how do they know she has been murdered? And who is this woman, the one who is charged with Mom's murder?"

"You need to remember that Dad is the source of this information and the police still think he may be involved."

"What is that supposed to mean? What did he tell you?"

"He said, she's a bull dyke."

"Oh for the love of God, does he have any idea how offensive that is? Does he even care? He's a misogynistic bastard," and then I catch myself, "I mean, if we are going to start calling people names. But more to the point, what does this person have to do with Mom?" I wipe

231

my eyes and blow my nose as I try to get myself under control.

Natalie silently pushes another napkin across the table to me as the one I'm holding is soggy and completely unusable now.

"Pop said that the police dogs tracked Mom to this woman's cabin on the Sacandaga River. It's downstream from the campground where Mom went swimming. Then they found traces of Mom's blood in her cabin and Mom and Dad's address was programmed into the GPS in her truck." Joey sits down at the table next to his wife and daughter.

"Oh...," is all I can say.

"I know," my brother responds as he reaches for Natalie's hand.

"I'm going to go put the baby down," Natalie says as she stands. She is crying as she leaves the kitchen. "I'm sorry, it's just that I love your mom, too."

"It's okay, Natalie. I know you did and Mom loved you," I say and Joey nods in agreement.

Once Natalie has left the room, Joey and I continue. "What does this woman with the cabin on the river have to say for herself?" I ask.

232

"According to Pop, she's not talking. Pop says she's a lesbian and she probably thought Mom was hot."

"That's rich, because as far as I know the man never gave her the time of day."

"Well, clearly that's not true. They had three kids, after all."

"Yeah, well we're all in our thirties, so if he ever had eyes for her, it was a long time ago. Pop had so many extramarital affairs."

"How do you know this?"

"How do you not?"

"There were a few instances when I was a kid when I saw him put his arm around some random woman. But they always pushed him away. It looked like they were just goofing around, like it was no big deal. I asked him about it once when I was in high school and he made some comment like *'boys will be boys.'*"

"If you were in high school, Dad must have been in his fifties. That doesn't qualify as a boy in my book, more like a philandering scumbag. Anyway, I have friends who used to run into him out and about. He didn't know them, but they sure knew him. He was out makin' a spectacle of himself, Mister Lover Boy Magee. The old goat was out there gettin' handsy and makin' a public display of affection with women half his age."

233

"You're not saying that Mom was ... interested in women, are you?"

"You mean a lesbian? You can call it what it is, it's not a dirty word."

"I know. I didn't mean to imply anything. I'm just trying to understand."

"No, rest assured our mother was cis normal, hopelessly heterosexual, although I'm sure she wasn't any more interested in him than he was in her. I don't know how she could stand him."

"How do you know this?"

"I just know."

"Now let's get out of here and go see our old man. I need to hear this from him. I need to look him in the face. He might be able to fool the police, but he won't fool me. I want to know what he knows and ask that son of a bitch some questions of my own. The police told him not to leave town. I want to know what they know, and I want to know more about this woman, too."

"You're sure you want to see him? I mean, he doesn't know your trans, right?"

"Right now, he has more to be concerned about than I do, don't you think?"

"You're right.  So, finish your breakfast and let's head down to the house."

"After that I want to go back to the police station. I'd like to get some information on this woman they're holding."

# Chapter 37
## Joey

I have reservations about this plan, but Andy seems dead set on confronting Dad about what he knows about Mom's disappearance. Hasn't there been enough turmoil and drama already, without going head to head with Dad about how his only daughter is now his son? He's going to blow a gasket as soon as he lays eyes on Andy. This can't go well.

I kiss Natalie goodbye. "See you later this afternoon."

"Good luck," Natalie whispers softly in my ear. The warmth of her breath makes me reach out and hold her tightly to my body and I feel her yield softly to my embrace. I'd like nothing better than to abandon this fool's mission and take my lovely wife back to bed. I groan as she looks up at me.

"Later Love, later," she says quietly so only I can hear and I gently release her.

Passing through the family room the boys call out in unison, "Bye Dad. Bye Uncle Andy."

Andy smiles and ruffles little Kyles's shaggy blond hair.

"That's enough television for one morning, now turn it off and go outside and play," I say to my sons. They grumble, but do as they are told. "Now mind your mother and we'll play some catch and get a pizza tonight." Instantly their childish pouting faces change. One moment they're sad and the next elated. I only wish all of my problems were so easily remedied.

Reluctantly, I get into the passenger seat of Andy's rental car and fasten my seatbelt. "You know, this goes against my intuition and any good judgment I may have once possessed."

"Since when have you possessed any judgment, let alone good judgment?" Andy asks as he lightly slugs me on the shoulder.

"All I can say is– this isn't going to go well."

"Look I've spent my whole life trying to please good old daddyo and have been supremely unsuccessful. I no longer care if he approves of me or accepts me. That's on him. I figure there is no time like the present when what we all should be focused on is– where the hell is Mom?"

"You really don't care what he thinks?" I'm finding this a little hard to believe.

"It's not that I no longer care, of course part of me will always care. But I want to be loved and supported for who I am, not who I pretended to be. If he can't love me, I will find other people who will, people who will love me just as I am. Besides, a major part of my therapy has focused on learning to love myself. I have and I do. It's more important to me what I think of myself than what anyone else does, including dear old dad, or perhaps I should say, especially dear old dad."

"Wow Andy, good for you. Maybe I should go to therapy and try to let go of all the gnashing we all endured from Nash."

"Maybe, but as I've said before you and Sammy got off easy compared to me and Mom. It was easier for me once I got out of here and didn't have to endure his nastiness on a daily basis..."

"You don't think Mom just decided she'd had enough? You don't think she just up and left him, do you?" I know this sounds crazy as I say the words aloud for the first time.

"I don't know...it's crossed my mind. But I think she would have left with more than just the swimsuit she was wearing. Don't you?" Andy grips the steering wheel tighter and puts the turn signal on as we change lanes.

I can't help but notice how his hands still have a rather feminine appearance and I worry about his safety if others might suspect he is trans. "Maybe. Maybe it's just wishful thinking on my part; Mom living out her retirement with some rich, handsome old dude who satisfies her every whim somewhere in the Caribbean."

"Wouldn't that be nice. A fantasy I'm afraid. Mom could never get Dad to take her anywhere, not even out to Denver to visit me or out to California to visit Uncle Douglas. His idea of a vacation was going to North Carolina to watch another football game. Sounds like Mom's version of Jean Paul Sartre's _No Exit_?"

"What?" I ask as I have no idea what Andy is talking about. "I never read it."

"Her own personal hell from which there is no escape," Andy clarifies.

"You don't think she liked going back to her alma mater, not even a little bit?"

"Hell no. She always talked to me about returning to the south of France."

"When was she in the south of France?" I ask as I wonder what else I don't know about my own mother.

"When she was in college before she got knocked up with me."

"She never told me she ever went to France and she never told me about ..."

"How Dad got her pregnant before they were married?" Andy asks.

"I feel like an idiot. How come I don't know these things?"

"You are her son, I *was* her daughter. We talked about a lot of stuff that she didn't share with you or Sammy. Mothers and daughters have different relationships than they have with their sons."

I look over at Andy as he wipes a tear from his cheek.

"I used the word *was*."

He is really choked up and having difficulty continuing. I'm choked up too, but for a different reason. There is so much I never even thought to ask my mother about. She had a full life before she became our mother. A life I have never really considered enough to even ask about. What is wrong with me?

Andy breaks into my private litany of all the ways I failed my mother saying, "I was her daughter. But I am no longer a daughter and Mom might be dead. So much has changed for me in the two years since I saw her last and so much has changed for all of us in the last few days."

We travel on in silence, neither Andy nor I daring to speak for fear we both might start sobbing and be unable to stop.

When we pull into the neighborhood where we grew up. The trees are a little bigger and the landscaping has matured but other than that everything looks about the same. I'm flooded with memories of a peaceful suburban life, at least that's the way I remember it. "What is the line from that old song by John Cougar Mellencamp?"

*"Oh, but ain't that America for you and me.*
*Ain't that America somethin' to see.*
*Ain't that America the home of the free.*
*Little pink houses for you and me..."*

I hum the tune and Andy joins me singing all the words that I've forgotten as we pull into the driveway of our childhood home.

"Do you think all the fathers in these houses subjected their less than perfect families to the same macho bullshit that Pop inflicted on Mom and us?" I ask.

"It's doubtful it was all the same once the front doors were closed. But they may have rendered some other personalized form of domestic dominance and torture on their loved ones. Who knows? Could have been drug or alcohol abuse or maybe just the fallout from a bad day at

241

the office. Anyway I'm sure many of the kids raised here are now trying to come to terms with their own childhood traumas and willingly paying their therapists' country club fees."

"You sure you want to be a member of this old boys club?" I ask.

Andy laughs and rubs his whiskered chin then beats his now flat chest with his fist. "Too late to turn back now. But I need to talk to my doctor about upping my testosterone so I can quit crying like a girl."

"Maybe I need to get some too. I've been on the brink of tears ever since we learned that Mom was gone."

"Let's go in there and see what Dad has to say about that."

"Do you want me to go in first and let him know that you are here, you know...kind of prepare him so he doesn't lose his shit as he's been known to do."

"Nope..." Andy looks like he has more he wants to say, instead he swallows and his protruding Adam's apple now moves visibly up and then down on his neck. "No, let's go." He opens the car door and steps out of the car and I do the same.

The front door opens while we're still on the front walkway and Dad steps out on the porch wearing a pair of

UNC gym shorts in Carolina Blue and a sleeveless wife beater undershirt.

The irony is not lost on me.

# Chapter 38
## Kaye

I savor the last of my duck confit and Perrier. Just sitting here and people watching allows me to relax for a moment longer as I try to decide what to do next. I am starting to feel the time difference and the corresponding jet lag is beginning to catch up with me as it is now early afternoon. I had better find some place to stay the night. I'd love to go see the impressionist paintings and the works of Claude Monet at the Musée d'Orsay. The museum is so close, just across the river. But I'm so tired now and I fear, if I don't get some sleep, I will begin to make mistakes. Any sight-seeing will just have to wait for another time. I will do a bit of shopping before I catch my train tomorrow. I can buy some different shoes then. I pay the waiter in cash and leave.

Leaving the café, I walk a couple of blocks before turning onto Rue Rouget de Lisle where I can see a red sign for the Hôtel Mayfair from the corner. It looks lovely and so French with its limestone façade, black wrought iron balconies, and lush window boxes overflowing with green foliage and red geraniums. Still, with a name like Mayfair, they certainly must be catering to tourists. Hopefully someone speaks English as I am finding my French is long out of practice and I'm having some difficulty making myself understood. I pray there is a vacancy and it's not too expensive.

I muddle through my inquiry to find they've just had a cancellation. One room with one single bed for 187 euros. The conversion to dollars is simple today as one euro is pretty close to one US dollar. I'm too tired to be a bargain hunter. I desperately need to sleep. I give the desk clerk my passport to copy and pay him in cash.

"Would you like help with your bag?" he asks as a bell cap stands at the ready.

"Non, merci. I can manage," I say as we both look at my leather satchel. I offer no further explanation about why I have no additional luggage. Perhaps he thinks I am meeting someone for an afternoon tryst. I wish and then almost laugh out loud at such ridiculous notion. He hands me an old school heavy brass key fob with the key for room 347. I make my way to the elevator.

The lift is no larger than my broom closet back in the states. I step in and pull closed the heavy metal gate of gleaming brass. It unfolds into a pattern of repeating diamonds locking me in. My hands start to sweat and my breathing speeds up. Oh God, my claustrophobia is mounting— fear of being trapped.

I have experienced this before.

I flashback to the night Nash raped me, it was just after Andy was born.

My panic increases.

He was drunk and I wanted nothing to do with him in his drunken state, but he wouldn't take no for an answer. He lay his prodigious, corpulent body on me pinning me down while he thrust himself into me until he passed out. I couldn't move.

I shudder at the memory.

Trapped beneath him I panicked until my screaming and the clawing my nails into him finally caused him to roll off of me.

"It's only three floors," I tell myself. "It's only three floors." Repeating it over and over again like a mantra until we arrive and the doors open.

Fear of being trapped.

Just like I was before.

Just like I've been for the last forty years.

These thoughts come to me like a download on a computer.

Although I've thought about that night so many times, I hadn't connected it to my claustrophobia until just now. I've finally put it all together.

I exit the lift, shaking as I make my way down the long hall looking for my room. There it is 347.

I put the old key in the lock and turn it until I feel the lock release. I take a deep breath and exhale slowly to release the memory before I step inside.

The room is small and under the eaves but well-appointed with red and ivory toile wallpaper and crisp white bed linens and a fluffy duvet. I open the door to the bathroom and to my surprise and delight there is an old clawfoot soaking tub. I set my bag down on the floor and put the stopper in the drain and begin to fill the tub. The water warms quickly as the tub fills. There on the vanity is a jar of bath salts. Removing the lid I inhale deeply—ah lavender. I use the scoop and put a generous amount into the running water and the scent of lavender fills the bathroom as the mirror and the windows begin to steam.

While the tub fills I step into the bedroom to undress. I hang my dress in the armoire as I will need to wear it again tomorrow. Then rinse out my under garments and hang them on the heated towel rack before brushing my teeth. Tomorrow I will be clean and ready to go. But for now I slip into the tub, relax, and begin to dream about all the possibilities that await me in my new life.

It's hard to believe that only a few days ago I was feeling so stuck, living in suburban New York with a man who never loved me. So much has happened in the last few days and so much more awaits me. What that will look like I cannot say, but it will be nothing like the life I've left behind. I make this sacred promise to no one but myself.

I must have drifted off as I wake and the water has grown cold. I chastise myself for such carelessness. This could have ended badly, I drain the water from the tub and dry myself off. The bed has been turned down and there is a single red rose in the vase on the bedside stand. A foil wrapped chocolate from *La Maison du Chocolat* rests on the pillow. Even though I have already brushed my teeth, I unwrap the chocolate. It melts on my tongue. It is delicious. This place is worth every penny.

Even though it is only early evening, I slip naked beneath the weight of the duvet and drift quickly off to sleep.

I wake in the morning as the sun beams in through my window. I neglected to draw the curtains before I went to bed last night. I check the clock on the bedside table, it's already 8:30 and I have a busy day ahead of me. I slip on

the white silken robe that hangs in the armoire and decide
to call down for room service. I order a cappuccino and a
croissant.

I could get used to this.

I sit down at the desk to make another list of
everything I must accomplish today. First things first, I call
the concierge. "When is the next train to Geneva?" I ask
him to check into this for me. While still on the phone
there is a knock at my door. "Will you excuse me for a
moment?" I ask, completely abandoning any attempt to ask
in French.

A handsome young Frenchman stands outside my
door. I am completely taken by his dark features and
rugged sensual beauty that it takes me a moment to notice
his uniform and the fact that he is here simply to deliver my
breakfast. I pull my robe closed tightly around my body,
aware of my own nakedness beneath the silken fabric. He
looks at me and smiles as he enters the bedroom and places
the tray upon the desk. Perhaps he is used to causing this
kind of reaction in women, but I feel absolutely unbalanced
by his very presence.

"Merci," I say, my voice is barely above a whisper.
He nods and smiles again as he turns to leave. The door
closes behind him.

Feeling weak in the knees and overexposed in nothing but a robe that traces every curve and nuance of my naked body I practically fall onto the chair beside the desk. "Oh my God what is wrong with me? " I say aloud before I see the receiver is off the phone and sitting on the desk. I remember the concierge is waiting.

"Allo?" I say breathlessly hoping he has hung up and I can call him back. But no, he heard the whole thing.

"Are you all right Madame?" he asks.

"*Oui, merci.* Were you able to book me a seat on a train to Geneva?"

"There is a train leaving every two hours from Gare de Lyon. When would you like to leave?"

I take a moment to think about the shopping I need to do. It is now nearly nine o'clock. "How long will it take me to get to Gare de Lyon from here by taxi?" I ask.

"Not long. Twenty maybe thirty minutes."

"Is there a three o'clock train?"

"Non, but there is one leaving at 16:18 or 4:18 this afternoon."

I nod recalling the French use of the twenty-four hour clock. "What is the expected time of arrival?"

"Well Madame," he chuckles, "Expected is the operative word here. The train is *expected* to arrive at 20:05 this evening. Give or take. This is France after all."

"Around eight o'clock. Good. Please secure me a ticket on that train. I will be down shortly to settle up on my bill."

"Very good, Madame."

I hear the phone click off as I take the silver warming cover off the plate that holds my croissant and two ramekins. One is filled with raspberry jam and the other with whipped butter. I take a moment to sip the cappuccino and savor the still warm croissant. How I have longed for the simple pleasures of this life—a hot bath, the fragrance of lavender, a silken robe, soft bed, the dark, the quiet, good coffee and a warm croissant with butter and jam. Can it get any better than this?

Maybe it can. The very notion makes me smile as my mind turns to that handsome Frenchman. Not him, per se as he is way too young for the likes of me but maybe he has an uncle, an older version, one with a few more miles on him.

One can dream.

I pull myself back to the reality of my situation.

I need to get going.

I'm already way over budget and I have no idea how much money my dear sweet father has bequeathed to me.

Once I get to Geneva I must get a phone so I can reach out to Ellery and let her know I've arrived and all is well. Then she can contact Andy and Andy can contact the boys.

A pall of guilt passes over me. I feel so selfish. I've been thinking of no one but myself since I arrived.

The little voice inside my head speaks up, unbidden, *it's about time.*

This is true, and I know it.

Still, I'll need to get some clothes if I want to pass as a French woman and get rid of these shoes before I break an ankle or fall flat on my face.

# Chapter 39
## Ellery

The next hour makes me feel like I'm playing a role in a tv crime show as I'm fingerprinted and photographed for mug shots and given an orange jumpsuit and a pair of canvas tennis shoes without any laces.

After this, I'm shuffled down the hall for something the booking officer called *pretrial services*.

"Take a seat. Someone will be in to see you soon," the officer states with his hand still on the door handle. He turns and I hear the lock latch behind him.

I can only speculate what kind of *services* I will be offered here as I wait in yet another windowless room for someone, anyone to show up. It has already been a long couple of days and I'm beyond exhausted. I sit on the hard, metal folding chair, then make a pillow with my arms and lay my head down on the table. I desperately need a shower. I've read that there is something different about the odor one emits after a good day's work and the smell of fear. Today, I reek of fear. God help me if I can't figure a way out of this mess. It's really a conundrum for me. Do I save myself and give up Kaye or do I protect Kaye and hope they won't convict me based on circumstantial evidence? For God's sake, they can't convict me if they don't have a body. Can they?

Just as I'm about to drift off to sleep I hear a key turn the lock and another officer comes into the room. "We've checked your record and you don't have any outstanding warrants. In fact, we don't have any record of you at all. What are you— some kind of a recluse?"

"Something like that," I say intending to say nothing more. It isn't hard to remember that these guys are not my friends and are not looking out for my best interests.

"I understand you haven't eaten yet. So we'll get you something to eat before we take you to your cell. You'll be arraigned in the morning. Do you have any questions?"

I pause a moment to think. I have about a million questions, but which ones should I ask? "I have yet to speak with an attorney," I state, realizing this is not a question, but he answers anyway.

"That's because it's a Sunday. Someone from the Public Defender's Office will be in to see you tomorrow morning before the arraignment.

"Do I have anything to say about who will represent me?"

"Only if you can pay for it. Otherwise, someone will be assigned to you."

I think about my meager savings. I know of no one I can ask or would ask for help. I am completely estranged from my siblings and have been since I left Saint Paul de l'Île-aux-Noix as a young person. Mom passed years ago and my father disinherited me decades ago when he confronted me about being a lesbian. I suppose I could ask Henri for help, but I wouldn't. I wouldn't accept his help even if he offered it. I just couldn't.

"I can't afford to hire a lawyer. I'm sure whoever they assign will be okay. I didn't kill anyone and the truth is a defense, right?"

He just smirks and makes my skin crawl.

"Any other questions?" he asks as he stands to leave.

"Just one, I thought I was going to be allowed to make a phone call."

"You haven't gotten your phone call?" he asks in a tone that resonates with disbelief.

"No."

He shuffles through his papers and must determine that what I say is true. "Okay," he says. Then he takes a cell phone from his pocket and asks whoever answers to bring in a phone.

While we wait for the phone I try to remember Henri's number.

"Could I have a piece of paper and a pencil?" I ask. He nods and pulls a small pad and a pen from the breast pocket of his uniform and hands it across the table to me.

I carefully write down the words—*Get One Tank For Me Please Get Me Another Soon*. I count the words. There are nine words and a one for international calling to Canada. A look of confusion crosses the officer's face. "Just a little memory trick I use," I offer as an explanation.

The door opens and a woman hands the officer an old school black phone. He places the phone in front of me on the table then plugs the cord into the phone jack on the wall. He sits back down and waits.

"Could I have some privacy please?" I ask.

Again he smirks, "Sure *lady*." He says *lady* as if it is a joke. I hear him say, "privacy," and scoff with a barely audible laugh as he exits the room. Then I know what I only previously suspected; there is no privacy here. The police will be listening and this call will be recorded.

I pick up the paper and dial the corresponding numbers–1- Get-4, One-1, Tank-8, For-3, Me-6, Please-7, Get-4, Me-6, Another-2, Soon-7. I hear the sound of the phone ringing and say a silent prayer that Henri will pick-up.

"Allo?" Henri answers as he sounds a little confused, perhaps because he doesn't recognize the number.

A recorded voice comes through the receiver, "You are receiving a phone call from an inmate at the Fulton County Correctional Facility. Press one to accept the call."

I hear the beep in my ear.

"Henri?"

"Yes," he sounds hesitant.

"It's Ellery. Do not say anything. This call is likely being recorded."

"Okay," he says and I can hear the worry in this single word.

"Please don't worry." I try to be reassuring. "I'm being held for the murder of a woman I have never met. A woman by the name of Amy Cooper."

"Oh, I see," he says and I know by the tone of his voice that he understands completely. "Have you heard from our friend?" he asks.

"Not a word, but they have my phone."

"I see," he says, not quite sure what to say next.

"I'm being arraigned in the morning."

"I'll be there."

"No, my friend. Don't. Just don't." And then the phone starts to beep in my ear indicating my time is almost up. "Henri, will you please take Skye? She is with Patrick Duffy at the market up in Speculator."

"Of course, Ellery. I'm on my way and I'll see you in the morning."

And then the phone goes dead.

"Damn it, that man is so hard-headed. He never could take no for an answer."

# Chapter 40
## Nash

Oh my God, my head is killing me. I didn't drink that much last night, did I? I can't really remember. Amy was always hassling me about drinkin' alone. But there was no one here to *bitch* at me last night, no one gettin' up in my business and sayin', 'don't you think you've had enough?' Lost in my own reverie I get up from the kitchen table to look for the Advil and pour myself a cup of coffee when a car I don't recognize pulls up in the driveway. I've had just about enough of these news hounds sneakin' around here lookin' for a story. Those busy bodies need to mind their own fuckin' business.

I open the garage door and walk out onto the driveway to confront these two nosey bastards.

"What are you a couple of Mormons? Makin' early morning house calls on the bereaved?" I shout hoping they get the message that they're not welcome.

They just stand there, like a couple of idiots not sayin' anything.

"Get the hell out of here. You're trespassing!" I shout a little louder. The words are no sooner out of my mouth than I see *Mrs. Kravitz* come around the bend, she's out walking her little wiener dog. She stops on the sidewalk in front of the house and lets her little beast take a shit in my front yard. Perfect timing, now she has an excuse to stand there while her dog does its business allowing her to eavesdrop. She's the neighborhood snoop and always sticking her nose in where it doesn't belong then flapping her gums to anyone who'll listen.

"Aren't you gonna clean up after your damn dog?"

"I'll get it Nash," the old biddy calls back in response. I wait for her to bend over and clean up its poop.

"Good Morning Mrs. Baker," the guy on the passenger side of the car says.

Oh it's Joey. Didn't even recognize my own kid until I heard his voice. I guess I did have too much to drink. I rub my eyes and try to focus. Who's he brought with him? The other guy looks familiar, but I can't place him.

"Good Morning, Joey," she responds. "So sorry to hear about your mother. Amy was such a wonderful neighbor. If there is anything I can do…" her voice trails off as she continues on down the sidewalk with the leash in one hand and a bag of dog shit in the other.

I turn my attention back to Joey. "What are you doin' here?"

"I need to talk to you."

"About what?"

"Mom..."

"You could have called, I'm not even dressed yet." I'm still wearing the clothes I slept in, a pair of old gym shorts and a stained undershirt. I hadn't noticed it was stained until just now. I must have dropped some tomato sauce from last night's pizza on it. I try to rub what remains from last night's dinner off of the undershirt. It's not goin' anywhere. I attempt to pull it down, still it barely covers my belly

"Sorry about not calling. I figured you might be sleeping. It's been a tough few days but we need to talk..." Joey says.

"Who's your friend?" I can't imagine he'd bring a stranger into my home, particularly now with everything that's been goin' on.

Everyone goes silent and holds their ground until the other guy says, "It's me, Dad. Andy."

"What the fuck..." I can't believe my eyes. I shake my head in disbelief before I turn and walk back into the garage and hit the button closing the door between us.

I head directly to the toilet and puke my guts up, heaving and gagging until there is nothing left but bile. That girl will be the death of me. She always was a freak. She needs to get on the next plane and go back where she came from. I collapse on the bathroom floor feeling nothing but shame and humiliation. How could she? How could she do this to me?

# Chapter 41
## Andy

"That didn't go particularly well," I say to my brother.

"I'm sorry Andy. You know how he is," Joey walks around the car to comfort me.

"I'm afraid I know exactly how he is. He's treated me like this all my life. If he doesn't like someone or something he just closes them out." A tear forms in my eye and slips down my cheek. "At least he didn't beat me, this time."

"He was probably afraid you might defend yourself and beat the crap out of him." Joey smiles and taps my bicep. "Nice guns."

I can't help but laugh. "Wouldn't that have been a nice turn of events, retribution for all the times he beat the hell out of me."

"Maybe you could smack him a few times for Mom while you're at it," Joey says.

I smile as I know he is trying his best to be supportive. This is all new territory for him, too. "Let's get out of here and leave well enough alone."

We drive out of the neighborhood in silence until it's time to make a decision about which direction to go and what to do next. I pull over into the park-and-ride lot so Joey and I can discuss our options.

"Do you want to go home?" I ask my brother.

"Not really," Joey responds. "Natalie has planned to take the kids to the community pool for their swimming lessons this morning and then back home to put the baby down for a nap. We'd only be disrupting her day. Babies thrive on routine and so does Natalie."

"Gotcha. Well, it isn't quite nine o'clock. Let's head up to the Fulton County Courthouse and see if we can catch the arraignment of the woman they're holding for Mom's murder. We didn't get any information out of Dad, but maybe we can learn what the police have on this woman. At the very least, we should be able to get a look at her."

Joey nods in agreement. So, I enter the destination, Fulton County Courthouse, into the GPS. Looks like we can take the backroads until we get to I-5 Northbound. "Should take us less than an hour if we don't run into traffic or construction." I pull out of the parking lot back onto Glenridge Road.

"Well Dad should be relieved, I don't think Mrs. Baker had any idea who I was."

"If she did it will be all over the neighborhood by the time Dad has a shower."

"Remember how Dad used to call her *Mrs. Kravitz*, after the nosey neighbor on *Bewitched*?"

"Used to? He still does. They've been neighbors since we were kids and he still has no idea what her real name is."

"I don't know why I had assumed that anything had changed. He looked pretty rough this morning. Do you think he's grieving? Maybe I'm being too tough on the old guy. After all, Mom *is* missing and may be dead."

"I don't think so, I think he probably tied one on last night and is nursing a hangover. He only cares about himself. You give him too much credit. He's the same old asshole he's always been. Look, he just walked away from us and closed the garage door in our faces."

"Wrong pronoun brother. He walked away from me. He closed the garage door in my face."

"Sorry, Andy. He hasn't seen you in over two years. Maybe he just needs some time to process things."

"Now you are giving him too much credit. He may have lost his wife, but we've lost our mother. He is our father, for God's sake. He could have shown *us* some

265

compassion for what *we* are going through, but he can never see anything from anyone else's perspective. It's all about him, it always has been, and we'd both be better off if we accepted the fact that it always will be."

# Chapter 42
## Ellery

I'm startled as I wake to the sound of an alarm. It takes me a moment to remember where I am. The clock outside my cell flashes a digital signal indicating it's six o'clock. I didn't know if I would sleep in here. This is a scary place but the other women seem to have given me a wide berth. They're probably afraid of me. I know how I look. I've seen the looks and barely audible whispers behind the shield of their hands. "Is that a man or a woman?" People have questioned my gender all my life. It's no different in here. Perhaps my ambiguous nature will at last prove beneficial and people will just leave me alone.

"Who's the new cellie?" one of my cellmates asks another.

"The fresh meat?" the second one responds.

I glance in their direction. These women look rough. Both are significantly younger than I am, heavily tattooed, and the younger of the two is badly in need of a dentist.

"That old bitch? She's hardly fresh meat."

Sound bounces off the cement block walls and the guards talk. Word travels quickly around here and it is already well known that I've been charged with murder.

"Take it easy, Glory. She's in for the long haul."

"Really?"

"Yep, she killed some woman."

"No shit. She doesn't look the type."

"Bet I could take her."

I keep my back to the wall, my head up, saying nothing, nothing at all. The last thing I need is to provoke a fight in here.

The guard unlocks the cell and the six of us are sent down the hall to shower. The shower room reminds me of gym class where everyone showers together. I guess this public nudity will put an end to their questioning my gender. There is a sign on the wall indicating that the showers are on a three minute timer. I turn and face the wall and keep the custody of my eyes. I need to hurry or I won't have any water left to rinse. The water is cold, too cold for the harsh bar soap to lather. I use it anyway to wash my body and my hair. Grateful that my hair is short, I wash it and rinse it easily in the three minutes allotted. I follow another woman as we walk in procession out of the shower room and are handed a package of laundry containing a thread bare towel, clean underwear, socks, and another orange jumpsuit.

I dry off and dress quickly. I'm chilled to the bone and my skin is red and itches from the harshness of the soap. I take the now damp towel and dry my hair, then use my fingers to push it into place. I've never been fancy, and although there are no mirrors, I'm fairly certain my hair looks no different than it usually does.

The women laugh and joke with one another but no one speaks to me. I can't help but wonder what atrocities they committed that landed them in this hell hole. Or maybe some of them, like me, are falsely accused or perhaps unfortunate victims of circumstance.

After we shower we are shuffled off to breakfast. As we make our way to the dining hall I listen to the other women's grumblings and learn that all inmates shower twice weekly. Our cell block showers first thing Monday and Friday mornings. On these days, we are the last one's in for breakfast and there isn't much left.

Today we are served oatmeal, an orange, and two slices of wheat bread with margarine and some jam. The oatmeal is cold and the bread is stale. I eat it anyway. Before I'm finished a guard approaches and informs me, "Breakfast is over, McMasters. Your attorney is waiting for you in the fishbowl."

"What's the fishbowl?" I ask as I push myself back from the table and stand.

"The meeting room with the big glass window so we can keep an eye on you and make sure you don't try to off your attorney," the guard says with a laugh.

I bend over to pick up my tray, still filled with half-eaten food.

"Leave it," she says. "Gordon, clear this up before you go."

"Thank you," I say to the woman who has just been ordered to clean up after me. The woman called Gordon lifts her chin to acknowledge me. I can't help but wonder what will be expected of me in return.

The guard gives me a shove in the back to get me moving. None of the other women speak to me as I leave the dining hall.

Through the plate glass window I can see a young woman in a navy blue suit seated at the table. I enter the room and she stands as she looks at the papers on her clipboard.

"Ellery McMasters?"

"Yes, that's me," I say.

"Please take a seat." She gestures towards the chair. "My name is Megan O'Riordan. I'm the public defender who has been assigned to your case. I will be representing

270

you this morning at the arraignment before Judge Fredericks. Do you understand the charges?

"Yes." My voice comes out as a croak. "I think so."

"Let me explain. You are being charged with first degree murder of Amy Elizabeth Cooper."

"I have never met anyone with that name, let alone killed anyone."

"I understand. Therefore, when the judge asks you if you understand the charges you are to say 'yes', indicating only that you understand. Then he will ask you, 'How do you plead?' to which you will respond, 'Not Guilty.' That is all that we are doing this morning."

"Will I be able to get out on bail?"

"Highly unlikely given the seriousness of the charges. You should be grateful that the state legislature repealed the death penalty back in 1972."

"I'm having a hard time being grateful for anything right now, particularly since I didn't hurt, let alone kill, anyone."

"I understand."

"Since you're the Public Defender, how do you plan on defending me?"

"We will have to see what evidence the Prosecutor has against you before we can plan an effective

271

defense. I should be getting that information later this morning. After that, we'll talk."

"How can they charge me with murder when they don't even know if this woman is dead? I understand she just floated down the river and disappeared."

"It's a stretch, but it's been done before. Let's see what they've got connecting you with the victim. Come on now, we're due in court."

# Chapter 43
## Kaye

Since my train doesn't leave until after four this afternoon.

I decide to make a day of it. I don't think I've had so much fun shopping since I went with my mother and was looking for a prom dress or maybe when we went shopping for clothes to take to college. I don't know what made me think of this. All my old memories have been stirred up and reshuffled, perhaps it's simply because I'm preparing for a new adventure and stepping into the unknown. Only this time I'm older, much older, and I vow to be wiser. This may be my last great hurrah and I don't want to mess it up.

I browse through a number of boutiques while the attentive shopkeepers bring me one beautiful garment after another to try. Finding things I like has never been an issue but I must travel light until I am more settled. One helpful woman suggests a few additional things to complete the ensembles until at last, I have made my final selections.

I wait for her to carefully wrap my new things in tissue paper and hand me the handled shopping bag printed with the name Lafayette on one side.

I can almost hear my mother's wise counsel about always buying quality and how less is more. I chuckle quietly, I think she was quoting Coco Chanel and now here I am in Paris. Not that my budget allows for anything from Chanel, still I think my mother would approve of the dresses, blazer, slacks, and lingerie I have chosen.

Nash on the other had would have a stroke at how much money I've just spent on myself. We often fought about money when the kids were little. The consequences were so brutal that I gave up buying almost anything for myself except the basic essentials, but even that never stifled my desire for beautiful things.

I pay the woman in cash and head to the corner and cross the street to a shoe store. The day is warming up, and although it is August and things will be cooling off soon, I opt for a pair of low heeled sandals in a neutral color. Perhaps I'll buy some ankle boots once I get to Switzerland; once I get some more money.

"*Puis-je utiliser les toilettes*," I ask the woman at the shoe store. She hands me the bag with my new shoes.

"*Bien sûr*," she responds and points the way towards the back of the shop.

"*Merci*." I take my bags back to the ladies room and change into my new linen dress and the matching taupe shoes before I tie a taupe and navy scarf I had just acquired around my neck and wrap the dress and shoes I had been wearing with the tissue paper and place them inside the shopping bag. I take a moment to admire my reflection in the mirror. This dress fits me perfectly. I reapply my lipstick and run a brush through my hair. I check my teeth and smile. Even I wouldn't recognize this new version of myself.

Claudette's words ring in my ears about needing to look French, and not like an American. She was so haughty, and still, she helped me.

Satisfied with my appearance, I leave the ladies room. I thank the saleswoman again as she stands behind the desk at the register as I pass by.

"*Vous êtes ravissante, madame.*"

"*Merci.*" I feel myself beginning to blush. When was the last time anyone even noticed my appearance, let alone said I looked lovely? I pause a moment to think about this, and then I smile as I remember Henri. He said I was lovely.

The shopkeeper smiles and waves good-bye.

Stepping out onto the sidewalk I hail a cab.

"*Gare de Lyon, s'il vous plaît.*" I catch the cabbie's eyes in the rearview mirror and he nods.

The traffic is light and we arrive within twenty minutes and a full thirty minutes before my train to Geneva is due to leave. I check the monitor just inside the station. My train is on time and leaves from platform nine.

The station is air-conditioned and I begin to feel a chill. I take my new navy blazer from my shopping bag, grateful I'd asked the saleswoman to remove all the tags when I purchased it. The voice over the public address system announces the arrival of the 20:18 to Geneva and I move quickly caught up in the rush with all the other passengers moving towards the platform.

It isn't long before I find my seat on the left hand side of the train by the window. The concierge has booked me a seat in a couchette, where the seats can be pulled out and converted into a bed, even though this is less than a four-hour journey. I close the door, sealing me off from the aisle. I'm pleased when no one comes to join me. I tell myself this is because my French is rusty.

What if someone wanted to ask all those questions that people do? They think they are only making small talk and normally I would welcome it, but not now. I am running away and I want to go unnoticed. I want to pass as French. I don't want to give myself away by saying something stupid. Right now I just want to get to Geneva, get my money and completely disappear. Once settled in with my navy leather tote and my shopping bag secured safely beneath my seat, I take a deep breath to calm my mounting anxiety. I feel the train begin to move. I'm really on my way.

In my head I convert the 24 hour clock to something more familiar. If it's 4:18 here in Paris. If all goes well, in a few hours I'll be in Geneva.

My heart starts to race as I can hear the conductor as he makes his way down the aisle. He opens the sliding door and approaches my seat to collect my ticket.

"*Billet, s'il vous plaît.*"

I hand him both my ticket and my passport. We will be passing into Switzerland, after all.

He punches my ticket but takes one look at the Canadian passport I extend towards him and shakes his head. "*Non, Madame. Ce n'est pas nécessaire.*"

Relieved, I put it back in the pocket of my satchel along with my US passport in my other name—Amy Cooper. I zip the pocket closed and return the bag to its resting place beneath my seat.

It's mid-morning in New York. I wonder if they've given up looking for me. I do some quick calculations in my head. I've been missing for less than ninety hours. I'm sure someone has called the kids and my brother. Are they worried about me or just shaking their heads at my foolishness to go swimming when the river was high and the current was so rapid?

If one of my children was missing I would be beside myself with grief. How could I have done this to them? I'll call Ellery as soon as I get to Geneva, I need to get a phone. I'll want to get one where I can access the internet, one with GPS and a map so I'll know where I am.

I begin to relax and drift. The melodic sound and rhythmic vibration of the train on the tracks eventually lulls me off toward sleep to that sweet place where you are neither fully awake nor fully asleep. I'm in that place where my grasp of reality is only tenuous and dreams seem so very real, where anything seems possible.

I don't know where I'm going, but I know I'm going away. Somewhere within my still conscious subconscious I think I know that I am dreaming. I know I'm on a train and the train is taking me somewhere I've never been and away from something I desperately need to leave. There is the thrill of excitement of starting over when you are no longer young. There is something exhilarating about re-inventing one's self and consciously choosing what you will do with your life. When choices are made not out of naivete, but with the wisdom that can only be gathered through the oft difficult experiences of life.

I am vaguely aware that we have left Paris and the French countryside rolls on for as far as I can see filled with flowering fields of yellow gold Colza until the train pulls into a rural station in some small provincial town. The sign at the station reads *Paroy-en-Othe* and a few passengers gather up their belongings and depart. There on the platform is a little girl about eight or nine years old and she is holding the hands of her two little brothers . The smaller one can't be more than three. He is crying, too. The older boy must be five or six. He looks stoic and unmoved. I open the window to talk to the children but the window is sealed shut and will not open. I frantically try to get their attention. I need to tell them not to worry. I will send for them, but then the train pulls away and I know they haven't heard me. The children just stand on the platform bereft , heart-broken, and confused.

I wake up sobbing.

My heart hurts as the vision of the children is implanted in my memory.

A man entered my couchette sometime while I was sleeping. He is disturbed by my tears. He leans over and speaks to me in French. "*Ne pleure pas Madame. Ce n'était qu'un rêve, un mauvais rêve.*" He moves over beside me and hands me a freshly laundered handkerchief from the breast pocket of his blazer.

There must be a look of confusion on my face as I have no idea what he has just said.

"*Anglais?*" I ask.

"*Pardon Madame,* I thought you were French." He smiles gently before saying, "Do not cry, Madam. It was only a dream, a bad dream." He translates and takes my right hand as I wipe my tears on the handkerchief he has offered.

"I'm sorry. I'm missing my children. I just had a dream about them, only they were so much younger. They're all grown now but in my dream they were little children. They were sad and I couldn't get to them. I couldn't comfort them and it seemed so real."

He listens as I ramble on. This is the kind of thing Nash would have had no tolerance for, my prattling on about my dreams. And yet this man sits and listens as if what I'm saying interests him.

"I have children too. I'm headed to Geneva to visit my eldest son, Luc and his partner. I haven't seen them all summer and it's been too long."

I look down at the handkerchief in my hand. It is monogramed with the initials JMP. "Thank you for the use of your handkerchief," I say as I try to hand it back to him. I'm feeling a little embarrassed to return a used handkerchief.

"No, no. Keep it. I have plenty. *Ma mère* sends me a new box every Christmas. She always told me to carry a clean handkerchief in case a lady was in need."

"Your mother raised you right. I can see that."

He smiles. "Where are my manners? *Je suis Jean Paul Moreau.* And you are?"

I swallow hard before answering. "Kaye Hill."


And so it begins, I start my new life as Kaye Hill.

I chat with this delightful man and it isn't long before he's pouring out his story.

"I was born in French Algeria. *Ma mère* was French and *mon père* was Algerian. We moved to Paris when Algeria was granted its independence in 1962. I was just a small boy at the time. My earliest childhood memories are of Paris and still there are those who still consider me a foreigner. *C'est la vie.*"

If he came to Paris in 1962 as a young boy, then we must be about the same age. He wears it well as his hair is still mostly dark except for a little gray around the temples and in his beard. He is fit and I can't help but notice his beautiful brown skin, tanned by the sun and the warmth of his chocolate brown eyes.

As I listen to his story, his French sounds impeccable to me. Yet, there is an openness, a friendliness about him that is uncommon among the French. I can't help but wonder what telltale gestures or nuances will give me away as *not French* or *one who does not belong* before I even open my mouth to speak.

He pauses and I know it is my turn. This man, this gentleman, is expecting me to reciprocate and tell him my story. There is something sensitive and sensual about him. What is it about him that I am drawn to?

There are his manners, and the way he looks into my eyes.

He leans in to listen to what I have to say.

I want to trust him.

We will go our separate ways soon enough. What can it hurt?

So, for the next couple of hours as we travel on towards Geneva and with great trepidation I begin to weave together a story about who I am and why I am in Europe. I omit much of what has just happened. When I do open up I offer a sanitized version of life—divorced, three children and from Pennsylvania.

Is it a lie to say I'm from Pennsylvania rather than New York? After all, I was born in Pennsylvania.

I try to stay as close to the truth about my life and my family as I can. I fear if I don't that I will mix things up and be called out as a fraud and a liar should this whole delicately constructed tale begin to unravel before my very eyes.

# Chapter 44
## Kaye

I crawl beneath the sheets in yet another small European hotel. This time I'm just down the street from the USB Bank. Tomorrow I will go there and see what my dear sweet father has left for me to rebuild a life for myself.

I am exhausted from the day's journey and still my mind won't rest. Although it was well after ten by the time I had a late dinner and checked into the hotel, it is still only late afternoon in New York.

Lying there on the crisp white bed linens images and bits of conversation from the day play on and on in my head.

Jean Paul had asked me for my phone number before we said good-bye in the train station in Geneva.

"Perhaps we could rendezvous once you are settled in Provence," he'd suggested. I'd only given him a thumbnail sketch of where intended to land. Provence sprawls along the Mediterranean coastline in southeastern France. I dream of living in and among the rolling hills, the vineyards, and fields of lavender.

"I'm sorry," I confessed, "I do not have a phone."

He'd looked at me as if I had three heads.

"Really?"

Who doesn't have a cell phone in this day and age? Still I offered no further explanation. He only shrugged and asked no further questions as he handed me an ivory-colored business card embossed with gold lettering and his contact information.

"I do hope you will be in touch," he said before he leaned in to kiss me on both sides of my face before departing.

I stood there for a moment and watched him go. His son, Luc, and Luc's partner were there at the station to pick him up for what appeared to be a happy reunion.

Luc's partner is another man. I don't know why I'd assumed his partner would be a woman, but I did. I'd told him I had a daughter, Andrea, but spared any details about her complicated life. Perhaps because she's been gone so long now that I really don't know any of the details. When she was growing up there was so much that we just didn't talk about. Still, I've long suspected that Andrea may be a lesbian. Her persona, or at least the way she comes off to others, is significantly more masculine than Joey, not more so than Sammy but more than Joey. Joey is my sensitive child. Andrea has always been more direct and pragmatic. I don't know why I think of that as more masculine, maybe because her approach to life is so different from my own. And then there is Sammy, and he is his father's son. What did Nash used to say? "Sammy's a man's man. You just don't understand him." I don't know if I understand him or not. As difficult as it is to admit, there are times when I really do not like my own son. Even now as I lie in this bed on the other side of the world, I cringe when I think about how tough and demanding he can be with his own children.

Jean Paul didn't mention that his son was gay in the three hours we spent in conversation. Perhaps he didn't know how I would react to that. Andrea and I have never talked about her preferences perhaps because she doesn't know how I would react. I love my daughter, no matter what. She needs to know that.

Perhaps we never talk about it because of Nash. I always needed to protect her from her father.

I fear there are a lot of Nashes in the world.

I fear for my daughter's safety.

I fear I have failed my daughter as I let my own cowardice overtake my better judgment. In this moment, guilt threatens to overwhelm me.

Beginning again, I vow to step into my own beliefs about love and inclusion. I think about Ellery, Henri and

Claudette and how they have made this new beginning possible by opening their hearts to a stranger. No longer will I allow my fears to keep me from speaking my truth and doing what I know is right.

Unable to sleep, I get up from the bed and go to find that new phone I purchased in the train station. I need to call Ellery and let her know I've arrived. She will get in touch with Henri and make a call to Andrea. Andy knows how to keep a secret. I believe she has been keeping her own secrets for years. How many times over the years has she begged me to leave her father and take her with me? More than I can count. Once she was grown, even when I didn't have the backbone to leave, she did. She is far braver than I have ever been.

Is this true?

Maybe, at least until now.

I need to make this up to her.

Letting her know I am alive and safe is the first step. She will know what to do, how and when to tell the boys. Joey must be worried sick. I wonder if Sammy even knows I'm gone, or cares.

Nash will just want the money.

Good luck finding me.

I attempt to peel away the hard plastic packaging surrounding the cell phone. I can't wait any longer to let

Ellery and my family know I'm okay. Eventually, I resort to tearing open the hermetically sealed package with my teeth. Long gone are the days when you could carry manicure scissors, let alone a Swiss Army knife on the airplane. I remind myself to buy a pocket knife tomorrow before I leave Switzerland for the south of France. No doubt it will come in handy and may save my teeth.

But not now, again I must use my teeth to open the prepaid sim card. Once I place it in the phone, I must plug it in to be charged. I wait for it to charge while taking a minute to speak aloud the mnemonic Ellery had me memorize so I would remember her phone number:

"Edith has enough cash. How bad can Edith be?"

I count the words on my fingers. Nine.

Shit.

That can't be right. I count them again. Nine.

There are supposed to be ten.

Have I forgotten a word?

Damn.

Panic begins to set in. How could I be so stupid?

I take a deep breath and write the words down on paper.

"Edith has enough cash. How bad can Edith be?"

Still only nine.

I know this. I tell myself. I know this.

288

I lie back on the bed and say a simple prayer into the great unknown.

Help me. Please.

I write the words down on paper again. The phone lights up indicating it is fully active and I can make a call, if only I remember.

And then like a download from the great beyond. I remember.

I add in the missing word.

"Edith *always* has enough cash. How bad can Edith be?"

Ten words.

All ten are there.

I look at the numeric keypad on the phone and write the corresponding number directly over each of the words on the page-- 324-324-2232

I add a 1 for the international country code and dial the number.

Initially, I'm relieved when it begins to ring, but after the first ring it goes directly to voicemail.

"This is Ellery. You know what to do." And then there is that familiar long beep.

I pause a moment before speaking.

I had expected her to pick up. I'm caught a little off guard and uncertain what I should say.

"Uh..." I stammer and then begin again. "*Bonjour, mon amie. Je vais bien.*" And then my French fails me and I revert to my native tongue. "Please call me back once you get my message. Please."

I do not leave my number as it will be attached automatically to my voicemail message.

I terminate the call.

Holding the phone in my hand, I climb back into bed and pull the blanket up around me. I'm certain once she plays my message she will call right back.

But the phone is silent.

An hour passes and then another. Eventually, I fall asleep with the phone in my hand.

When I wake in the early morning hours, just as the sun peeks over the mountain, I see that the phone is dead.

Damn.

I'm certain I've missed her call, but perhaps she got mine.

I plug my phone back in and wait for it to charge.

# Chapter 45
## Joey

Sitting with Andy in the courtroom my heart aches for her,

I mean him. Dad can be so cruel. I know Andy has endured years of emotional abuse. She, I mean, *he* is so tough. Damn, there I go using the wrong pronoun again. This is going to take some time for me to get it right. Still, this morning was particularly rough.

We don't have to wait very long before the bailiff comes into the courtroom and announces that we are all to rise for the honorable Judge Fredericks. An older gentleman with a full head of silver hair in a black robe enters from a paneled door behind the judge's bench. He takes a seat while we stand and then he bangs the gavel announcing, "Court is in session."

With this Andy and I do as all the others do and take our seats.

"Bailiff, call the first case," the judge announces as he probably has done many, many times before.

"State of New York vs Ellery McMasters."

A man in uniform walks an elderly woman in an orange jumpsuit into the courtroom. She is tall, with short white hair and her hands are handcuffed behind her back. The officer walks her to the center lectern where a young woman in a navy blue suit stands.

"Do you think that's her?" I whisper to Andy behind the cover of my hand.

He shrugs his shoulders indicating he doesn't know any more than I do.

The woman in the blue suit says, "We waive the reading of the charges."

The judge asks, "Ms. McMasters, do you understand the charges which have been brought against you?"

Andy nudges me and nods. I read his lips. "That's her."

The woman in the orange jumpsuit says, "Yes, your Honor." Her voice is coarse and low but loud enough to be heard throughout the courtroom. She's no shrinking violet. Could she really have killed my mother? Something within me isn't convinced. I don't know why, but somehow I think if my mother had been murdered that I would know it. I would feel it and I don't. I can't explain it, maybe it's just my intuition. Or maybe I'm just crazy.

The judge nods. "And how do you plead?"

"Not guilty, your Honor." Again her voice is clear and strong.

"So noted," he says before dropping his head to his notes before he turns in the direction of the prosecutor. "Am I to understand you do not have a body, just a missing woman?"

The prosecutor stands, "Yes, your Honor, but we believe we have more than enough evidence to try this case and secure a conviction."

"You will need to convince the Grand Jury of the merits of your case, Mr. Stone."

The defendant turns and whispers something to her attorney. The woman in the blue suit looks exasperated but nods to her client and says, "Judge, my client is requesting to be released on her own recognizance as she has no prior convictions and has lived in the community for the last forty years."

The prosecutor jumps to his feet. "Judge, could you remind Ms. O'Riordan that this is a murder case? To release this woman on her own recognizance is simply ridiculous. Do you intend to help her get rid of the body, too?"

"That is quite enough, Mr. Stone. I'm sorry, Ms. O'Riordan, the prosecutor has a point. Your client is facing serious charges. Bail is denied. The defendant is remanded into custody until she stands trial."

The judge lowers his gavel with a bang and turns to the clerk, "Next case."

With that the handcuffed woman is led away by the same officer who brought her in. As she leaves the courtroom, a large mountain of a man stands and calls out to her, "Stay strong, Ellery. I'll get this sorted out."

She pauses momentarily and looks him in the eye and shakes her head, "No, Henri, just no. Please. Just take care of Skye." She sounded so resolute when she was speaking in court but now she pleads with this man and sounds absolutely dejected.

It isn't until we've left the courtroom and are back in the car that I replay the whole interaction over and over again. What did he mean, "I've got this?" I ask Andy.

"Who?"

"The big guy with the white beard. The one who looks like Santa Claus or a lumberjack."

"I don't know who you're talking about?"

"Didn't you hear her? She called him *Henri*. Unusual name for these parts, he sounded French or something. Maybe Quebecois? And who is Skye?"

Andy turns his face back to the road, but I can't let this go.

"Even the judge seemed to think it was a stretch to charge someone with murder when they don't have a body." Andy and I had come here hoping to hear what evidence they had tying this woman to our mother. "We still don't have any more information than we had before."

"I can't help but feel this is one of those, all too frequent, examples of shoddy police work and a rush to judgment," Andy says as he runs his hand through what remains of his hair. He's had it cut into a fade and it suits him.

"I agree with you. I just can't believe Mom's dead. I think I would know if she were."

"It's strange you would say that, because I was just thinking the same thing. Maybe we just don't want to believe it's true," Andy says as he pulls up to the stoplight.

"I won't believe it until they find her body. Until then, I'm holding onto hope."

"Want to grab some lunch?" Andy asks.

"You mean before we head back to my house and the three-ring circus that awaits us there?"

Andy just smiles.

"Absolutely, I need some quiet to process everything that has gone on this morning."

"And we need to figure out what we are going to do now."

# Chapter 46
## Henri

I stand there watching as Ellery disappears from the courtroom. I have never felt so helpless in all my life. She has been my dearest friend since childhood. This cannot be happening, not to this good woman who has never hurt another living soul in her entire life. The look on her face before they took her away is burned into my memory. She has always been so brave and now she is afraid. I begged her to stay strong and told her I would get this sorted and still, her last words ring in my ears.

*'No, Henri, just no. Please. Just take care of Skye.'*

By the time I make my way back to my truck I am shaking with rage at the injustice of it all. How can she be charged with the murder of a woman who chose to disappear from an abusive husband and a life that did not serve her. Since when is that against the law? There is no evidence that a murder has been committed. They do not even have a body.

Sitting in my truck my mind shifts to Kaye and I am overwhelmed with feelings of tenderness for her. I find myself fantasizing about her and the new life she will create in the South of France. I have the audacity to imagine myself accompanying her there ... holding her hand as we walk up a country lane amidst the vineyards heavily laden with ripening fruit or sitting in a sidewalk café enjoying a cappuccino in the morning sun. I shake my head and chastise myself for such foolishness. What would a woman like Kaye see in an old goat like me?

Then these images fade as quickly as they'd appeared only to be replaced by visions of my dearest friend, Ellery, locked up in some god awful women's prison in that orange jumpsuit. Her eyes are wild with fear, much like they were just moments ago in the courtroom.

Although, I don't really know her, if Kaye is anything like the woman I've imagined her to be, she would never allow this injustice to take place. I know she wouldn't.

It is in this moment that I know I have to find her. She is Ellery's only hope.

Pulling out of the parking lot, I turn north towards the little town of Speculator. I promised Ellery I would look after Skye. I have some serious thinking to do. Right now, I don't know how I will take care of her pup *and* take off to Europe to look for Kaye but I'm not going to worry about that now. This is a solvable problem. It is only a minor obstacle I tell myself, trying to convince myself that it is true.

I spend the rest of the drive up into the Adirondacks attempting to concoct some kind of a plan.

It's only early August and already I can see how a few of the maples are beginning to turn. There are leaves trimmed in shades of red and yellow dotting the evergreen mountainside. The autumn is so beautiful up here in the north country. I wonder what autumn is like in the south of France.

My mind drifts back towards Kaye and the mission that awaits me. I try to recall my conversation with her when we were on board the Été Lune. My memory is spotty about where she said she was headed. What is wrong with me, it was only a few days ago? I shouldn't have brought the wine. Still, it added to the intimacy and perhaps the reason I feel so connected to this elusive woman who has disappeared under the cover of darkness.

Somehow I know she was headed to Provence, although I can't recall the conversation. Perhaps she told this to Ellery and Ellery relayed it to me. But Provence is a large region and I do not know the city or village. I fear this may become something like searching for a needle in a haystack, as they say. Still, I will need to try. Kaye is a beautiful woman and an American with limited French. She will have difficulty passing unnoticed among the provincial people.

When I pull into the convenience store in Speculator I can hear Skye barking in the back room. My eyes are drawn to a rack holding the local paper, *The Hamilton County Express*. There on the front page is a photograph of the woman I know as Kaye. The headline reads: *Woman Missing from the Sacandaga Campgrounds* and below that the next line reads *Local Woman Charged with her Murder*. I pick up a copy of the paper and head inside and approach the counter.

"Just the paper?" the man behind the counter asks.

"I'm looking for Patrick Duffy," I respond.

"Well, you've found him," he says as he looks me up and down.

"My name is Henri Pelletier. I'm here to pick up Ellery's pup, Skye."

He does not smile but holds my gaze. "How do you know Ellery?" he asks.

"We've been friends since we were children," I say then, fearing perhaps I have said too much. I don't know this man and I don't want anything I say to come back on Ellery or on me.

He simply nods and to my great relief he doesn't pursue this any further. Instead he says, "Then you know that she could never have done what they're accusing her of."

"Oui, she doesn't have it in her to hurt anyone."

"I've trusted that woman with my dogs. They love her and I trust their judgment. They'd growl and take the leg off of someone capable of that kind of evil. She didn't do it."

"Yes sir, we agree on that."

With this Skye begins to bark again.

"She's not used to being penned in. She's been Ellery's constant companion. Ellery takes her everywhere. Skye's always in her truck sitting up front in the cab with her head out the window. You should've heard her cryin' and carryin' on last night. Won't eat. Poor little thing is missin' Ellery."

"I was just up at the courthouse. I promised Ellery I'd look after Skye until we get this sorted out."

"So be it. You tell Ellery, Alice and I aren't buying a word this bullshit. We know she didn't do it and we'll see her soon."

"Will do," I say and yet, I don't know if I will be able to communicate with her about anything while she is incarcerated.

Patrick walks back to the store room and brings the little white dog out on a leash. I bend down to pick her up and she immediately begins to lick my face.

Patrick begins to laugh, "I guess you're okay, dogs are a good judge of character. If you're okay with Skye, then you're okay with me."

"How much do I owe you for the paper?" I ask as the little dog wiggles in my arms.

"Nothin'. It's on me. Give Ellery our best," he says as another customer gets in line behind me and I make my way out the door with Skye.

Skye cozies up on my lap as I start up the truck. I take a moment to program the GPS on my phone to find the route home.

Before we head that way I take a moment to look at the newspaper. The caption below the photograph gives Kaye's other name— Amy Elizabeth Cooper. The photo looks something like the woman I know as Kaye but a younger version. This picture must have been taken at a wedding or another special event as she is all dressed up and has had her hair done. This is a godsend, I will take it with me to the south of France. Maybe someone will remember seeing her.

She is unforgettable.

At least to me she is.

# Chapter 47
## Kaye

I can't sleep. I roll over again and take a look at the clock.

It's half past two and I've been awake for hours. I can't shake the feeling that something is dreadfully wrong.

I get out of bed and check that I still have my old passport, my US passport. It's zipped into the inside pocket of my handbag. I pull it out and look at it. It is issued in my old name, my married name— Amy Elizabeth Cooper. I'll need to present it at the bank in the morning.

I put it back inside my purse and zip the pocket closed before climbing back into bed.

I really have no idea what to expect as I don't know anything about what's involved when someone attempts to access a Swiss bank account. My imagination is off and running as I ruminate on everything that could possibly go wrong. My list of worries is mounting.

Has someone informed the bank that I am missing?

Will they be on the lookout for me?

I doubt it.

My father was successful in his business.  He and mother lived a life of privilege. There were expensive cars, a membership to the country club, and summer vacations in Europe. My parents even funded my children's college education when Nash neglected to save and provide. But Dad was adamant, he would not be leaving anything to Nash, that's why he set up this account for me.

But I have no idea how much money that might be.

Dad begged me not to marry Nash, even when I was already pregnant with Andrea. He made no secret about how he felt about my husband.

I've read about people where their parental estates have been unequally distributed between the siblings. It has crossed my mind more than once that he may have left the lion's share of his wealth to Douglas.

Maybe Dad was expecting Douglas to look after my interests and manage my share of the inheritance.

Maybe Douglas will give me an allowance as if I am a child.

What if Dad left it all to Douglas?

How will I support myself?

I've never held a real job.

Nash wouldn't stand for it.

If I had my own money, Nash would've lost control of me long ago.

I was too impetuous.

I chastise myself again for poor planning.

I should have thought this through.

I drift off to a fitful sleep filled with angst only to wake a few hours later to the sound of the alarm on my new phone.

My eyes spring open as I struggle to turn it off the offending sound.

It takes me a moment to figure out just where I am.

I'm still exhausted. Images from my dreams linger.

I was wearing a dark apron that was covered with flour.

I was working in a French bakery making baguettes.

I have no agency over my life.

Another nasty man was threatening me and making rude sexual innuendos.

He was my boss at the bakery.

I take a few deep breaths.

I pray this was only a dream, and not some kind of premonition about what my future holds.

I shower and dress before heading down for breakfast. Although I'm still tired from a poor night's sleep, I decide to forgo the coffee. I'm anxious enough without it.

~ ~ ~

Carrying all my worldly possessions, a new bank card, and enough euros to last me for a while, I leave the United Bank of Switzerland in Geneva with a smile on my face and a sense of joy that radiates from my whole being. I feel like skipping, but I am still much too reserved for that. This whole thing has gone off without a hitch. My father has left me a very wealthy woman. The banker acted like this is the kind of thing he handles every day, like it was no big deal. But it is a very big deal to me. I've gone from feeling hopeless and stuck to feeling an immense amount of gratitude and freedom. Now, I'm free to do whatever I want. How could my fortune have changed so much in a few short days? My father's voice rings loud and clear in the recesses of my memory, *"You can leave anytime you want to, just say the word and I will help you."* I guess I just wasn't ready until now. But now what?

I should call Andy. She will never betray me to her father. I just need to let her know that I'm okay. She worries about me; she's worried about me her whole life. I'm sure Ellery has called her by now, still, I'd like to hear her voice and let her know I've finally done it and that I'm going to be just fine.

I walk across the street to the *Parc de Beaulieu* and wander the tree-lined sidewalks while relishing my good fortune before taking a seat on one of the benches. The gardens overflow with color as the summer annuals are all in full bloom. There are beautiful beds filled with multicolored zinnia, geranium, cosmos, daisy, black-eyed Susan, petunia, and begonia. For a moment, I miss my own garden which I so carefully tended throughout the years. I shake off these memories. I won't indulge them now. Although the day is still warming up, I know that autumn comes quickly in the mountains. There are probably only a few weeks left of summer or at least until the evening temperature falls below freezing and the frost kills the flowers. A gentle reminder to enjoy the day, yet plan for the future.

I remove my new phone from my bag and think again about calling Andy. I used to have everyone's phone number memorized, but that was decades ago, before cell phones. All our relevant data is now stored so we no longer are burdened with the task of remembering. I don't even know my own daughter's phone number or anyone else's for that matter. I open up the Google App and search for the name of the law firm Andy works for in Denver. I guess this is what they mean by a world wide web. Using the tip of my finger, I click on the link and the phone responds by asking if I want to call the number. In no time at all someone answers.

"The Law Offices of Prescott, Evelyn, and Conrad. This is Michelle. How may I help you?"

"Ah..." I hadn't thought this through. "May I speak with Andy Cooper, please?"

"I'm sorry but Andy isn't in today. He won't be back in the office this week. Would you like me to put you through to his voicemail? He calls in and is picking up his messages while out of town."

Did this woman just say *he?*

"I'm sorry, but I'm looking for Andrea Cooper."

The receptionist lets out a sigh of exasperation. I can almost see her rolling her eyes at me. "He goes by Andy, now. Would you like to leave a message?" Her tone is snarky and I know she is annoyed with me, but again she has referred to my daughter as *he*.

"No, that's okay. Do you know when Andy is expected to be back?"

"I'm sorry. I don't know. He was called away suddenly for a family emergency."

Oh God. The silence hangs across the phone line. I don't know what to say now.

307

"Ma'am?" The receptionist waits for me to say something.

I just hang up.

He.

That pronoun again. Does that woman even know Andy?

A family emergency.

What in the world is going on?

Is Andy in New York because of me?

Of course she is.

Does she know I've finally left her father?

Why didn't I tell her?

Damn it. This whole thing is so unsettling.

I get up and walk around the gardens as I try to decide what to do next.

I press the numbers corresponding to the mnemonic I'd memorized for Ellery's phone number. The call goes directly to her voicemail.

"This is Ellery, you know what to do."

"I'm okay. This is my new number. I need you to call me back. Please..."

Damn, why isn't she picking up? Maybe her phone is off. Maybe the battery is dead.

Now what?

I take another walk around the perimeter of the park before deciding there is no sense waiting around. I've been waiting my whole adult life for this moment, and I have no intention of wasting any more time. I leave the park and hail a cab.

Speaking neither Swiss nor German, I attempt to communicate with the cabbie in English. "The train station, please." I catch his eye in the rearview mirror and he smiles and nods.

It takes only a few minutes and we arrive. I pay the driver in cash and head into the station. Now what? Where am I going?

Looking up at the departure board, I see there is a train leaving in fifty minutes for Marseille.

I have wanted to live in the south of France for so long, somewhere in Provence, but where exactly?

With no place to sit I lean against a wall and open Google Maps on my phone to be certain I have this right. It is then and there that I decide Marseille is probably a good place to start. The town of Martigues is nearby, only about an hour away. Martigues is about half the size of Marseille and somehow I think that might suit me better. I don't know why, but I think I'll be less conspicuous in a smaller town. Researching a little more I quickly learn they call Martigues the Venice of France as it has a series of canals connecting the Mediterranean Sea to an inland body of water known as the Berry Pond. Although I've not been there, I've seen the pictures and it looks charming.

Perhaps I can find a bed and breakfast or a small inn in Marseille for tonight and head into Martigues in the morning and look for someplace to rent if it suits me.

I take a deep breath as the magnitude of starting over where I don't know a soul begins to seep in and threatens to overwhelm me. I tell myself to let it go. This is what I've been waiting for. Staying with Nash was not an option as that man was clearly intent on continuing to exert his will over me and dominating me for the remainder of my life. Why in the world should I be having second thoughts about leaving now?

I activate my new bank card and then wait in line to purchase the ticket at the kiosk.

I don't know where the day has gone as it dawns on me that I haven't eaten much today and I'm starting to get hungry. So, before heading towards security and onto the platform to await my train, I head to a deli counter and purchase a chicken wrap with cucumber and pesto to take with me.

If all goes well, I should be in Marseille before midnight.

# Chapter 48
## Nash

The afternoon sun beats down into my bedroom as I lay on my bed dripping in my own sweat. I roll over to look at the clock. Holy crap it's already half past four. I rub my eyes in disbelief as I try to come to terms with why I'm sleeping in the afternoon. Shadowy images from the last few days begin to take shape in my memory— Amy, searching for her in the rain, barking dogs, the interrogation, being locked up in a jail cell— and Andrea.

Oh fuck.

I drag my ass out of bed and into the bathroom. It smells of vomit. Shit— was I that sick? I flush the toilet and turn on the shower. The taste of bile fills my mouth and I'm afraid I may barf again.

How could she? How could she have turned herself into a ... I don't know what she is now. She's not a man, for god's sake she's a freak. That's what she is, a god damn freak of nature. I suppose she always has been.

I spit into the toilet and take a deep breath. I don't want to deal with this, any of this. I grab my toothbrush and put on an extra-large glob of toothpaste to try and rid myself of this vile taste in my mouth. If only cleaning up the rest of my life could be so easy.

The steam from the shower fills the bathroom. I nearly scald myself as I step into the shower and quickly turn the temperature down. I really need to get someone out here to fix this. One moment I'm burning myself and the next minute the water is ice cold. I barely moved the goddamn handle and now I'm freezing. I turn the handle back and I can already feel the temperature changing. I grab the body wash that Amy has left sitting in the corner of the shower. I breathe it in. It smells like flowers. It smells like her. I rinse it off. That's all I need, to be smelling like my dead wife. I grab my shampoo and wash my hair. By the time I finish all the hot water is gone. The towel I used yesterday is still damp on the bathroom floor. I use it to dry my face and my hair. Ugh. The towel smells a little like mildew or something. I step from the shower and take a good look around the bathroom, how did this place become such a shit show in only a few days? I guess I'll need to find someone to clean this place up or hire someone.

There was a time when fathers could rely on their daughters to step up and take their mother's place. My sister did when Mom died but Andrea has never been like that and it certainly isn't now. Andrea was never like Amy, or any woman I've ever known for that matter. I wouldn't want Andrea living here even if she was willing. I just don't. Still, I'm not sure how I'll manage now that Amy's gone.

By the time I've showered and shaved it is after five. I do a quick calculation and figure out it's only two on the west coast. Amy's brother, Douglas, should still be at his hoity-toity office in Silicon Valley. I dread calling that prick. The last time I spoke with him he threatened me and told me I wasn't gettin' any of their old man's money.

God damnit, Amy and I were married for almost forty years. That has to count for something.

Maybe I should call a lawyer. Dealing with lawyers can cost a small fortune and I still might not get any money.

It's not too early for a drink. It's already after five. I'm going to need some fortitude if I'm going to deal with *The Duchess*. Amy always hated it when I called her brother that. Neither of them could ever take a joke.

I go to the liquor cabinet. What happened to those two handles of Jack I bought for the camping trip? Oh well, they're not here. So, instead I opt for a hefty pour of Wild Turkey 101 on the rocks.

Here goes nothing. I find *The Duchess* listed under contacts on my cell phone and before I can change my mind I'm calling my brother-in-law.

Some sweet young thing picks up on the third ring. "Tech Net, may I help you?"

"May I speak with Doug Watson?"

"Who may I say is calling?" she asks.

Shit. I should have thought this through. He'll never pick up if he knows it's me. So, instead of giving this young woman my real name I say, "Tell him it's Detective Randall from the New York State Missing Persons Unit."

"One moment please."

I wait on hold for what seems like ten minutes. I'm surprised *The Duchess* would keep the chief investigator in his sister's murder waiting but I guess cops don't get much respect these days either.

At last someone comes back to the phone, "Nice try asshole. Have you ever heard of caller ID? Welcome to the technological revolution."

"Sorry, Douglas. I just wasn't sure you'd take my call. The last message you left me wasn't exactly friendly."

"You're right. I almost didn't take your call. I'm not feeling the least bit friendly towards you. And why should I after the way you've treated my sister and even your own child, you misogynistic bastard."

314

I swallow hard as I try to think of how to continue.

"Look Doug, in spite of what you may believe about your sister's disappearance, I had nothing to do with it. As you may or may not know, they charged an old woman with Amy's murder, a lesbo dyke really. The case is set to go to trial."

"I'm well aware of this. But I don't believe for one minute that you are innocent of any wrongdoing. You made my sister's life a living hell for years to say nothing of the way you treated Andy."

"What you think of me as a husband or a father is not really the issue here. Amy was my wife for almost forty years, and I am going to need some information from you. I know you managed some of Amy's assets. I'm going to need account numbers and access to those accounts so I can settle her estate."

"Really Nash." He waits and I can almost hear him fuming on the other end of the line. "This is outrageous, even for you. Are you really going to attempt to settle her estate and confiscate her assets before her body has been found, before you inform your eldest son that his mother is missing and is presumed to be dead, before you have planned a funeral or memorial service to honor her, and comfort those who grieve? Unless you have taken out a life insurance policy on your wife, you will not be seeing one

315

thin dime of my sister's money as you are not a named beneficiary on her trust. She saw to that years ago and any money she may have inherited from our father was left to her alone in a Swiss Bank account which you will never access. So, as I've said before, Father and I were on to you. You'll have to make do with anything you've managed to squirrel away on your own. Amy always said you probably still had your first communion money. Given how stingy and cheap you were with Amy and your children, I'm sure you'll be okay."

And with that the phone goes dead.

I slam my fist down on the kitchen table and the bourbon splashes out of my glass.

My first communion money? What was she talkin' about? I'm not even Catholic.

What else did that bitch say about me?

I toss back what remains of my drink and then pour myself another before going to change my clothes.

I'm going out tonight. Maybe I'll head over to Dozers in Saratoga Springs.

A couple of drinks, a little live music, and the company of some lonely, lovely ladies might do me a world of good.

This poor old widower might have some fun tonight after all.

# Chapter 49
## Henri

"What am I going to do with you?" I look down at Ellery's little white dog who is snuggled up on my lap as we make our way down the highway. "How in the world can I take you with me to Europe to look for the elusive Kaye Hill?" I need to think this through. I pet Skye's little head as she looks up at me with what I read as concern. No doubt she is as worried about Ellery as I am. Perhaps she is worried about her own future, too. Poor little thing, she's just spent the last few days locked in the storage room of a convenience store. I wonder how she'll like spending her days on a fishing boat. "What do you think about that, my little friend?" Skye wags her tail like she knows what I'm talking about before she settles back down to sleep on my lap.

Tying myself up in the details of my current predicament, I decide to call Claudette. Not that she is likely to offer me the comfort or kindness I sorely need, but the woman is decisive and she's known for her clear thinking. Maybe she'll help me cut through this quagmire I find myself stuck in. Maybe Kaye told her where she was going on the drive to the airport in Montreal. Maybe, just maybe, she'll know what I should do.

The phone rings and rings and I fear Claudette is monitoring her calls and has no intention of picking up. How could I blame her? Every time Ellery or I call her we always need something from her. This time is no different.

Just when I'm ready to give up, someone answers.

"*Allo?*"

"Claudette?"

"*Oui.*"

"Sorry, it didn't sound like you. It's Henri."

"*Oui*, I know. What do you need from me now?"

I take a deep breath. Claudette isn't just direct but she is surly, too. I look over at the newspaper folded on the dashboard. I can still read part of the headline—"Local Woman Charged with Murder."

"Have you been following the papers?"

"Which paper?" she asks.

"Sorry, stupid question. Ellery has been charged with Kaye's murder and has been taken into custody. It was the lead story in the local paper, the *Hamilton Gazette.*"

"Where are you?"

"I'm up in the Adirondacks, in New York. I came to see Ellery and pick up her little dog."

"You need to hang up now. Don't call me again. You understand, her neck isn't the only one on the line."

"Ellery won't talk. You know her."

"Just meet me at the marina. When can you be there?"

"I'm almost in Vermont, so I'm at least an hour away."

"I'm leaving now. Just get there, Henri."

"Okay."

"And for the love of God, don't be off chasing rainbows. Just get there."

The line goes dead.

I should have figured that Claudette's major concern would be for herself, and not for Ellery, and certainly not for Kaye. I hope involving Claudette wasn't a mistake.

There isn't much traffic as I head for the border. I make good time, arriving just after eight and the last few minutes of daylight creates a rosy glow on the horizon as I approach the Canadian border control.

"Passport?" the border control agent commands.

I hand it to him and he scrutinizes it carefully before scanning the barcode.

"You entered the US early this morning?"

I nod and say, "Yes sir."

"What was the purpose of your visit?"

"I needed to pick up this little dog." Skye climbs onto my lap and sticks her head out the window at the agent to say hello.

"Do you have his vaccination records?"

Oh *merde*. I hadn't thought of this. "I am sorry sir, I do not. I am doing a favor for a friend who cannot take care of her beloved dog at this time. I am certain the dog is fully vaccinated. She treats this little pup as if she were her own child."

The guard smiles at me for the first time in this entire encounter.

"She's lucky to have you for a friend, as is this pup. Go on." He waves me through and I breathe a sigh of relief as I head for home and the marina. I'm not sure the US border patrol would have been so understanding.

By the time I've reached the marina, the sky is dark on this moonless night. The place is nearly deserted except for a couple of yahoos drinking and carrying on aboard one of the boats tied to a mooring. Still, Skye appears apprehensive as we walk down the dock to the slip with the Été Lune. She sits down refusing to go any farther until I bend down to pick her up. Carrying her, the poor little dear quivers in my arms. So many changes in the last few days. I can't help but wonder how Ellery is faring in prison, and Kaye in France. Did she even get there? Wherever *there* might be.

There is a light on in the cabin on my boat. Claudette must be here already. No sooner do I step onto the deck does the door to the cabin swing open and Skye begins to growl as if she intends to protect me from whomever is inside.

Before even saying hello, Claudette begins barking out orders as if she is the captain of this vessel instead of an intruder.

"You brought the dog?" she snarls.

"I told you, I promised Ellery I would take care of Skye."

"Well keep it away from me. I don't want to get dog hair on my new dress."

Claudette looks like she has dressed to go out on the town. "Thank you for coming. It looks like you had plans this evening."

"Never mind, I can reschedule for another time. I pulled up a couple of articles about the American woman, what's her name?" She turns to an open page on her laptop and answers her own question. "Amy Cooper."

"Yes, that's her name."

"I don't know how they can charge Ellery with her murder when they do not have a body. The United States," she says with disgust. "Cannot a woman just disappear if she wants to? Why is someone always at fault?"

I know better than to answer as Claudette realizes what she has just said.

"My situation was different, human trafficking. This is not the same."

"Perhaps they don't know that. Either way, Ellery will be convicted if we cannot find Kaye so she can present herself and exonerate our friend. Did Kaye tell you where she was planning to go? All I know is she was planning to head to Provence."

"Let me think, we didn't talk about much. I only spoke with her in French, and her French was piss poor at best. I figured the less I knew about her the better."

I should never have involved Claudette. I take a seat at the table and fold my hands. "She traveled in France as a young woman, perhaps she will go back to the area she knows."

"*Oh Mon Dieu*, Henri. That was when she was at University and what is she now, over sixty? The world has changed and so has she. *C'est impossible.* This is a fool's errand like going on a wild goose chase."

"Still, I must go and see if I can find her."

"Do you think Ellery will talk? Give us up? I know you said no, still when facing a murder conviction and life in prison, who knows what she will say to save her own skin?"

"I don't think she will betray us, but neither will I allow her to take the blame for something she is incapable of doing. My only concern is what will I do with Skye while I look for Kaye?"

"Take the little beast with you. He's small. People fly with their animals all the time now. I can get him a little service vest, one for an emotional support animal."

"She..."

"Whatever."

"Hmm, I didn't know you could do that. I haven't flown anywhere in ages."

"The world has changed. About time you get with the program."

She turns her face back to her laptop and starts typing away while I take a moment to think about how in the world I might find Kaye and where I should begin to look.

"There is a flight Wednesday out of Montreal. I think you should be on it. Will that give you enough time to get your affairs in order? Do you have your passport?"

I nod my head and Claudette gives me a look. She is irritated and impatient.

"I'll need your name as it appears on your passport, if I am going to book this ticket."

I reach into my back pocket and retrieve my passport as I'd just used it at the border to cross back into Canada.

I extend it towards her and she snatches it from my hand.

"Let me get my credit card." I reach into my pocket for my wallet.

"No, I've got this. You are doing this to save *all* of us, in the last ten years I have built a life for myself. It's a life I like and I intend to keep it. Covering your expenses while you find a way to get us out of this mess is the least I can do. You and Ellery saved me once, it's time for me to repay the debt. Ellery needs us. You are doing the hard part. Go find that woman. I'll pick you up Wednesday evening at seven, little beast and all. Be ready."

She hands me my passport and I open the storage box beneath the settee and pull out my old lockbox. I fiddle with the lock, my combination is the year of my birth. Hardly secure, but there it is. I put my passport inside, right on top. I'm going to need it again soon.

Claudette stands to go.

"I'll need to bring vaccination records for Skye with me." The little dog jumps up on my leg at the mention of her name. "I was just asked for them by the Canadian border patrol."

"No problem, that's an easy one, I know someone who owes me a favor."

Of course she does. Again, I nod and with that she is up and gone without saying goodbye.

The sound of her high heels click along the dock and then grow faint and disappear as she heads towards the parking lot to retrieve her car.

# Chapter 50
## Kaye

I find my seat on the train and am relieved that no one is sitting next to me, at least so far. What little I am carrying is easily stowed in the overhead rack before I settle in. I am seated next to the window and it isn't long before the train pulls out of the station and I can see the snow-capped mountains in the distance. The sun is beginning to set and the western sky is already a beautiful pink and gold. Perhaps this is another sign that something wonderful awaits me. There is one beautiful vista after another and I am mesmerized by the grandeur of the Alps.

It doesn't last for long. The train enters one tunnel after another encasing all the travelers in darkness for what seems like a long time. A chill envelopes me and a shiver runs up my spine, a whooshing sound vibrates on my ear drums. I travel headlong into the unknown.

Tunnels and beautiful mountain vistas mark the early part of my journey from Geneva to Marseille. I take my phone from my bag and attempt to take a couple of photographs through the window of the train. I've never had an iPhone before. Nash always said they were too expensive. Too expensive for me, but not for him. Besides, he thought I didn't need one since all I ever did was "sit on my ass at home." I heard him say that so many times. I can almost hear his voice as the words ring out even now.

I shake my head in an attempt to dispel all memories of him. It's taken me so long to leave him, I'm not going to allow him to take up any more of my head space and spoil this for me.

I check the pictures I've taken. Most are a little blurry, but a couple of them are pretty good. The blurring of the colors makes them look like some kind of impressionistic painting. Maybe I can use one or two of them as a reference photo and learn to paint. I haven't painted since I was in college. I used to be okay, not great but okay. I never really devoted myself to the task and learned how to paint, still I always liked painting. Maybe I could give it another try. What else am I going to do now that I'm on my own?

I start to indulge the fantasy of living in Martigues as I imagine myself painting beside the canals, going to the beach on the Mediterranean, or enjoying a glass of wine in a sidewalk café. Eventually, I allow the sound of the train moving me closer to my new home to lull me off to sleep— click-click-click.

I wake in a panic. I'm unable to determine where I am or why. It takes me a moment to reorient myself. My breathing slows as I regain my composure. What had I been dreaming? And then I know what has been vying for my attention for so long. I've been so wrapped up in the daily drama of my own life that I've failed to put the pieces together until now. My only daughter, Andrea, is living as a man. Why has it taken me so long to see the obvious? Is this why she hasn't been home in over two years? The receptionist at the law firm called her Andy, and referred to her as *he* and *him*. Maybe I could have helped her... him. Whatever. It doesn't matter, she will always be my child and I love her... him.

I need to let her know that.

This pronoun thing is going to be hard for me. Maybe if I *see* Andy living her life as a man it will be easier for me to think of her as a man. Oh god, if I am having this much difficulty just thinking of my daughter as a man, I can only imagine how hard it must be for her to change her gender. Or am I just extrapolating my own feelings onto her, maybe it feels good, maybe even wonderful, to finally be living in a gender that feels like it fits who she has always been. Why has it taken *me* so long to see what has been right before me? f

328

I think about calling her office again, but there is no privacy here. More passengers boarded while we were stopped in Lyon and I was asleep. Now a woman sits across the aisle. She turns and looks over at me, but does not smile. For Andy's sake as well as mine, this is not the kind of conversation I want to have where someone might be eavesdropping.

I decide to send Andy an email. I need to let her know that I'm alive and well. I need to apologize for letting her go through this transition all alone. How could I ...?

A voice in my head begins to play the litany of all my faults and failings. God knows I've heard them all before. As if I need a reminder of how inept I am, Nash was always there to enumerate my flaws. I can still hear his voice,

"What kind of a mother are you?"

"You always ..."

"You never ..."

I fumble around on my phone until I figure out how to set up an email account.

I type in my new name, Kaye Hill.

I am no longer Amy Cooper. All those things that Nash said about me no longer apply. I am no longer Amy

329

Cooper. I am remaking myself and my life. Perhaps Andy and I are not so different.

My thumbs are too big for the tiny key pad on the phone. I have to start over multiple times and with each attempt to get this right my frustration mounts. At last, I am satisfied. My email address is KayeHill65@post.com. I tried multiple variations of my new name before I was able to come up with one that wasn't being used by someone else. It didn't work until I decided to add the number 65. My birthday is rapidly approaching and I want to honor myself and my courage. I will soon be in my sixth-fifth year of my life. This is the year of my rebirth. This is the year I will reclaim my life and begin again.

It takes me about an hour to finish the letter to Andy as I try to get clear on what I want to tell her. Just before hitting the send button I decide to delete the subject line. I know she had a secretary or someone who screened her calls, but does this person open her email too?

No wait! That's old school and no longer politically correct. Andy has had a variety of personal assistants since she's worked at Prescott, Evelyn, and Conrad. I leave the subject line blank and hit send. Immediately, a prompt appears saying *Empty Subject* and asks if I want to send this email anyway. I take another moment to think about this.

Just to be safe, what if someone other than Andy is looking at her email.

This message is private, just between Andy and me. I don't want to expose her as *trans* in case I'm wrong or in case they don't know.

I tap on the "yes" button and confirm. The email is sent from my phone.

By now the sun has set and the train is dark except for a few overhead reading lights shining down and the glow of cellular phones. Using my phone I book myself a hotel in Marseille on Hotels.com. I congratulate myself for joining the twenty-first century. Maybe I'm not as stupid as Nash always said. Feeling satisfied, I turn off my phone to save the battery before sitting back and closing my eyes. It's been a busy day.

# Chapter 51
## Andy

Once we get back to Joey's, I head into the guest room to pack. They haven't found her body so we can't have a funeral for Mom. We could have a memorial service. What do they call those? A celebration of life— but I don't feel the least bit like celebrating. I feel cheated and robbed of the only person who has always loved me.

I need to leave New York and head back to Denver before Sam gets back in town. Sammy and Pop are cut from the same cloth, poor bastards. They always have been. It must suck to be so narrow-minded and self-righteous. I've dealt with enough of their bullshit to last me a lifetime. This last go round with Dad has left me feeling raw and vulnerable. I'm still having a hard time believing Mom is gone. I could kick myself for not getting back here sooner to let her know I've transitioned and I'm happy.

At least I was before all of this.

I could kick myself for not being here for her.

I need to get home.

I need to get back to feeling like myself again. Joey understands. Today was almost as hard on him as it was on me. He spent most of the afternoon beating himself up for not standing up to Pop, and allowing dear old Dad to talk to me like he did.

Whatever. I'd hoped Pop would come around but I can't see that happening anytime in this lifetime.

Joey has offered to deal with Sam. We finally got through to him on the phone on the way back from the courthouse. When we told him about Mom, he was stoic and unemotional. He said he'd cut his vacation short and be back late tomorrow night. Sammy doesn't know I'm trans. He still called me Andrea. I just want to be gone before he sees me and unleashes his cisgender wrath and privilege on me. I don't want to become the issue that distracts from the fact that Mom is gone and may have been murdered.

Shit, I need to go home so I can be comfortable in my own home and in my own skin, and can grieve and process the fact that my beloved mother isn't here any longer. God damnit. Why did I stay away so long? I always thought we'd have more time. I always thought she'd leave him and would move to Denver. She stayed to protect me, this I know. She never got the life she deserved. I feel responsible for that.

I lay down on the bed and begin to cry. First one loud sob is released from somewhere deep inside of me and then another. I'm losing it. Once my tears begin to flow, I'm afraid they may never stop.

~ ~ ~

In less than an hour, I'm finally able to pull myself together. I packed and get ready to go. I carry my suitcase into the kitchen where Natalie is at the stove cooking something that smells of garlic and Joey holds his baby daughter in one arm and sips a cocktail with the other.

"Andy," Joey says as a look of alarm crosses his face. "Natalie has dinner almost ready. Don't you, dear?"

Natalie turns around still holding a wooden spoon. She looks from me to the suitcase I'm dragging behind me. "You're not leaving, are you?"

"I'm sorry. There's a non-stop flight on United from Albany to Denver. It leaves in a couple of hours. If I hurry I can make it."

"Please. Don't go," Joey pleads.

My tears threaten to start all over again.

"I'm sorry Joey. I need to get home. Maybe if I throw myself into my work, maybe I can find a way to get through this. I can't stay. I just can't."

"Okay. I'm sorry you're leaving. When will you be back?"

"I don't know. I'll be back if they find Mom or her body or if there is a memorial service, and certainly for the trial... if the case goes to trial."

"What?" Joey asks. "You look like you want to say something else."

Natalie turns back towards the stove and stirs whatever it is she is cooking. She's sensitive and intuitive as she attempts to give Joey and me what little bit of privacy she can.

"You don't think Mom will just show up and this whole thing is just some big misunderstanding do you?"

A slow sad smile crosses Joey's face as he slowly shakes his head. "I'm sorry, Andy. I wish it was so, but I don't see that happening."

"I got to go," I say. Natalie takes my infant niece from Joey, so Joey can enfold me in his arms. We both cry.

I kiss Natalie and little Leah good-bye. "Kiss the boys for me. I'll be back soon." I wipe my eyes with my shirt sleeve then grab my suitcase and head for the door. "And don't take any shit from Pop or Sammy," I call back to Joey as I close the door behind me.

~ ~ ~

By the time I retrieve my car from long term parking and make my way back from the airport it's already after midnight and that puts it after two in the morning

335

back in New York. I've had enough coffee today that I fear I may not sleep at all tonight. I'm sad, edgy, and wanting nothing more than to just crawl into bed and escape from the reality I find myself in. I hit the button for the garage door. The interior light goes on and the door opens. To my surprise, Michelle is standing there wearing a sheer summer nightgown.

I pull the car in and grab my bag. "Hey," I call to her. "I didn't expect you to be here."

"Is it okay? Do you want me to leave?" she asks.

"No, it's fine really. I just didn't expect you, that's all."

"You didn't sound very good when I spoke with you earlier. I didn't want you to come home to an empty house after everything that's happened. I was worried about you ..."

She lets this hang there and I don't know if she is looking for reassurance that it's okay she broke into my house or that I'm glad to see her or what. This whole world of trans dating is all new to me. I don't know the protocol or what the rules are or even if there are any.

"No, I'm glad to see you. It's been a rough couple of days." I tell her and I am. She looks lovely standing in the doorway. I put my bag down and give her a hug. She holds me tight and for a little longer than I expect. I can feel the warmth of her body against my own before she releases me. Standing on her tip-toes she reaches up and kisses my cheek.

Maybe she missed me.

Maybe this isn't as one-sided as I feared.

We make our way into the kitchen when she asks, "Would you like a glass of wine? I opened a bottle earlier."

"No thanks," I say as I look at my mail that Michelle has neatly stacked on the kitchen counter. There are just a couple of bills, advertisements, and a letter from *One Colorado*, an advocacy organization for LGBTQ+ rights. They're probably looking for another donation. I restack my mail without opening any of it. I'll deal with it in the morning.

"Do you plan to go into work tomorrow? I think you're entitled to a week of bereavement time, if you need it or want to take it," Michelle asks as she snuggles up close to me.

"I'll be going in. I'm sure there are plenty of things I need to do. Besides, I think work may help me take my mind off of everything. You're going in, right?"

"Yes. If I don't work, I don't get paid."

I nod as I remember the personal assistants are hourly employees, unlike the partners and associates at the

337

firm. This is getting complicated and I fear I may have crossed a boundary that should not have been crossed.

"Thanks for coming over," I say and I mean it. "You have an early start tomorrow, why don't you go back to bed. I'm going to shower and then I'll be in."

She smiles seductively as she brushes past me on her way to the bedroom.

I take a long hot shower and begin to relax from the flight and too much coffee. To my relief, Michelle is nearly asleep when at long last I crawl into bed. She wraps her body around mine before she drifts back to sleep.

# Chapter 52
## Nash

I pour myself another drink before I go to get dressed for a night on the town. It dawns on me as I rifle through my closet looking for something to wear, if I get lucky tonight I can bring someone back here. Amy's gone and there's no need to sneak off to a motel anymore. I'm free to do as I please. I'm a single man.

I need to do some laundry as all the pants that fit me have been worn and are a rumpled mess. I try on several pairs and discard them on the bed, most are too tight. At last I find a pair of white pants that sort of fit. I can still wear white pants for a couple more weeks. I can still hear Amy's annual reminder not to wear white pants after Labor Day. And it's not after Labor Day, yet. I zip them up and secure the button below my belly. I stand in front of the full length mirror.

I really need to stop drinking beer, although I can't imagine my life without it. Maybe if I switch to a *Lite* beer I can lose this belly. I hate that stuff, I might as well drink water and that's not gonna happen. I grab a handful of fat around what used to be my waistline and shake it. Just more of me to love. I give myself my sexiest smile I can muster and then laugh at the notion of bringing some sweet young thing home with me. Critiquing the reflection of my half-naked body in the mirror. I decide I'd better keep the lights off in here if I'm lucky enough to charm someone into coming home with me tonight.

There's a clean orange golf shirt in my dresser drawer. What do they call this fabric? Double knit or something? I think this one was a freebie from some dude trying to sell me something. I take another look at the logo— it's a leaking faucet and says *Brothers Plumbing Supplies* beneath it. Oh well, it's the only one that's clean.

I take another look around the bedroom. The dirty laundry is piling up, the bed is still unmade, and there are a few dirty dishes sitting on the bedside stand. I don't have time to clean it up now, not if I'm going to get over to Saratoga Springs.

I guess I'll have to get a room tonight if...if I get lucky.

I've never had trouble in the past. A guy can dream, can't he?

I finish what remains of my drink and leave the empty glass on my bedside stand with a couple others. I'll get 'em tomorrow.

I back the car out of the garage and nearly run into *Mrs. Kravitz,* or whatever her name is.

"Oh Nash," she calls out to get my attention.

I put the car in park and hit the button to lower the window before I turn to face her.

"Where are you going?" she asks.

I don't reply and just stare her down.

Where I am going is none of her damn business.

"Never mind," she says as she shakes her head. "I know this must be such a difficult time for you with Amy gone and the boys in town..."

She yammers on. I'm starting to wish I *had* hit her. If she doesn't get to the point soon I'm going to put the car in reverse and just keep going. I don't have time for this nosey do-gooder.

Without saying anything, I just watch as she gets even more flustered.

"I've made you my cheesy chicken casserole. Should I bring it over? Now?"

"No." If she sees the inside of my house she'll be appalled and will be calling the health department. "Thank you, uh...Mrs..." I stumble around a bit. I want to use her name, but all I've ever called her is Mrs. Kravitz and I can't call her that. "Maybe tomorrow."

"Of course," she says as she slowly backs away from the car. "You know we all loved Amy. She was such a dear..."

I nod and close the window before she can say another word.

I'm already halfway down the street and in my rearview mirror I see the old biddy is still standing in my driveway watching me drive away.

~ ~ ~

I wake up alone feeling sick to my stomach and feel like I might puke, again. It must have been bad chicken. I mumble that old line from college. All the guys used to use it at the frat house when they'd had too much and couldn't hold their liquor.

Did that woman put something in my drink?

The room smells of smoke and a ratty old polyester bedspread lies in a heap on the floor. I guess it's been a few years since I've been to this place. I think it used to be nicer.

I head into the bathroom. Something has been written on the mirror with red lipstick—*tuff luk sucker*. Poor little bitch can't even spell. There's a cigarette floating in the toilet and the mirror is cracked. Damn her, this is a non-smoking room and I'm gonna get charged for the damages.

342

Memories from my evening at Dozers begin to come back to me through my still drunken haze.

It'd been slim pickin's at the bar. It was a race weekend in Saratoga and the place was packed. I had to buy three or four gals a drink just to get one of them to talk to me. And none of them was even remotely good lookin'. Then this little beauty in a short skirt strolled in, just when I thought I was goin' home alone. She was a foreigner from somewhere but she was young and cute so I didn't care. I had to drive out of town a ways to get to the Red Roof Inn as everything else was already booked.

She wasn't bad in the sack, but then she wanted to be *paid*. I laughed when I told her, "I've never *paid* for it in my life and I wasn't about to start now."

That's not exactly true but I wasn't going to tell her that.

She had a little hissy fit and tried to kick me in the nuts. I put an end to that. I'm guessing I'm not the only one who's hurtin' this morning. What did she call me on her way out the door— something about an unhung hero? I didn't know what she was talking about. I thought it was just her accent or something.

But ... I think she was insulting my manhood.

Damn that little slut.

I guess I fell asleep after that.

343

I rinse my mouth out and wash my face before I leave the bathroom. I'm lookin' pretty rough and feeling even worse. When I go to get dressed I find my orange shirt rumpled on the end of the bed, but I can't find my pants. I look under the sheets and beneath the nasty floral bedspread that is strewn across the floor. God damn it, my pants are gone! I head back into the bathroom to check for them. They're not in here, either.

When I can't find them anywhere it dawns on me that she probably took them.

"That goddamn whore stole my wallet, too."

I'm fuming mad and I need to get out of here. Thank God my car keys are still on top of the TV. I try to wrap one of the bath towels around my waist. But the towel is so skimpy it's never going to fit all the way around me. I need to use two towels, one to cover the family jewels and another to cover my ass. I step into my shoes leaving my socks behind. With my key ring looped through my fingers, I hold the towels with both hands, one on each side of my waist before I make a dash out of the room and across the parking lot and to my car.

Some smart ass little girl in the parking lot sees me and yells to her father, "Look Daddy, that man doesn't have any pants on."

I struggle to unlock my truck and in the process I drop both towels.

The little girl screams in horror as her father attempts to cover his daughter's eyes.

# Chapter 53
## Ellery

Day after day, the program around here doesn't seem to change one iota.

With no one to confide in, I have started to keep a journal. I can only hope it will help me hold onto my tenuous grasp of reality.

I feel like a child again where someone else is dictating when I need to get up and what time I have to go to sleep. Meals are served in a cafeteria and there is never any choice, you either eat it or you go hungry. Sometimes going hungry is preferable to feeling sick to my stomach when even my trips to the toilet are regulated by someone else. The food is God awful and my appetite is off. Perhaps I'll shed some weight while I'm here but this is a pretty costly diet plan. This place has cost me my freedom. I can't think of anything more valuable to me than my freedom, except maybe my integrity.

I'm not a woman who needs a great deal of excitement to keep me from getting bored but the monotony of this place is even more than I can bear. We are allowed out in the yard each day for about ninety minutes, give or take. When the gigantic razor wire gates open there is the mass movement of hundreds of inmates out into the yard. I keep my head down and shuffle out carried along by the pushing and shoving of the others. This is supposed to be our recreation time and our time to socialize. But, for me it feels scary and dangerous.

Some of the inmates have used their internet privileges to read the news, while I can hear others gossiping to one another as they try to figure out who I am and why I'm here. There is plenty of speculation, although I offer no confirmation, people still make rude comments directed at me. I feel like I'm trapped on a middle school playground with a cadre of mean girls who can find nothing better to do than pick fights with one another over things of so little consequence.

I feel like I've been here before.

Images from my past take shape in my memory, childhood taunts delivered on the playground from other little girls about my size. I can still hear their high pitched little voices and see their frilly little dresses as they hurled questions at me about whether I was a girl or a boy. The sound of their laughter still rings in my ears. I remember running away and hiding in one of the recessed doorways on the other side of the school until a teacher came out to

347

find me. I returned to class with my ruddy tear-streaked face amid the whispers and teasing for being a cry-baby. I've learned to keep to myself out of self-protection. The unkindness of those children led me to years of self-doubt and self-loathing.

It didn't get better as I grew older. When I was just seventeen, there were two young men working at the marina who jumped me and intended to rape me. I can still feel their rough calloused hands when they grabbed me that night. I can smell the liquor on their sour breath as one of them held me down while the other tried to get my clothes off. Their voices fill my memory as they yelled at me and shouted words of encouragement to each other to bolster their bravado. I'd heard their banter on the docks of the marina all summer long. They were convinced they could straighten me out, turn me into a proper girl. All I needed was to be fucked by a man and they were both volunteering their services, whether I wanted them to or not. I just didn't know what I was missing, then Henri showed up.

Over the course of my lifetime I've learned to keep to myself. This place is dangerous for people like me.

We are allowed library privileges and reading has long been my greatest pleasure, but even more so now that I'm incarcerated. Many of the books in the library are geared to a young adult audience and written at a child's reading level. I'm certainly not an expert, but some of the books are stories I read growing up. Right now I'm re-reading *A Wrinkle in Time* by Madeleine L'Engle. It's a story of the battle of good and evil. I loved it as a child and it's even better the second time around. I guess when you've been around the block a few times there is just so much more to hang the lessons on. Evil is not just some childhood fantasy but very real. And so is goodness.

I think I read somewhere that *A Wrinkle in Time* is a banned book, although I can't for the life of me imagine why.

Reading fiction allows me to escape my current reality, if only these other women would just keep their mouths shut.

I don't understand it all. They speak their own language in here, but I can get the gist of it from either tone or context and most of it is unspeakable and degrading. The offering of sexual favors for protection is common. I wouldn't have a cup of coffee with most of these women let alone be intimate. The way I figure it, the longer I can feign ignorance the better off I'll be.

There is a level of brutality in here and many of these women wield their words as weapons. They say the most hurtful things to one another; it could make my hair curl. I laugh as I put the words down on paper, as I think it's an expression my old Granny used to use when something shocked her. Old Granny, I'm probably older now than she ever was as she  passed on in her mid-sixties. It's funny how different time looks on the other side of one's youth.

I'm certainly no psychiatrist but it doesn't take any expertise to see that this place is full of women with personality disorders and every other garden variety of mental illness. Diagnosed or undiagnosed, I can't help but believe that there are many in here who could benefit from therapy, and, likely, psychotropic medications to keep their demons at bay.

I need to quiet this tone of judgment for if I don't get out of here, I may end up just like the rest of them and that is the frightening reality of my situation.

Yesterday they moved me to a new cell and I have a new roommate. I guess she is my *cellie* to use the common vernacular. Her name is Veronica but for some reason they call her Phrone. She acts as if I should know that Phrone is a common nickname for Veronica. I guess I've only ever known one person named Veronica and that was all she was ever called. I've never heard of anyone named Phrone. I guess I have a lot to learn about the world and certainly this world I now inhabit.

Anyway, Phrone and I haven't exactly hit it off.

Phrone is twenty-three and in spite of the fact that she's more than four decades younger than I am and at least fifty pounds lighter, she insists that she is keeping the lower bunk.

As she told me in no uncertain terms, "You can get your fat ass up there or sleep on the floor. I'm not moving."

So much for respecting your elders. I guess she's in here on an assault charge and domestic violence. Apparently, she attacked her live-in boyfriend with a pair of scissors when she read his email and learned that he was seeing another woman. She recounted the story within the first fifteen minutes of meeting me. This woman shows no remorse for the pain she caused someone she once loved. Her only regret is that she got caught and that she hadn't killed him and the other woman, too. Then she went on to elaborate on how she'd finish both of them off when she gets out of here in another 1825 days. This girl, Phrone, is scary.

I know she expects me to tell her why I'm being held. She asks a few probing questions which lets me know she's heard the rumors about me or read the stories about the missing woman on the internet. Although she doesn't ask me directly, she wants to know what I've done with Kaye's body. Fat chance I'm going to tell this woman

351

anything. I've read enough crime thrillers to last me a lifetime and I'm well aware of how the jailhouse snitch testifies against another inmate in return for an abbreviated sentence. This is pure manipulation, whether truth has anything to do with it or not. I have her number, Phrone would say anything to serve her own purpose and get out of here. Even if it means throwing me under the bus in the process.

Evil is alive and well, and flourishing in this women's prison.

I ignore her as I roll over in my bunk to face the cinderblock wall and pretend to sleep. I miss my little Skye and I can't help but wonder how she and Henri are getting on. And then my mind turns to Kaye, and a smile comes to my face as I picture her wandering the lavender fields of Provence. I've never been there except through the writings of others. Still the pictures that form in my head are beautiful and I can almost smell the lavender wafting on the breeze. I smile as I think of Kaye, at last getting some beauty and peace in this lifetime. If somehow I helped Kaye escape the life she was entrapped in, this is something I can hold onto and feel good about.

~ ~ ~

I must have fallen asleep because I wake to the sound of the guard's voice. "McMasters, get up. Your lawyer is here to see you."

I rouse from a deep sound sleep. I must have been dreaming as I was back in my own home with Skye and Henri, and Kaye was there, too. We were celebrating something, although it's unclear to me what it was. I sit up on the side of my bunk as my feet hang over the side.

Phrone swats at my left ankle. "Get your goddamn feet out of my face!"

"Sorry," I mumble as I make my way to the end of the bunk and climb down.

"Come on McMasters," the guard says, "you don't want to keep your lawyer waiting."

I adjust my rumpled orange jumpsuit and step into my prison-issued canvas loafers. The guard cuffs my hands behind my back then gestures that I'm to go first. She follows closely behind me down the dimly lit corridor. It's late afternoon and the cell block is quiet as other inmates read, write or nap. A few people call out to me in some derogatory fashion or another. It's amazing how brazen some people can be when locked safely behind their cell door and there is no immediate fear of retaliation.

The guard unlocks the door to a small conference room where my attorney sits at a linoleum-topped table. I take the seat across from her and the guard makes eye contact with my attorney. She's dressed in the same navy blue suit she wore for my arraignment.

"We won't need long," she says as she throws her long dark hair over her shoulder.

The guard locks us in.

"How are you holding up, Ellery?" My attorney looks down at the papers in front of her to make sure she has my name right.

"About as well as can be expected," I reply. I wonder why she's here and why I've been summoned.

"As you know the prosecutor has gone before the Grand Jury and they believe they have enough evidence implicating you in the murder of Amy Cooper to bind you over for trial."

"I know we've been all through that."

"The Prosecutor is under a great deal of pressure to get this case resolved as it is already being tried in the media."

"I have limited internet privileges so I really don't know what is being said."

"There is a great deal of controversy about charging you with first degree murder when they don't have a body. People all over the country are weighing in on your case and the likelihood of a conviction." She states this as if I should have already surmised the legal arguments being made. "The Prosecutor held a press conference this morning and stated on national television that he is certain he has charged the right person given the evidence. He's confident a jury will convict without a body. Still, I think he may have doubts. He had one of his assistant prosecutors approach me this morning after the news conference. He's offering a plea deal."

"I didn't do it. I didn't kill anyone. How many times do I have to tell you that?"

"Hear me out, Ellery. If you plead guilty to second degree murder rather than first degree murder, they are willing to commute the sentence from life to 15 to 20 years."

"No. I didn't kill anyone. You do understand that, don't you? It might as well be a life sentence for in twenty years I'll be 88. If I live that long."

"With allowances for good behavior, you could be out in thirteen to seventeen years," she offers.

We sit in silence for a moment as once again I try to wrap my head around the situation I find myself in. I could just tell them that the woman they know as Amy Cooper is living somewhere in the south of France. For another moment I mull over the ramifications of doing so. I can't do that to Kaye, that woman has a right to live her life without fear of that abusive husband of hers. I can't expose Henri or Claudette. They, too, have broken the law and risked so much. Not just for Kaye, but for the others, too. There is too much on the line. Too many good people would go down if I talk and try to save my own hide. I won't do it. I can't.

"No. I didn't kill that woman. I'm not taking the deal. I'll take my chances with a jury of my peers."

"Okay. This will be a difficult case for the prosecution as they have no body, but it is also a difficult case to defend. You have given me nothing, absolutely nothing to work with..."

She lets the words hang there. I know she expects me to help her out, but I can't betray Kaye not while Nash is still out there and intent on her demise. I have known men like him. I won't sacrifice Kaye to save myself. Besides, I don't know if I could locate her even if I wanted to.

When it becomes obvious that I have nothing else to say, my attorney calls for the guard to unlock the door. She stands up and gathers her papers before she looks me in the eye and shakes her head as if she can't understand me at all. Then she walks out of the conference room without even saying good-bye.

# Chapter 54
## Kaye

I wake early as a breeze off the sea wafts in through the open window. The lace curtains flutter gently as the morning sun shines through them casting shadows across the bed. I pull the linen sheet up around me as I feel the cool crispness of the morning. It's in the air. Floating in almost imperceptibly, but I can feel it this morning. Summer is waning and autumn is coming. I love the change of seasons, each bringing its own delights.

I lie there for a moment savoring the peace and stillness of the morning. I think of how long I've dreamt of living in the south of France and now, against all odds, here I am. Again, the old song by Judy Collins plays on in my head and before long I'm humming it and then singing along.

*"My father always promised us that we would live in France. We'd go boating on the Seine and I would learn to dance..."*

Perhaps not the Seine, as I am not in Paris, but perhaps I'll take a river cruise on the Rhône or even sail on the Mediterranean. Perhaps I'll learn to dance or maybe I'll learn to paint...

It isn't long before I begin to hear the sounds of the birds calling to one another and the sounds of the city waking up as people head out onto the streets to begin their day. I guess it's time I get my day started as well.

I shower and dress in something I purchased in Paris. I'll need to do some shopping for some casual clothes and perhaps a sweater before I board the train for Martigues.

I checked the train schedule last night and there is a train leaving at eleven and another at one. I plan to be on the early train so I can look for an apartment if the town suits me.

I indulge in another light breakfast of a croissant and a cappuccino at a sidewalk café just down the street from my hotel. This could get to be a habit with me, a very pleasant habit. After breakfast I wander the streets of Marseille as I wait for the shops to open. This is a delightful city and already I wish I had more time just to peruse and poke around. I read the menus posted outside of some of the restaurants taking note of which ones I'd like to return to.

The shops open between nine and nine-thirty, or whenever the shopkeeper decides. It doesn't seem to matter what the posted hours are, people open their little establishments when it suits their schedule. These are not the generic stores owned and operated by large multinational corporations found in nearly every strip mall across the United States where the hours are dictated and sacrosanct. Yet another difference between life in Europe and life back home; it may take some getting used to but it seems more humane.

I can remember how Nash ranted on and on about how Tim Webster was late getting the hardware store open and how he'd fired him on the spot. No excuses were ever accepted unless he was the one offering them for both major and minor transgressions. I certainly won't miss that.

I wonder what he won't miss about me... probably plenty.

I stop into a little boutique and pick out a pair of black leggings, some lingerie, a black cardigan, two camisole-type tops for yoga, and a couple of tunics with ¾ length sleeves, one in royal blue and the other in sea foam green.

In my head, I catch myself trying to justify my purchases. These tunics are just long enough to cover my backside should I get caught wearing my leggings in public.

I should be able to wear them into September when the weather will begin to change.

I used to have to justify anything I bought for myself or Nash would go crazy.

Enough of that nonsense. I no longer have to answer to him. This is not extravagant and besides I can afford it. I put everything on the counter and give the woman my credit card.

Next door is a small bookstore; I venture in. As one might expect, nearly everything is in French. I pick up one book after another and realize that although I can pick out many of the words I will need to get a French-English dictionary and spend a great deal of time translating and I'm still not sure I will understand the nuance of the story.

There is an attractive woman in her early fifties behind the counter, she asks, "*Puis-je vous aider?*"

I'm sure she is asking if she can help me, but my French fails me so I ask, "Do you speak English?"

"*Oui*, yes. May I help you?" she asks and smiles warmly.

"Thank-you. I'm moving here, not here exactly but to Martigues and my French is very rusty..."

"Rusty?" She looks confused.

I shake my head, of course she doesn't understand my use of the word. I try again. "I haven't spoken French

360

for many years and have forgotten most of it. Do you have a French-English Dictionary?"

"No Madam. Most people use a translation App on their phones rather than a dictionary. You have a phone, *non?*"

"Yes, of course."

"Let me show you."

I hand her my phone and she brings up the App. It appears so simple and straightforward that even I should be able to use it.

"Thank you," I say and smile. "I would like to purchase some books in French, so I can practice. Perhaps something easy to start."

"Fiction?" she asks.

"*Oui,*" I say, trying my best not to be the ugly American who expects everyone to speak my language. She leads me to a section containing books for young people. I can't help but notice how friendly and helpful people are here in the south of France.

"Some of these have been translated from English into French and are written for children. This may be a good place to start."

"Thank-you, I'll take a look."

I pick up *Les Misérables* by Victor Hugo. I know the story. I saw the movie and love the music. I open the cover and read the first line, "An hour before sunset, on the evening of a day in the beginning of October..." I'm able to read it without needing to translate. Perhaps this will be a good place to begin.

As I'm standing there between the shelves of books when the shopkeeper returns. "You know this book is on the banned book list in the United States."

"Oh for the love of God," I shake my head in disgust. "In that case I definitely will take it."

"Sounds like you and I are cut from the same cloth. Who are these people controlling what we can and cannot read?"

"I've lived forty years with someone who tried to control my every move. I certainly don't need my government trying to control what I can read about."

This kind woman gives me a slow smile and nods as if she understands. "We also have a small section of books in English if you're interested."

"I am, thank you." Again I follow her to another shelf of books and choose two novels, one is historical fiction about the French Resistance during the Second World War and the other is a mystery, a crime thriller. "This should keep me busy for a few days," I say as I approach the counter with my books.

"I don't know if you might be interested but the *French Alliance Aix-Marseille* offers French language classes. I've heard they are very good. Perhaps you could travel in from Martigues once or twice a week, if you like."

"Could you write the name down for me?" I ask. This may be a very good idea.

"*Oui.*" She looks up the website on her phone. "There is a class starting in September. Here let me send this to you. What is your phone number?"

"I'm sorry, but I don't know it yet. I just got this phone yesterday and I haven't memorized it." I'm starting to feel flustered for being so incompetent. I drop my shopping bag and start to rifle through my purse to see if I can find the paperwork I was given when I purchased the phone. "Surely it must be on one of these papers."

"Here," she says, "let me see your phone."

I hand it to her.

"I will text myself from your phone and then I will have your number." She smiles at me kindly. "It must be difficult to be in a new country where you do not speak the language. It will get easier."

She hands me back my phone and I hear the little bell chime indicating I have a text message. "Very good, you've been so kind."

"My pleasure," she says as she hands me a business card with her name on it. "On the back I have written your new phone number, so now you will have it."

I take a look at it and then tuck it into my wallet next to my credit card. "Thank you Simone. You've been so kind and helpful."

"Stop in again when you are back in Marseille and let me know how you are doing. Perhaps we can share a meal or have a glass of wine when you're in town."

"I'd like that," I say. "*Au revoir*," I call to her as I readjust my packages and head out the door and onto the street.

It is already ten o'clock and I need to head over to the train station, *Gare de Marseille-Saint Charles*. I practice using my French, if only in my head. On my way there, I pass a little art supply shop. I check my watch. Do I have time? Only if I hurry so I stop briefly, for I have promised myself that I will learn to paint again.

The promises one makes to themselves are sacred and should never be broken.

I purchase a sketch pad, a couple of small canvases, a package of assorted brushes, five small tubes of acrylic paint in red, yellow, blue, white and black as I can create all the colors by mixing these, and a package of drawing pencils. I'd love to spend the day poking around in here but the train will not wait for me and besides, I can't carry much more.

I had planned to walk as the station isn't far but I am overburdened with packages, so I hail a cab instead.

It isn't long before I'm on the train and headed to Martigues. The ride should only take about forty-five minutes.

On my phone, I open my email, hoping and praying there will be some word from Andy.

Nothing.

Maybe she is angry with me.

Maybe she doesn't understand how I could have just up and disappeared.

Maybe she feels abandoned.

Maybe she doesn't want to talk to me.

Maybe it's all just too much to process and she, no he, is just getting on with her life, his life and he thinks I should just get on with mine.

Maybe I should reach out to Joey or Sam.

Maybe they will tell their father.

Maybe... .

# Chapter 55
## Nash

This is so humiliating, first getting robbed by a whore and then dropping those towels and exposing myself in the parking lot of some fleabag motel. The sound of that child screaming still rings in my ears. I pull my orange golf shirt down in an attempt to cover myself. I still can't believe that bitch took my pants and my wallet and left me without any money.

I'm still nauseous and a little dizzy from drinking last night. I haven't had anything to eat since yesterday afternoon and I'm sure my blood sugar is low. Doc Adams warned me about my weight and how if I didn't lose some weight I'd be a full blown diabetic before the year's end. I guess this is what he was talking about. If I don't get something to drink I'm likely to crash my truck and I'll never make the drive home.

I scrounge around the cup holder to see if I can come up with enough change to buy a Coke at McDonalds. Some of the coins are sticky and covered with lint and hair while others are stuck to the bottom of the cup holder. I dig them out with my fingernails. I count out a dollar forty-seven in coins. They are gross and nasty as they stick to my palm. I pull over to the next McDonalds and head towards the drive through. There on the dollar menu I see that I can get a large Coke for a dollar. I guess this is my lucky day. I place my order and drive around to the window to pay for it and pick it up.

I hand the kid a handful of sticky nickels, dimes, and pennies.

He gives me a look like I've just handed him a pile of shit. Fuck him if he can't take a joke.

He hands me my drink and a straw and I'm out of there.

By the time I pull into my subdivision, I'm starting to feel a little better until I round the corner and see a police car in my driveway.

Shit. Now what am I going to do?

How am I going to explain the fact that I'm drivin' around without any pants on?

I can't pull into the garage because my truck won't fit in there.

Oh fuck, here comes Mrs. Kravitz with her goddamn casserole.

367

I think about driving past the house when the cops see me and approach on the driver's side of my truck. I pull my shirt down as best I can and unroll the window hoping he doesn't look inside and I won't have to get out of the cab.

"Mr. Nash Cooper?" the younger one asks.

"Yes, officer," I say as politely as I can.

"Were you up at the Red Roof Inn in Glen Falls?"

"Yes, sir. But I can explain."

"And at the McDonald's in Lake George?"

I drop my head. "Officer, I can explain."

"Oh, I bet you can." He looks inside the car and he knows. A shit eating grin crosses his face. This guy is tryin' to humiliate me and he is enjoying it. "Step out of your truck, Mr. Cooper and keep your hands where I can see them."

I do as I am told with my hands held high. This lifts my shirt exposing everything I've got. Right now I'm pretty shriveled up and it doesn't look like much. Poor Mrs. Kravitz stops dead in her tracks and I hear her scream just before she drops the casserole dish right in my driveway. This asshole cop is laughing so hard he can hardly contain speak. His partner is all business.

"Can we *please* go in the house?" I ask. "Can I just open the garage door?" Now, I'm practically pleading. "The opener is on the visor." I'd like nothing better than to get inside my house and bring this to an end. If that cop doesn't stop laughing at me I might just punch his lights out.

"Let's just go in the front door," the first cop says.

"You have your keys, right?" his partner asks, stating the obvious.

I nod as I walk towards the front door with my bare ass hanging out the back and my keys held high above my head.

"May I put some pants on?" I ask the officers who follow me into my living room.

"Yes, please do. Then come back out here. We have a few questions we need you to answer."

The older cop gives a subtle lift of his head in my direction and the younger guy, without saying a word, follows me towards the bedroom and stands in the doorway. It's obvious, they don't trust me.

I find a pair of dirty gym shorts in the now overflowing laundry basket. I try to decide how I'm going to explain my stolen pants as I pull my shorts on.

"We got a call early this morning from the emergency room at the Saratoga Hospital. A young woman was beaten. Her face is in pretty bad shape. She said she met some guy in an orange shirt at Dozer's last night and went to the Red Roof Inn with him. The manager there said he didn't remember you. I got the feeling that ratting out some of his regulars might be bad for business. But it just so happens that another fella was checking out when we arrived. He remembered a guy wearing *only* an orange shirt. He told us the story of some poor sap who was out in the parking lot without any pants on. He wrote down your license plate number and was planning to call us. He said you exposed yourself to his nine year old daughter."

"Stop running your mouth, Johnson," the older cop warns his partner. "So, Mr. Cooper, here we are killing two birds with one stone, so to speak. Care to explain?"

I drop my head into my hands as I try to come up with some kind of an explanation.

"Let's start with Ms. Smirnoff..." the older officer says.

"That can't be her real name, that's just what she was drinking. She was a prostitute." No sooner do the words leave my mouth then I realize that I've just admitted to something illegal. Shit. I purse my lips together and shift uncomfortably in my chair.

"That's not what she said, Mr. Cooper. She said you didn't pay her."

"I didn't. She came with me willingly, you know, just two consenting adults."

"Can you explain why you hit her in the face? Or was this something consensual, too?"

"Do I need a lawyer?"

"Maybe. Do you want to tell us about exposing yourself to a nine year old girl and why you have been seen out and about without any pants on?"

"That bitch, Miss Smirnoff, or whatever her name is, stole my pants and my wallet. I was trying to get to my car so I could go home when I dropped the towel. It was an accident, honest officer."

"Mr. Cooper, I'm not sure you know the meaning of that word. If you were just driving home after an evening filled with unfortunate events, why did you stop at McDonald's and expose yourself to the young man at the drive through window?"

"I did no such thing. I'm no homo. I'm not into men or kids, either. I wouldn't do that." I protest.

"Well, the young man has provided us with a statement along with your license plate number. Seems they have a close circuit camera and one of those convex mirrors. We've seen it all, Mr. Cooper, and it isn't pretty.

"Ms. Smirnoff is meeting with a counselor from our victims assistance unit. We are uncertain at this time if she will press charges against you for assault or not. But the father of the nine year old little girl needs no convincing.

Indecent exposure is a serious criminal offense and exposure to a child can mean you're going to jail," the young guy explains.

Without waiting to see if I have anything else to say, the older cop reads me my Miranda rights. "Nash Cooper, you are under arrest for two counts of indecent exposure. You have the right to remain silent. Anything you say can be used against you in a court of law..."

Blah, blah, blah. I've heard this all before, twice in less than a week. The young cop handcuffs me, clicking them tightly behind my back before they escort me out to the police car.

Sure enough, Mrs. Kravitz has done what she does best. A whole troupe of old biddies from the neighborhood are standing on her front porch gossiping.

I want to flip them off and tell them to mind their own business but the handcuffs are digging tightly into my wrists.

"You'll keep your mouth shut, *buddy*, if you know what's good for you." The young cop presses his gun into the small of my back.

"Is that really necessary?" I ask about the gun as he shoves me into the back of the car and locks me in.

The police car pulls out of the driveway after engaging both lights and flashers and I can't help but wonder what these two know about Amy.

# Chapter 56
## Andy

When I awake the house is quiet. My phone is on the nightstand. I pick it up. It's already nine-thirty and Michelle has obviously already gone into the office. She starts every morning at nine where I can wander in any old time I choose unless I'm due in court or have appointments scheduled. One of the benefits of being a partner, albeit a junior partner.

Today my calendar is relatively clear.

I check my email. There's nothing there of any importance. Just a few love notes from my good friends at J. Crew and Ann Taylor to let me know they're having another sale.

I put my phone back on the bedside table and turn over to look out the window.

My thoughts turn to my mother, again. I just can't believe she's gone. I feel so abandoned and adrift. The truth is I abandoned her. I left her because I couldn't bear to be around him. He never loved me, at least not in any way that ever felt like love. And he never loved her either.

Even as a child I knew this. Images of him coming home drunk and picking fights with her fill my head. I thought I'd worked through all of this with my therapist and yet here it is again. I know it's not the child's job to protect the parent. Still she was so vulnerable and hurt by his unkind words. I know he hit her and pushed her around. And I know for a fact that he cheated on her. He's still a monster and Mom bore the brunt of it over and over again. Is it possible she finally had enough and just up and left him? Was this some act of self-preservation? I know that's why I moved across the country. Is this all just wishful thinking on my part? Wouldn't she call me and let me know she was okay? Well, I went through a sex change operation and am living as a man and I didn't tell her. I haven't even seen her in the last two years. Maybe she doesn't feel she owes me anything. Why would she? None of us has been there for her. In our own way all of us were just trying to distance ourselves from Dad.

I get out of bed and get myself dressed. Michelle has left a note on the kitchen counter—

> See you at work. Take your time.
> There's nothing on your calendar until
noon
> and no one expects you in any earlier.

Love,

M


Oh God, there it is. The "L" word.

I need to think this through. For the first time in my life I'm in a romantic relationship with someone who sees me and seems to accept me for who I am. I thought I wanted this. I've been telling myself this for years and now all I can think about is bolting. But where the hell would I go? This is my house. I live and work here, but so does Michelle. She doesn't live *here* exactly but she's been staying over and is getting comfortable. But we work together and worse. She works for me. The firm has rules about partners having relationships with subordinates. They'll keep me but she'll be looking for another job.


I fix myself a cup of coffee and take a seat at the kitchen counter. I call Joey. I told him I'd let him know I got home, but I was too tired last night.

"Hey Joey," I say when he picks up.

"Hi Andy. I was going to call you. What time did you get in last night?"

"I don't know. It was late. I slept in this morning. Just having my first cup of coffee as we speak."

"I decided to go in a little late myself. Sammy came by this morning on his way to Dad's. He wanted the low down on everything. I tried to bring him up to speed before he talks to Pop."

"How'd that go?"

"He was as stoic and unemotional as always."

"That's not a surprise. Anything else on Mom since I left?"

"No." He lets the word hang there and I can sense he wants to tell me something more.

"Anything you need to tell me? Seems like you're holding back on me."

"God, Andy, I hate to tell you this..."

"Tell me."

"Dad got arrested."

"He killed her?" I'm nearly shouting into the phone.

"No. No, God no. Nothing like that. He was arrested for public indecency."

"What the fuck did he do?"

"According to Dad, now consider the source, he met some woman at a bar and took her to the Red Roof Inn in Lake George."

"He always was a class act. Mom hasn't even been gone a week."

"Again, according to Pop, she was a prostitute but he didn't know that when he left with her."

"Who did he think he was leaving with, some virginal fairy princess?"

"Anyway, when he refused to pay her, there was some kind of a physical altercation."

"Let me guess. He hit her, didn't he?"

"He was a little vague about that part. He said something about her not pressing charges."

"Our father's a real stand-up guy."

"Anyway, according to Dad, she took his pants and his wallet, when she left. He had to leave the motel wearing nothing but a towel, which he inadvertently dropped in the parking lot while trying to get in the car."

"Good Lord, can this story get any worse?"

"I'm afraid it can. He exposed himself to a nine year old little girl and a sixteen year old boy who was working the drive-through window at McDonalds."

"He went through the drive-through at McDonalds without any pants on. What is wrong with the man?"

"He needs to get his head out of his ass. Anyway, Sammy is meeting with a bail bondsman."

"Don't ask me for any money. He can just sit there in jail and rot for all I care."

"I know Andy, I know. Particularly after how he treated you and all the horrible things he said."

A moment passes as I try to digest the latest dirt blowing through my family's ongoing saga.

"Andy?"

"I'm still here. Just trying to take it all in."

"I spoke with Sammy..."

"About?"

"Your transition. I figured it would be better if he heard it from me than from Pop."

"I see. Pop would have told him and God knows what he would say about me. It wouldn't be good." I take a deep breath before I ask, "What'd he say?"

"Nothing I want to repeat."

"I figured as much. Sorry you have to be put in the middle of all of this, Joey."

"I'm just starting to understand how Mom must have felt."

"Always in the middle, trying to keep the peace?"

"That about sums it up. Listen Andy, I've gotta go. Sammy's trying to ring through."

"Call me later. Bye."

I take another sip of my now lukewarm coffee. I feel so all alone.

Sitting there, I peruse the unopened mail I left on the counter last night. There are a couple of bills and a letter from *One Colorado*. I open the letter first. Initially, I thought this was probably an invitation to their annual fundraiser as *One Colorado* is an advocacy organization for LGBTQ+ people. However, it is not. They are looking to hire an attorney and my name has been put forth by someone on their board of directors as a potential candidate for the position.

Huh, is this serendipity or what?

I've been practicing family law for over ten years now, sometimes it feels like I'm on the right side of the issues and sometimes I feel like I'm being bogged down in the marital squabbles where none of the participants are particularly honorable. It wears me down. Perhaps working for this organization would be a good move for me. I certainly understand some of the issues and have lived through much of the prejudice and discrimination.

Besides, the truth is I think I want Michelle in my life. Whether things work out with us or not, I can't have this good woman losing her job because of me.

I pick up the phone and call *One Colorado*. I want to let them know I'm interested.

# Chapter 57
## Henri

It will probably take me a good week or so to get my affairs in order and to prepare for a trip abroad. I don't know how long I'll be away.

Wednesday afternoon while I'm down at the marina with Skye, Claudette comes roaring into the parking lot. The dust from the gravel road is flying and she nearly runs over one of the boys who works here.

Stepping from her black Peugeot she calls to me, "Henri, I have booked your flight. You leave from Montreal on Wednesday."

I approach her and we exchange kisses on either side of our faces. "*Bon,*" she says. "You may act like a French man but dressed like this..." She shakes her head, tossing her dark hair over her shoulder and leaving the remainder unstated.

She loops her arm through mine and I can smell the sweetness of roses from her perfume as we walk up the dock towards my boat.

"So good of you to come , *ma chérie,*" I say.

Claudette is brusque as she pushes me away. She is suspect of all endearments.

I offer her a soft laugh as I know this about her as we have been friends, or at least friendly for years. Today, she is true to form but alas, so am I.

"You need to finish up and get ready to leave. No more wasting time. No more dawdling. *Oh mon Dieu*, poor Ellery is imprisoned and here you are, out enjoying the afternoon sun," she scolds me.

"Oh Claudette, I am not dawdling. It is almost September, and fall closes in pretty early in the north country. It's not uncommon for the temperatures to drop below freezing and we often have snow in October."

"Tsk-tsks," Claudette mutters at me as if my concerns are of little consequence.

"I cannot leave my boat without winterizing it. If I was a wealthy man I could have Jean Paul handle this for me, but I am not."

"Jean Paul? Who is this Jean Paul?"

"He is the mechanic here at the marina," I say, as a way of an explanation.

Claudette steps in front of me and crosses her arms across her breasts. I want to laugh as this tiny woman in her bright pink sundress attempts to intimidate me. "Enough

Henri. If it is only the money, for the love of God, hire him and I will handle it."

I nod and acquiesce. "As you wish, *Madame*."

"I'll pick you up. Five o'clock sharp next Wednesday evening. Be ready to go." She stands there looking me up and down and shaking her head. "For God's sake, Henri, get a haircut and buy something suitable to wear. No one is going to take you seriously or want to help you find this woman if you look like you've been sleeping under a bridge."

I guffaw when I hear her description of me. It's my turn to shake my head. I can't help but laugh. "Come now, Claudette, I've just stepped off a fishing boat. My clothes may be worn but they're not dirty." Clearly Claudette has grown accustomed to her life of wealth and privilege and has never been in the company of anyone who is homeless and lives in abject poverty.

She smiles as I laugh.

"You will need to do better than that if you intend to insult me," I say as I give this petite woman a squeeze on her shoulder.

She hands me a credit card in my name and a sealed envelope. "Use this. It's tied to my account."

"Claudette, I can't..." I start to protest and refuse but she's not having it. She holds up her index finger to silence me before she turns and walks away.

"*Je ne sais pas* if you will even find this elusive woman, but you may be gone for a while and Europe is *très* expensive." She mixes French and English with ease as so many of us Francophiles do in this part of Canada.

I stand there with the card in my hand and watch as she heads down the swaying dock in her matching pink high heels as her pink dress flutters with the onshore breeze.

She starts her car and roars out of the dusty parking lot with the same exuberance she drove in with. That woman is a force to be reckoned with.

I head into the cabin of the boat with Skye at my heels. I sit down at the table and the little dog jumps up onto my lap. She's a curious little critter and wants to see what Claudette has left me. I open the envelope and inside I find that Claudette has made arrangements for my flight to Paris and for little Skye to fly in the plane with me. I haven't been on a plane since I was in high school and heaven knows that was some time ago. I don't think anyone ever conceived of emotional support animals flying around the globe back in the day. Perhaps Ellery is the one in need of emotional support given her imprisonment for a crime she is incapable of committing. *C'est dommage*— too bad Skye and Ellery can't wait this out together. Still, I can't leave the pup at home. I made a promise to Ellery that I'd look after Skye and I intend to keep my promise.

I've never been to Europe, but I fear Claudette may be right. I hardly look like I am homeless, and yet, I can't imagine walking the streets of Paris or the villages of Provence looking like I've just stepped off a fishing boat.

I decide to take Skye home before I head into town and see if I can get into the barber shop before they close.

~ ~ ~

Taking a seat in the barber's chair, I have a good long look in the mirror as Luc wraps the cape across my chest and secures it around my neck.

"Just a trim? The usual?" Luc asks as he runs the comb through my hair.

"My beard was dark when I first decided to grow it, then gradually it changed to salt and pepper, and now I fear I have begun to look like dear old Santa Claus."

Luc just stands behind me smiling. "What are you thinking, Henri?"

Without a well thought out plan, I decide to let Luc shave off the full beard I've worn for decades. "I think it's time for a change. Time to see who I've become."

"You're sure?" he asks. And rightly so, as Luc is nearly as old as I am and has been cutting my hair and trimming my beard for years.

"No, but do it anyway. A friend of mine just told me she thought I looked like I was homeless."

"Must have been a woman. A tactless woman," he adds as he gently shakes his head.

I give him a nod and smile. "Well, that is an apt description of Claudette. Let's just do this." I grasp my beard with my right hand and pull it down towards the ends.

"It's only hair, if you don't like it you can always grow it back." He turns me away from the mirror and bends the chair back as he begins to cut away at my beard with scissors. Tufts of white hair litter the front of the cape and fall onto the floor.

Once most of my beard has been trimmed away, Luc applies the shaving cream with an old school cup and brush before pulling out a straight razor and removing what remains of my once full beard. Before he allows me to see his handiwork, he turns the chair back to the sink and washes my hair and trims it up.

"Well, what do you think?" He says when at last he turns me back around so I can look in the mirror.

386

"I'm not sure I recognize myself. I think I look younger without the beard. Not young exactly, but younger."

"Want me to color it for you? That will make you look younger. Some men are doing it?"

"Ahh, no, I think I'll pass on that."

As I leave the barber shop, I think about what Claudette said about my clothes. They are pretty well worn, but patched and cleaned. I own a pair of pants and a jacket that I save for weddings and funerals, but I bought those years ago. No doubt they are hopelessly out of date. Perhaps I'll run into Montreal this weekend and do a little shopping and get myself a few new things to go with my clean-shaven face and my whole new look.

If I'm able to find Kaye, I do hope she'll recognize me.

# Chapter 58
## Kaye

Arriving in Martigues, I am overwhelmed by the simplicity and beauty of this little provincial town. The canals are lined with old pastel colored buildings that glow in various shades of dusty rose, pale aqua, and golden hues in the afternoon sunshine. Juggling all my purchases I walk the sidewalks that run along the canals and cross over bridges where painted wooden boats are docked, making my way to the bed and breakfast where I've booked a room. I understand why painters flocked here during the nineteenth century and still do today.

My host, André, a middle aged man with a handsome face and prematurely grey hair, is here to welcome me when I check into the inn.

He asks for my passport and a credit card, then engages me in some casual conversation asking about my itinerary and if I'm enjoying my visit so far.

The woman at the bookstore was so helpful that I may have let my guard down as I offer this man more information than I probably should. "I am thinking of relocating here. I hope to find a realtor who can help me find an apartment."

He nods and smiles indicating he understands as he comes out from behind the reception desks to help me to carry my parcels up the stairs to my room. He unlocks the door for me and I am delighted to find my room has been beautifully appointed and has a private balcony that overlooks the canal.

"*Oh mon Dieu*, such a beautiful view," I gasp.

He opens the floor-to-ceiling glass doors to allow a soft breeze to blow in.

Before he leaves he informs me, "This room is available through the month of September. If you are in need of a place to stay while looking for an apartment, you may book with me. Directly. I can do better on the fees."

I nod. I understand. He wants to avoid having to pay the booking agent.

"May I let you know in the morning?" I ask.

"Of course, *Madame*." He smiles and gives me a slight bow as he exits my room.

Will I be able to sleep here? Is there some reason why this room hasn't been let for the month of September? Still, the view is exceptional and it would make my life easier if I could have some time to look around and get acquainted with the city before committing to a lease.

I debate lying down and taking a nap, but decide against it. I want to sleep well tonight and if I sleep now, I may not. Instead, I decide to freshen up, change into the casual clothes I purchased this morning, take one of my new books and go out for a walk.

Following the canal towards the sea, it doesn't take me very long before reaching the *Beach of Ferrières*. The sand is white and fine and the Mediterranean sea is crystalline blue. The water looks so appealing that I'd like nothing better than to just go for a swim.

The last time I went swimming was in the cold dark rushing waters of the Sacandaga River and now I am here on the Mediterranean. The water is calling to me, again. But this time it will be different.

I make a mental note to look for a swimsuit, buy some sunscreen, and a straw hat.

With a long slow deep breath, I begin to relax. I think I'm going to like it here.

Taking my new book, *Les Misérables*, I head for a park bench under a grove of olive trees where I can sit in the shade and still see the sea and hear the waves gently lapping the shoreline. Men, women, and children walk the beach and through the park hawking their wares, snacks, and drinks. There are also carts with colorful umbrellas all along the walkway with vendors selling ice creams, cream-filled beignets, and other essentials.

I spent the remainder of the afternoon watching the people and thinking about starting my life over here in the Town of Martigues. Since leaving Nash, I feel as if I have been walking on a tightrope, needing to keep my attention tightly focused on the next step to avoid falling and having to face the unmitigated rage of my husband. I can almost conjure up an image of him, both red-faced and raging. I can almost hear him shouting, 'How dare you?' While I cower and pray to just disappear. And now, against all odds, I have done just that, I have just disappeared.

Somehow, it just doesn't seem real, but it is.

I can't help but think about my children, all grown now with lives of their own. I check my cell phone, one more time, to see if I have an email from Andy. There is nothing. I think about contacting the boys. They are hardly boys any more as both of them are busy with families of their own.

Busy. That's the operative word. I've rarely seen either of them since they married and even less since they've had children.

Nash deserves some credit for trying to maintain his relationship with the boys. He still organizes an annual *Boys' Day Out* every July where he takes Joey and Sam into the city for some excessive beer drinking and a Yankees' game.

Andy and I were never invited. From the time that she was a little girl, Andy always begged to go along and cried with bitter disappointment when Nash refused to let her. She was a better ball player than Joey ever would be and she actually followed the game.

Again, thoughts of Nash fill my head. I can only imagine what Nash is telling the boys about me now.

No doubt there will be lies about what a bad wife I was to him. He will manipulate the truth, like he has done so many times in the past. I can envision him casting himself as the unwitting victim, unable to imagine why I might just up and leave or perhaps he will elaborate on how he is the poor grieving husband who has no idea why *I* would leave *him* after he suffered through nearly forty years of marriage to such a cold-hearted wench.

I try to shake this off. I don't want thoughts of Nash to spoil my beautiful day. It has taken me forty years to be free of him, I refuse to give the man any more head space today.

Attempting to push these painful thoughts from my head, I pick up my new book and start to read a few chapters before I head back to my room.

On my way back up canal street, I pass one painter after another just finishing up the final details on their canvases before the sun is gone. Inspired by the plethora of painters and all the beautiful scenery, I stop in an art supply store and purchase a portable easel complete with retractable legs and an attached sketch box for my supplies. The gentleman behind the counter refers to this as "a Julian easel or a French easel" and declares it *"Exemplaire for en plein aire."*

The sound of French is positively poetic.

Tomorrow, I will head out early to find a magnificent view of the sea. I will set up my new easel and catch the morning light. I, too, will paint *en plein aire.*

# Chapter 59
## Nash

four months later

"Hey Dad."

I hear Joey call to me from the front door. Before I can even get up out of my *Lazy Boy*, Joey has let himself in. I remind myself to change the locks on the doors, I can't have him just coming and going from here like he lives here. For all he knows I could be gettin' busy with a lady friend. I shove the girly magazine beneath the cushion and head into the kitchen.

"I stopped at Hannaford's Market to pick up the groceries you wanted." His voice is muffled as he calls to me with his head inside the refrigerator. He has deposited the grocery bags on the kitchen counter and is already putting things away.

Looking through the bags to see if he has forgotten anything, I ask, "Did you get the Budweiser? I don't see any."

"You can't be drinking with that electronic tether around your ankle. I bought you some O'Douls, it's non-alcoholic beer and they're already in the fridge. There is a second case still in the garage."

"O'Drools? Non-alcoholic beer, now that's an oxymoron if I ever heard one. Ugh. Hand me one, will ya?"

Joey emerges from the refrigerator with a can of the fake beer in his hand. "It's kind of early in the day to start drinking, don't you think?"

I snatch the can from his hand and crack it open and slug about half of it down. "Don't start with me." I let a loud burp escape before taking another swallow from the can. "What else am I supposed to do with this thing on?" I lift the leg of my pajama pants to expose the electronic tether around my ankle. "I've got nowhere to go and nothin' to do. They've got me tied to the house for another couple weeks."

I pick up one of the green cans to read the label. "I know Dad, just take it easy. O'Doul's is supposed to have only 0.4 percent alcohol. I don't know how many cans it will take to set off the alarm but you don't need any more trouble right now."

"Yeah, yeah, I know."

Joey finishes putting the groceries away. He clears a pile of old mail from the kitchen table then wipes the table down with a wet sponge before he grabs himself an orange and a napkin and takes a seat.

"Have you given any thought to how you'd like to spend the holidays?" he asks me. "I know that Mom always took charge of making sure we had a nice Christmas, and this will be our first Christmas without her."

"I don't know, I suppose you could bring the wife and the kids over here. Maybe Sammy's would come, too." We both look around the house. I can read the disgust on his face.

"This place is a bit of a pig pen," I say.

"Maybe you should hire someone," Joey suggests.

"What about Natalie, she doesn't have a job."

"My wife?" Joey sounds incredulous that I would even suggest that his wife help me out. "Actually, she does work. She is a mother, the mother of my three children."

"Take it easy, don't go gettin' your panties in a twist. Your mother had three children and was able to keep this house clean."

"You do understand the difference don't you?" Joey is nearly shouting at me. "My wife keeps our house, it is not *her* job to clean *your* house."

"Never mind," I say as I get up to get myself another beer. "I'll have this ankle bracelet off in a couple weeks and I may go down to Florida for the holidays."

"Really? Why Florida?" Joey asks.

"I might retire there or maybe North Carolina once your mom is declared legally dead. I hope to get my hands on her inheritance. I'm thinking of hiring a lawyer, someone to help me get what I'm entitled to."

Joey rolls his eyes. "Don't you think this family has incurred enough legal expenses this year?"

We've been all through this. Amy's brother, dear old Douglas, insists their old man set it up so I'd never see one red cent of that money. The apple didn't fall far from the tree. They're a couple of bastards, the both of them.

But I sure don't need a lecture from my kid, so I decide to change the subject.

"What do you hear from your brother and sister? Neither of them ever call me."

"Of course you meant to say, *my brothers*, right?"

"Whatever."

"Andy started a new job, as an attorney for someplace called *One Colorado*. It's an advocacy organization for LGBTQ+ people."

"I'm sorry I asked. God dammit I'm going crazy in here all alone!"

"Sammy is still planning to take you to meet with your probation officer."

"That's not for another two weeks!"

"It could've been worse, you're lucky to be at home. They could've put you in jail for 90 days. For God's sake you were convicted for Public Lewdness. That judge took it easy on you because of Mom. He must have thought you were out of your mind."

"You don't know what you're talking about. I didn't do anything. I was ..."

"Save it, Dad. We've been all through this. I was in the courtroom. I heard the evidence."

We sit in silence for another minute. I'm lonely as hell, and yet, when my son comes to visit and bring me some groceries all we ever do is argue.

"About Florida..." Joey makes another attempt to turn the conversation back to neutral territory. "Do you even know anybody in Florida?"

"Well, I met this woman online, on one of those dating sites. I put together a profile and took a few selfies in the bathroom mirror, then ran them through one of those airbrushing apps. I looked pretty good, if I do say so myself. She's into me."

"For the love of God. You are an idiot. I'm out of here."

Joey shakes his head in disgust.

He leaves the kitchen.

The door slams. He's gone.

# Chapter 60
## Kaye

It's a beautiful sunny day, unseasonable I've been told for late December. By the time I arrive at the café, Simone is already there waiting for me.

"*Bonjour mes amies*," I say to Simone and kiss her cheeks as she stands to embrace me.

"*Mon amie*," she corrects me. "Last time I checked I am still only one person.

I laugh, "Oh, I know that and I've just come from my French class, too."

"You look lovely, Katrina. You exude the very essence of ... *je ne sais quoi? Joie de vivre.*"

I smile and take a seat at the table before dropping my book bag and easel beside my chair.

"What are you drinking? It looks delicious."

"It's a Bordeaux." Simone lifts her glass for a sip and smiles with satisfaction. "And it is."

I wave the waiter over. "Bonjour Jacques."

"Katrina," he smiles, "what can I bring you?"

I order a glass of Bordeaux for myself.

"Day drinking? That's so unlike you," Simone comments without reproach.

"I guess I feel like celebrating."

"Really Kaye, you look so full of life, so happy. Has something happened? Did you hear from Andy or your boys?"

"No, I'm afraid not. But I am happy, happier than I've been in a very long time. I have come to believe that happiness is a choice, and given all the challenges I've overcome just to be here, I'm choosing to be happy."

Although I haven't shared *everything* with Simone, we have grown to be close friends over the last few months. She knows that I was in a bad marriage for a long time. She knows enough about Nash to understand how I value my new found freedom and independence.

"It shows in your face. You have a confidence about you that has blossomed since you've moved here."

"I can't thank you enough for all you've done for me, but mostly for your friendship."

"I've done nothing," she poo poos the whole idea. "You moved here, all on your own. You arranged for a beautiful apartment overlooking the canal. You've enrolled in French language classes and you're almost understandable, at least some of the time." She laughs and gives me an affectionate squeeze on the hand. "You are learning to paint and you have made friends: André, Gérard, and me. You should be proud of all you have accomplished."

"*Merci* Simone. I don't know if I should be proud or not, but I do feel happy, at least most of the time."

"I see, I see. Perhaps this is not enough, perhaps you need something more, perhaps you need to take a lover."

I nearly choke on my wine at Simone's suggestion. "I don't know about that. I've only ever been with one man and we both know how that turned out."

"Only one?" She shakes her head in disbelief. "*C'est impossible.* You need a French lover, at least one. Maybe two."

Now we are both laughing.

We sip our wine and watch the people, both lost in our own thoughts...

It's been almost four months since I moved to Martigues and I love it. There are days when I almost need to pinch myself as I can't believe my good fortune.

André, the owner of the bed and breakfast where I stayed when I first arrived, introduced me to a friend of his, Gérard, who had a vacant apartment. Both Gérard and André have introduced me to so many people that I am never lacking something to do or someone to do it with.

My two bedroom apartment has beautiful natural light and overlooks the canal. One of the rooms I use as my bedroom and I've set up a studio in the other. I often start painting *en plein aire* in either Martigues or Marseille and finish up the final detail work in my studio. I'm not great by anyone's standards but I'm getting better and having fun doing so.

I take the train into Marseille twice a week for the French language classes that Simone recommended. She and I have become friends and I usually have lunch with her before class or meet her for a glass of wine afterwards whenever I am in town.

I suppose I should have corrected him but my French teacher, Maurice, when he assumed that my name is short for Katherine and has taken to giving it a French twist. He calls me Katrina and I have not corrected him and it seems to have stuck. Sometimes Maurice joins Simone and me for a glass of wine after class.

"You seem a million miles away," Simone says as she brings me back to the present moment.

"I guess I was. Just counting my blessings." I smile.

"Thinking about a French lover?"

"No, I don't think I'm ready and I wonder if I'll ever be. My marriage was so restrictive and my freedom has cost me. I don't think I need the complication."

"Who is talking about something complicated?"

"People are complicated. Relationships are complicated."

"Oh you Americans," she rolls her eyes and I understand from her tone that she thinks Americans take sex much too seriously.

But mimicking her tone and the accompanying eyeroll, I give it right back to her. "Oh the French."

Simone laughs. "I know someone. You should at least meet him."

"Maybe."

"Is that a firm, definite maybe?"

"Absolutely."

We both laugh and take another sip of our wine.

"What are your plans for the holidays?" Simone asks.

"I haven't made any plans. This will be my first Christmas without any of my family. I expect it will be difficult, but I'll get through it. I won't be the only single person spending the holiday alone."

"*Non, mon frère* always has a Christmas Eve party. Later, we will traipse over to *The Cathedral de Sainte Marie-Madeleine*, en masse for midnight Mass. It's fun, there will be caroling, good food, and plenty of wine. Come with Felix and me, please."

"Thank you. Can I let you know?"

"Hoping for a better offer?"

"No," I laugh.

"Perhaps my other friend will join us and you can meet him then."

"Maybe. I'm still hoping I'll hear back from Andy ... maybe *he* will fly over and we could spend the holidays together."

"Have you not heard back from her?"

"No. I think Andy is identifying as a man now. I called the law firm where she was working and was told, '*he* no longer works here.' I don't know what that is all about or how I might reach him now. The woman on the phone was curt with me when I asked for his contact information."

"*Je suis désolée*, Katrina." Simone reaches across the table to hold my hand.

"*Merci.*"

"Have you tried to call your other sons?"

"*Oui*, I called Joey but he wasn't home. I spoke briefly to Natalie but the baby was crying and we had a poor connection. I wasn't able to identify myself and I think she thought I was some kind of telemarketer or other unsolicited caller as she hung up on me muttering something about prank calls. I tried to call Sammy's house but no one answered. I know they monitor their calls. If they don't recognize the number they won't pick up, even if they're right there. I have to admit, I used to do that, too."

Simone nods in understanding. She doesn't need to say more.

The moment passes.

"It is what it is. I hate that saying, but somehow it seems apropos."

"Drink up, *mon amie*. It's getting cold and we should go if you are going to make your train."

I finish what remains of my wine and reach for my wallet to pay the bill.

"I've got this," Simone waves me off.

"Thank you. Next time it's my turn." I stand to leave and Simone helps me gather my belongings. She leans in to kiss my cheeks before she sends me on my way.

# Chapter 61
## Henri

Skye jumps up onto the bed to let me know she needs to go out. I check my watch and see that even this little dog has slept in this morning. I tousle her little white head. Perhaps she, too, is tired of all the traveling and moving from town to town. I pull on my trousers which are far too big now to wear without a belt. Just another reminder of how long I've been away from home and how many miles we've walked looking for this elusive woman. I make a mental note to replace these pants today, for a smaller pair. I stand in front of the full length mirror and decide that although the pants may not look very good, I haven't been this thin or fit since I was a much younger man. The combination of the weight loss and having shaved off my beard makes me barely recognizable, even to myself.

I finish dressing, clip the leash onto Skye's collar, and grab my bag before we leave this quaint little inn for our morning walk.

Once again, we head towards the water in yet another provincial town passing another Christmas market selling a wide variety of handmade gifts, none of which interest me. As we walk through the market Skye surveys the cobblestone plaza looking for a lost treat that may have fallen to the ground while I keep a look out for Kaye.

Marseille is picturesque as the morning sun christens the pastel colored buildings in a golden light. We walk past some brave and hearty souls who have already set up their easels hoping to catch the light and recreate the beauty of this day on their canvases.

We arrived late last night and the weather here is changing, and winter is closing in. I close the top button on my woolen coat and take a moment to wrap my scarf around my neck. Who knew it could be this cold on the Mediterranean?

The shop windows adorned for the season with twinkling lights, evergreen wreaths, and Christmas trees remind me that I am running out of time. Ellery's trial is set to begin the first week in January and I have still not found Kaye. God only knows what will become of Ellery if... I can't bring myself to even think of this.

Today I will look again.

Skye and I stop for a coffee and little breakfast, with a baguette with butter and fig jam, at a corner café. It's a little too cold to eat outside this morning even though they have the heaters on. The waiter looks at Skye who has settled herself beneath my chair and he gives her a nod indicating she can stay.

"*Merci,*" I mumble in gratitude as I am chilled to the bone.

He takes my order but before he can depart I ask, "*Avez-vous vu cette femme?*"

He takes the photo from me and looks at it for a long time before handing it back to me. "*Non, je suis désolé. Je ne connais pas cette femme.*" His tone is gruff and definitive.

As he hurries back toward the kitchen, Skye emits a low growl. I gently pat her head to soothe her. She senses something and so do I. There was something about the way the man scrutinized the photo before declaring he did not know the woman. I don't know if I believe him.

He brings my coffee but does not make eye contact. This would not be unusual in Paris, but provincial people have a tendency to be more friendly. I keep an eye on him as I wait for my breakfast.

He steps outside and onto the sidewalk to make a phone call. He is only gone for a minute. Am I reading more into this than I should?

The photo I have of Kaye, the one from the newspaper article, has become creased and the edges are worn from beating around in my bag the last few months. I don't know how many times I have shown it to innkeepers, barmaids and shop owners only to be met with blank stares and a shake of the head. I thought at least someone would have seen her and remembered her. She is a beautiful woman, unforgettable, really. At least she is to me. Perhaps the photograph doesn't do her justice. Perhaps she has cut or colored her hair. Perhaps she has simply disappeared, just as she had planned. Perhaps it doesn't matter as I am nearly out of time. And so is Ellery.

By the time I have finished eating, the rain has begun to fall. It is cold, gray, and miserable outside. For a moment I think about retracing our steps. In spite of the rain we take another route and walk along the canal. All the painters have packed up and left.

We don't get very far before the sky opens up and the rain pours down. I take this little dog and we head into a bookstore hoping for some reprieve before heading out again.

"*C'est ok?*" I ask as the woman behind the counter eyes the dripping wet dog.

"*Oui, laissez-moi vous prendre une serviette.*" She smiles and quickly returns with a towel.

Once I have thanked her and dried myself and Skye off a little, I peruse the shelves for something to read. Given the weather, it doesn't look like Skye and I will be going out again today to look for Kaye.

I make my selection, *Le Grand Monde* by Pierre Le Maitre and place the book on the counter. "Looks like we are staying in today." I speak to the dog in English.

"You are American, *non?*" The kind woman behind the counter asks in English with an unmistakable French accent.

"*Non, je suis Canadien,*" I respond.

"We don't get too many tourists in December. You should come in the spring or summer when the weather is fine. Most tourists come for the beaches and the sea." I hear a phone ring behind the counter but she does not pick up.

"I'm actually trying to find a friend of mine, perhaps you have seen her?" I pull the worn photograph from the leather bag that hangs from my shoulder and hand it to her.

"*Non, je suis désolée.*" She hands the photo back to me but holds my gaze for a moment and I get the feeling she is sizing me up. Does this woman know something? Is there something she's not telling me?

She turns away and rings up the sale. I hand the woman twenty-five euros.

I put the book and the photograph of Kaye back into my bag and zip it closed.

I decide to give it one more try. "If you should happen to see her, I am staying at Hôtel du Sud Vieux Port."

"I am sorry sir, but I do not know your friend."

This woman who started out so kind has turned cold. I think about telling her my name but decide against it. She already thinks I'm a creep.

Skye and I head out of the bookstore. The rain has slowed to a drizzle and the sky is a bit less ominous. We walk for a few more hours, in spite of the rain, just hoping for a glimpse of Kaye.

# Chapter 62
## Simone

No sooner does that *man* leave the bookstore with his little cur in tow than I pick up my phone to call Kaye. The phone rings and rings. "*Oh, mon Dieu*, please pick up." I offer up a little prayer. My hands shake as I hold the phone. I take a deep breath and try to calm myself.

Should I tell her that someone is looking for her?

Was that man her husband?

Has he tracked her down?

I don't want to frighten her, but I am afraid for her.

My call goes to her voice mail. "Kaye, *c'est Simone*. Call me, *s'il te plait*."

I hang up.

I curse that man out loud, "*Espèce de salaud*."

My heart is racing and I am shaking with fear.

I send her a text— *Call me! C'est important!*

She doesn't reply.

Perhaps, I should go to Martigues and warn her.

I would have to close the shop now, but it's the weekend before Christmas.

It could be my busiest shopping day of the year, in spite of the weather.

What choice do I have?

Besides, I don't even know if she's home.

With that, the bell over the door announces the arrival of more shoppers. Are they seeking refuge from the rain or are here to buy some last minute Christmas gifts?

There is a steady stream of shoppers throughout the day. I hear my phone buzzing behind the counter but I cannot find a way to get to it. Even if it is Kaye, I can't deliver her this message with the store full of nosy shoppers. I'll have to call her back later tonight.

Just before closing, Jacques, the waiter from the corner café rushes in. He shakes the rain from his umbrella and sets it just inside the door. Clearly, something has him upset.

"Simone, I've been trying to call you all day."

His eyes dart around the shop sizing up my other customers before taking me by the hand with great urgency and pulling me behind the curtain and into the storage room.

In a hushed whisper he says, "There is some old guy in town asking about your friend, Katrina. He came to

413

the café early this morning with a picture of her from an American newspaper. I think she is in trouble."

"*Oh, mon Dieu.* He was here, too." I take a deep breath to steady myself. "What did you tell him?"

"Nothing? I told him I didn't know her, that I'd never seen her."

"Good. I told him that too."

"I've tried to call Kaye but she's not picking up. Perhaps she is out shopping or home painting with the music on."

"Either way, the shops will all be closing soon for the Christmas holiday and the weather is cold and nasty. Perhaps she will just stay inside and this man will go back where he came from or move on to another town."

"We can only hope."

"Poor Katrina. There is something vulnerable about her. I can't quite put my finger on it and now this man is out hunting her down. I don't like it, not one little bit."

"I know, when she first moved here she seemed so shy and fearful but she has really started to come into her own."

"Do you think she may have been abused by her husband?"

"Do you think that guy is her husband?"

"Who else could it be?"

414

# Chapter 63
## Kaye

∽

## later that evening

"*Allo?* Simone, *c'est Katrina.*" I laugh as I seamlessly begin to use the French version of my new name.

"*Oh, mon Dieu, mon amie.* It is so good to hear your voice. I've been so worried."

"What is it, Simone?"

"I have been trying to reach you. Where have you been?"

"I'm sorry you were worried. I left my phone at home and decided to treat myself. I went to the spa today..."

"I am sorry to interrupt your evening, but I have to tell you something."

There is something in the tone of my friend's voice that makes me sit up and take notice. I slip the flap of the book jacket into my book to mark my place and set my wine glass back onto the coffee table.

"What is it?"

"Someone is in Marseille and he is looking for you. He came into the bookstore today. He carried a tattered photograph of you from an American newspaper. He was also at the café this morning and spoke with Jacques."

In spite of the fire blazing in my fireplace, my blood runs cold. "Was it Nash?"

"I don't know. He was a big man."

"Tall and heavy?"

"Tall, but not heavy. He might have been at one time as his clothes looked like they were too big on him."

"I suppose Nash could have lost some weight. He was always talking about losing weight but could never seem to. He always blamed it on me and my cooking."

"He was older. Maybe in his sixties."

"Older, eh? In his sixties, like me?"

"Oh, don't take offense, Katrina. I know you are in your sixties, but you are beautiful and have a young spirit. This man looked tired and beaten down. His face was weathered, like he had spent too much time in the sun. He was clean shaven and had blue eyes."

For just a moment I wonder if perhaps it was someone else. Could it be Henri? He has beautiful blue eyes, but he was a mountain of a man with a full white beard. Simone had said clean shaven, so I quickly dismiss the thought. "I suppose it must have been Nash. Nash has blue eyes. I was always reminding Nash to wear his sunscreen when he went out with the guys to play baseball,

416

but he never listened. He has probably come looking for me in hopes to claim his share of my inheritance. Who else could it possibly be?"

"*Espèce de salaud,*" Simone mutters under her breath.

"I suppose even if it's not Nash, it could be someone he has hired to find me."

"Or hunt you down and hurt you."

"Or that. It must have hurt his pride that I just up and left him. He always did have a very fragile ego. He could be seeking revenge for the very public humiliation he likely has endured."

"I don't have a good feeling about this. You need to be careful, for you are being hunted."

I nod and murmur into the phone that I will be. "Thank you Simone. Will you thank Jacques for me, too?"

"Of course. Have you given any more thought to coming to my brother's party? Tomorrow is Christmas Eve."

"All things considered, if Nash is around and looking for me, I think it would be best if I stay home until I'm certain he's moved on."

"There is probably some wisdom in that, still, I will stop by in the early afternoon on the way to the party as I have prepared a basket of treats for you along with some

417

*foie gras* and a *Bûche de Noël* that I've picked up from *Patisserie Torres*. I'm bringing one to you and one to my brother's for his sweets table."

"Oh Simone, you do not have to do that."

"Nonsense, Felix and I will be coming into Martigues for my brother's party anyway and we'd love to see you and wish you a Joyeux Nöel. I'll call you from the train. Stay inside and keep the door locked. Call me if you need anything, anything at all. Remember there may be a predator in your midst."

# Chapter 64
## Henri

It's only just after four in the afternoon and already the

December sun has set. The street lights are on and the light

reflects brightly on the wet pavement. It has been raining

off and on all day. I'm feeling sad and dejected and I'm no

closer to finding Kaye than I was four months ago when I

first arrived. My little friend and I tuck into a small café for

a bite to eat before heading back to the inn.

"*Bonsoir Monsieur*," the waiter says as he hands me a

one page menu. "*Je suis désolé*, we are closing in ten minutes

for the Christmas holiday. We still have a nice *coq au vin* or a

*cassoulet* but not much else I'm afraid."

I look down at Skye, "What do you think my little

friend? Shall we have one of each?"

Skye licks her lips and settles down on the floor

beneath the table.

"Don't let me hold you up," I say to the young man

at the table and he smiles. "If you could just box up an

order of each then we will take them with us and dine in

our hotel."

"*Merci Monsieur*, my wife will be happy that I am home early tonight as we are headed to her *Maman's* for the holiday."

In no time at all he returns with our dinners all boxed up and ready to go. "*Joyeux Nöel and Bonne Année.*"

By the time we get back to the inn, I'm soaked to the skin and so is poor Skye. She looks like a drowned rat and is shaking with the cold.

I spoke with a few people today and showed them Kaye's picture. I told them where they could reach me. I thought I saw a moment's hesitation in the waiter's face at the café this morning and then again with the nice woman in the bookstore but the more I pushed the more adamant they became that they had no idea who I was looking for.

I did my best. The truth is I am just not cut out for this kind of work. Someone else may have been successful, but alas I have been unable to find the ever elusive Kaye Hill. Heaven only knows what will become of my dearest friend, Ellery.

I stop by the reception desk to retrieve my key.

The *concierge* looks Skye and me up and down with an air of disapproval as we stand there dripping on the carpet. He can't make me feel any worse than I already do.

"*Bonsoir Monsieur*, may I have the key for room 312 *s'il vous plaît?*"

He nods and turns to the old style wooden cubby holes behind the desk to get my room key with the large brass key fob.

"Are there any messages for room 312?" I ask.

He turns back to the cubby hole and retrieves a note from the box.

Why did he not just give this to me when I asked for the key?

He hands me a note on a folded sheet of pink paper, then turns his face to something of utmost importance on the screen of his computer and I feel dismissed by this arrogant man.

I wait until Skye and I are inside the lift before I open the note and read it. It is from Claudette. It simply asks that I return her call. Still, I can almost hear her voice and I know this is not a request but a demand that I do as I am told.

I am cold and weary. I take a towel from the bath and dry the little pup before I change out of my wet clothes and into something dry.

She climbs up onto the bed and buries herself beneath the covers. I guess she needs to get warm more than she needs food right now.

I sit at the desk and pull out the take-away boxes, the paper napkin and the plastic utensils. I eat from both

421

boxes being certain to keep some for my faithful companion for she will be hungry when she wakes up. Some food only tastes it's best when it is freshly prepared but not *coq au vin* or *cassoulet*. These two dishes must have been cooking slowly for hours upon hours as the meat is tender and flavors are beautifully melded, either that or I'm just plain starving. I think the young man who served us must have been very grateful to be going home early for he has gifted us with exceedingly large portions. I eat until I can eat no more and still there is plenty left for Skye. I put the box with what remains onto the tile floor and fill her water dish. It will be ready and waiting for her when she wakes.

I check the time. It's nearly six o'clock which means it is almost noon in Montreal. I take a deep breath before calling Claudette. Like the arrogant *concierge* at the reception desk, Claudette cannot make me feel any worse than I already do. I have failed at my mission, but most importantly I have failed Ellery.

I punch her number into the phone.

"*Allo?*"

"*Claudette, c'est Henri.*"

"I know who this is. Where have you been? I've been texting you and I called you hours ago."

"I'm sorry. I guess I didn't check the phone. I have been out in the cold and the rain looking for anyone who may have seen Kaye."

"And..."

"Again, I was unsuccessful."

"I've had word from a friend who looked in on Ellery yesterday."

"Who? Did she visit her in prison?"

"Henri... You know better than to ask too many questions."

She scolds me. Claudette and all her secrets. "Okay, but just one more."

"What?" she asks impatiently.

"How is she?"

"I was told she is looking pretty rough. Apparently, she's lost a lot of weight. Her face and her arms are pretty bruised up. According to my friend, she looks like she's been beaten, more than once."

"Who told you this?"

"I'm not at liberty to say, but the bruises are different colors indicating they are in various stages of healing. Some of the bruises are from old beatings and some are more recent."

"Oh my God, the poor dear, she never hurt anyone in her whole life. What is wrong with people?"

"People fear what they don't understand," Claudette says and I can hear her voice crack and soon we are both crying for our friend.

"She is the best friend I have ever had, and I've failed her," I say as a loud sob breaks loose against all my efforts to try and keep my emotions in check.

"You need to come home. I've booked a flight for you and Skye to leave tomorrow morning from the *Marseille Provence Aeroport* at 6:00 AM. With the time change and without any unseen delays, you will arrive at Albany International at 6:55 PM. I'll pick you and Skye up and we will spend Christmas Day at the prison with Ellery."

"Does Ellery know about this?"

"Of course not. She would never agree to this, but she needs us now. I'm done playing by her rules. Her trial begins on January 3rd. Her attorney has agreed to put you on the stand as a character witness on Ellery's behalf. She'll need to prepare you. I had hoped you would find Ms. Kaye Hill, or whatever her name is but to no avail. Now you and I need to strategize with this *baby lawyer* on how we are going to keep Ellery from spending the rest of her life in prison."

"Okay."

"Is that all you can say, just okay?"

"I am trying to process this change of plans."

424

"You can take all the time you need on the way home on the plane to *process this change in plans.*" Claudette oozes with attitude before continuing. "I have made arrangements for you and that little dog. Jerome will meet you in front of the *Hôtel du Sud Vieux Port* at 3:00 AM and take you to the *aeroport.* He has your tickets and a crate for the little beast who will ride under your seat. See you tomorrow night." And just like that she is gone and I am left with the dial tone ringing in my ear.

# Chapter 65
## Kaye

Any and all of bliss I had felt after a day at the spa had

rapidly dissipated and was now long gone following the phone call from Simone. I spent a restless night thinking about Nash and my children. A litany of questions was looping through my head. I'd no sooner get to the end of the list of questions then I would start all over again at the beginning. I think they call this rumination. But just knowing what it is doesn't seem to help me stop worrying.

What is Nash doing over here looking for me? I know I always used to sing that old song about living in France, but had he really been listening? It seems so unlike him.

And what had Simone said? 'He was a big guy and his clothes were too big.'

Nash had been complaining about his weight ever since he stopped playing football, and that was almost forty years ago. He hasn't been able to shed a pound in decades. Does it really make sense that he would lose so much weight in a few months that his clothes would be too big for him?

Some people lose weight when they are grieving and under stress, while others gain weight. Nash has always been a stress eater.

Maybe he is ill, or maybe something is wrong with his business or one of the kids.

Maybe he knows about Andy...

And the list ran on and on throughout the night. When I finally did fall asleep it was nearly morning and then my worries invaded my dreams and I woke in a fright.

I drag myself out of bed and wrap myself in a warm cashmere robe that I treated myself to. It's new and feels so luxurious and comfortable on this cold gray morning. I feel so self-indulgent and for a moment I think about returning it. I no longer need to justify my spending to anyone, let alone my ex-husband. I clip the ticket from the sleeve.

But he is not really my ex-husband; we are not divorced.

I think about how Simone said 'I should take a French lover or two.'

Well, I certainly can't do that if I'm still married to Nash. I suppose I could— others do. But it doesn't seem right, at least not for me.

I make myself a cup of coffee and sit looking out the window overlooking the canal. The carillon of church bells plays an old French Christmas carol— and I find myself singing along.

"Bring a Torch, Jeanette, Isabella..."

I hum along until I remember a few more lines.

"Jesus is born, and Mary's calling.

Ah! Ah! Beautiful is the Mother.

Ah! Ah! Beautiful is her Son!"


I don't think I've heard this song since I was a girl. My mother used to play it on the piano and sing. And just like that my spirit lifts for today is Christmas Eve and I am here in Provence where the song was written.

I don't know how I know this, but I just do.

I look out the window and see the children dressed as shepherds and milkmaids. They are lining up in pairs to parade towards the church singing with the carillon of bells.

I think of my own children, my three beautiful sons.

I dress quickly in some warm clothes. I want to see the children. I pull on my coat and head outside to watch the children and take some photographs with the camera on my phone.

Later, I will try and paint the scene.

The children sing in French and the words come back to me.

"*Un Flambeau, Jeannette, Isabelle...*"

Returning to my apartment, I see Simone and her husband, Felix, standing in the lobby.

"Katrina, we almost gave up on you. I was starting to worry as I was so certain that you would be staying in today, considering the predator, and all."

"Don't worry, I am protected," I tell my friends as I reach into my coat pocket and pull out the tiny Swiss Army knife I bought in Geneva.

Simone laughs, "And what would you do with that? Trim his fingernails?"

And then Simone enfolds me in her arms before she releases me to her husband's embrace.

"*Joyeux Nöel, mes amis,*" I say as I return their kisses. "Please come in." I gesture towards the lift.

"*Oh non,*" Felix shakes his head as he hands me the basket of goodies he has tucked under his arm. "We are already running late and we have two more gifts to deliver before we are expected at Simone's brother's house for the festivities. Are you sure you can't join us? The more the merrier."

"Non, Felix, we discussed this. It is too dangerous for her," Simone scolds him gently before turning her attention to me. "Katrina, you know we would love for you to join us tonight. But I don't like it. Someone is showing a picture of you to total strangers and asking for your whereabouts. There will be many people at the party and someone may recognize you from the photo. My intuition is acting up. I've learned my lesson— never ignore my intuition."

"Don't let me hold you up and please, don't worry about me. It's Christmastime and I'm happy to be here in my home. I've even hung a wreath above the fireplace. I'll enjoy the fire, a glass of wine, and maybe finish that book you recommended. Enjoy the party and *Joyeux Nöel*"

We kiss one another before they depart.

"Thank you for this lovely gift," I call to them as I raise the basket that is now looped over my right arm.

I make myself a simple dinner and enjoy the *foie gras* Simone and Felix brought for me with a glass of wine and a slice of the *Bûche de Noël* for dessert. Then I finish up some detail work on a painting of a boat docked on the canal that is sitting on my easel. Once I have cleaned up, I sign into Google, using my phone, to do a little research on how to get an online divorce.

# Chapter 66
## Nash

The door clicks behind me and some drug laden youngster looks up from where he lies on the lower bunk.

"Ho, Ho, Ho, if it isn't old Saint Nick in an orange jumpsuit. Merry Christmas old man. What'd they pick *you* up for?"

I climb up to the upper bunk as beds shift under my weight.

This kid is about my Joey's age. I try to ignore him but he starts kicking my mattress from beneath me and won't let up.

"Hey, I'm talkin' to you old man. What are you in for?"

"None of your business."

"I saw your ankle bracelet. Did you violate?"

"It's embarrassing. I was on a Zoom call with this beach babe. She was a real hottie I'd met on *Match*. It was Christmas Eve and I wanted to get in the mood. So I poured myself a short one."

"You were drinkin' and wearing the anklet? Man, you're an idiot. Even I know better than to try and pull a stunt like that."

"I tried to explain it to the cop who came to the house. I thought he'd cut me a break, given it was Christmas and all. I told him it was medicinal, just tryin' to keep the shakes away."

"I take it he wasn't buyin' it."

"If he had, I wouldn't be back in here. First drink I've had in a month. When he told me he was takin' me in, I figured what the hell so I downed what little remained in the bottle. At least I've got a buzz on."

The kid laughs. "Man, you've got *cajones* buddy."

"What are you in for?" I ask the kid.

"Got pulled over for rolling through a stop sign. I was on my way to a party and I was playin' Santa and bringin' the party pack."

"What's a party pack?"

"A little of this and a little of that— you know, the good stuff. They got me on possession with intent to deliver. I've been here before. They'll probably plead me down, but I'll be here for a few days and so will you."

"Why is that?"

"It's the holidays, buddy. Ain't nobody goin' to court until after New Year's."

"Shit."

"Why are you wearing the anklet, anyway? Clearly, this ain't your first rodeo."

"Never mind. It was a misunderstanding."

"It always is." The kid laughs.

"Anyway, I've got to get out of here. My wife's murderer is going to trial next week and I need to be there so I can see that lesbo bitch go down."

"Wait a minute. Is your wife that lady who disappeared in the river last summer?"

"Yeah."

"That story blew up on social. I've been followin' it on Facebook. Man, I'm sorry. They never found her body, did they?"

"No."

"And now here you are, the *grieving husband* who's trying to hook up with some bimbo on *Match*?" The kid laughs.

He's really starting to annoy me. I roll over and face the wall. Again, he kicks me through the mattress.

"Man, I was sure you offed her. A lot of folks did. And here you are, locked up again. Karma, man, karma."

# Chapter 67
## Joey

The house is finally quiet and the kids are all tucked into bed and little Leah is in her crib. Natalie joins me on the couch. "Maybe we should turn in. Tomorrow will be an early start as the boys have been talking of nothing but what Santa Claus is going to bring for weeks now." Natalie snuggles in close and I can feel the warmth of her body and smell her perfume.

"They were even out in the yard tonight looking to see if they could spot Rudolph's nose among the stars."

"When Andy called over the Thanksgiving weekend and we'd made plans to get together, I have to admit I wasn't sure how it would all work out," I confess. We'd decided to celebrate Christmas at our house this year and then Andy would stay for the trial.

"It's just easier this way. Santa will visit our kids at our house and they get to stay home tomorrow and play with their toys. I think we made the best decision we could have, considering..."

Natalie had called to invite Sammy and his family to join us for Christmas dinner, but when he learned that Andy was coming with his girlfriend, Michelle, Sammy decided his family would celebrate at Pop's house instead.

"Sammy's personal code of ethics is hard for me to reconcile. I guess he finds Pop's behavior— cavorting with a prostitute and public indecency with children less offensive than Andy's decision to become a man. Whatever. If he doesn't want to come for Christmas, I'm okay with that. I'm just as happy to spare Andy, Michelle, and the kids the drama."

"I think Sammy was just looking for a reason not to come. I think Andy's great, and Michelle's a sweetheart."

"Poor Pop had been hoping the judge would have his ankle bracelet removed before Christmas and he'd be able to leave the house. He said he was hoping to go to Florida and meet up with some woman he met through an online dating service."

"No such luck, the judge decreed that your father had to stay under house arrest until the trial. His ankle bracelet is due to be taken off on the 3rd, just before the trial begins."

"He can wait. It's only a little more than a week now. Besides, I don't think he's allowed to leave the county."

"Sorry, but I'm not sure he thinks those rules apply to him."

"He thinks he's special. He always has."

"Can we change the subject, I'd rather not let thoughts of your father ruin my holiday."

"Sure. I'm glad Andy brought Michelle. The boys love them both."

Andy and Michelle arrived here yesterday afternoon. They'd taken a red-eye flight from Denver and rented a car at the Albany airport. Apparently, they'd gone directly to the Crossgate Mall as they arrived with a carful of wrapped Christmas presents for the kids. They even had a couple of things for Natalie and me.

"They came with a carload of gifts. What's not to love?" Natalie says, then adds, "I think it is more than the gifts. Andy is attentive and listens to the boys and so does Michelle."

"Andy looks ... good. He passes for a man. He has always been big, almost six feet tall, so it's probably easier for him than it might be for others. I don't know what I'm talking about. I love him, always have. If he is more comfortable being a man than he was being a woman, who am I to judge?"

My wife coos some kind of assent. We have talked and talked about my sister transitioning to be my brother and we are on the same page. We love him and so do our children.

"And Michelle, I like her."

"She's sweet." Natalie says and I can see she is starting to drift off towards sleep.

"I just wish everyone could be as open minded as you."

"What's not to love?" Natalie snuggles up close to me on the couch as she falls asleep in my arms.

"Come on sleepyhead, let's go to bed."

# Chapter 68
## Ellery

It's Christmas day, and it's not much different than any other day in prison, at least it isn't for me. They were playing Christmas carols over the public address system at breakfast. The breakfast was better than usual. Today we got the choice of one link of sausage or a slice of bacon.

Some of the other women were chatting about seeing their children during the visiting hours today. It might be good for these women but I can't believe it is very good for the children. But what do I know? I never had children. I guess I can be grateful for that, at least I haven't disappointed anyone else.

I sure would love to see my little pup. Just the thought of Skye brings a smile to my face. I know Henri is being good to her. It's in his nature to be kind.

My cell is quiet this morning like most of the cell block as many of the women are visiting with their families. I had just sat down at my desk to write in my journal when one of the guards unlocks my door.

"Come on McMasters, you've got visitors."

438

I look up from my desk and stand to face her. "Really? Who?" No one has come to see me since I've been here except my lawyer. And that poor young woman looks terrified every time she's in here. She can't seem to get in and out of here fast enough.

"How should I know? Do you think I'm keepin' your social calendar?" She gives a little  snort as she tries to be funny and I laugh.

"Well, that wouldn't keep you very busy."

"Come on, they're waitin' on you in the visitors room."

I turn my back towards Louisa and she clips the cuffs around my wrists. She unlocks the door and escorts me down the hall while I try to figure out who might be here. "I hope it isn't some of those Jehovah's Witnesses trying to save my immortal soul."

"Good luck with that," Louisa snorts again.

My orange jumpsuit pools around my ankles and over the tops of my canvas shoes as I make my way down the corridor. I've lost some weight since I've been in here and have taken to rolling my pant legs up so I don't trip, but I didn't do that this morning. I didn't think I'd be going anywhere.

I can't imagine who's here to see me.

439

It's probably the Jehovah's Witnesses or maybe the Mormons.

Louisa unlocks the visitors' room and we enter.

"You have one hour," Louisa says as she locks me inside.

There at the visitor's table sit Henri and Claudette. And Skye!

"Oh for heaven's sake!" Skye jumps out of Henri's arms as I bend down to pick her up. She jumps all over me and licks my face as I burst into tears. "How in the world did you two manage this?" I ask.

"I've told you before, I know people who know people," Claudette says and raises her shoulders as if this is no big deal.

I take a seat at the table while Skye continues to wiggle with joy in my arms.

"I don't know if you are happier to see her or if she is happier to see you," Henri says as tears begin to fill his eyes. "How are you my friend?" Henri asks as he reaches over to touch my hand.

"Better now, thank you both so much for coming. Henri you've shaved and lost weight. You look like you did when we were kids and worked at the marina up in *St-Paul-de-l'Île-aux-Noix.*"

"Non, not hardly. But you have lost some weight, too. Are you well?"

"As well as can be expected. What can I say? I miss my own cooking, but I'm getting by."

"And you, Henri?"

"I don't suppose that Claudette told you, but Skye and I have been in France, walking the streets of every little village in Provence."

"You've been looking for Kaye?" I ask.

Henri nods and a tear slips from his eye. "To no avail, I'm afraid."

"Thank you. Thank you for trying." I hold my little dog a little tighter and bury my face in the fur on her head.

Henri and I are both crying now but Claudette is not having it. "Enough of that. Your trial is ten days away. And we have work to do." She moves a yellow legal pad from her lap to the table in front of her. "We only have an hour, so we need to get busy. What kind of a defense is your attorney planning?"

"Oh her, I think she's still hoping I'll plead."

"To what?"

"Second degree murder. I'm charged with first degree murder which, if convicted, I would spend the rest of my life in prison. If I plead to second degree murder I could be out in twenty years. I'm sixty-eight years old—

either way it's a life sentence. I've told her again and again that I'll take my chances with a jury given I didn't kill anyone and they don't have a body."

"Oh Ellery, I so wish we could have found Kaye. She would be here if she only knew what you are up against..." He lets the words hang there a moment before he adds, "You could tell them what really happened."

"I won't do that to Kaye, and I won't implicate you or Claudette either."

"I repeat my question," Claudette says, "what kind of defense is your attorney planning to offer?"

"I think she is hoping the prosecution's case will fall apart and create reasonable doubt among the jury. She's hoping they won't convict me as all the evidence they have is circumstantial and it's hard to prove murder without a motive or a body." I attempt to sound more positive than I actually feel.

"Has this woman ever tried a capital case before? Ever defended anyone wrongly accused of murder? Ever gotten anyone off?" Claudette fires these questions off while she taps the point of her pen angrily against the legal pad.

Next thing I know Claudette is up and starting to pace around the room when Louisa, the guard, unlocks the door and shouts, "Sit down in that chair right now or I'm pulling the plug on this little party."

Claudette snarls at the guard and takes her seat.

"I don't think my attorney has ever been in front of a jury for anything more heinous than an underaged kid charged with possession of alcohol."

"God help us," Henri says. He drops his head into his hands.

"Maybe you can get out on appeal for ineffective assistance of counsel," Claudette says before she shakes her head and begins wringing her hands. "Non, non, let me think..." Several minutes go by and no one says a word.

Skye is sleeping on my lap now and I pet her tenderly. How I have missed my little friend.

Claudette pulls herself up to the table. "She needs to create reasonable doubt. This case has been all over social media."

"I don't even know what that is," I admit.

"Facebook, Twitter, Instagram, that kind of thing. Anyone who has ever had any contact with that husband of Kaye's finds him to be despicable. He is the reason Kaye chose to disappear. She could not bear one more day with that man. Since she disappeared, he's been charged with soliciting a prostitute and indecent exposure to minor children. He's a monster."

443

Claudette taps her long manicured fingernails on the table in front of her. Henri and I keep quiet as, clearly, she is thinking.

"All we really need to do is create reasonable doubt to show that she was afraid of him and had reason to want to disappear. It isn't against the law to disappear," Claudette says aloud, but to neither of us. She is trying to put this together for herself.

"Did Kaye ever say that her husband abused her?"

"She never said so but it was implied."

"Perhaps her children or a neighbor saw or heard something over the years and could testify to that. Perhaps there are medical records of questionable injuries that could be put into evidence."

"How have you come up with all of this?" Henri asks Claudette.

"I read a lot of crime novels," Claudette admits as if this is the most natural thing in the world and she assumes everyone must.

Henri looks uncomfortable. Clearly, he has not considered concocting an alternative story to persuade the jury they have charged the wrong person. Even if the person they intend to implicate is Nash.

"How can you fill your head with such darkness?" he asks.

She just shrugs.

I turn when we hear the key in the lock and the door opens. "Time's up, McMasters. Hope you all enjoyed your little party."

I kiss Skye on the head and hand her back to Henri's waiting arms.

"Merry Christmas my friends. Thank you so much for coming."

"I have already scheduled an appointment with your attorney for Tuesday. Time to light a fire under her and get you out of here." Claudette stands and straightens her shoulders like the mighty warrior she is.

"Thank you," is all I can muster.

"It's payback time," she says, then links arms with Henri in solidarity.

"Keep the faith, Ellery," Henri says while he snuggles Skye in his other arm. "We will see you in court."

Louisa clears her throat and grows impatient so I place my hands behind my back and she cuffs me for my stroll back down the long hall to my cell.

My heart is full. It has been a Merry Christmas indeed.

# Chapter 69
## Kaye

The sun rose brightly over the Mediterranean this morning. The streets are quiet as all of the New Year's eve revelers have gone home and are probably still lying in bed nursing their hangovers. I'm happy to wake clear headed and relieved that the holidays are finally over. I have survived, let the New Year begin.

Try as I may I can't quite come to terms with the thought that someone has been in Marseille looking for me. Is it Nash? Simone seems to think so, but I'm not sure. Simone has never met Nash or even seen a picture of him. She said this man was thin, and Nash has never been thin, not even in college.

Perhaps he hired someone to look for me, a private eye or something.

Still, when I tried to call Joey on Christmas Day and the phone went directly to voicemail, I decided against leaving a message. For all I know, Natalie may have included Nash in their holiday plans and he was the last person I wanted to talk to.

The weather has been cold and rainy for about a week now. I've been hiding out in my apartment for days, partly because of the weather and partly for fear of being spotted by whoever was looking for me. This time alone had given me plenty of time to think.

I complete the papers for an online divorce that I'd downloaded from the internet. From everything I've read, it's legal in the State of New York. I'll ask for nothing, except to be free of him. Nash can keep everything we've accumulated and saved during the forty years we were married. This should appease him. He has no legal claim to the money my father had left me. From what I'd learned from my research on the internet, inheritance is not seen as a marital asset.

Apparently, I can file electronically but I'll have to figure out a way to have him served.

I don't want to see him or let him know where I am.

This will be the tricky part.


This morning is glorious, so after my morning coffee I gather up my Julian easel and head down to the canal to paint. Slowly the city starts to come alive as the pedestrians amble their way along the canal. There are a lot of tourists in town this morning and it is clear that a cruise ship is in port. I catch snippets of conversation in English as some of the women pass me bemoaning the fact that the shops are not open on New Year's day.

Lost in my work, I paint quickly trying to capture the morning light on the water, not allowing my paint to dry so I can blend the various shades of blue. Two women stop behind me and watch.

"That is just beautiful. I'd love to learn to paint, but all I've ever painted was a bathroom." The one woman laughs to the other.

"I thought maybe I'd take some lessons, now that I'm retired. But Billy will never spring for something so frivolous. He's still griping about all the money he's had to spend taking me on this cruise."

"Maybe you can talk him into it after we visit the vineyard. Get him good and drunk on all the free wine they'll serve at the tasting and he'll agree to anything."

"I think he'd just as soon be home watching the Rose Bowl and drinking Budweiser with his pals this afternoon."

They are Americans, likely from New York or New Jersey. I lived there long enough that I can recognize their accents. But it's more than that...I turn my head to look at them.

"Amy?!" one of the women says as we look into one another's faces. "Oh my God, Amy! Is it you?"

My heart leaps into my throat. It's Betsy Madden. She and Billy were at the campground the day I disappeared.

I shake my head dismissively and speak to her rapidly in French, "*Je crains que vous ne vous trompiez Madame. Je m'appelle Katrina.*"

I turn away from them and back towards my easel. My hand trembles as I begin mixing paint on my palette.

The other woman attempts to translate, "She says you are mistaken. Her name is Katrina."

"Well, I'll be damned. She looks just like a woman I knew back home, Amy Cooper. I told you about her. She's the one who disappeared on the river last summer. Some old lesbian killed her and they never found poor Amy's body. The murder trial is supposed to start this week."

"Oh my God," the other woman says in horror as the story is repeated.

"Well, they say everyone has a twin and this woman could be Amy's."

"Her doppelganger?"

"Her what?"

"Doppelganger, it means look alike or twin."

449

They begin to walk away, but Betsy turns to look back at me and shakes her head. "Well, I'll be damned. She sure looks like Amy."

My heart is racing as I watch them turn up a side street and disappear.

Oh for the love of God, what have I done?

Oh God, no!

What have I done to Ellery? She has been charged with my murder.

What have I done to my children? They must think that I am dead.

I feel like I might vomit.

My head is spinning as I throw all my paints back into my box, collapse my easel and tuck my still wet canvas under my arm. My legs are trembling as I make my way home.

# Chapter 70
## Andy

I sit in the courtroom with Joey. I don't intend to miss any

of this. Joey may have to leave this morning and go to work depending how long the jury selection process takes. He's made arrangements to be here throughout the trial, but he doesn't get too many paid days off.

My new employer, *One Colorado*, has been great. They told me to take all the time I need.

Michelle left on New Year's day. She had to be back in the office yesterday. She is a love. She's my love. Joey and Natalie and the kids really seem to be taken with her, and she with them. She has been so supportive through all of this craziness.

Dear old Dad is back in the slammer. What kind of an idiot drinks when he is on house arrest and is wearing an ankle bracelet? He called Joey and is trying to get released for the trial. He said something about being called as an *expert witness*. He's delusional. In what fantasy land is he an expert on anything?

The courtroom is packed with family, friends, reporters, and the simply curious. We all stand as the judge enters and the court is called to order.

The first order of the day is the selection of the jury. Each of the potential jurors has been assigned a number. They are seated together in the front of the public seating area. The court clerk draws fourteen numbers from a wooden box and each potential juror makes his or her way to the jury box as their number is called.

"Good Morning. I am Judge Templin and I will be presiding over these proceedings. He looks to the court clerk and commands, "Swear in the jurors."

Once this is completed the Judge resumes, "This trial is expected to last a week or perhaps even longer. Jury service always interferes with our personal lives and work. So, mere inconvenience does not excuse a person from jury service. If it did, we would not have a trial by jury for the benefit of our citizens for over 240 years. The question therefore is: aside from mere inconvenience, is there something that is so critically important that it would create an exceptional hardship for you to serve on this jury?"

He waits a moment and one woman raises her hand. "I am the primary caregiver for my mother. She lives with me and suffers from dementia."

The judge nods, "Thank you. You may be dismissed." He turns towards the clerk, "Call the next juror."

A middle aged man approaches the jury box and is sworn in.

The judge begins the litany of questions to assure all jurors are capable of being seated on the jury for the duration of the trial. "Do you have a health matter that would be harmed by service on the jury, or that would interfere with your ability to be here every day and serve as a juror? Do you take medication that would make it difficult to concentrate or otherwise be attentive during the proceedings or during deliberations? If you are required by a doctor to avoid stressful situations, will the trial, or the give and take of the discussions during jury deliberations, be too stressful for you? Do you believe that you may know the defendant, a lawyer, a member of the court personnel, or the judge..."

I have heard all these questions *ad infinitum* during law school and when I went to trial in my former position. I can practically recite them in my sleep and thus I start to zone out.

Next the prosecutor and the defense attorney get a chance to ask the potential jurors questions and either accept them or dismiss them for cause or bias or they must use one of their three peremptory challenges where they do not have to give the juror or the court any reason for their dismissal.

Several of the jurors admit to having followed the case in the media and have already formed an opinion about the defendant without even hearing the evidence. One man expressed blatant prejudice against "women who have sex with other women."

The jurors shift in their seats and look uncomfortable as the man is dismissed by the defense attorney for cause. I cringe as I wonder how this woman can possibly get a fair trial. I can hardly control myself as I want to jump up and object. But the defense attorney doesn't even know enough to object as the entire jury pool has just heard this inflammatory remark that could prejudice them against her client. I take a deep breath and remind myself to check my sympathies as the defendant has been accused of killing my beloved mother.

Within the hour the jury is seated and Judge Templin says, "We will reconvene after lunch with opening statements."

Joey and I leave the courtroom and walk down the street to find some lunch.

"How about *The Victory*? I think it's a sports bar," Joey says.

"A sports bar? I don't think so. Just add a few macho guys reliving how the Giants got beat out in the playoffs and a little too much booze, and that's how people like me get beat up. Let's keep going. It looks like *The Bishop* is open for lunch."

When Joey and I get back to the courtroom, Natalie is already there and so is Pop. He's still dressed in his lovely prison garb. Looks like Sammy is a no show. I shouldn't be surprised and can't really blame him. He's trying to distance himself from all the family drama. I catch Pop's eye as he looks up and over at us. He nods in our direction. It is then that I see he is handcuffed to the officer.

My mother is dead, an elderly lesbian is being tried for her murder, and now our father sits there in his orange prison jumpsuit and handcuffed behind the defense attorney. I feel so conflicted.

What the hell is going on?

Whose witness is he?

The bailiff brings in the defendant. She's a tall androgynous woman. Her hair is white and she is badly in need of a haircut. She wears a white blouse and a gray pants suit. Her clothes are too big for her and look like they were bought off the sale rack at JC Penney's. My heart goes out to her and the old adage plays on in my head...*there but for the grace of God go I.*

Where has this come from?

This woman is on trial for killing my mother. Still, had I not had gender affirming health care would I grow old as this woman has?

Her gender and her sexual orientation have nothing to do with the reason she is here, or do they?

I push these thoughts from my head and try to focus on the proceedings.

The prosecutor is a forty-year-old guy with short hair. He is dressed in a conservative navy blue suit. He stands and approaches the jury to deliver his opening remarks.

"Your Honor, and Ladies and Gentlemen of the Jury, my name is Charles Stone. I am representing the prosecution and the people of the State of New York. I am the victim's attorney.

"In this case I will prove that the defendant, Ms. Ellery McMasters murdered Mrs. Amy Cooper.

"Mrs. Cooper was camping with her husband and their friends up on the Sacandaga River on July 17th last summer. It was a hot day and she went down to the river to swim when she was caught up in the rapidly moving waters

456

and ended up on the shore of Ms. McMasters' cabin. The Northville Police Department's canine unit was able to trace Mrs. Cooper's scent to Ms. McMasters' cabin. Ms. McMasters has repeatedly denied any knowledge of Mrs. Amy Cooper, and, yet, our forensic evidence will show that Mrs. Cooper was inside Ms. McMasters' cabin as there has been a DNA match from Mrs. Cooper to blood found in Ms. McMasters' home. We will also show that Mrs. Cooper's fingerprints were found in Ms. McMasters' GMC truck and that Mrs. Cooper's home address had been programmed into the navigation system of Ms. McMasters' truck.

"Ms. McMasters' continues to deny knowing anything about Mrs. Cooper and her disappearance despite forensic evidence that places her in Ms. McMasters' home and her vehicle.

"There has been no sign of Mrs. Cooper since she floated down the Sacandaga River and she has not been in contact with any of her family or her friends since last July leading us to the only logical conclusion that Ellery McMasters has murdered Mrs. Amy Cooper.

"At the end of the trial the State of New York will ask you to find the defendant, Ellery McMasters, guilty of first degree murder."

The prosecutor nods solemnly to the jurors before returning to his seat at the table. His co-counsel gives him a smile of approval and I know, he thinks he's nailed it.

I look over at the defendant where she sits with her attorney. She looks ashen and unwell. Her skin tone matches the gray pantsuit she wears. The defense attorney stands and approaches the jury box. She looks positively frightened, like she is the one on trial instead of the defendant.

"Good Afternoon your Honor, and Ladies and Gentleman of the Jury. My name is Megan O'Riordan..."

And before she can go any further one of the older men in the jury box raises his hand and says, "Can you speak up? I can't hear anything you're saying."

And with that the poor woman looks completely undone. But she takes a deep breath and begins again in a much louder voice.

"Good Afternoon your Honor, and Ladies and Gentleman of the Jury. My name is Megan O'Riordan. I am here representing the defendant Ms. Ellery McMasters. There are just a couple of things I feel I must remind you of: the first is that the defendant, Ms. McMaster's must be presumed innocent until she is proven guilty. And the second is that the burden of proof lies with the prosecution. If the prosecution does not prove their case beyond a reasonable doubt, then the law demands that you must acquit my client and send her home. I will be asking you to consider the following things as you listen to the prosecution present their case against my client: The first is that there is no proof that Mrs. Amy Elizabeth Cooper is even dead. No body has been found. The second is that people disappear every day, sometimes of their own volition. Mrs. Amy Cooper may have chosen to disappear and this is not a crime. The third thing I'd like you to consider is that Ms. McMaster's does not have a motive to hurt, let alone kill, Mrs. Amy Cooper. The fourth thing you need to ask yourself is —who would benefit if something untoward happened to Mrs. Cooper? Mrs. Cooper's father recently passed away leaving her an undisclosed inheritance. Number five—are there other people who may have hurt or killed the missing woman? If necessary, we will call witnesses to testify that Mr. Nash Cooper, the missing woman's husband, is a more likely suspect as he has a lengthy history of abusing his wife both verbally and physically. And lastly, the prosecution has indicated they intend to use forensic evidence to place my client, Ms. Ellery McMasters, in the presence of the victim. But evidence can be tampered with and could have been planted at the defendant's home and in her car. All of this we intend to explore if the case should proceed that far.

Please remember if you have *reasonable doubt* that my client is innocent, then you are obliged by the law to acquit."

Her demeanor is tentative and her voice is soft but she has a good handle on the facts and did a pretty good job outlining her case. But this stuff about my dad as a suspect... I'm still just mulling it all over in my head when the defense attorney turns away from the jury. My father in his orange jumpsuit stands up dragging the corrections officer with him by his handcuffed wrist.

"You are the scum of the earth," he screams at the defense attorney who is now shaking with fear.

The judge slams his gavel. "Bailiff, remove that man."

I am aghast and so is everyone else in the courtroom as the corrections officer and the bailiff wrestle my father to the ground as he continues to shout indignities. "This is the biggest bunch of bullshit I've ever heard. I never touched my wife." With his one free hand my father points at the defendant. "I'll give you a motive, that woman is a pervert. That's what she is."

The jury sits wide-eyed as my father is thrashing about and is practically carried from the courtroom.

Again the judge bangs the gavel. "The jury will kindly disregard that outburst. We are done for today and will reconvene at 8:00 tomorrow morning when the prosecution will present their case. Counsel, in my chambers."

# Chapter 71
## Kaye

My head is spinning as I try to wrap my head around all that has transpired in the last few days. Once I got back to my apartment on New Year's day it didn't take me long to figure out how to Google my old name, *Amy Cooper*, and read about all the havoc I've caused in the lives of those who only tried to help me. The whole thing fills me with profound regret and remorse. Poor Ellery, locked up in prison for months upon months and now facing a murder trial for a crime she never committed.

Why didn't she just tell someone what I did and where I was?

She was supposed to call Andy. Didn't she?

And what about my children? Do they think I've been murdered? I pick up the photo of my children from my bedside table and hold it close to my heart.

I took this photo with me from the bedroom I once shared with Nash.

Didn't anyone notice it was gone?

I figured Ellery would get word to the kids.

That was the plan.

Do they really think Ellery killed me?

Of course they do. Everyone must.

I would be beside myself if I thought something like that had happened to any one of them.

How could I have been so naïve to think my behavior wouldn't have consequences for others? The truth is the only person I was intent on leaving was Nash. After all he has put me through over the years, leaving him seemed like something I should have done years ago. I figured he would be just as happy to have me out of the house and out of his life.

But it looks like he has really made a mess of things, in ways that he will have to own as they have nothing to do with me. Bastard.

It didn't take me long before I knew what I had to do. The trial was set to begin in two days and I have to get back there and set things right. I have no choice. It's the only answer.

I search the internet to purchase a plane ticket. It seems as if everyone is trying to get back to the United States after the holidays as so many flights are completely booked.

After much negotiation with the airlines, I pack quickly and take the train to the airport. In the end I have to fly from Marseille to Istanbul on Turkish Airlines where I have a fifteen hour layover. Then I have an eleven hour flight from Istanbul to Washington DC. I was seated in the back of the plane in a middle seat. I guess I should be grateful I got on the flight at all. Then there is a three hour layover before I catch a commuter plane for quick flight up to Albany. The whole ordeal takes over 35 hours not including the time it took to get to Marseille and to get through security on the front end and immigration once I arrive back in the States.

By the time I arrive in Albany it's nearly midnight on January 3rd and the trial has already begun. I only hope I won't be too late. I grab a taxi at the airport and the cabbie delivers me to the Hilton, just a few blocks from the courthouse. I think about looking to see if I can find anything about it on the local news but I can't keep my eyes open one moment longer.

I set my alarm for seven the next morning but the jet lag is overwhelming and it's nearly nine o'clock by the time I've showered, fixed my hair and makeup, and gotten dressed. I need two cups of strong coffee just to get me out the door.

It's a typical New York winter and the sidewalks are still buried in snow which completely covers my open-toed shoes. I certainly hadn't planned for a trip back to New

York this winter. I wear the warmest sweater I brought with me beneath my trench coat and I'm still freezing.

The guards at the courthouse send me and my pocketbook through the metal detector and then direct me to Judge Templin's courtroom.

I carry my coat over my arm, take a deep breath, and try to muster up all the courage I can before I enter the courtroom.

The heavy wooden door closes behind me.

I take another deep breath to try and calm myself as I take another tentative step up the aisle.

The presiding judge wears a black robe and sits high up on a platform behind his mahogany desk. A uniformed policeman is on the witness stand and a man in a navy blue suit stands before him with his back to everyone but the witness and the judge. At a table to the left I can see the back of Ellery's head and beside her is a young woman. I presume she is her attorney.

Before I can decide what to do now, the policeman on the witness stand stops speaking mid-sentence and just looks at me.

It's then that everyone in the courtroom turns and looks in my direction.

A shocked silence hangs in the air.

I look into the wide-eyed faces of so many people who just sit there with their mouths wide open, some I know and many I've never seen before.

Then Andy jumps up and runs to me. "Mom!" he shouts and folds me into his arms. Overwhelmed with emotion I start to cry.

"I love you, Andy," is all I can get out between sobs.

"Amy!?" Nash calls out, in a tone that indicates that he can't believe his eyes, but neither can I as my ne'er do well husband is sitting there handcuffed, and wearing an orange prison jumpsuit.

I turn from him and meet Ellery's eyes, then she drops her head into her hands and begins to cry.

"Kaye," three voices proclaim with great joy from over near the defense table.

Then Judge Templin hits the gavel and shouts, "Order in the court! Order in the court!"

People on both sides of the aisle are crying and so am I. The judge bangs his gavel again and asks in a booming voice, "And who madam might you be?"

I clear my throat and answer, "My name is Amy Elizabeth Cooper." And the courtroom erupts in applause as both Joey and Andy wrap their arms around me.

The judge turns to the policeman sitting on the witness stand. "Office Conroy, will you please step down from the stand."

Silence falls over the courtroom as everyone waits to see what will happen next.

"Everyone take your seats or I will clear this courtroom." The judge barks from the bench. "Bailiff please escort Mrs. Cooper to the witness stand and swear her in."

Trembling, I follow the bailiff to the witness stand.

"Please raise your right hand. Do you swear to tell the truth, the whole truth , and nothing but the truth?" the bailiff says.

I do as requested and respond, "I do," as my heart thunders in my chest.

The judge nods to the prosecutor, "Your witness Mr. Stone."

The prosecutor approaches and asks, "Are you Amy Elizabeth Cooper?"

"I am."

"The same Amy Elizabeth Cooper who has been presumed to be dead?"

"I am."

"Where have you been these last five months?"

"I have been living in France."

"Ms. Ellery McMasters has been charged with your murder, did you know that?"

"Not until a few days ago."

"Do you know Ms. McMasters?"

"I do."

"Ms. McMasters has maintained that she has never met you, can you explain this?"

"Ms. McMasters was telling the truth. I never told her my name was Amy Cooper, she only ever knew me as Kaye Hill."

"And why did you present yourself as someone other than who you are?"

"I decided to disappear. I had lived over forty years as Mrs. Nash Cooper or Mrs. Amy Cooper and I'd had more than enough of that. My marriage was in shambles and had been for a long time. My husband was abusive and I was afraid of him. My children were grown, and I believed that I'd fulfilled my obligations to them. I wanted a new life, a life of my own choosing where I didn't have to live in fear and where I was beholden to no one. I decided to disappear. I accept full responsibility for that decision and apologize to everyone but especially to Ellery who has endured a great injustice in an effort to keep me safe."

It was then that the woman in the dark blue suit seated next to Ellery stood and said,

"Your Honor, I move that all charges against Ms. Ellery McMasters be dropped as clearly Mrs. Amy Cooper is very much alive."

The Judge bangs his gavel and again addresses the prosecutor, "Mr. Stone?"

"No, objections, Judge."

"Ms. McMasters, please stand."

It takes Ellery a moment to get to her feet and then the judge addresses her, "Ms. Ellery McMasters all charges brought against you in this case are dismissed. You are free to go with our most sincere apology."

"Mrs. Cooper or perhaps you prefer Ms. Hill, you may step down."

"This is outrageous!" Nash shouts as I walk past him.

My sons are up and out of their seats wrapping their arms around me.

"Where is Sammy?" I ask Andy and Joey.

"He didn't come," Andy says. "A little too much drama, I guess."

"Please come with me and meet my dear and loyal friends," and I take my boys by the hand to introduce them to Ellery, Henri, and Claudette. I wrap my arms first around Ellery who returns my embrace with tears in her eyes.

469

"You are a sight for sore eyes," she says as she holds me tight.

"I am so sorry," I whisper in her ear, "I had no idea. I came as soon as I found out."

"Henri, you look so different, so young."

"Skye and I have been walking all around France looking for you," he says as he opens his arms to embrace me.

"So it was you," I say as the pieces begin to fall into place.

I reach for Claudette, but she smiles and waves me off. "You did the right thing. Ellery was right about you, she said you were a good woman. And you have proven to be just that, a good woman."

"Come and meet my *sons*, Andy and Joey," and with that I introduce my boys.

Ellery shakes Andy's hand. I watch as their eyes meet in a moment of profound understanding and then they embrace as both of them well up with tears. "Thank you," Andy emits a long heartfelt sob. "Thank you for protecting my mother."

I hear Ellery respond, "Your mother is a good woman, she stayed with your father all those years so she could protect you. I wish I'd had a mother who loved me like that."

Joey holds my hand while Natalie hovers nearby. "Come let me take all of us to dinner. I am staying just around the corner at the Hilton. There is so much to talk over."

"I'll call for a reservation," Natalie says as she looks in her purse for her phone. "For seven?" she asks while counting us up.

Judge Templin bangs the gavel once more and the courtroom quiets before he says,

"Mrs. Cooper, may I have a few minutes of your time in chambers?"

"Yes, of course." I say as I reach into the navy leather satchel that Claudette bought for me six months ago and pull out a packet of papers. "Andy, could you give this to your father?"

My son looks it over and then begins to smile as he walks over to his father still handcuffed to his chair and says loud enough for everyone to hear, "Nash Cooper, you've been served."

# Chapter 72
## Kaye

The courtroom bursts into applause and raucous cheers as Nash is served with divorce papers. I look over at Judge Templin who covers his mouth with his hand to hide a smile. "Ms. Cooper..."

I follow him into his chambers.

"Ms. Cooper or should I call you Ms. Hill?"

"I'm going by Kaye Hill now and will have my name legally changed."

"Okay, then, Ms. Hill, you certainly have created quite a stir today."

"I'm sorry, your Honor. Up until three days ago I had no idea that anyone thought I had been murdered..."

He holds up his hand to stop me. "It isn't against the law for someone to choose to disappear, however your decision to do so has wreaked havoc on many people's lives. I understand from the testimony you gave that your husband was abusive. Given what I have witnessed in my courtroom and have subsequently learned about your husband's behavior since your disappearance, I can begin to understand why you may have chosen to disappear and why you just had him served with divorce papers. Still, I believe there are significant issues you will need to resolve and people you will need to apologize to and reconcile with before you can get on with your life."

"Yes, sir."

"For this reason I am going to recommend that you seek some counseling. Although you may have just filed for divorce, it appears that your husband still has anger issues and it is unlikely that he will remain in the county jail too much longer. I want you to be safe. Therefore, I would like to refer you to a domestic violence counselor. Our Victim's Assistance Unit makes this kind of referral regularly and they know people who are good at this."

"Yes, sir. He is the reason I fled the country and the reason I stayed away."

"Now that you have returned, do you intend to reside in the State of New York?"

"No, sir. I will probably be here for a couple of weeks. I want to spend some time with my sons and their families but it is my intention to return to France and make a life for myself there."

He nods. "I have never presided over a murder that had a happy ending. This is a first. See my clerk on the way out of chambers for the counseling referral. Best of luck to you Ms. Hill."

When I exit the judge's chambers the corridor is crowded with reporters trying to take my picture as they attempt to get a story for the evening news. Andy sidles up next to me and ushers me past the throngs of reporters.

"No comment. No comment." He keeps his arm tight around my shoulder as we exit the courthouse. A car is waiting as we make our way down the courthouse steps with Joey and Natalie inside.

"To the Hilton," Andy says as if Joey is his designated chauffeur.

"Everyone has already gone over and they're waiting for us," Joey says as we pull away from the curb.

"Everyone?" I ask.

"Everyone but Dad," Joey says.

"He's back in jail and it looks like he'll be there for a while longer," Natalie adds.

# Chapter 73
## Kaye

Once back in my hotel room, I have a quiet moment to reflect on the day.

We had such a lovely evening.

Throughout the evening all the details came to light about the chaos my disappearance had caused the people I love. I clearly hadn't given any of this adequate consideration. I begged for everyone's forgiveness and my children asked for mine for they had never really understood the level of my desperation.

I tried to explain how I never would have consciously allowed them to suffer as I now knew they had.

I told them that I had tried to call Ellery. Only now did it come to light that she never got my calls after her phone was taken from her when she'd been arrested. I had been holding on to the mistaken belief that she had been in contact with Andy and Andy had contacted his brothers. This had been our plan.

I explained how I had called Andy's office repeatedly and hadn't gotten through and then was told that he had changed jobs, but I wasn't told where he had gone or how I could get in touch with him.

I explained how I had sent long emails to Andy's work email but never received any reply.

Andy had looked confused when he asked, "What name did you send them under?"

"Kaye Hill," I told him.

"Hmm, I don't know how I would have missed them. I check my email multiple times every day. What did you put in the subject box?"

"I left it blank. I didn't know if one of your assistants might be reading your email. I was just trying to keep our family business private."

Andy slowly nodded his head as he put the pieces together and now had clarity on yet another one of my faux pas. "Any unsolicited email coming into our office without anything in the subject line and an attachment goes directly into the spam folder and is automatically deleted. It's not that I missed your emails, I never received them. I'm so sorry Mom, you must have felt so alone and abandoned."

I'd explained how I tried to call both Sammy and Joey, but given the unknown phone number I was calling from, no one in their families had picked up my calls and I was afraid to leave a message.

I was afraid if my sons knew where I was that their father would harass them to find me.

When I'd finished my children were beginning to understand just how afraid of their father I was.

"Only a desperate person would do such a desperate thing," Andy proclaimed. "I am just so grateful that you are alive and well and back in our lives."

And everyone cheered and raised their glasses to my homecoming.

It was then that Sammy arrived. He had that deer in the headlights kind of look as I stood and went to him.

"Mom," he said tentatively as if he couldn't quite believe it was really me. He gave me a stiff little hug which felt rather perfunctory. It was more than a little bit awkward as I could tell he was angry for what I had put the family through. I pray that given some time he will be able to let it go, but it may take him some time. Sammy has always been the most conservative of my children and I know he still longs for a loving intact family. But we have never been that, in spite of the façade I tried my best to present.

Over the course of the evening Sammy and Andy seem to have started to reconcile their differences. It did my heart a world of good to see them embrace before leaving.

I heard Sammy say, "I don't really get it, but I still love you."

It's a start and you have to start somewhere.

I had thanked and apologized to Ellery, Henri and Claudette repeatedly throughout the evening. Everyone was getting ready to leave, and Ellery looked so tired when I went to her and held her hands. "Why didn't you just tell them that I had gone to France?" I asked.

"When I saw you lying there on the beach you looked so frail and vulnerable. And then you told me your story and my heart went out to you. You have lived all of your adult life with a man who is so unworthy of you. You had stayed to protect a vulnerable child. You were a hero in my eyes. Like I told Andy, I wish that someone had loved me that much. I have lived a peace-filled life of my own choosing and I thought you deserved the chance to do the same."

I hugged her and I was sobbing while the others looked on. While in her arms she'd whispered, "You are not the first person we have helped escape a difficult situation. You are one of us now and we can't risk exposing our operation. There will be others, there always are."

I turned to Henri who stood there so gallant in the well-tailored navy suit he wore to court. "And you, my friend, spent months and months walking the provincial villages looking for me."

He smiled, "You are a remarkable woman, Kaye. Your friend in the bookstore said I should come back to Marseille when the weather turns nice..."

"Ah Simone," I started to fill in the blanks. "My door is always open to you, Henri. I hope you will come and stay for a while."

I remember how he leaned in and kissed me on both cheeks. "You can count on it," he whispered in my ear then held me tight in his arms and I breathed in the clean masculine scent of him. I can still feel the warmth of his embrace.

I moved closer in towards Claudette, when she held up one finger to let me know I was close enough.

I whispered, "I don't know how to thank you," just loud enough for her to hear.

In response she replied, " Remember, real friendship is reciprocal, sometimes you are the giver and sometimes the beneficiary. We will call on you when we need you..."

I gave her a slow nod of my head.

"Welcome to *notre alliance*," Claudette says as she turns and heads towards the door.

Ellery just wanted to go home. Who could blame her?

Henri had been staying there the last few days so he would be close enough to drive in for the trial. Henri had spent the day before the trial getting the place cleaned up, the water turned on, chopping some wood for the wood burning stove, and getting some food in. What a wonderful man. He had prepared for Ellery's homecoming, just in case... just in case they were able to create a reasonable doubt in the mind of the jurors...just in case she was released.

Skye would be at the cabin waiting for them and Ellery couldn't wait to see her.

It was then that Claudette drove Ellery and Henri back to her cabin in the woods.

All Ellery had ever wanted was a quiet life. And then I had floated up onto her beach last summer and thrown her life into complete chaos. Now, at last, she was going home. She is the most selfless person I have ever known. She is my hero.

# Chapter 74
## Kaye

I sit in the drafty waiting room wearing a dress that isn't nearly warm enough for this New York winter.

My mind is wandering as I think about Andy. He has called his partner, Michelle, and she is flying in from Colorado this morning. We are supposed to have lunch together after my session. He wants me to meet her before I head back to France. I think about Henri and the way he held me when we said our goodbyes. I wonder if he was feeling it too. Is this what they call chemistry?

Just then a pretty woman about my age opens the door and calls my name, "Kaye Hill."

I stand and follow her back to her office.

"Please take a seat," she says and gestures towards a comfortable chair upholstered in a rich burgundy velvet. "I'm Dr. Carlita Fox. Can you tell me why you are here?" the therapist asks as she takes her seat behind her desk.

"Judge Templin suggested that I should talk to someone and his clerk arranged for the referral."

"I see, so this consultation wasn't court ordered, only suggested. Do I have that right?"

"Yes, I haven't been charged with anything, however, the judge described my behavior as impulsive and erratic. I was a victim of domestic violence and he thought I could benefit from seeing someone."

"Oh," she says, unable to cover her surprise "Kaye Hill, otherwise known as Amy Cooper." She is starting to put it together. "You're the woman everyone thought was dead and they charged another woman with your murder. I read about you in my news feed. You've created quite a stir around here. Where would you like to begin?"

"I guess I'd been thinking about it for a while, just not in any serious way."

"No wait, start at the beginning."

"The beginning of, what, my entire life?"

"No, but we may get back to that. How about just that day?"

"Oh, *that* day ... well, let me think. It's been a while ago now and you know how memory is."

"No, not really."

"It can play tricks on you, memory plays fast and loose with the facts, leaves things out that may or may not be significant. Memory is overcome by emotion and always favors the storyteller. Just as long as we're clear about that."

"You're stalling, is there something you don't want to tell me?"

"Of course."

"Perhaps it would be best if you just begin.

"Okay. It was the middle of July, and it was already hot and it was only nine AM. I was standing at the sink washing up the breakfast dishes. Judy Collins was playing over the speakers and I was singing along softly, lost in daydreams of my own.

"... *my father always promised me that we would live in France, we'd go boating on the Seine and I would learn to dance...*"

# ACKNOWLEDGMENTS

I would like to thank my friends in the Tuesday Writers at the Laura Riding Jackson Foundation in Vero Beach, Florida for patiently listening to this story as it unfolded week after week. Thank you for your kind words and thoughtful critique. My writing is better because of you.

A special thank you to my nephew, Philip Selander for his graphic design and the creation of the cover.

And all my early readers- your comments are invaluable as I enter into uncharted territory hoping to do justice to the struggles of our common humanity and trying to get it right.